The Tides Between

Between

ELIZABETH JANE CORBETT

Published by Odyssey Books in 2017
www.odysseybooks.com.au

This is a work of fiction. Names, characters, businesses, places, events and incidents are either the products of the author's imagination or used in a fictitious manner. Any resemblance to actual persons, living or dead, or actual events is purely coincidental.

A Cataloguing-in-Publication entry is available from the National Library of Australia

Series: Corbett, Elizabeth Jane. The Tides Between
ISBN: 978-1-925652-22-2 (pbk)
ISBN: 978-1-925652-23-9 (ebook)

Cover design by Elijah Toten

To my mum, Linda, from who gave me the privilege of being half Welsh; to my dad, David, who was so very English; and to my husband, Andrew, who is Australian. My heart belongs with him also.

They'll turn me in your arms, lady,
Into an esk and an adder.
But hold me fast and fear me not,
I'll be your bairn's father.

They'll turn me into a bear sae grim,
And then a lion bold
But hold me fast and fear me not,
And ye shall love your child.

Again they'll turn me in your arms,
To a red hot gand of airn,
But hold me fast and fear me not,
I'll do you nae harm.

At last they'll turn me in your arms,
Into a burning gleed,
Then throw me into well water,
O throw me in with speed.

And then I'll be your ain true-love,
I'll turn a naked knight:
Then cover me wi your green mantle,
And cover me out of sight.

'Tamlane'—Robert Burns

CHAPTER 1

Deptford – 30 August 1841

Silence. Bridie glanced back over her shoulder, no feet crunching on the dirty cinders, no shadow shift in the dormitories. On tiptoes, she prised open the locker door. It rasped, the sound like a hacksaw in the empty yard. She froze, waited, eased her notebook from its hiding place.

If only it wasn't so big—breadboard big, and bound in thick brown leather. Her dad should have realised it would be difficult to hide. No, her dad wasn't to blame. He didn't know he was going to die. Or that she would emigrate to Port Phillip without him. He certainly couldn't have imagined Ma still hating him, even now, eighteen months after his passing.

'Alf Bustle!' She heard her stepfather's name called.

Bridie bundled the notebook into her flannel petticoat and shoved it to the bottom of her emigrant-issue canvas bag. Its corners bulged. She tweaked at the fabric, shifted her wad of scrap paper and stepped back to survey her handiwork. It would pass, so long as Ma didn't check her bag 'one last time' before boarding.

'Bridie! Where's Bridie?' Ma's voice shrilled out from the mess hall.

'Here,' Bridie called, wriggling through the family groups awaiting their boarding call.

'For goodness sake. Where have you been? And why did you take that bag again? Anyone would think it held the queen's own wardrobe, the way you're hovering over it—not spare petticoats and cotton shifts.'

'I'm fine. Keep your voice down. I had to go to the privy.'

'Again! Anyone would think you were costive. And that bag looks like it's been dragged through the dust. You haven't been upsetting things, I hope?'

'No.'

Ma's eyes narrowed. 'Three days, we've been at the emigrant depot. Three days, with you fidgeting about like a dog with fleas. I don't know what you're up to, Bridie, but there's something you're not telling me.'

'I'm nervous, that's all. About the journey.'

'Your ma's nervous too.' Alf's big, blunt hand grasped her shoulder. 'She's scarcely slept a wink these past nights for worrying we've left something behind.'

'Well, I haven't. So she can stop meddling. I'm old enough to look after my own belongings.'

'Your ma's expecting, lass. We must make allowances.'

Allowances! It was like travelling with the one-eyed crone of Ben Nevis. Bridie shrugged, dislodging Alf's hand. He was always interfering in a big, dopey old-dog way, as if he could somehow worm himself into her dad's place.

She fell into line ahead of Rhys and Siân Bevan, the young Welsh couple assigned to their mess of ten people.

Siân Bevan was raven-haired and dainty, like a fairy, and although her baby was due around Christmas, like Ma's, she didn't seem nearly as fractious. Her husband Rhys was a musician, like Bridie's dad. More than once, while listening to the strains of his violin above the clamour of the mess hall, Bridie had fancied herself the focus of his intense, dark gaze. As if he'd somehow guessed her secret, or been gifted with second sight—seeing beyond her nervous locker-side vigil and the shipboard routines of the emigrant depot and into her world. He hadn't, of course. This was real life, not one of her dad's fairy tales. Yet as the line of emigrants left the depot's grey stone walls, his gaze seemed to prickle the back of her neck.

Bridie fixed her eyes straight ahead, resisting the urge to shift the weight of her bag, or glance down to check whether the book's corners were making peaks in the canvas. As they trudged through the miry streets of Deptford, the rasp and chink of the naval dockyards was replaced by the trundling of a brewer's cart and the urine stink of tanneries. Dockworkers leered and pointed from the doorways of grimy taverns. Pot boys shoved past, eager to collect their coin. Women winked, wiping blood-red hands on their aprons. Bridie clutched her bag strings, fearing she might slip on the glistening cobbles at the entrance to Butchers' Row.

At the slick green steps of the watergate, they were hailed by a grinning, gap-toothed waterman whose plush cap didn't quite cover his large weathered ears. Alf balanced, feet apart on the steps above the tideline. He took Ma's bag and helped her into the waiting wherry. It rocked.

Ma shrieked. 'Lord, Alf! I'm going to drown.'

'Don't panic. Here, Mary love, take the waterman's hand.'

Ma clutched his hand, took a series of teetering steps, and lowered herself into the wherry. Alf stepped down, Thames water lapping at his boots, and passed Ma's bag to the waterman. Twisting round, he held out a hand to Bridie. She staggered back, clutching her bag to her chest. Here was a danger unforeseen.

'Oh, for goodness sake,' Ma called from the river. 'Hand over the bag. Alf won't run away with your small clothes.'

'It's fine, Ma. I can manage.'

'Don't be nervous,' Alf added. 'I'm here to catch you.'

She wasn't nervous. At least, not about falling into the Thames. Her notebook weighed a ton. Would Alf notice? Maybe not. He was pretty stupid. But, no, she couldn't take the risk. She stepped forward, determined to brazen it out, then felt a slender hand grasp her shoulder.

'If you don't mind, Mr Bustle, I'd like to settle my wife Siân on the boat first.' Rhys turned, a smile arching his brow. 'That's if Miss Bridie doesn't object?'

A smile. What was he playing at? Now she'd have to front up to

Alf all over again. Meanwhile, Ma's eyes were tight as buttonholes. Bridie shuffled backwards. Rhys helped Siân into the wherry, passed her his violin and canvas bags, and swivelled back round.

'Your turn, Bridie Stewart.'

'Mine?'

'I'll hold your bag while you step into the boat.'

'Oh.' A short giddy breath. Her hand shook as she held the bag out to him. He swung it onto his shoulder and winked. She blinked. Had she imagined it? No, his eyes were alight in an oh-so-serious face. She grinned, bunched her skirts, and clambered into the waiting wherry. Rhys leapt in behind her, plunked the bag at her feet and sank down on the bench opposite. That was it—all over in the sleight of his hand. Bridie traced the outline of her notebook through its layers of padding. Perhaps there would still be some magic in her world after all.

* * *

Their ship, *Lady Sophia*, was anchored about forty feet out from the watergate. Her curved wooden sides cast the wherry into a damp shade as they pulled alongside. A whiskery sailor lowered a wooden plank seat for the women who were expecting. Siân took her place and, with a series of heaves and chants, was hoisted up onto the ship's main deck. Then it was Ma's turn to board. Her shrieks joined the mournful cry of gulls as the plank seat swung up into the air and disappeared over the side of the ship.

Alf stood, face to the sky, bellowing his encouragement.

'Thank you,' Bridie mouthed as Rhys helped her fasten her bag to the end of a hook.

He nodded, his face seeming to pale as he glanced at the rope ladder. 'You first, Bridie Stewart.'

The ladder swayed. Bridie's head swirled. No! She mustn't panic. Taking a firm hold of the rung, she began to climb, desperate to reach the top before Ma started checking their luggage.

A gnarled hand helped her step from the ladder on to *Lady Sophia's* main deck. Pausing to catch her breath, Bridie saw sailors hauling on ropes; barrels and boxes were being lowered into the cargo hold of the ship, along with sacks, freshly sawn timber, hens in coops, sheep trussed and waiting, while a carpenter with nails in his mouth made finishing touches to a series of pens. She scarcely had time to take it all in before the next boatload of emigrants surged up the ladder. She grabbed her bag and joined the group gathered at the hatchway.

Steerage was a long, low, tunnel-like compartment squeezed between the main deck and the cargo hold of the ship. Narrow timber bunks lined the perimeter. A table with fixed wooden benches ran like a train track down the centre of the deck, but there were no cupboards or lockers, apart from the privy closets. No bulkheads to separate the families from the single men berthed in the forward part of the ship. Not even a curtain to shield the single girls in the after part of the deck. Only a low, thin partition separated one bed from the next.

At the sight of it, Ma laid her head on Alf's shoulder and wept.

She wasn't the only one to break down on seeing their accommodation. All around Bridie, women fumbled for hankies while husbands shoved hands in their pockets and tried to keep a smile in place.

Bridie felt her own eyes begin to mist.

No, she mustn't cry. She had to find a hiding place for her notebook. But how? And where, in this un-private space?

Weak sunlight struggled through the hatchways and scuttle holes. In between, murky oil lamps cast hazy circles of light. Bridie shoved her way through the press of people, squinted at the name labels affixed to each bed end, and found her berth in the family section, amidships. Stepping onto the bench, she hoisted herself into the top bunk she'd be sharing with Annie Bowles.

By rights, seventeen-year-old Annie should have been travelling unaccompanied, like the other single girls. But for some reason her vinegar-lipped aunt had offered Alf a gratuity to act as her niece's guardian. She would stay with them until she found work in Port Phillip, so long as she remained helpful and obedient. Bridie didn't think the latter would be a problem. Annie kept her head down and her eyes lowered when she spoke, probably due to the livid smallpox scarring on her face.

Bridie ran her fingers along the edge of their straw mattress. The bottom boards were slats, no hope of tucking the notebook beneath. Besides, Alf and Ma were sleeping in the bunk directly below hers. She couldn't risk it plopping down on their heads.

Annie smiled, jerking her chin toward an overhead beam. 'There's a peg. Hang your bag next to mine. I won't touch it, I promise.'

Bridie flushed, ducking her head. Had she been that obvious? Did everyone know she was hiding something? Not just the second-sighted Rhys Bevan.

'I'd offer to help … But if your Ma found out, she'd be cross, I think.'

Cross wasn't the word for it. Ma would be furious. Just like she'd been that final Christmas. Her dad had been so happy that night— no whisky scent to his breath, or slurred speech, only the fever flush of his cheeks to speak of a long and bitter illness. One minute he'd stood, eyes a shine, brandishing a flat, brown paper package. Next thing Ma's face had become ugly and twisted.

'We can't afford gifts,' she'd snapped, 'with you forever drinking.'

'It's a notebook, for her stories,' her dad yelled back. 'Why must you always spoil things?'

In the end he left, slamming the door behind him. Bridie lay awake, listening for the returning stumble of his feet on the landing. He didn't climb the stairs that night, or ever again. When they carried him home the next day, he'd turned blue with cold. Three days later he was dead.

* * *

Rhys didn't follow them down the ladder into steerage. Once Siân had made up their lower bunk next to Alf and Ma's, she took his dinner plate onto the main deck. After a hasty meal of mutton and potatoes, Annie followed, along with the rest of steerage. Bridie longed to join them. To get a final glimpse of London before Doctor Roberts, the ship's surgeon, arrived and the tugboats towed them down the river. But she couldn't risk leaving her notebook unguarded. The glint in Ma's eyes signalled imminent danger.

'Have you made up your bed yet?'

'Yes.'

'Well, for goodness sake, leave that bag alone for ten minutes. Come on, there's a good girl. Help me scrub this table.'

Bridie scrubbed until her arms ached, not only their section of the table, the entire length of steerage. Ma pulled out beakers and quart pots and wiped them with a damp cloth. After which, she tutted at the miry deck boards and set Bridie to work with a broom. Ma followed with a dustpan and brush, even poking her nose into the male and female hospitals at either end of the deck.

By suppertime, Doctor Roberts still hadn't arrived. Bridie and Annie set the table. Ma ladled leftover stew onto their plates. Their messmate, Pam Griggs, tied bibs around her children's necks. By the time Rhys and Siân joined them, supper was well underway. Though, it was hard to believe Rhys was the same young man who had winked on the watergate stairs. He didn't talk during supper, or smile, not even once. Though she told him her dad had been Scottish (a bit like Welsh) and had played the flute at Drury Lane. Rhys's white-knuckled hands gripped the raised table edge. His dark eyes seemed to stare right through her. Halfway through dinner, he lurched to his feet, grabbed his violin from his bunk, and stumbled toward the hatchway.

Siân's anxious eyes followed him along the deck.

After supper, the ship's mate announced that Doctor Roberts had been unexpectedly delayed. They would spend their first shipboard night anchored on the foetid brown waters of the Thames.

People muttered and cursed, pulling out maps, diaries and letter books to while away the hours. As the day's shadows lengthened into the purple of early evening, light from the scuttles and hatchways faded. Groups huddled over mugs of tea, talking of home and the ones they had left behind. Others slapped newfound companions on the back and recited the virtues of Port Phillip like a creed. Some, like Ma, held back a fresh flow of tears.

'I'm looking forward to it,' Pam Griggs said, pushing a straggle of hair back from her face.

Ma nodded, summoning a smile. She clearly didn't trust herself to speak.

'It'll be warm and sunny. No problem getting the clothes dry.'

Still no answer from Ma.

'Tom wants to work as a station hand. A man can earn forty pounds a year working out in the bush. Imagine that! No more strikes or fretting about the rent, no more haggling over the price of bread. We'll eat meat three times a day.'

Ma didn't care about the money. Bridie could tell. Or about the meat. She certainly didn't care about Tom Griggs' job. Her chin quivered as she stared down into her milky mug of tea. Bridie might have felt sorry for her, if not for the notebook. But, really, it served Ma right. She ought to have thought before she decided to emigrate. Before she married Alf. He'd been on about Port Phillip from the beginning. Long before Bridie's dad died, when he was simply another lodger in the house. A big, dull, friendly man who spoke of lost opportunities, endless hours working in the market shop, and the need to make a fresh start.

In the end, Ma had married Alf—and agreed to emigrate, although she wasn't content. The idea of sailing halfway round the world frightened her, as did living in a strange, back-to-front place without cobbles, carriages or shops. Mostly she worried about the baby. Bridie wondered whether this one would live.

Her eyes found the back hatch. It would be nice to go on deck, see the river at dusk. Ma didn't look capable of bag inspections this

evening and Pam Griggs' bird-like chatter showed absolutely no
sign of ceasing. Yes, why not?

* * *

The main deck was cool and quiet after the close, dark fug of
steerage; the ship's three great masts tall and stark like winter trees
against the dusk-lit sky. Laughter and pipe smoke curled up from
the sailors' quarters beneath the fo'c's'le. A horse whinnied in its
makeshift stable. Through her half-open door, Bridie glimpsed
Mrs Scarcebrook, the ship's pretty-as-a-china-doll matron, reading
in her deckhouse cabin.

Between deckhouse and horsebox, two small boats lay lengthwise in preparation for the morning's departure. A hound had been
kennelled beneath one of the boats. The other filled with cages of
ruffling hens.

Bridie gazed out over the blackened river. Mills turned slowly
on the Isle of Dogs opposite. Small piers and granaries broke the
smooth, dark silhouette of its shoreline; the sight strange and foreign, as if they had already crossed an ocean. Somewhere, beyond
the docks, mudflats and the City of London, lay the cobbled streets
of Covent Garden. The streets her dad had walked, their lodging
house within calling distance of the theatres. The musical, magical
cellar where she'd etched his fairy tales onto the crisp new pages of
her notebook and run her finger over his final message and still felt
his presence, long after he was gone.

She didn't know how long she stood there, only that the light
thickened and the night air fell like a chill shawl on her shoulders.
Turning back toward the hatchway, she heard an eerie drawn-out
sound from beyond the deckhouse. She halted, nerves feathering
her spine. A long, slow note pierced the evening. The fiddle? Ah!
Rhys. He was playing an air, an-oh-so familiar air, from the *Beggars' Opera*. One her dad had played so many times—toward the
end with tears coursing his cheeks.

She walked slowly toward the sound.

In the shadow of the deckhouse she stopped, her breath coming hard and fast. Every piece of music held a story, her dad told her—a thread that attached itself to the heart. She'd become attuned to those threads, growing up to the strains of Mozart's *Magic Flute*, and Purcell's music for *The Tempest*, hearing tales of fairy queens, Arabian nights and midsummer dreams—and this was a sad song, quite apart from Peachum and his cronies in the *Beggars' Opera*. A long haunting melody that spoke of a sadness and longing.

Head bent, eyes closed, Rhys's lashes made a smudge against the night-white of his cheeks. It might have been the melody, or simply her fear of discovery. Maybe the memories of her dad. But she saw a struggle in the lines of his body that went beyond the music. Something in the long, measured stroke of his bow that put her in mind a sapling bent hard by the wind. She found herself dissolving at the sight.

She stood for an age, with her fist jammed in her mouth, trying not to sob aloud. Forever, it seemed, until the music drew to a gentle close. She didn't clap, though his performance surely deserved it. She turned quietly to leave.

'It's called "*Ar Hyd y Nos*"', his soft voice followed. "All through the Night", you might say in English.'

Bridie stopped, hugging her arms to her chest.

'Welsh, it was, long before Gay made use of it in his opera. A love song, recorded by Mr Jones in his *Relicks of the Welsh Bards*. I've heard it many a time, though I'm not convinced of the lyrics. It speaks sorrow to me, quite apart from the romance. Death, perhaps, or ambition gone wrong? A secret? What do you say, Bridie Stewart? Am I being fanciful on the eve of a long and difficult journey?'

He knew. How did he know she'd been listening?

'I'll not force you to speak, *bach*. Only seeking your thoughts, as you're haunting the deck along with me.'

Silence. He waited. She stepped forward, pulse thrumming.

'I can't stay out long, Mr Bevan, because of Ma. But I liked your playing and I agree about the melody. It speaks sorrow to me too.'

'Indeed!'

'My dad was a theatre musician. So I've heard that tune loads of times. I've always fancied it a lament—for a fairy who had died.' She stopped, aware of how foolish that must sound. For some reason, she didn't want to appear foolish before this soft-voiced young man with truth-seeing eyes. 'I suppose, if there are Welsh words written in a book, I might be wrong. About the fairies, I mean. Not about the sorrow.'

He laughed. 'You mustn't apologise, Bridie Stewart. Where I come from, beauty is often attributed to the fairies.'

Was he in earnest? She peeped up at him through her lowered lashes. Found his smile, a pair of warm, dark eyes, an eyebrow raised in query. But how to explain about her dad's love of fairy tales? How, in the early days, before he got sick, her world had been filled with wonder and stories, how they lived still in her memories?

'We played this game, in the cellar of our lodging house in Covent Garden, with spangles and feathers and a magic stone. My dad made it up to keep me amused while he was practising. If I played quietly, without once interrupting, the fairies would leave a gift for me. Nothing fancy, only baubles and trinkets. Back then, I thought even his music came from the fairies.'

For a while, Rhys didn't speak. Turning, he laid violin and bow in the case at his feet. 'Is that what you're hiding, Bridie Stewart? A gift from the fairies?'

'Yes.'

'Something forbidden, you couldn't bear to leave behind?'

'Forbidden, yes, but not bad, Mr Bevan. At least, I'm not doing any harm. It's a notebook, filled with fairy tales. My dad gave it to me before he died.'

'And now you are leaving the home of your childhood, with its cellar and magic fairy memories, and you wish to carry his presence to the far side of the world?'

She nodded, a lump forming in her throat. He knew. How did he know? How did this young man understand what Alf and Ma couldn't?

'Ma wants me to forget him, Mr Bevan, and his stories. But I won't, ever. Even if I have to keep my notebook hidden in Port Phillip.'

'Rhys, Bridie Stewart. You must call me Rhys, seeing as you've made a smuggler of me.'

'Oh, yes, of course. Thank you … Rhys. I won't ask you to hide anything else, I promise.'

Hands in his pockets, he gazed out over the blackened water. 'We all have secrets, Bridie Stewart. Yours is safe with me.'

* * *

The tables had been cleared by the time Bridie climbed into her bunk. Ma's grief had driven her deep into sleep. Alf sat, woe-faced, on the bench beside her, his big blunt hand stroking her shoulder. In the upper bunk, next to Bridie's, Pam Griggs was brushing and plaiting her hair. Her husband Tom had donned a striped green nightcap. Keeping her back to the open deck, Bridie undid her bodice, pulled a nightdress from her bag and slipped it over her head. She touched a finger to the corner of her notebook before snuggling down beside Annie.

'This time tomorrow we'll be at sea,' the older girl whispered. 'Are you nervous?'

'A little, yes.'

'My aunt told me there will be savages in Port Phillip, with spears and wild dogs. We'll live in tiny wooden huts, in the middle of nowhere, never knowing when we are going to be attacked.'

Bridie shivered. Annie's aunt didn't sound like a cheerful woman. Although, Alf had told similar tales. She could scarcely credit them, nor imagine living in such a strange place. Would she still be able to feel her dad's presence without the music and magic of the cellar? Or would she reach the other side of the world and find everything had changed?

The ship's carpenter extinguished the lamps. Steerage lay in darkness, with only a dimmed light to mark each hatchway. Bridie heard whispers and muffled sobs, the ship's bells tolling the half hour. She lay awake, listening to the deep, dark lap of the Thames and the groan of their vessel adjusting to the tide.

Sometime around midnight, she heard a stumbling around the main hatch. As the footsteps drew closer, she realised they belonged to Rhys. His appearance provoked a whispered explosion in the bunk next to Alf and Ma's. Bridie didn't understand the Welsh. But she fancied Siân was trying to reason—and that Rhys was in no mood to listen.

She woke again in the early hours of the morning. Groping her way back from the privy, she collided with Rhys.

'*Sori,*' he gasped, panting, as if he'd been running.

Bridie watched him stagger along the deck, boots in hand. He might have been going for a stroll in the moonlight. But Bridie didn't think so. His jerky flight up the ladder made her think of *secrets*, and the words *long and difficult journey.*

CHAPTER 2

*B*ridie woke the next morning to the clamour of six bells. She blinked, rubbed her eyes, saw the brooding deck boards above, her bag hanging from its peg, felt the empty rumple of blankets on Annie's side of the bed. All around her, women wriggled into shifts and bodices. Bleary-eyed men pulled shirts over tousled heads. On the deck below, Pam Griggs struggled to dress her children.

'Stand still, Billy. Let me button your trousers. Thumb out of your mouth please, Lucy. I can't fasten your bodice. Oh, thanks, Annie. She needs a fresh pinafore.'

By the time Bridie had dressed and slithered down from her bunk, two-year-old Lucy was perched on Annie's lap, thumb wedged firmly in her mouth. Giggling and squirming, her face pinked with pleasure as Annie played *This Little Pig* on her toes.

'What about me?' Billy's head popped up smiling like a Jack-in-the-box. 'I got little pigs too.'

'If you want a turn, you must ask politely.'

'Can I 'ave a go please, Miss Annie Bowles?'

Annie laughed, patting the bench. 'Yes, come on, sit here beside me.'

Billy grinned, wriggled onto the bench, and held out a grubby foot. 'I got five little pigs. I've counted. But I mightn't giggle like Lucy, or squirm nearly as much. Coz I'm older than her.'

Fresh bread had been delivered to the ship while they slept. Ma hacked their loaf with a long-handled knife. Alf scooped leaves into the teapot while Tom fetched boiling water from the galley. Bridie helped Siân set plates out along their section of the table. Rhys was nowhere to be seen. Had he returned to steerage in the early hours of the morning? Or stayed on the main deck? The tight press of Siân's lips suggested the latter. From the dark shadows beneath her eyes, Bridie guessed neither the Welsh girl, nor her husband, had enjoyed a good night's rest.

After breakfast, Siân held up a shiny new penny and announced that she and Rhys were going to throw it over *Lady Sophia*'s bows as they got under way.

'For luck,' she said, her eyes a flash of sudden tears, 'and goodbye. Maybe also for wishing.'

Imagine that, a whole new penny—and a wish. Bridie thought her heart might stop. She didn't have a penny (and one look at Ma's face told her it wasn't worth asking). But if she stood beside Rhys and Siân as their penny spun through the air, she might borrow some of its magic. If she closed her eyes, hands gripping the bulwarks, and made a wish, then maybe, just maybe, her notebook would stay safe on its peg for the remainder of the voyage.

* * *

Doctor Roberts arrived while they were finishing the breakfast dishes. He sat, straight as a yard rule, though the wherry bobbed on the morning tide, one gloved hand gripping the rim of his silk top hat, the other resting on a silver-handled cane. He might have been a pleasure seeker out for a jaunt along The Strand, if not for his portmanteau and the set of travelling drawers he had hauled over the side of the ship.

Within half an hour of boarding he called a cleaners' meeting. Alf's name topped the list. His big, round face glowed with pride as if he'd won a prize. Ma kissed his cheek and straightened his cap as if he were an overgrown schoolboy. It was all rather embarrassing, as far as Bridie was concerned, and annoying—because Ma wouldn't go on the main deck without him and, if Ma wouldn't go on deck, neither could Bridie. She was trapped between decks.

If being trapped wasn't enough to ruin her morning, Ma's mood certainly would have. She wasn't crying anymore. Neither was she happy. This morning, her tears had turned to ice—and she was snapping.

She'd re-rolled their mattresses at least twenty times since breakfast. Swept beneath their bunks until Bridie feared the boards might wear thin. Taken the mugs from their hooks and polished them as if they were silver instead of tin. Now, she'd run out of tasks and turned her attention on Bridie—and their luggage.

'There's a bonnet missing. The one I embroidered for the baby's christening.'

'It'll be in our trunk, Ma. In the cargo hold.'

'No. I'm sure I kept it out.'

'You couldn't have.'

'It'll be in your bag, Bridie. Get it down, please.'

Her bag!

Bridie's stomach lurched, her gaze darting along the raised table edge. She found the back hatch. The hatch! Where on earth was Alf? He ought to have returned long before this. For once, she'd have been thrilled to see his round, earnest face. She might even have managed a smile if he'd arrived at that moment, though she didn't normally encourage him, because, although boring and stupid, he did have a soothing effect on Ma.

Lady Sophia creaked and groaned, swaying in her mooring. Overhead, shouts competed with the thud of feet and the occasional clank of a brass bell. Sounds of cheering drifted down through the hatchway, the toot and bellow of river traffic. From somewhere far off, Bridie heard a rhythmic chugging sound.

'The tugs! Listen, Ma. Can you hear them?'

'Don't change the subject,' Ma snapped back.

'Don't you want to say goodbye to London? The things we'll miss?' Bridie lowered her voice. 'I'll look after you, I promise. Alf's probably forgotten we're waiting between decks. He'll be searching the crowd, even now, Ma, worried sick.'

'If Alf said he'd meet us in steerage, he will, Bridie. There are no two ways about it.'

This was true. Alf was horribly reliable. He went to church on Sundays, worked in the market shop on weekdays and stayed home of an evening. He hardly ever went out drinking. If Alf said he'd be in a meeting, that's where he'd be—standing to attention like one of the palace guards, as if the whole voyage depended on him.

There was only one consolation in this gloomy picture. If Alf was in a meeting, so was Rhys. His name had also been on the cleaners' list. And if Rhys was in a meeting, he couldn't be throwing pennies. Which meant she might still be able to make her wish.

'You can't stop the ship, Ma. Even if we have left the bonnet behind.'

'And you'd rather I didn't search your bag, is that it?'

'No!'

Ma's eyes narrowed. 'I've been watching you, Bridie—refusing Alf's help at the watergate, hovering over that blessed bag for hours on end. You've been skittish as a colt since we left Covent Garden, as if you're hiding something—and I've got an inkling what that something might be.'

'I've lied. Is that what you're saying? Been sneaky?'

'Yes. That's exactly what I'm saying.'

Ma gathered her skirts and stepped on to the bench. Bridie lunged forward, grabbing her arm. 'No! Don't climb up. It's ... dangerous.'

'Then perhaps you'll get the bag down for me?'

They stood, eye to eye, in a bubble of silence. The tugs had drawn alongside, their rhythmic wheeze all but bursting through the sides of steerage. Bridie heard a bark of orders, the rattle of anchor chains, a high, shrill cry of many voices, and all the while her fingers shackled Ma's arm, as if she could stop the moment unfolding.

She couldn't. Her dad's death had shown her that. Some things kept on happening, no matter how tightly you held on. This was one of them. And, no matter how much she valued her notebook, it wasn't worth a tiny coffin.

She stepped onto the narrow bench, grabbed the bedpost and hauled herself onto the bunk. She couldn't crawl fast. The overhead beams were too low. Although she'd heard Alf say the clearance was generous for steerage—around eight foot. She paused, adjusting her petticoats. Maybe if she handed the bag over, head held high, Ma would lose interest, give it only a cursory glance? Or maybe she could delve into the bag now, while Ma wasn't looking, and shove the notebook under her bedclothes? She glanced back over her shoulder.

Ma teetered on the bench, her eyes a steely gleam. She wasn't losing interest, or not looking. She wasn't going to miss anything.

Bridie's vision blurred.

She yanked the canvas bag from its peg, crawled along the bed and jumped down, hitting the deck with a thud.

'It's all right, Ma. You sit down. I'll unpack.'

'No. Let's get to the bottom of this.'

Out came Bridie's wad of scrap paper, her towel and cake of yellow soap. Next came her clean white shift, two pairs of worsted stockings, a pinafore and her starched cotton cap. Ma's hands delved to the bottom of the bag. Her fingers closed around the single remaining item—a flannel petticoat, with something hard and flat at its core.

Bridie's heart hammered. Her fingers clenched. She didn't move or cry out as Ma unrolled the petticoat and let it tumble to the ground. The notebook sat like a breadboard on her palm.

'I told you to leave this behind!'

'I couldn't, Ma. It's precious.'

Ma's lips thinned. 'I've been patient, Bridie. God knows how patient. I let you spend hours in that blessed cellar, when you should have been helping me with my piecework. Given you time and extra candles, though we could ill afford them. But it's been eighteen months since his death and you still haven't adjusted. Or made an effort with the new father in your life.'

'I don't want to adjust. Or forget my dad.'

'You haven't got a choice, girlie. We're leaving.'

'No. I haven't got a choice. About Alf, or emigrating. But I'm not going to leave my notebook behind, just because you hated my dad.'

'Me? Hated him! Don't be ridiculous.'

'It's true, Ma. You know it is.'

'Truth! You want the truth? *He* didn't love *us.* That's the only truth I see. If he had, he wouldn't have gone out that night.'

'He only went because *you* nagged him.'

'What of the other nights? Days spent staring at the wall? All our hard earned money spent on whisky? Is that what love looks like? He picked a funny way of showing it.'

'It was your fault! You told him to stay away that night. I heard you. "Don't come back," you said. "We're better off without you.'"

'If not that night, it would have been another. Why can't you see it? He'd given up, Bridie. He wanted to die.'

'No! My dad loved me. He'd never leave me on purpose.'

'He would—and he did. These words prove it.' Ma wrenched open the notebook, jabbing at the message on the flyleaf. '"She held him fast, tho' the wild elves laughed and the mountains rang with mire. She held him fast though he turned at last to a gleed of white-hot fire.'" Her lips curled. 'A reference to "Tamlane", isn't it? His favourite ballad? As if he were some blighted Scottish hero, instead of a man who didn't know his duty.'

'He was sick, Ma, and sad. It doesn't mean a thing.'

'"Dark nights, cruel winds, shadows overwhelming,'" Ma continued as if Bridie hadn't spoken. 'Then, here's the choicest part, "Write them down and think of me and how I have ever loved you.'" She looked up, triumph lighting her eyes. 'That's not a Christmas message. That's a goodbye.'

'No!' Bridie backed away, clapping her hands to her ears. Why did Ma always do this? Why must she always spoil things? Her dad loved her. He never meant to fall down drunk in the street. When they brought him home, blue with cold, he'd fought to stay alive with every breath of his being.

* * *

Bridie crawled into her bunk. She shivered, curled up small, teeth chattering—cold, so cold, despite the thick wool blanket. Shock. It must be shock. She'd heard Ma talk about shock before. She'd heard her say nasty things about her dad too. In the early days, when he first got sick, Bridie had witnessed their arguments first hand. She remembered Ma's shrill voice and twisting fingers. Her furious attempts to snap him out of his despair. But in all that time, amid all the terrible things that had been said, she'd never accused him of wanting to die before.

It wasn't true! Despite Ma's cruel words. Even in the final days of his illness, when coughs wracked his body and blood smeared his handkerchiefs, he'd dreamed of returning to Drury Lane. But what if all that time he'd been lying? If he'd written her Christmas message, knowing one cold night in the middle of winter would be enough to kill him? If he'd handed it over with love in his eyes, all the while planning to leave her … forever?

No! She'd never believe it. Yet, now the words had been said, she didn't know what to do with them, how to make sense of them. Only lie in her bunk, letting them curl around her like tendrils of smoke and cast their pall over everything.

Alf didn't notice. He came bustling along the deck, full of his own importance as always, seeing neither Bridie curled up in her bunk or Ma's stiff, upright form.

'Mary, sorry to keep you waiting. It's a long story. You'll never guess. Doctor Roberts has asked me to be his chief cleaning constable. He's a bit of a dandy to look at, love. But a professional man nonetheless. He took me aside, said he'd read my character references, thought I was a cut above the others. He wants me to be his eyes and ears in steerage. Imagine that! If only Mr Pitt had heard those words. He'd not have overlooked me then, would he, love? Or promoted Johnnie Blackett ahead of me. Mary?'

Bridie heard a pause. Alf's big dull mind trying to comprehend.

'Mary, love, what's wrong?'

'Oh, Alf, I've lost the baby's bonnet. And … Bridie's been sneaky.'

'Bridie? Sneaky! Don't tell me she's hidden the bonnet?'

'No, it's worse. Much worse.'

'What, love? Tell me.'

'She's brought her notebook on board, Alf. The one I told her to leave behind.'

'Oh, I see. Well, it's disappointing, I have to admit. You've been so patient with her. I'd hoped she would make a clean break of things once we left Covent Garden.'

'She accused me of hating him, Alf. Said I caused the argument.'

'There now. We know it wasn't that simple.'

Bridie didn't stir. As if from afar, she heard Alf's ambition, Ma's obvious distress. Her mind registered the overhead trample of feet, the close up flap of steam paddles, heavy lines dragging against the side of the ship. Somehow, somewhere, she knew this was linked to a magic penny. But she no longer cared. Curled around the ache at her core, she heard only a measured pulse and the low distant murmur of another world.

'I'll have a word with her. We can't have you upset. I'm going to be busier than ever in this new position. Where is Bridie anyway?'

'In her bunk, Alf, sulking. I've said too much. But you know how she gets my blood up. Still, at least she knows the truth now. I've set her straight on that score. There'll be no more mooching about, thinking her dad was God's own gift to the world.'

The deck boards creaked. Bridie glimpsed Alf's slowly turning form. She scrunched her eyes tight. Heard a sigh.

'Look at me, please, Bridie.'

'Go away.'

'I know you're upset. But we can't have arguments. Your Ma's condition is delicate.'

'She started it.'

'Can you climb down, please, Bridie? It's hard talking to a heap of bedclothes.'

Bridie sat up, shoved aside the rumpled blankets and slithered down from her bunk. Alf stood in the aisle, her notebook clasped like a Bible in his hands. Beside him, Ma bristled like a brush, her eyes red-rimmed.

'Your stepfather's here now, Bridie. He'll decide what's to be done.'

'No.' Bridie grabbed for the notebook. 'It's mine. Give it back.'

'Of course it's yours.' Alf laid a gentling hand on her arm. 'No one's disputing its ownership, and I'd like to give it back to you. But first we need to sort out this little … misunderstanding. You know why, don't you, lass? You're not a child anymore. You're old enough to be honest—and to trust me.'

The unexpected kindness brought a wash of tears. It wasn't real kindness, of course, only a pretence to get her on side. As if that were possible, when even now he fanned her notebook with his big, blunt fingers, as if he owned it, as if he had a right, seeing each carefully penned story without the music and magic of the cellar— and all through the lens of Ma's bitter memories.

'No, Alf! Don't read it!'

Alf stepped back, surprise widening his eyes. 'Don't take on, lass. I'm only trying to help.'

'You don't understand. It's private.'

'I do understand. More than you realise. But your Ma's upset. We need to put her mind at rest.'

Bridie's fingers curled. She wanted to lash out, yank the note-book from Alf's grasp, sprint along the deck. But what then? Find Rhys? No, he had his own troubles. 'You say you understand, but you wouldn't let me bring the notebook. You say you want to sort things out, yet you always take Ma's side on everything.'

'It's not a matter of taking sides.'

'Really? You never back me up, or see things my way. That's why Rhys had to …' She stopped, shuffled. Her eyes found the deck.

'Rhys! The Welsh lad? What's he got to do with this?'

'He … well, he may have helped me … at the watergate.'

'Helped?' Alf turned puzzled eyes on Ma. Unfortunately, she wasn't so slow to grasp the situation.

'Hah! Him, a married man, his wife about to have a baby. He ought to be reported for interfering. Still, I'm not surprised. Welsh—and a musician. He was bound to be shifty.'

'No, Ma. He wasn't shifty. He was kind. And he understood about my dad and my notebook … even about the fairies.'

'Stories! Fairies! Magic pennies! You think I didn't realise? "Don't you want to say goodbye to London? The things we'll miss?" In a few years you'll be married, with a husband and children to feed. There'll be no time for wishes then, my girl. Or magic pennies.'

'My dad made wishes. Even after he was married.'

'Exactly! A mistake from the beginning. With me too young and foolish to see the signs. A little less wishing and a bit more elbow grease might have put some food on the table.'

'Oh good, so I'll marry someone boring.'

'Not boring. Sound.'

'And stupid!'

'Enough.' Alf stepped between them. 'Let's not say things we don't mean.'

Bridie meant every word, and more besides. She blinked, looking up at Alf through a prickly haze.

He held up a silencing hand. 'No, Bridie. I want you to hear me out.' He swivelled back round. 'You too, Mary, before you start. This is a family matter. I'll not be reporting it to anyone.'

'You're the chief constable. You could have Rhys struck off the list.'

'It's too late, I'm afraid. He didn't turn up for the cleaners' meeting. Doctor Roberts is a strict man, Mary, and I hope a fair one too. I'll go a long way with his backing in the colony. But he doesn't strike me as a man for second chances. Perhaps it's just as well, under the circumstances.' He shrugged, thick lips pursed, and studied the notebook. 'This seems harmless enough. As far as I can tell, it's only fairy tales. That's right, isn't it, Bridie? Scottish fairy tales?'

She nodded, throat tight. 'My dad's favourites.'

'It's a lovely sentiment, lass, and I can see you've put a great deal of effort into preserving his memory. But your ma's right. You're too old for fairy tales. They didn't help your dad and they won't help you either.'

'Please. I can't leave it behind.'

'You're a clever girl.' Alf continued as if she hadn't spoken. 'Your ma kept you at school long enough to learn your sums. You could marry well in Port Phillip. You'd be an asset to a man with a business. There's no rush, of course. You've only just turned fifteen. But girls do marry young in the colonies, I've told you that already and, as your father, I intend to see you make the most of your opportunities. Is that clear, Bridie? Do you hear me?'

She couldn't answer. Tears fell thick and fast.

'Correct me if I'm wrong,' Alf droned on. 'But there are blank pages in this notebook.'

There were. She'd written small, drafted each story multiple times before entering it in her best copybook hand. Hoping, always hoping, there would be something more—a story she'd forgotten, perhaps, a treasured phrase, or ballad.

'I'm not an ogre, Bridie, despite your best efforts to paint me as one, and as we're setting out on a one-way journey, I'd like to make a fresh start. What do you say, lass? Are you ready to compromise?'

Understanding came slowly, letter by letter, then the whole word: *compromise*—agreement, understanding, settlement. She looked up, searching Alf's round, earnest face. 'You mean … you're going to give it back to me?'

'On one condition, that you work with me from now on—learn the names of the ship's sails, record daily temperatures, note geographical details of the lands we pass en-route. There will be so many interesting things to record, Bridie. Sensible, adult things to improve your mind. What do you say, lass? Shall we make a daily log of the voyage?'

Say? What could she say? Alf's words dropped like pebbles into her stunned silence. It was horrible. She shuddered. Too horrible to think about. Yet, so typical of Alf—this terrible misguided kindness.

'Well?' Ma's sharp voice interrupted her thoughts. 'What do you say? Your stepfather has made a generous offer.'

'Yes, thank you.' Head down, Bridie muttered the expected response.

Alf smiled, holding the notebook out to her. 'Right, it's agreed. A fresh start.'

At last! It was hers. Bridie snatched the notebook and spun round, hard and fast. Saw the nearby hatchway. Alf blocking her path. Head down, she shoved past him. Heard Ma's cry of alarm. Didn't look back. She flew up the hatchway ladder and stumbled blinking into the sunlight. Even then, she didn't stop. She shoved forward into the press of people, not caring whose toes she might tread on. Or who she might hurt. In the shadow of the quarterdeck stairs, she sank down, tears coursing her cheeks.

Too late for wishes, or magic pennies. Too late to find Rhys and Siân. But at least she held the notebook in her hand. Discovered, sullied, its final message horribly diminished—but hers, still remarkably hers. She would never share it with Alf. He wasn't her dad. She'd rather throw her notebook into the sea than let it fall into his big, blunt, interfering hands.

CHAPTER 3

*H*idden. Thank God he was hidden. Rhys leaned back against the horsebox, pressed his feet down onto the deck and tried to stop his knees from shaking. It didn't work. He drew a ragged breath, pressed harder, his fingers clutching the coarse fur of the black bitch curled up beside him. Hours, he'd been squeezed into this rectangle of space between ship's boats and horsebox. Ever since his panicked early morning flight from steerage. Hours, with his fists clenched and his feet jammed against the deck boards, waiting for the clamp on his airways to ease.

He'd heard his messmates line up for breakfast rations, the click of the capstan on the fo'c's'le, a drag of anchor lines against the side of the ship, feeling a jerk as the tugs took up the slack in the tow ropes, their vessel turning slowly toward the sea. He'd heard his name called too. Doctor Roberts. The ship's surgeon. The voice sounded oddly familiar. All around him, the whoops and cheers of his fellow travellers told him they were leaving. That he should be in a meeting, providing for his family. Or throwing a penny over the bows of the ship as Siân had planned.

For luck! Dear God, he needed more than luck this morning.

Still, he'd managed to pull his boots on. He couldn't have done that an hour ago. Maybe the worst of the panic was passing. Though he still couldn't crawl out from his hiding place. Or face his messmates. The thought of returning to steerage made him tremble like an old man with palsy.

He'd have to face it, eventually. Tonight, the next night, four whole months of nights—maybe as long as five? How many was that? A hundred and fifty nights. Dear God, how would he ever endure it? More to the point, how could he still be so pathetic? He wasn't down a mineshaft, or locked in a cupboard. Tad wasn't standing over him, belt in hand.

Crist, the memories, always the memories.

He breathed deep, fixed his eyes on the chink of blue sky above, and tried to stop his teeth from chattering. They had chattered the night he left Cwmafan. His knees had knocked beneath the table too. No! He mustn't think about Cwmafan. *Nefi*, how could he not think of it? The terror, the beatings, the flight. This morning, it was like the years between had never happened. All that schooling his face and pretending, gone. Vanished. As if Tad still had the power to force him underground.

He saw their grey stone cottage in the hills above Cwmafan, a child of six being dragged toward the pit head, himself running— always running, the sneering faces of his brothers, Mam taking his place down the mine. Rhys moaned, pressing his hands to his face, saw a seed cake with the number twelve pressed into its crust, his new work clothes hung in readiness behind the door, Tad's Bible open, accusing, his fist slamming down on the rough wooden table top.

'We'll have no more running, son. No more hiding behind your mam's apron strings. You're a man now, time you did a man's work. And, God help me, I'll cure you of this cowardice, even if I have to chain you to the coal face.'

Rhys had run—at midnight, on his twelfth birthday, taking his grandfather's fiddle and a hunk of barley bread from the pantry. He'd joined a party of drovers, travelled all the way to London, where Tad's vengeance could never reach him. Left Siân, the friend of his childhood, who had known of his fear and not despised him, who had shared his love of music and stories, who had needed to escape as much as he did, left her with only a tiny wooden love spoon and a promise he would one day return.

Eight years it taken him to fulfil that promise. Though it was never once forgotten. Eight years in which he'd taught himself not to shudder at the smell of coal dust, or jump at the sound of a door slamming, in crowded rooms to always stand within sight of an open window. He could never have worked on the Thames Tunnel; he knew his limits. But he'd carried churns from Evans the Milk's cellar countless times. Once or twice, he'd managed to fetch coal from the bunker without betraying himself. With time and maturity, he'd hoped his fear of enclosed spaces was fading.

Wrong. This morning, Rhys knew he was still a coward.

* * *

'Rhys, *cariad?* Are you in there?'

'Yes.'

'I've been searching all over for you. You've missed breakfast. And the cleaners meeting. We've a penny to throw, remember?'

Rhys sighed, lacing his boot. He could manage that now. Though his fingers still felt numb. He crawled to the end of the horsebox and forced his quivering legs to stand. 'I heard my name called, Siân. I'll see the surgeon after we've thrown the penny.'

'*Arglwydd mawr!* Look at you, milk white, chest heaving like a set of bellows. Did you get any sleep last night?'

'It's shock, that's all—wood, dark, like the inside of a cupboard. It's bringing back memories. I'll be fine once we get underway.'

'Fine! Truly? Hold out your hand.'

'No need. You can throw the penny.'

'Hold out your hand.'

It jiggled. He couldn't stop the penny from jiggling. Why wouldn't his hand stop shaking? He'd taught himself to recover, disguise the signs. Why couldn't he do so this morning?

Because you're a coward. Tad's voice sneered in his head. *Can't face another night on this ship.*

Rhys's fingers curled around the coin on his palm.

'We don't have to do this, *cariad*. It's too hard. We'll leave the ship at Gravesend, when the captain and paying passengers board.'

'*Iesu*, Siân! Think what you're saying. To raise our children in London's low lodging houses, is that what you want? To never know where our next meal is coming from? My pay barely able to cover the rent?'

'We could go back to Wales. If only you'd swallow your pride. That's where we belong, Rhys. With our own people, speaking our own tongue. Not in some *Seisnig* colony, on the other side of the world.'

'I said no!'

Rhys groped blindly for the whitewashed wall of the deckhouse. Of course, he wanted to leave the ship. His every instinct urged him to disembark. But he couldn't go back to Wales. After all they had been through. How could she even suggest it?

'What about your birth, Siân? Is your memory that short?'

'I have your name now, Rhys. No more need for shame.'

'And the rumours?'

'Never mind the rumours. You, I'm thinking of. The cost.'

'Go, then! Go back to Wales! You never wanted to emigrate. I see that now. You were counting on me to fail. Well, I won't, Siân. Even if this voyage damn near kills me. I haven't forgotten how ugly those rumours were.'

She gasped, backing away from him, her eyes wide as a fawn. Rhys shoved the coin in his pocket and pushed his way into the crowd. Cost! As if the rumours surrounding her birth hadn't already cost them. Dear God, even in London there had been whispers. Why couldn't she see? He was taking her away from all that. Forever. To a place where the worse could never be proven.

A coward can only run so far. Tad's voice sneered again. *In the end he must turn and face his fears.*

Tad was right, damn him. Like Jonah, he'd landed inside the belly of a great fish. Well, to avoid one thing, he must face another, it seemed. To win a new life, he must find the courage that had so far eluded him. Please God, he'd manage to do it with a degree of dignity.

* * *

Rhys didn't know how he shoved his way through the crush of people. Or indeed, how much time had passed. Only that he found himself clinging to the base of the fo'c's'le stairs. People, so many people. All around him, emigrants laughed and cheered, pressing up against him. Sailors dragged lengths of chain along the deck forming them into coils with short iron hooks. A red-faced ship's officer barked orders, scowling at those who hovered underfoot. Rhys's eyes found the horsebox. Half an hour, that's all he needed. A space to settle his thoughts.

No. Time to be strong. A man. He turned his face toward the saloon.

He'd missed the cleaners meeting. But Doctor Roberts might be willing to overlook that in light of his own tardy arrival. Rhys worked his way aft—past the horsebox, boats and deckhouse, the sealed up cover of the cargo hatch. At the main mast, he stopped, eyeing the closed double doors of the saloon. The stern cabins were out of bounds for steerage travellers. The depot master made that clear in his instructions. But the captain and paying passengers hadn't yet boarded. Doctor Roberts would most likely be alone in his cabin, buried beneath a mountain of paperwork. Rhys's fingers closed around the penny in his pocket. For some reason he didn't relish the notion of approaching Doctor Roberts. Something in the surgeon's clipped no-nonsense tones had brought a shock of recognition earlier. A dull unease in the pit of his belly told him the surgeon was not a friend to him.

He pushed through the saloon doors, heard them close behind with a click. He shivered, resisting the urge to turn, yank the doors open and stumble gasping into the fresh air. No, he wouldn't run. This was a room, not a tiny airless cupboard beneath the stairs.

An oak table lay lengthwise across the wood-panelled space.

Beyond it, a narrow corridor opened backwards onto a row of cabins. Rhys fixed his eyes on the filtered green light of a porthole and followed the table clockwise, past the sideboard and the steward's pantry, to where a seam of light threaded beneath one of the foremost cabin doors.

He stopped and knocked. 'Doctor Roberts?'

No response.

He knocked again, louder. 'Doctor Roberts, are you in there?'

He heard footsteps, a muttered curse. Something dragged across the cabin floor. The latch lifted. A pair of haughty brown eyes glared out at him.

'About time, young man. I've been waiting over an hour.'

'Sorry, sir. I ought to have come before this. But my wife's expecting.' Rhys swallowed, cursed himself for the lie. 'It's been a difficult morning ... for both of us.'

Doctor Roberts blinked, shook his head. 'Wife? Difficult morning!' He raised an empty tumbler. 'Over an hour, I've waited and, by Christ, I need a refill.'

'Sorry, sir. Rhys, my name is. Rhys Bevan. I'm here for the cleaners meeting.'

'Ah!' Doctor Roberts' expression cleared. 'The inconsiderate young man who kept us all waiting.'

'Sorry, sir. It won't happen again.'

'It certainly won't, Mr Bevan. The meeting is over.'

Doctor Roberts swung the door closed. Rhys sprang forward, jammed his foot in the gap. Doctor Roberts stepped backwards. Rhys fell, sprawling into the tiny cabin, his shoulder hitting the desk. The surgeon's papers fluttered to the floor.

Rhys held his breath, heard a cough, the gyroscopic swirl of his penny on the boards. He reached out a shaking hand. The toe of Doctor Roberts' red velvet slipper got there ahead of him.

'*You* are trespassing.'

'A second chance, Doctor Roberts. That's all I'm asking.'

'First, you keep five good men waiting on what you have

correctly described as a difficult morning. Then, you force your way into my cabin. Now, you have the temerity to expect employment.'

Rhys rose, forcing himself to meet the surgeon's gaze.

Where had he seen this man before? The deep, humourless lines about his mouth were familiar, along with the whisky-soured fug of his breath. But when? In what place? Rhys studied the surgeon's face. Nothing came. Only a sharp wave of revulsion that made him want to spit, followed by a dread, cold certainty—this man was not what he seemed.

'Expecting, my wife is, Doctor Roberts, as I mentioned earlier. I'd appreciate the chance to earn a gratuity.'

'Your financial embarrassments are of no concern to me.'

'No?' Rhys stooped, gathering the scattered papers. Many bore the familiar crest of the Emigration Commission. He laid them on the desk alongside a sheaf of passenger records and a slim volume entitled *Instructions for Surgeon's Superintendents on Emigrant Ships*. As far as he could tell, none of the official documents had been marked. A wad of credit notes seemed to have claimed Doctor Roberts' immediate attention, his blotter bore a criss-cross of tiny calculations. 'You'll not have found my replacement yet. Seeing as you've been so busy here.'

'I doubt you can conceive of the responsibilities I am managing.'

Rhys glanced at the blotter. 'Two hundred and thirty souls, is it, sir? With the possibility of two births en-route? One of which involves my wife and child? Let me see, what would that be—'

'A hundred and fifteen guineas, Mr Bevan. More than you've seen in your lifetime.'

Rhys nodded, indicating the wad of credit notes. 'Though, not enough to cover your expenses, I'm guessing. That's why you were late, is it, sir? Needing to conclude your business dealings? Or is it an escape you're after?'

Doctor Roberts stiffened. 'You overstep yourself, Welshman.'

'Not at all, only setting my need in its proper context.'

'The colony needs labour, Mr Bevan. That's why you are

emigrating. Though your safety is far from guaranteed. Dysentery and typhus thrive in conditions such as steerage, along with measles, mumps and scarlatina. An infection could wipe out your entire family.'

The curl of Doctor Roberts' lips suggested this would be the desired outcome. 'Fortunately, Her Majesty's Government has learned a great deal about the transportation of human cargo in recent years. I have been given authority to impose a rigorous sanitary regime. I intend to exercise that authority, Mr Bevan, and to claim a just reward for my efforts. For that, I will need the best of men. Not upstarts who don't know their place. Have I made myself clear?'

'Perfectly. I have the measure of you completely.'

Doctor Roberts lifted the toe of his slipper. 'Take your penny then, Mr Bevan, seeing as you're so concerned about your finances.'

'I'll not grovel at your feet, Doctor Roberts. No matter how great the authority you wield.'

'You may regret that, Welshman.'

Rhys shrugged, turning away. 'Perhaps. But I'll leave the penny with you, if you don't mind, seeing as you'll be overseeing my wife's confinement. It'll ease my mind, to know to know I've paid a little extra toward your services.'

CHAPTER 4

Their seasickness started amid the grey-green waters of the Nore. As Alf stood on the main deck and watched the coastal scenery unfold, he saw people's smiles lose their shape, a whiteness coming into their cheeks. The morning's chatter faded into an uneasy silence.

Young Bridie was one of the first to take sick. She crawled into her bunk before *Lady Sophia* had threaded her way through the sandy banks at the mouth of the Thames. Mary followed soon after, along with Pam Griggs who, in between gut-wrenching heaves, held first Billy, then Lucy, as they spewed onto the deck.

'It's mind over matter,' Tom Griggs said, holding out a hawse bucket. 'As you can see, Pam, I've got a cast iron constitution.'

Pam glanced up, scowling, and wiped the spittle from Billy's lips. 'More like hot air, if you ask me.'

'Don't look at me like that, Pam. I'm only trying to help.'

'Then do us a favour. Stop your blathering.'

After that, it was like a row of dominos. One by one, Alf watched his fellow travellers fall. Politely at first—dashing for the privy, or reaching for the nearest pot or pan. But their manners didn't last beyond the hour. By evening, they were heaving and puking the length of steerage.

The high, rolling swell of the channel didn't help matters. Nor the overnight storm that tossed *Lady Sophia* like a twig on the waves. Alf lay in his bunk, listening to Bridie's choked sobs and the empty retch of Mary's stomach while seawater oozed through the sides of the ship and a witch's wind shrieked high in the rigging.

When the carpenter came down to light the lamps the following morning, his presence was met by a chorus of groans. As Alf walked the deck offering words of comfort, he saw misery in people's faces, along with the aching, unasked question: *Will it be like this for the whole voyage?*

'Not long,' he said. 'Surgery at three bells. Doctor Roberts is bound to have something in his cupboard.'

He stopped beside Bridie's bed. 'Are you getting up for surgery, lass?'

'No!'

'It won't last forever. Here, sit up, have some tea.'

'Go away. I'm dying!'

Alf sighed, turning away. Why was she always so dramatic? Anyone would think she was the only one affected. Still, it was hardly surprising, considering the fancies she'd been raised on. That would change now they had left Covent Garden. No more theatres to invoke her father's presence, or cellar infused with his memory. The idea of turning her notebook into a voyage log had been an inspiration. Though, it may take time for Bridie's enthusiasm to match his own. He'd bring her round.

He stooped to rouse Mary. 'Surgery time, love.'

'I can't sit up, Alf. The deck's spinning.'

'Nonsense. We've got a qualified surgeon on board, compliments of Her Majesty's Government. We'd not have been able to afford that in Covent Garden, would we, love?'

'We'd not have needed to if we hadn't come to sea.'

'Yes, but think of the benefits. The prosperous new life we'll have in Port Phillip.'

'Do me a favour, Alf. Don't remind me. I've enough on my plate this morning.'

'Oh, yes, of course. Let's get you up then.'

Alf knelt on the bench, tucked his hands under Mary's shoulders and eased her into a sitting position. She moaned, eyes closed. Alf felt a jerk, saw her throat convulse. A gush of warm bile hit his chest.

Mary's lips quivered.

'There, now. Don't cry.' Alf laid her back down and pulled the blanket over her shoulders. 'Doctor Roberts is bound to have a pill or a powder in his cupboard. I'll bring it back down, shall I?'

* * *

The dispensary was a deep, full-length cupboard set into the starboard side of the deckhouse. After Alf had changed his shirt, he helped a line of lesser sufferers drag themselves up the hatchway ladder onto the main deck. He took his place at the end of the queue. Watched traveller after dejected traveller step forward, heard Doctor Roberts' matter of fact replies.

'Rest is the only cure, I'm afraid. Yes, I'm sure your wife is suffering. But do take heart. It won't last forever. She'll be on her feet in no time.'

At last, it was Alf's turn to step forward.

'Ah, Bustle. How are we this morning?'

'I'm fine but—'

Doctor Roberts held up a gloved hand. 'Not you too, Bustle. Honestly. I don't know what people thought. Coming to sea is a wretched affair.'

'Yes, I see. Suffering is to be expected.'

'Good man.' Doctor Roberts clapped him on the shoulder. 'I knew I could rely on you. A cut above the others, I said, and by Jove, I mean it. You'll have your work cut out for you, though, Bustle, with so many affected. Still, you'll have helpers, I expect?'

'Three, sir. Annie, the lass travelling with my family, is up and dressed this morning. As is Harvey Rolf, one of the other steerage cleaners.'

'Three! Dear me.' Doctor Roberts tutted, shaking his head. 'These winds aren't helping, coming from the west as they are. Still, at least you've got helpers. Three, you said, Bustle. Who's the other one?'

'Tom Griggs, one of the married men in my mess. But he's not a great help. He seems to think seasickness is all in the mind.'

'I see. Not a consoling attitude. But there's an element of truth in his supposition. You must keep people's spirits up, Bustle, along with their fluids, and, it goes without saying, I want the deck sanitised. Cleanliness and order, those are my prescriptions. If you can manage that, people will rally in no time.'

* * *

Things hadn't improved by the following morning. Alf fetched boiling water from the galley. Once the leaves had steeped, he and his helpers carried tepid cups of tea to people lying in their bunks. In between rounds, Alf emptied the privy buckets, swabbed the deck with chloride of lime, and lit the aromatic swinging stoves.

Doctor Roberts held surgery twice daily at the appointed times. But after the first morning, only Rhys struggled up the ladder on to the main deck where he sat, huddled at the bulwarks, rising occasionally to vomit into the sea. Everyone else stayed inert in their bunks, calling down curses on Doctor Roberts' head while, with their next breath, they implored the Almighty to come to their aid. By evening of the second day, many sobbed aloud, certain their lives would end. When the bell rang for supper, Siân dragged herself upright. Face pale, swaying with fatigue, she produced a waxed packet of leaves.

'Horehound, Mr Bustle, and ginger. One of my aunt's favourite remedies. Mix it with black tea and sugar. It'll settle people's stomachs.'

The black tea did nothing to disguise the bitter tastes of horehound and ginger. But to Alf's surprise, people accepted the infusion readily. In many cases, it seemed to be helping, though not in Mary's. Her skin looked putty grey in the lamplight and felt hot to touch. Maybe he should ask Doctor Roberts to pay her a visit?

No, he mustn't panic, or jeopardise his position. This was normal, Doctor Roberts said, to be expected.

The gales worsened overnight. The carpenter battened down the hatches and covered the scuttles. Bridie and Annie shrieked in the bunk above. As the ship pitched and shuddered, Mary's head lolled like a doll's. Alf held her fast, fearing she would be flung from their bunk.

At breakfast the following morning, Tom Griggs moaned, and spewed his porridge onto the deck.

'Where's the bleedin' surgeon?' He gave a gurgling half-cry. 'A man could die down here for all he cares.'

'It's the storm, Tom. Upsetting your stomach. Here, have some tea.'

'Gawd! Not that muck.'

'Not muck. Medicine. Siân's remedy.'

'I don't care if the bleedin' Virgin Mary herself prescribed it. I ain't having any.'

'Come on, set an example. Billy's watching—and Lucy. Doctor Roberts said to keep your fluids up.'

Tom grabbed the bench and dragged himself upright, drool glistening his lips.

'Fluids! I'll tell you about fluids. I've just lost 'em. And you can tell your fancy Mr-Top-Hat-and-Tails surgeon that there's sick people down here, really sick, your wife included. And if he wants to set an example, he can bloody well come down here and look after us properly.'

A sudden lurch made Alf fling out a hand. He grabbed the bed-post, keeping his head down lest Tom read the confusion in his face. Maybe the other man was right. Maybe he'd let things go too far. Mary was sick, really sick—and Bridie. Now even Tom Griggs was vomiting.

* * *

The overnight gales had been fierce. Choppy morning-after seas made it almost impossible to stand. Hands wide, legs apart, Alf watched Doctor Roberts insert a key into the salt encrusted lock. The cupboard doors creaked open, revealing the shelves in serious disarray. This morning, one of the large stoppered bottles had broken. Doctor Roberts picked up a shard of glass and dropped it into the bucket he was using as a bin, his movements abrupt, testy, his eyebrows almost touching over the bridge of his nose.

Alf swallowed, his mouth filling with cobwebs. Maybe this wasn't a good time to ask about Mary. He should wait, perhaps, until afternoon surgery. No, that was a feeble excuse—*Sorry Mary, I couldn't talk to the surgeon, his brows were too low.* Besides, what did he have to fear? Doctor Roberts clearly thought well of him. 'Good man,' he'd said, followed by 'a cut above the others'. He wouldn't have said those things unless he meant them, or asked Alf to be his 'eyes and ears in steerage'.

Alf coughed, clearing his throat. 'Good morning, Doctor Roberts.'

'Ah, Bustle. How are my patients this morning?'

'Much the same, I'm afraid.'

'You've kept their fluids up?'

'Yes.'

'Then there really is nothing more we can do.'

'Ordinarily, I would agree with you, sir. You've so been generous with your instructions. But … it's my wife Mary I'm worried about.'

'No doubt you are worried. But we mustn't let emotion cloud our judgment.'

'No, of course not.' Alf reached out, steadying himself against the solid wall of the deckhouse. 'But she's expecting, you see, and hasn't been at all well, what with the strain of the move, and now these storms. She can't keep a thing down. I wondered, well, I'd hoped, if it wasn't too much trouble—'

'Yes, yes. I appreciate your concern.' Doctor Roberts interrupted with a flick of his hand. 'But a sea voyage is hard on women who are breeding. You knew that before setting sail, I presume?'

'Yes, no, I mean, definitely, sir. Siân, the little Welsh girl is also badly affected. I see that, now you've pointed it out. But she's not the only one.' Alf thought of Tom, Bridie, the two hundred or so others lying wretched in their bunks. 'Some … well, even some of the stronger ones are beginning to feel discouraged.'

'Nonsense. You must be firm. Surely, you've explained the temporary nature of the situation?'

'Yes, I have, but I think they might need—'

'What they *need* is a change.' Doctor Roberts turned, eyes narrowed, pointing. 'Like that stubborn Welsh lad over there. He's a strange, haughty sort of fellow. A troublemaker, Bustle. Mark my words. You'll do well to keep an eye on him. He didn't take kindly to being dismissed. Made the most astonishing accusations. And now here he is, huddled on the main deck. It's a bit odd, don't you think?'

Alf didn't know what to say. He'd had little chance of getting to know Rhys before setting sail. He seemed a polite young man, though rather pale and withdrawn, when he thought about it, and there was, of course, the strange business with Bridie at the watergate. But if asked to describe the Welsh lad, Alf didn't think the think the words 'odd' or 'troublemaker' would have topped the list.

'He seems to like the fresh air.'

'Precisely!' Doctor Roberts all but pounced. 'Tell your wife and any others who are complaining that they will feel a marked improvement out on the main deck.'

Alf glanced at Rhys, his face pale and green against the hard dark wood of the bulwarks. He didn't look any better for being outdoors. 'I think, well, if you don't mind me speaking freely … I think they might like to hear it from you.'

Doctor Roberts sniffed, his nostrils pinching.

'You disappoint me, Bustle. Really. I thought you'd jump at the chance of extra responsibility. Your references certainly indicated a capacity for hard work. But if you're going to complain at the first sign of trouble. Or let family matters interfere.'

'No! I won't, truly. I'm honoured by the trust you've placed in me. Only, I thought, perhaps, you mightn't realise ... how sick people were.'

'Your concern is noteworthy, although somewhat misguided. I will therefore put the slight down to ignorance.' Doctor Roberts' lips thinned. 'As surgeon superintendent on a voyage such as this, I must juggle a number of responsibilities. Many of which, from your limited viewpoint, you can scarcely appreciate.'

'Yes. Thank you, sir. I'll bear it in mind.'

'Very well. Now that's established, let's move onto the unfortunate matter of your wife.'

Alf eyed him warily. What was this? A sudden change of heart? He didn't think so. Doctor Roberts' lips were pulled downwards, as if the whole situation had given him a sour taste.

'The seasickness will pass, Bustle, as I've told you already. It's merely a matter of time. But talk is costly. No matter how careless. It can undermine the morale of an entire voyage. Since, in this instance, you've let it get out of hand, I must now make a practical demonstration of my care. Tomorrow, you will therefore gather all but the most seriously affected on deck.' Doctor Roberts paused, consulting his watch. 'Say at two bells, on the forenoon watch?'

'But—'

'I want you to set up screens and tubs for bathing, Bustle. People will feel better for a bathe. Once they're clean and comfortable, you may sanitise steerage, while I talk to those most in need of reassurance. Then, once the deck has been fumigated, I will visit those confined to their bunks.' He stood, a hand on each lapel, his buttons winking in the bleak, mid-morning light. 'Well, Bustle, what do you say?'

'Yes, sir, thank you, sir,' Alf muttered the anticipated response, all the while wondering how he was going to motivate a sickly, demoralised group of travellers to take a sponge bath in the chill wind.

The outward bang of an intermediate cabin door jolted Alf from his thoughts. He glanced up to see Mrs Scarcebrook, the ship's matron, staggering onto the deck. She looked dreadful, almost skeletal. Though she'd set her bonnet at a fetching angle, there was no disguising the scooped out hollows of her cheeks.

Doctor Roberts pushed past him with an outstretched hand. 'Mrs Scarcebrook! This will never do.'

'I'm quite well, Doctor Roberts. Only a little unsteady on my feet.'

'Not well enough, dear lady. Not nearly well enough. Even your friends at the commission would not expect you to work in this state.'

So, it was true. She did have friends in high places. How else could this sweet, honey-haired young woman have been employed as matron on a crowded emigrant vessel? Her husband had gone ahead of her to Port Phillip, if the rumours were to be believed, and found himself unable to meet her travel expenses. Though how she was going to oversee the welfare of the forty-eight single girls was anyone's guess. Doctor Roberts was clearly of the same opinion.

'You are gravely ill, Mrs Scarcebrook. I'll not have you out of bed until you are recovered.'

'You're too kind. But I daren't abuse my position.'

'Nor shall you.' Doctor Roberts patted her gloved hand. 'A person in my position has many cares—surgery sessions twice daily, a ream of paperwork to present at the end of the voyage, a host of other sundry emergencies. If you will share my burdens, of an evening, perhaps over sherry and biscuits? Lend your pretty hand to my paperwork? You'll be doing me an immense service.'

'Oh.' She flushed, dropping her gaze. 'You do ease my mind. For I must confess, I have no great experience of nursing.'

'And neither shall you, my dear. It's preposterous. One of the emigrant women can take your place. What do you say, Bustle? A married woman, perhaps? As befitting a matron's status.'

Alf shook his head. 'There are none enough, sir. Apart from the lass travelling with my family.'

'The disfigured one?' Doctor Roberts grimaced.

'Annie, sir.'

'Oh, well, she'll have to do.'

CHAPTER 5

*B*ridie's days passed in a blur of seasickness and storm. She wouldn't look at Alf when he brought the tea around, or talk to him. This was his fault, all of it—the leaving home, the seasickness, and now this horrible salt-water bath on the main deck.

'Come on,' he said, pulling back her covers. 'There's a good girl. Leave your notebook. You'll feel better for a bathe.'

'No!' Bridie grabbed the blanket and dragged it back over her head.

'Please, lass, everyone else is getting up.'

Bridie wouldn't budge, not when Alf wheedled. Or when he brought his big round face in line with hers. She heard Tom Griggs' muttered curses, Pam's tearful attempts to explain to the children, an all-around moan of people easing themselves upright. Still, she wouldn't leave her bunk. Even when Alf tugged at the covers again.

'Look Billy's up. And Lucy. You're the only one making a fuss.'

'What about Ma? She doesn't have to bathe!'

'Your ma's expecting. We can't put her health at risk. But look, here's Siân. She's never seen anyone behaving so badly.'

Alf shifted on the bench. Bridie felt a cool hand touch her cheek.

'Not badly, Mr Bustle. Only cross, she is, see, and poorly. Maybe a little frightened? Sickness takes us all differently.'

Bridie jerked upright. 'I'm not frightened!'

'There you are, only needing a bit of encouragement, she is, see. Leave us now, Mr Bustle. She'll be fine with me.'

Siân's face looked pale and drawn. But her eyes were soft with understanding. Her hand closed around Bridie's. 'Come, *cariad*, it's a bath we're having. Whether we like it or not. Bring your notebook. There's a good girl. It'll make you strong.'

Bridie wept as she dragged herself up the hatchway ladder and as she stripped down to her small clothes. Huddled against the bulwarks, she cradled her notebook to her chest and tried to feel her dad's presence. He wasn't there—not in the lurching grey menace of the sea, or in the scudding clouds overhead. Even the still, small voice of her imagination had fallen silent and, all the while, Ma's words coiled like a snake in her head.

He'd given up, Bridie. Why can't you see it? He wanted to die.

The hard yellow soap didn't foam like at home. The flannel scoured her goose-bumped flesh. She shivered, teeth chattering as she fumbled back into her bodice and skirts, the sensation like a thousand pricking pins.

Steerage smelled better on her return, she had to admit. Little by little, warmth stole back into her tingling limbs. She still couldn't rise, or join her messmates at the table. She could barely manage the short, lurching trip to the privy. The deck boards were so slippery, and the whole vessel tilted on an angle, as if the passengers were little silver balls and Neptune had decided to play a game with them.

'It's all to do with the wind and how they set the sails.' Alf explained with a horrible, toothy I-want-to-be-your-father smile. 'We'll write about it, once you've found your sea legs.'

Bridie had no intention of writing about the sails—with or without her missing legs. But she felt too weak to argue with Alf. Besides, the information was useless. Whether their ship was tilted by wind, Neptune, or God himself, it made no difference. Her legs still sprawled all over the place.

Things improved once the storms had passed. Bridie's world stopped swinging like a gong. She managed to rise, dress, and walk the entire length of steerage. Her days fell into the steady rhythm of bells, mealtimes and rostered duties. Except now she faced long afternoons in the sun. Long, lonely afternoons in which mothers nursed babies under awnings, men smoked pipes and discussed their prospects while little girls played endless games of pat-a-cake, and their brothers squirmed like maggots underfoot. Endless, empty afternoons, in which Bridie watched the sailors pick at oakum, gazed up at the men in the rigging, or stood with her back to the galley and listened to the black cook sing, until her legs ached and she longed to sit down. But where? And who with?

On the whole crowded vessel, she didn't have anyone to sit with, or talk to. She was the odd one out.

Ordinarily, this wouldn't have mattered so much. Even at the charity school on Hart Street, she'd been the oldest girl by a couple of years. But then she'd had her notebook for company. Now she couldn't read past the message on the flyleaf without hearing the echo of Ma's cruel words.

When night is dark and the wind blows hard and shadows overwhelm you—there are always stories. There was nothing sinister about the first part. Her dad had been sick and sad. He always took comfort in stories. But the next bit, *write them down and think of me and how I have ever loved you*, gave her an echoing, empty wellshaft feeling in the pit of her tummy.

She had to admit, it sounded an awful lot like goodbye.

Why? Why would he write such a thing unless he was leaving? And if he knew he was leaving, he must have known he was going to die. Which meant he couldn't have loved her, at least, not enough to stay alive …

No! Ma was wrong. People had accidents all the time. It didn't prove a thing. Not that they had given up. Or that they wanted to die. One day, she'd have answers to Ma's accusations. Meanwhile, she needed company. She'd go mad listening to the voices in her head.

At the base of the main mast, she picked out Rhys and Siân. All through the miserable days of seasickness and storm, she'd been aware of the Welsh couple suffering in the bunk below. She'd seen

Rhys's face drain of colour each time the hatch covers were rammed into place, Siân cradling his head in her hands. She remembered the coolness of those hands on her own cheek, the Welsh girl coaxing her out of bed. She'd hoped, once the storms passed, they would go on being friends. But these days, Siân only had eyes for Rhys. Even from a distance, Bridie could sense her concern. She kept glancing sideways, her eyes alert to Rhys's every movement, as if he were sugar and might dissolve any minute. As Bridie watched, she leaned close and pointed out a gull flying above the salt spray. Rhys smiled. His face momentarily lost its haunted expression.

Bridie's heart twisted. If only she were that gull. If only Rhys would look up and notice her standing alone. She didn't want to pester the Welsh couple, or sit down uninvited. But if she were to stroll past them on this sunny afternoon while Rhys was still smiling, maybe, just maybe, Siân would glance up and beckon her over.

Stepping away from the deckhouse, Bridie picked her way through a group of freckle-faced Scotswomen clustered about the cargo hatch. She followed the smooth, curved line of the bulwarks aft, stopping just short of the quarterdeck stairs. A plume of salt spray misted her cheeks. From amid a group of single girls, Annie's hand rose, beckoning.

Bridie swivelled away, heat creeping her cheeks. She didn't want to sit with Annie. Though, the older girl always made a point of inviting her over. Bridie didn't feel right sitting among the single girls with piled up hair and laced-tight waists. Besides, they were boring. As far as she could tell, they only ever talked about one thing—the single men.

'*Bridie!*' She heard her name called.

Without looking back, she began to weave her way through the bonnets, boots and sensible skirts of the single girls.

At the back hatch, she stopped to catch her breath amid a welter of soft-spoken Gaelic. Rhys and Siân sat forward of the main mast, looking out over a pile of rolled-up canvas. Would they look up? Invite her over?

She walked forward in a slow straight line, drew level with the mast. Rhys was close, so close, she could have reached out and touched him. She stopped, shuffled her feet, examined the smooth round head of a belaying pin. Coughed, shuffled some more, ran her hands along the taut lines of rigging, heard the high, thin snatch of her name again: '*Bridie!*'

She glanced down, tutting, and shuffled over to the pile of canvas, placed her notebook on the roll directly in front of Rhys. She raised her boot, tied one careful bow, and doubled it. Checked her other lace. Grabbing her notebook, she peeped sideways at Siân.

The Welsh girl caught her eye, smiling, and nudged Rhys. 'Look, *cariad*, here's Bridie, come to say hello.'

'Bridie!' Rhys gave a start of recognition. 'Bridie Stewart?'

'Yes.'

'And her fairy notebook?'

Bridie flushed, turning the notebook over in her hands. It sounded foolish without a gathering dusk and the haunting strains of '*Ar Hyd y Nos*'.

'Your ma relented in the end, I see, Bridie Stewart.'

'Yes. I mean, no. Well, anyway, Alf let me keep the notebook.'

He smiled, a tired smile, that didn't quite reach his eyes. 'Happy, I am, to see it safe.'

Bridie swallowed, looking down at her feet. The notebook was there, in her hands, but it was far from safe. Ma's words had twisted her dad's message all out of shape. She couldn't hear his voice anymore when she turned its pages, or feel his presence. But how to explain? And would he be interested?

She heard her name again. Closer this time. '*Bridie!*'

She turned, smile fading, and found herself face-to-face with Annie. The older girl laughed, shaking her head.

'I called your name ever so loudly. You looked so sad and lonely hovering about the main mast. I'm sitting over there with the single girls. Why don't you join us?'

Bridie bit her lip, glancing from Annie to Rhys and back again.

How could she refuse? Annie's offer was so kind, genuine. She'd have to join the older girl, unless Rhys spoke up now.

'I'd ask you to stay, Bridie Stewart. But I'm poor company.'

She nodded, pressing her lips together.

'Remember, I told you before setting sail, this was going to be a long and difficult journey.'

So now she knew: Rhys didn't want her friendship. Poor company, he called it. A long and difficult journey. Though, Siân didn't agree. She gazed at Rhys with such tender concern that there was no room for anyone else. Certainly not a fifteen-year-old girl with a big silent notebook and a welter of aching doubts.

* * *

Eunice was queen of the single girls. As far as Bridie could tell, her sovereignty rested on a pair of fluttering blond eye lashes and the smug certainty that her bosom was three times bigger than anyone else's. This made her an authority on all things unmarried and male. Though in truth, the single girls had little opportunity to mix with the single men. They cooked, ate meals, and did their chores separately. Even here on the main deck, they sat with the respectable buffer of thirty-six families between.

This didn't stop speculation, the endless deliberations over which young man was the drollest, or most athletic, or who would make the best husband. Today, Eunice held court from the bottom step of the quarterdeck stairs. As Bridie and Annie slipped in behind the group, Mr Rolf was the young man in question.

'He's handsome,' Eunice said, running her hands over her hips. 'But he's not my type. Besides, I'm going to marry a squatter.'

'A squatter? Whatever d'you mean, Eunice?'

'You know. One of those rich gentlemen's sons with all the sheep. Besides, I think Mr Rolf fancies you, Hilary.'

Hilary, a long, thin girl with rabbity front teeth, pinked with pleasure. 'Oh, no. I'm far too plain.'

Mr Rolf was a tall, solid young man with ears like paddles. He looked about as interesting as a tree trunk. Bridie had heard Alf sing his praises a number of times, which meant he must, indeed, be very dull, though this didn't seem to have occurred to the blushing Hilary.

Bridie glanced sideways at Annie. The older girl always kept her head down, bonnet shading her face during these discussions, as if trying to avoid notice. But the curve of her lips told Bridie she might be willing to marry a tree trunk if the opportunity arose.

Another girl, Ruth, knelt up and peered along the deck. 'Oh,' she gasped, sitting down with a bump. 'It's him—Mr Todd. He waved at me.'

As one, the girls knelt, craning their necks.

'Which one, Ruthie? Point him out to us.'

'The tall one. With a red kerchief.' Ruth fanned her cheeks. 'Lord, he's handsome.'

Bridie sighed. The single girls were all so silly. Even sensible Annie seemed to have had her brains addled. Was this what growing up was like? Why on earth would Ma and Alf want her to behave like this? Still, in other ways, it made perfect sense. Ma had been little more than Annie's age when she'd first married Bridie's dad. She claimed to have been young and foolish then, that the marriage was a mistake. Although, the way Bridie saw it, the foolishness had nothing to do with being young. Ma had married Alf within weeks of burying her first husband and was showing no signs of regret.

'What about you Annie?' Ruth's laughing voice interrupted her thoughts. 'Who do you fancy?'

Annie gave a start of surprise. 'Oh. No one in particular.'

'Go on! You'd be right desperate to marry, doting on Pam's children the way you do.'

'No. Not at all. I'd like to work as a nursemaid in the colony.'

'But, you'll want children?'

'Yes, of course, one day. But—'

'There's only one way to have children,' Hilary piped in from the side, 'and I don't mind admitting, I'm desperate.'

The girls shrieked, drumming their heels on the deck. It was so unkind, dragging Annie into the conversation when she'd been trying to stay out of it—and to call her desperate. As if she had no chance of marrying. Bridie reached out, grasping the older girl's hand.

'Now, girls,' Eunice called above their laughter. 'There's no cause for concern. Port Phillip is crawling with young men. The emigration agent told me. There isn't a single girl in the colony over the age of sixteen years. Sixteen, girls! Imagine that! Even Annie will find a husband there.'

Sixteen!

Bridie gasped, jerking her hand free of Annie's. She swung round, searching the older girl's face. Shame mottled her cheeks in high red patches and she had a trying-not-to-care press to her lips. But she didn't seem surprised by Eunice's summary of her prospects, or even alarmed.

But ... Sixteen? Married!

If there wasn't a single girl in the colony over the age of sixteen, that meant girls were courting at the age of fifteen—her age.

Realisation hit her in an icy wave.

All Alf's hints, all Ma's sly suggestions. Why hadn't she realised? There would be men lining the docks when *Lady Sophia* dropped anchor in Port Phillip Bay. Hundreds of big, dull men, all desperate to claim her hand in marriage.

'Fifteen!' She'd shout out through cupped hands. 'Only fifteen.'

Though by then, she'd be almost sixteen—the age for marrying and having babies. There would be no time for wishes then, Ma said, no time for stories—only a long dark future without music or magic or fairies.

CHAPTER 6

Annie cried all through supper and afterwards during mess duties. Bridie didn't blame her. She felt like shrinking down to Lucy's size and sucking her thumb after the afternoon's revelations. Though, as it turned out, Annie's tears had nothing to do with marriage, desperation, or Hilary's rabbit-toothed comments.

'You look right peaky,' Pam said, rubbing her back. 'Why don't you have a lie down?'

Annie sniffed, dabbing at her eyes. 'No, it's all right. I'm fine.'

'Still, I'm not surprised. You've taken on such a load at the dispensary. And my Billy's a cheeky monkey. You'll tell me if he gets too much, won't you, love?'

'No, please, Mrs Griggs. Don't blame Billy. I've got … a tummy ache.'

Ah! A tummy ache. Bridie knew what that meant. Not first hand. She hadn't started her monthlies. She thought, perhaps, it was just as well in the circumstances. Not even a big, dull man like Mr Rolf would want to marry a girl who couldn't have babies.

'Go on. I'll finish the dishes.' Pam eased the plate from Annie's hand.

Annie wouldn't stop crying. She scraped and stacked the plates while Pam protested, and Bridie did her best to help, and all the while tears ran in jagged lines around the pitted contours of her face.

Once the dishes were finished, Siân stepped in.

'Now, then, Annie *bach*. I've a red petticoat here to draw out the pain and an infusion to help you sleep. But no more crying, mind. Rest, you're needing.'

Annie sat docile as a child while Siân braided her hair, wrapped her in a red flannel petticoat, and tucked her into bed. Bridie climbed into the bunk beside her.

It wasn't late in the evening. She could have stayed at the table. Pam had risen, leaving a space on the bench opposite Rhys and Siân. But what was the point? Rhys didn't want her friendship. He'd made that plain this afternoon. He didn't even want to be in steerage. His white-knuckled fists clenched the raised table edge, his gaze straying toward the hatchway. He'd have been up the ladder in a flash, if not for the steady rain-beat on the deck boards overhead.

If she did take her place at the table, Ma would only arch her brows and say how nice it had been to see her sitting with the single girls that afternoon. Pam would glance up from her darning with a knowing smile. Before she knew it, Alf would join in, talking about her notebook and how she'd be an asset to man with a business.

Not that Alf posed a serious threat. Between exhaustion and Tom Griggs, he'd hardly had a chance to pester her about their voyage log. He sat, head in his hands, studying an old map spread out on the table in front of him, but every so often his eyelids drooped, as if the simple task of staying awake was beyond him. A fact that wasn't wasted on Tom Griggs.

'You can pretend to study that old map, Alf. But anyone can see you're done in. You'll drop dead from overwork if you don't take control of the situation.'

'The deck has to be cleaned. Doctor Roberts has strict instructions from the emigration commission.'

'And you're the muggins doing all the work—organising, motivating, inspecting, on top of your paid cleaning duties. You've gotta draw the line, get Mr Top-Hat-and-Tails involved.'

'Doctor Roberts can't scrub the deck.'

Bridie grinned. Alf really was very stupid.

'No, Alf. You're missing the point. And havin' been a junior retail clerk for so long, it's hardly surprising. But I was in the building trade, as I've told you a number of times, and I learned a thing or two about working men's rights.'

'Oh, good, we'll start a cleaners' union, shall we? Me, Harvey Rolf, and the other four men!'

'You can mock. But Doctor Roberts hasn't set foot in steerage since we left the Channel—and he won't unless you put your foot down. Tell him he needs to draw up a schedule and conduct regular inspections. Otherwise, you can't answer for our hygiene.'

'I can't tell Doctor Roberts what to do! He's an important man.'

'Important? Or are you too lily-livered?'

Oh, that was ripe! Bridie almost clapped her hands. Doctor Roberts wasn't too important to promenade on the quarterdeck with Mrs Scarcebrook, making her blush and giggle like one of the single girls. As for Alf, he'd work himself into the ground, just like he had at the market, rather than stand up to Doctor Roberts. Bridie peered over the bed end. A mistake. Ma glanced up from her knitting, brow creased.

'What are you sniggering at, Bridie? Take your head out of that ridiculous notebook, please, and come and sit with the adults for a while.'

'I'm not reading my notebook.'

'Then it must be Alf's situation you find amusing?'

Alf shifted, laying a hand on Ma's arm. 'Leave it now, Mary, love. We don't want an argument.'

No, Bridie didn't want arguments, or even to be noticed. She smiled weakly at Alf. Her second mistake for the evening. He beamed back at her, clearly seeing a way out of his torment.

'Your ma's right, Bridie. You'd benefit from a change of focus. Bring your scrap paper down here, there's a good lass. We'll make some notes for our voyage log.'

'What about the cleaning?' Tom poked him in the ribs. 'You still haven't answered me question.'

'I'm not a coward, Tom, if that's what you're implying. I'm simply conscious of my position. Something you may not understand for all your talk of working men's rights.'

He turned back to Bridie. 'Come on, lass, enough fairy tales. I saw you sitting with the single girls this afternoon. I doubt they had their minds on such nonsense.'

Nonsense! What about ogling Mr Rolf, all that cackling and drumming their feet on the deck.

'No!' The word exploded from Rhys's mouth.

Silence, heads turning all along the deck.

He flushed, ducking his head. 'Sorry. I didn't mean to shout. Only you're wrong, Mr Bustle, that's all.'

'Wrong? Regarding my own stepdaughter?'

'Fairy tales aren't nonsense.'

'Not in the strictest sense, young man. But they're hardly helpful for a girl Bridie's age.'

'We all need stories, Mr Bustle. They help us understand our lives.'

Alf blinked, clearly stumped by the turn of events. Beside him, Tom Griggs threw back his head and cackled with glee.

'Tell us a story then, Welshman. One that'll help poor Alf here understand his life.'

'Give over.' Pam nudged his arm. 'Alf's had enough of your tormenting.'

'No, Pam, I won't give over.' Tom's yellow-toothed grin widened. 'If this Welsh lad reckons he's got a story that'll help us understand our lives, I want to hear it.'

A story! Hope leapt like a hare in Bridie's chest. Though Rhys looked rather like he was going to be sick. His face pale, his Adam's apple huge in his throat. He swallowed, licking his lips.

'Fairy tales don't come made to measure, Tom.'

'You're the one making the claims, Welshman.'

CHAPTER 7

*L*ord, what had he done, speaking out? As if he had a right, as if he could help people understand their lives. Him, with his breath hard in his chest and his knees knocking beneath the table. Rhys turned pleading eyes on Siân. *Help get me out of this?*

She shook her head. '*Gelli di wneud e, Rhys.*'

Do it? No! He couldn't.

She leaned close, breath warm on his cheek. 'Dig deep, find the words within, the words we acted out as children on the mountain. The stories you told that company of drovers on the way to London. They are inside you, Rhys. Only be still, let them come.'

Silence. All around him, his mess mates' curious stares.

'Not long,' he heard Siân say. 'Only searching for inspiration, he is.'

Inspiration? Here, in steerage? He emptied his mind, softened his shoulders, his neck. Tried to hear words above the wing-beat in his head. Wisdom, Rhonwen, Siân's great aunt, had called the ancient tales. A torch. But could he find that wisdom here? Did he even have a right, when he hadn't spoken to his own father in years?

'You are not the wisdom, Rhys. The stories will speak for themselves.'

He nodded, held Siân's gaze, thought of wind—fresh, bracing, like on the mountain—Rhonwen's words filling him with wisdom and courage. Courage, yes, courage. He felt a familiar stirring—like sparks falling on tinder and producing a warm glow within.

Slowly, very slowly, as if pulling a cart laden with coal, he rose and shrugged out of his jacket. He stood, head bowed, trembling like an aspen leaf as Siân made her way to their bunk and returned with his fiddle. Her fingers were firm as she placed the warm wood in his hands, her presence a balm, soothing.

She began to hum.

Rhys closed his eyes, focused on the sound of her voice—soft, gentle, like a voice from another realm. The voice of his childhood. Never mind that his knees were quivering beneath his trousers. Or that his throat felt dry and resistant as old leather. The words were forming, still, small like a wisp of smoke at his core, yet there, unmistakably there, even in steerage.

He looked up into the hushed expectation of his mess mates' faces.

'Tom has asked for a story—one that will help us understand our lives. I cannot tell you Alf's story. Or, indeed, Bridie's. I can scarcely tell my own, for its meaning is not yet plain to me. But I can give you an ancient tale, of a prince with a hard, cruel father who raised a child other than his own. A good prince, an honest prince, Elffin ap Gwyddno.

'Elffin yr Anffodus, the bards liked to call him; though I would seek to show you otherwise. He was a hapless young man, not overly burdened by intelligence, who lived out his days under the lordship of Maelgwn Gwynedd.'

He was sweating like an old washerwoman at her tub. But as Rhys raised his bow and let the violin speak, he felt a tenderness spread through him, felt the heaviness that had been on him since boarding the ship roll back like canvas.

Felt courage returning.

He glanced about to see if his mess mates were following.

'Elffin ap Gwyddno! Elffin yr Anffodus!' Tom spoke aloud to no one in particular. 'Why don't he stick to plain English?'

'Wait!' Pam whispered. 'If you're patient, he'll explain the meaning.'

Rhys smiled. There was only one way to deal with a heckler:

answer them—in your own time, not theirs—without skipping a beat. Arms folded, the lines of Tom's face had fallen into a sceptical heap. But beyond him, Rhys saw heads lifting, fathers hoisting children onto their shoulders as, all along the deck, people jostled for a space on the bunks, benches and tabletops.

'Stand on the bench,' someone yelled out. 'We can't see back here.'

Rhys bowed, holding out a hand to Siân. She smiled, stepping up onto the bench, the small triumphant smile he knew so well. Rhys leapt up beside her and lent music to her song.

'*Misty May morning,*
Elffin's misfortune,
Take this tale as your own,
Wisdom and wonder,
Elffin's misfortune,
Find yourself in this story.'

'Now Elffin the Unfortunate was a plain, honest man,' Rhys continued, 'and therein lay his problem. For his father, Gwyddno Longshanks, had lost his prime lands through neglect and expected Elffin to make good his misfortune. To this end, Elffin was sent to the court of King Maelgwn Gwynedd. Alas, poor Elffin was neither a warrior nor a hunter. He was certainly not cut out to be a courtier. His prime quality was an honesty that did not allow him to speak with a double tongue. He served Maelgwn without distinction, married a woman without wealth or position, and settled happily on his father's remaining estates.'

"'Fool!' his father shouted. "Wasting every opportunity. How can we expect to prosper, if you will not exert yourself?"

"'I am content with my lot, Father, and to earn my bread in peace."

"'Peace! Contentment! What about when our enemies invade?"

"'Our prime enemy has been neglect. And you have allowed it to prosper."

'Now Elffin was a kindly soul and, despite his honest tongue, it grieved him to disappoint his father. He tended his hives, herds and flocks always hoping to win a measure of approval. But Gwyddno Longshanks was a hard, exacting man and, no matter how plump Elffin's cattle, nor how fine his fleeces, nor how clear and golden his honey, he took no pride in his son's achievements.

"'Tonight is May Eve," Gwyddno announced. "The door to the otherworld will swing open. If you cannot make a fortune in my salmon weir tonight, I will wash my hands of you."

'Now the salmon weir was Gwyddno's pride and joy. All day, Elffin toiled in preparation for the catch, resetting the weir poles and ensuring the wattle fences were in good working order. But his efforts were doomed from the outset. For that night, a vengeful witch cast her ill-born child into the sea. When Elffin and his father rode down to inspect the weir the following morning, they found nothing but a bulging leather bag hanging from its poles.'

"'You have broken the luck of the weir!" Gwyddno sneered, turning away in disgust. "Was a son ever so unfortunate?"

'Elffin's eyes stung as he pulled the leather bag from the water. Why must it always be like this? Could not fortune once favour him? To his surprise, the bag squirmed in his hands. Opening it, he found a baby nestled in its folds, a baby boy so beautiful Elffin's heart filled with love for him. Imagine his wonder and surprise when the child began to prophesy.

"'Elffin of steadfast heart,

Be not dismayed,

For I bring blessing.'"

A shiver worked its way up Rhys's spine as Siân took on the otherworldly voice of the child. She may not have been cast upon the sea by a vengeful witch, but she'd been abandoned at birth and raised by a wise woman, and there were rumours, terrible rumours that her birth was cursed.

"'Small and weak, as I am,

Washed up by foaming waves,

In your day of trouble,

I will prosper you,
More than three hundred salmon."

"'*Diawl!*' Gwyddno lurched backwards, making the sign of the cross for protection. "The child is bewitched! Throw it in the water!"

'Elffin turned, ready to fling the bag back into the weir. But as he looked down into the child's innocent face, his breath caught. Such beauty, his eyes so deep, soulful. A poet's eyes. How could they possibly abandon him?

"'He may not be what you expected, Father. As I am not what you expected. But I will not destroy him. Look, how he smiles! His brow so radiant. I shall call him Taliesin.'"

'*Misty May morning,*
Elffin's misfortune,
Take this tale as your own,
Wisdom and wonder,
Wealth for the taking,
Find yourself in his story.'

'As the child grew, it became apparent that he and Elffin were as unalike as earthenware and crystal. For although Taliesin possessed an honest heart, he showed no great talent for husbandry. He spun tales of flower maidens, bubbling cauldrons and otherworldly swine; named the stars from north to south; and wrote verse that none could ever rival. But although Elffin listened to these fantasies with wonder and pride, he doubted Taliesin would ever aid him in his day of trouble, let alone prosper him more than three hundred salmon.

'It was not until thirteen years hence that the original prophecy was put to the test.

'Having been summoned to Maelgwn's Christmas court, Elffin took no pleasure in the invitation, remembering only his awkward years as a squire in which he'd failed to distinguish himself. But as Gwyddno bade him attend, he set out determined to make the best of the situation. This he might have done, if not for the straightness of his tongue. For when others complimented Maelgwn's beautiful wife, Elffin pointed out that his wife, though not of noble birth, was every bit as pure and lovely.

"'Furthermore,'" the hapless Elffin ventured, "I have a poet at my hearth who outshines your learned bards in both wisdom and eloquence."

'On hearing Elffin's boasts, Maelgwn flew into a rage. Summoning his guards, he had Elffin fettered in and thrown into a dungeon. He sent his son, Rhun, in search of evidence.'

"'Go! Find this upstart poet, seduce this man's wife. If Elffin cannot support these claims, his life will be forfeit.'"

'But Maelgwn had not accounted for the poet being a thirteen-year-old lad. Nor that the wily Taliesin would hide his mother's virtue behind the pots and pans of the scullery. He certainly didn't expect that same lad to slip into Deganwy Castle and cause his bards to start babbling like fools.'

"'What is this?" Maelgwn demanded. "Why do you utter such drivel?"

"'We are bewitched." The chief bard swung round, pointing at Taliesin. "The lad in yonder corner is a demon. Every time he plays *blerwm, blerwm* on his lips, our speech is confounded."

"'Who are you?" Maelgwn demanded as Taliesin walked toward the dais. "From whence do you hail?'"

"'I am Chief Bard to Elffin,'" Siân replied, in the boy's clear unbroken voice. "My home country is in the region of the summer stars.'"

"'I see you have some powers and there is no denying your eloquence. But tell me, what is your purpose here among us?"

"'Elffin ap Gwyddno,
Lays in dark imprisonment,
Secured by thirteen locks,
For praising his bard,
I, Taliesin,
Chief Bard of the West,
Have come to release him,
From his fetters."

'"Chief Bard of the West, a bold claim indeed. How do you expect to release him, small one? With the strength of your song?"'

'"Words will indeed prove the key. But where is my father? Fetch him, if you dare?"'

'Here was sorcery indeed. Maelgwn's thumbs pricked. But he daren't refuse the challenge, lest he lose face before his subjects. Elffin was brought shackled from his prison.

'"So Elffin, it seems your poet is more boastful than you are. I confess to a curiosity. I am therefore willing to indulge his claims. If he can release you from your fetters, you will be allowed to return home unpunished. If not, your precious poet will join you in the dungeon."'

'Elffin trembled at these words. What a fool he'd been to speak out against Maelgwn. Taliesin would be imprisoned. There could be no other outcome. For no matter how profound his son's words, nor how powerful his imagination, they could not unlock his fetters.

'Taliesin was not so easily discouraged. He raised his arms and directed his voice above the roof trusses.'

'"Come strong creature,
From before the flood,
Without flesh, or bone,
Without vein, or blood,
Come strong creature,
From field and wood,
Who is strong, and bold,
Who is dumb, and sonorous,
Come! From the earth's four corners,
Mighty wind! Come!"'

'As Taliesin spoke, a wind swept through the hall. The great fortress of Deganwy shook on its foundations. Circling his father, Taliesin touched a finger to each wrist and ankle. The fetters sprang open. Elffin's chains fell tinkling to the ground. He rose, shaking his head in wonder and amazement.'

'"My son, my clever son. You have won us our freedom."'

"'A son is worth more than three hundred salmon. A poet's soul is to be prized above riches. For knowing this, Elffin ap Gwyddno, you will now be rewarded. Go! Dig a hole in the place I command you. A cauldron of gold will be the recompense for your misfortune.'"

'*Misty May morning,*
Elffin's misfortune,
Take this tale as your own,
Wisdom and wonder,
Wealth for the taking,
Find yourself in his story.'

'Elffin returned to his father's estates a wealthy man,' Rhys continued, as Siân's voice dropped to a hum. 'Though, he cared less about his new found prosperity than the son riding at his side. And although they were as unalike as earthenware and crystal, and although Taliesin showed no great talent for husbandry, they lived out the remaining days of his childhood in peace and prosperity. When the time came for Taliesin to take his place in the world of men, he did so without equal. So that Gwyddno never again doubted his son's luck at the weir that misty May morning, or cursed his misfortune ever again.'

* * *

Satisfaction rippled through the crowd as the story drew to a close, followed by an eerie suspension of sound. Head bowed, Rhys lowered his fiddle and waited. The clapping started, slowly at first, ragged, as if people were waking from an enchantment. It gained momentum, like a wave. Rhys let it break over him. He'd done it. Danced in the face of his fear. He felt flushed, new born, curiously alive. If he could hold onto this moment, he might yet make it through the voyage.

He jumped down from the bench, held out a hand to Siân. She laughed, skipping down beside him and cupped his face in her hands. Her kiss was light, inviting, her eyes a wick of invitation. Rhys wove his fingers through the dark muss of her curls.

'*Arhoswch!*' he mouthed the word. Wait sweetheart.

Releasing Siân, he stepped back and raised the fiddle to his chin. What to play? A jig perhaps, to meet the thrum of his pulse? No. Siân liked '*Ar Hyd y Nos*'. He'd play a jig later, and a polka. He'd play his whole repertoire. Steerage would take an age to settle. He'd not be making love to his wife with his mess mates still seated at the table.

Through half-closed eyes, Rhys watched Siân shrug into her nightgown. Heard Pam's muttered endearments as she tucked blankets around her children. Watched Alf's final, plodding round of the deck. He was a good cleaning constable and, as far as Rhys could tell, a good stepfather. Though, Bridie clearly didn't think so. Ignoring Alf's 'good night', she crawled into bed beside Annie.

Only Tom Griggs remained at the table now. Why, at this late hour? What could the man possibly have to say to him? Rhys changed his tune, to *Suo Gân*. A lullaby. Surely Tom would take the hint?

No. Tom Griggs was like a dog with a bone. Once he had something in his mouth, he'd not let go. Rhys watched the privy line dwindle down to nothing, heard bedboards creak as people settled for the night, the watch officer's slow, measured tread. Still Tom didn't leave the table. Rhys turned slowly to face him.

'Not bad, Welshman. Not bad, at all.'

Rhys nodded, unsmiling. How was this happening? He should be making love to his wife, not keeping Tom Griggs company.

'Alf's no prince. But he's plain and honest. Not overly burdened by intelligence.' Tom chuckled. 'I liked that bit. And Bridie's got her head forever in the clouds.'

'Stories don't come made to measure, Tom. I told you that at the beginning.'

'A hard, cruel father? Disappointment? Seems there's something of your own story in there too, Welshman?'

Rhys paused mid-stroke, the hairs on the back of his neck rising. 'Me? In tonight's story? No, mistaken, you are, Tom.'

'You can play the innocent, lad. But we had an old Welsh dairyman down our way, so I've heard that tale loads o' times. I don't recall much about fathers and sons in his version.'

'Perhaps that is your lesson for tonight?'

'Nah! My old man was as soft as soap.'

'And mine was neither a landowner nor a fisherman.'

'Nothing criminal, I'd stake me life on it. But you're running. From the girl's father, perhaps? Or something political? 'Ere! You ain't been running round calling yourself Rebecca, 'ave you?'

Rhys grinned. He couldn't help it. The man was sharp. And it seemed he had a knowledge of Welsh politics: the Rebecca Riots was a long-running protest in which the men of Carmarthen fashioned themselves as women.

'No dressing up for me, Tom. In London, I've been, these past years, earning my bread in peace. Mind, Tad was a great one for politics. He'd not have found fault if I'd called myself Rebecca.'

'But he did find fault? You'll admit that much Welshman?'

Fault. Yes, his father had found fault—and he was running. As if the admission were a plug being lifted, Rhys felt the evening's euphoria drain out of him, knowing he'd pace the deck again that night with terror squeezing his bowels, wondering whether this journey, his dream of a new life, was worth the struggle. Or whether he should have swallowed his pride, as Siân had urged, and found the courage to face his father.

No, there were still the rumours. Always the rumours.

'We are all of us running, Tom, from poverty and disappointment, perhaps, some of us from cruel expectations. It takes courage to see ourselves truly, to take pleasure in our modest achievements. I'm not sure I have that courage. Or that I will ever now find it. Pray God, I am wrong. That like Elffin, I will one day find wealth where I least expect it.'

CHAPTER 8

He'd stood up for her! Rhys had stood up for her. Putting Alf in his place by telling the story of a big, dim-witted man who'd raised a child other than his own. And what a story! The change that had come over Rhys. Bridie couldn't pinpoint the exact moment but, somewhere between Rhys's awkward interruption of Alf and the final, soft-voiced conclusion of his tale, a transformation had taken place. Gone was the the white-knuckled clench of Rhys's fists, the haunted uncertainty in his eyes. As he'd jumped from the bench, face alight, and held out a hand to Siân, it was like seeing the real Rhys for the first time.

As Bridie lay awake—eyes wide, skin tight, trying to capture each fluttering elusive butterfly moment of change—she found a new and fragile knowledge. She knew that this Rhys, the dark-eyed storyteller who had stood up to Alf, was the same young man who had helped her at the watergate and that now, despite every outward sign to the contrary, this Rhys, the real, storytelling Rhys, wanted to be her friend.

She woke the next morning in a flurry of excitement. Rhys wasn't in steerage. But that wasn't unusual. He often rose with the dawn. She gobbled down her porridge, grabbed her notebook, and scrambled up the hatchway ladder. She wouldn't have to sit with the single girls anymore, or watch the sailors pick at oakum. The real Rhys would call out to her from the base of the main mast. Siân's eyes would dance as they had during the story last night. There would be no more stilted conversations, no more answering on Rhys's behalf. It would be like the last few weeks had never happened, as if they had always been friends and, as they spoke the language of friendship, then maybe, just maybe, Rhys would help with her notebook again.

On tiptoes, Bridie scanned the deck. Siân sat at the base of the main mast. But Rhys was nowhere to be seen. Not at the galley; the breakfast line had dwindled down to nothing, and the privy doors stood wide open. Where on earth could he be? Turning back to Siân, she felt a twinge of unease. The twist of the Welsh girl's hands suggested she'd been sitting there for ages.

All through the long sweaty hours of the morning, Bridie waited for Rhys to reappear, ignoring Alf's pleas for help and Annie's beckoning hand. Not daring to turn her head or leave her place, lest she miss his return. She heard the ship's bells toll the half hour. Saw the mate taking a noonday sighting of the sun. Still Rhys didn't appear, not at dinnertime, or later on when Siân slipped behind the horsebox with a plate of food. Bridie watched another round of mess duties, the day's shadows lengthening through the long, slow sand-trickle of the afternoon. When Rhys finally appeared at suppertime, his face had grown tight and white and sad again.

Bridie's throat ached with unshed tears.

What had gone wrong? she asked in the toss and turn of that night. What terrible burden was Rhys carrying? Something so heavy that neither Siân nor his stories could rescue him. When would the real Rhys come back again?

She worked like an automaton, all through the next day—and the ones following. Dragging a comb through the tangled mess of her hair each morning, toying with the food on her plate during meals. She found it so hard to concentrate during mess duties that she mixed the currants in with their pease ration.

'What's got into you?' Ma snapped. 'Anyone would think you were a child Lucy's age.'

'Sorry, Ma. I'll pick the currants out.'

'Don't be ridiculous. No one wants your fingers in their pudding.'

Bridie's face burned. She bit her lip, as Tom Griggs made laughing jokes about their strange mixed-up dinner of currants and pease. Once the dishes had been cleared, Alf added to her woes by remembering their voyage log.

'Right,' he said, rubbing his hands together. 'Enough silly mistakes. You need a project.'

Project! Bridie's fingers curled.

'You saw the men taking a noonday sighting of the sun, the ship's boy up in the crow's nest. He's looking for something. Can you tell me what?'

'No.'

'Come on, you know the answer. We discussed this at breakfast time.'

'A whale, p'haps?'

'No, Bridie. It isn't a whale.'

'An albatross?'

'It's Corvo, remember? The northern most island of the Azores. You were going to write some observations. Have you done that for me?'

Bridie nodded, pressing her lips together. Why must Alf always do this? Why must he always be so mean? Hadn't he learned anything from Rhys's story? She didn't want to write down his stupid earthenware observations, or talk to him ever again.

'Well, where are they?' Alf reached for her notebook.

'No! Not in there.' Bridie delved into her pinafore pocket and pulled out a scrap of paper on which she'd listed the nine main islands of the Azores. They belonged to Portugal, whereas the Canary Isles belonged to Spain. It seemed the sea was full of small, scattered islands, like a giant's hopscotch, all belonging to different players. It might have been interesting if Alf wasn't so intent on turning her notebook into a voyage log.

She thrust the scrap of paper at him. He scanned the list. She'd listed the sailors' watches too, and their corresponding bell times. Alf's big, round old-dog eyes filled with pride.

'Well done, lass. You've made an excellent start.'

'Yes. Can I have my list back, please?

'No, let's write this up now.'

'It's okay.' Bridie plucked it from his fingers. 'I know you're busy, with … well, with the cleaning and everything. Besides, this'll need another draft. I'll rewrite it this afternoon, shall I? We can work on it together, when you've got time.'

Alf's eyes narrowed, suspicious. Bridie stretched her smile wide.

'Right. I've a meeting at four bells. After that, I'm on supper duties. But I'll be free all evening. I promise. We'll make our first proper entry tonight.'

Tonight. A proper entry. Bridie's face set like cement.

Alf would be too tired come suppertime. He always was. She should be able to gull him for a few more drafts. But, really, what was the point? Her notebook was dead. She couldn't hear her dad's voice anymore when she turned its pages. Or feel his presence. She may as well toss it overboard.

Slipping the list behind the notebook's cover, she marched along the deck, keeping her pace slow, deliberately even, though her knees threatened to buckle beneath her skirts.

The ship's waist wasn't wide: about twenty-five feet according to Alf's useless store of information. But it took an age to thread her way through the tangle of wind-sails and washing lines strung across the deck. At the bulwarks, she stood, looking out over the great green counterpane of the waves. It was so vast, undulating, like a pattern for eternity. It would make a fitting grave for her memories.

Neptune's kingdom beneath the sea.

She balanced her notebook on the high curved rim of the bulwarks. The ink would run, of course. Fish would nibble at its pages. She'd lose all her dad's stories.

Tonight, Alf had said. *A proper entry.*

She closed her eyes, imagined Alf's big blunt hand scoring the notebook's pages—words like archipelago, sextant and compass, all thick and black and ugly. A sob rose in her throat. One shove, that's all it would take. No more doubts, no more danger, no more questions.

Her notebook safe from Alf's horrible, prying hands.

No! She couldn't do it. She staggered back, clutching the notebook to her chest. It might be dead but it was still precious. She had to give it one more chance. But how? Where? Her eyes sought the base of the main mast. Siân wasn't in her usual place. She must be resting. But what about Rhys? Had he been in steerage at dinnertime? She'd been so caught up in the currant and pease disaster, she'd failed to notice.

But, no, she didn't think so.

She swivelled back round, threaded her way across the deck, circled the whitewashed deckhouse, the makeshift horse box, the two small boats lying lengthwise between. If Siân had taken to her bunk, Rhys must be behind the horsebox.

Alone.

She peered around the boat end. Rhys sat, knees bent, head in his hands, his feet resting on a lashed down pile of spars. He'd removed his cap and draped his jacket over the kennel. Beside him, a row of puppies tugged greedily at their mother's teats.

Bridie took a deep breath and blew out through her puffed cheeks. What now? Interrupt him? Ask for help again? Would he even be interested? Did it matter with Alf's proper entry looming? Rhys might be 'poor company' and he certainly seemed to be having a 'difficult journey'. But he'd stood up to Alf, claiming stories could help people understand their lives and, if that was the case, if stories did truly have that kind of power, then maybe, just maybe, his Taliesin story could help bring her notebook back to life.

She gathered her skirts and crawled into the narrow space. Her boots clunked on the hollow wood of the deck. Her notebook swished like sandpaper. Rhys didn't look up, even when the bitch gave a low warning growl. His stillness was like an apse or a sanctuary.

She inched closer, saw the hard yoke of his shoulders, his tense, ridged fingers.

'Rhys.' No reaction. 'Rhys.' She touched a finger to his knee.

His head snapped up, eyes darting, unfocused. They came to rest on her face. 'Bridie!'

'Sorry. I didn't mean to startle you.'

'No. It's me who should apologise. Hours, I've been sitting here, with others like yourself needing space and privacy.' He twisted round, grabbed his jacket and cap and began to squeeze past her.

Bridie knelt, blocking his path. 'Actually, it was you … you, I wanted to talk to you … about your story.'

He stopped, head to one side, his expression a mix of weary puzzlement. 'You liked it, I hope?'

'I did, yes, and what you said about stories … and everything. And well, I was wondering … just, wondering whether I could write it down … in my notebook.'

'My story? In your notebook?' His stillness returned.

'It's just, I think, I can remember how you told it. But … if I could ask questions, it would help.'

'Is that all?' His eyes searched her face.

She flushed under his gaze. Her finger found a knot in the deck, tracing it inwards, outwards, all hard and gnarled and complicated. 'It's just, well … sometimes, I can't feel my dad's presence anymore.'

A sigh, the weight of his body shifting. He settled back against the horsebox. 'I can tell it again if you like, and others. I have plenty of others.'

'Oh, yes, please!'

He smiled—not a tight, white-faced smile—a real smile that lit his eyes, like the flare of a torch, promising warmth and friendship, with only the white-knuckled clench of his fists to tell her how much the gesture was costing. She didn't understand his secrets. Only that they were real and nagging. But in that moment, she wanted him to understand the value of the gift he was offering.

'I haven't been honest with you, Rhys, about my notebook. At least, I haven't told you everything.'

'Indeed! How so, Bridie Stewart?'

'Remember I told you my dad gave it to me, just before he died? Well he did, that part was true. He was a musician, like I told you, until he got sick and sad and couldn't play his flute anymore. Sometimes ... he drank too much. But even then, even when he was sick and sad and drunk, he never stopped believing in stories. That's why he gave me the notebook, so I could write them down. But then he died, suddenly, well ... in an accident, and the notebook was empty.'

'So you filled it with his memory.'

She nodded, throat tight. 'At first, it was terrible. I couldn't remember anything. Only bits and pieces, as if the stories were all broken up inside me. But I wrote them down as they came.' She stopped, opened the notebook, passing over the terrible confusion of the flyleaf, to a list written in her looping twelve-year-old hand. 'Once I had the pieces, I could fit them together. Only by then, there were so many, I couldn't write fast enough. So I began to tell the stories over and over in my head.'

'So you wouldn't forget.'

'Yes.'

'Then, as you were able, you made them complete. Trying to catch every word, every phrase, exactly as they'd been told. But in the end, you found they were the same, but different, as if they had somehow become your own.'

'You know! How did you know?'

'Well, now, Bridie Stewart, I might have done something like it myself.'

'But ... my dad, he was a musician, not a storyteller. He never stood before a crowd, like you and Siân. Only told stories, softly, by the fire, for me and Ma. She used to like them once ... but not anymore.'

'She tries to forget.'

Bridie nodded, though his words didn't come close to explaining Ma's attitude.

'What about you, Rhys? Did your dad tell stories?'

'No, not Tad. Siân's great aunt, Rhonwen, was the storyteller. No matter how tired or busy or pensive, she always had time for the old Welsh tales.'

'What was your favourite?' Bridie leaned forward, hugging her knees.

'Well now, that's easy. There is a lake high up in a hollow of the Black Mountains called Llyn y Fan Fach. Once upon a time, a fairy woman came out of the lake and married a man. It reminds me of Siân—and her aunt Rhonwen.'

'Siân came out of a lake!'

'No.' He chuckled. 'There's *twp*, I am not explaining myself properly. The Lady of the Lake healed with plants, like Siân. She passed her remedies onto her sons, who became healers of great renown. The Physicians of Myddfai, we call them.'

'Oh.' Bridie bit her lip. 'That was silly.'

'Mind, I wouldn't be surprised if Rhonwen came out of a lake. She was the seventh child of a seventh child. Some say she had unnatural abilities. Rhonwen never needed to put an ox-blade in the fire to see what the coming winter would be like, or lay mistletoe beneath her pillow to shape her dreams. She simply knew things.'

'What about Siân? Does she know things?'

It was as if the wind slammed a door closed, changing the light in the room. She saw a flicker of alarm in his eyes, a tightening about his mouth.

'No. Siân was her mother's first child.'

Bridie shivered, feeling alone. Or maybe she imagined it? No, Rhys's face had shut down. As if he'd gone to a place far, far away. How to bring him back? She mustn't talk about the Lady of the Lake anymore, at least, not in relation to Siân. But she wasn't ready to lose his friendship again. She reached out, touching a finger to his knee.

'Please, Rhys. Don't go away.'

He blinked, the twitch of his limbs putting her in mind of some-one waking from a nightmare and passed a hand across his face. 'Sorry, Bridie Stewart. It's a terrible friend, I've been.'

'It's okay. We both have secrets.'

He smiled then, the light returning to his eyes. 'We do, indeed, Bridie Stewart. We do indeed. Right, enough of my foolishness.' He placed a determined hand on each knee. 'Let me guess, your dad was Scottish, so what was your favourite fairy tale?'

Her favourite? It was a fair question, seeing as she'd just told him about her dad. She ought to have seen it coming. But she hadn't—and now she didn't know how to answer him.

'Was it "The Black Bull of Norroway", by any chance?'

'No.'

'"The Fairy and the Miller's Wife?" Or what about "The Well at the End of the World?"'

'Not those either.'

'Well then, Bridie Stewart, I think you must tell me.'

What could she say? She'd had a favourite, until Ma twisted her dad's message all out of shape. The story of Tamlane—a youth cap-tured by the Queen of Elf-land and the brave young maiden who had rescued him. Her dad had reimagined it as part of her Christ-mas message.

She held her father, and lo! he turned to a wild bear waked with ire,
And she held her father, and lo! he changed to a lion roaring higher,
She held him fast, tho' the wild elves laughed,
And the mountains rang with mire,
She held him fast, though he turned at last,
To a gleed of white-hot fire.

Tamlane wasn't the girl's father, of course. He was her secret fairy lover. Yet still the story resonated. She felt its loss more deeply than all the others, if that were possible. But how to explain? The truth was far too painful.

'When I was little, I liked "Whuppity Stoorie",' she answered in a high, bright voice, 'because of the name.'

'Like "Rumplestiltskin". He nodded. 'A good choice.'

'Do the Welsh have a story like it, one with a secret name?'

'Indeed. It's called "Sili go Dwt".'

'"Sili go Dwt", Bridie repeated the strange sounding words. 'Does it mean anything?'

'Yes, Sili Somewhat Small, you would say in English. Once upon a time, a mysterious green fairy tricked a poor widow into giving up her only child—'

'Only, by the law she lived under, she couldn't take him until the third day,' Bridie interrupted with a quote from 'Whuppity Stoorie'.

'Exactly! But to save the child she must somehow guess the fairy's name. Only in the Welsh tale, she'd changed her form. For although a tiny fairy, she appeared very tall.'

'Oh. That's horrible. She wasn't playing by the rules at all.'

He laughed. 'No. It makes for a better telling. Though, in this case the story does end happily.'

Bridie shivered, recalling the first time she'd heard "Whuppity Stoorie"—the soft burr of her dad's voice, the scratchy feel of his jersey when she cuddled up close, the faint, musty smell of the theatre and fireside on his clothes. There had been no whisky stench to his breath in those days, or sickly smell of cough preparations. Only a delicious anticipation as the story unfolded, an agonised guessing of names, and Ma's laughing voice telling him not to let his imagination run wild. Yet, all the while, the twinkle in his eyes had told Bridie the story would have a happy ending.

'What's your favourite story now?' Rhys's soft voice interrupted her thoughts.

'Now?'

'You're not little anymore, Bridie Stewart.'

She'd forgotten this about Rhys, his uncanny ability to guess her secrets. Maybe he did indeed have second sight. Could he see into her life? But in claiming his friendship, she'd given him the right to ask these questions—and she must find a way to answer him.

'"Tamlane". Head down, she muttered the word.

'But not anymore?'

'No.'

'Though, it too has a happy ending?'

It sounded stupid. It was stupid. On the surface the tales had so much in common—love and enchantment, the power of never letting go, no matter how desperate or ugly the situation. Yet, how to explain? Time had shaped them differently. For "Whuppity Stoorie" had been a child's tale, one she'd grown out of with afternoon naps and comfort blankets, whereas 'Tamlane' had been her dad's story.

She had believed in it.

'When my baby brother died, Dad said he'd gone to live with the fairies. I was only little then, so I believed him.'

'And it eased the pain of your loss?'

She shook her head slowly. 'I didn't know why the fairies wanted our baby. But I thought, at least he was happy. Then my baby sister died.' She swallowed, looking up into his kind dark eyes, remembering the confusion, Ma's endless weeping, the winter of her dad's cough starting. 'She died before she was born. You know, a stillborn child. I was older then and I thought it mightn't be true about the fairies.'

'But you wanted to believe.'

'Then my dad got sick.' She stopped, drew breath. If only her throat weren't so tight, her eyes so suddenly swimming. 'Then my dad got sick and sad and I couldn't … well, I wouldn't …'

'Let him go?'

She nodded, not trusting herself to speak.

Even when he'd turned his face to the wall, she'd not let go; though Ma had given up and Mr Cooke the music director had paid a regretful visit, Bridie wouldn't loosen her hold. Even after the accident, she'd kept faith. Thinking, if only she'd had more time, if only he hadn't gone out that night, she might have saved him still. But now Ma's words had changed everything and she would never know. Whether he'd played her for a fool. Whether after all that blind, stubborn believing, he'd always meant to go.

'Painful, it is, when the words that once brought comfort seem to lose their voice. It's not the stories that are at fault. Or that we were foolish to believe. Only that we must learn to see with different eyes. Sometimes it takes time and the answers aren't always easy—that's part of the magic. But we are never too old for fairy tales, Bridie Stewart, no matter what Alf or your ma might say.'

There was more to say, so much more, and one day she'd find a way to tell him—about Ma hating her dad and Alf wanting to steal her notebook and how she couldn't even read it anymore without hearing the echo of Ma's cruel words. But now wasn't the time.

She leaned back against the horsebox and closed her eyes.

CHAPTER 9

*R*hys sat silently during supper that evening and all through the following morning. But a single nod at dinnertime told Bridie he hadn't forgotten his promise. She shovelled down her salt-beef, raced through mess duties, and grabbed her writing materials. The Bevans sat in their usual place, at the base of the main mast. Rhys, knees bent, shoulders hunched, a hand caught in the dark tangle of his hair; Siân perched on her knees, scanning the deck.

Bridie raised an uncertain hand. Was this it? Should she walk over? Or wait for Siân to notice her? As if on a string, the Welsh girl's head swung round. She turned, nudging Rhys. His head rose, eyes unfocused. A smile woke his features.

Bridie wormed her way across the deck, paying no heed to card games, sewing circles, or whose fingers she might be treading on. As she neared the base of the main mast, Siân called out, eyes ashine.

'Stories, for you, now, is it, *bach*?'

Sinking down beside them, Bridie scarcely knew what to expect. Would Rhys repeat the story word-for-word, pausing as if in dictation? Or expect her to remember everything, rattling off the Welsh names so fast she couldn't keep up with him? She glanced sideways. His tight face offered no clues, though; his mouth still retained a ghost of its smile.

'I know you asked for Taliesin's story, Bridie *bach*, and we'll come to it in time. But today, I thought we'd start with my favourite—"The Lady of Llyn y Fan Fach".'

Bridie frowned, picking up her pencil. 'The story of the woman who healed with plants? And passed her remedies onto her sons?'

'You needn't fret. I'll not be giving you a history lesson.'

'But ... if her sons were famous, they must have been real people?'

'So they were, in the thirteenth century, under Rhys Grug of Dinefwr. Physicians of great renown.' He smiled. 'Sometimes, with us, it's hard to know where history ends and the story begins. "The Lady of Llyn y Fan Fach" is one such tale, full of otherworldly tests and reversals of fortune. It's no easy task to woo a fairy woman, you understand. Let alone for her to dwell in the land of men.'

He glanced at Siân.

'You're not the only one asking for stories, *bach*. We've had requests, from others in steerage. We'd like to tell a story every Friday until the end of the voyage.'

'Stories! Every week! And you want to start with the lake woman? Is that what you're saying?'

'Yes. If you don't mind helping with the preparation.'

'Me? I can't pronounce the name of that lake, let alone write it down.'

Rhys laughed. 'First you must experience the story, then worry about writing it down.'

'How will I remember if I don't take notes?'

'Start in your heart, feel the parts. Once you've heard it a couple of times, you'll come up with your own version of the tale.'

'But ...' Bridie stopped, chewing her lip. This wasn't what she'd had in mind.

'Did you write notes when your dad told stories?'

'No.'

'Then that is how we must begin.'

Siân began to hum. Arms on his knees, Rhys fixed his gaze on the deck. Bridie saw the nervous swallow of his throat, his too-tight fists, heard the sudden sharp intake of his breath.

'High up in a hollow of the Black Mountains is a tiny, mysterious sheet of water pressed into the surrounding crests like a giant's thumbprint. Llyn y Fan Fach, people call it, the lake of the small peak. Once upon a time, a widow lived in the shadow of those dark peaks, a poor widow who, having lost her husband to the sword, vowed her son, Ianto, would not earn his bread by soldiering.

'Being a gentle, sensitive young man, Ianto had no lust for battle. He liked nothing more than to graze his cattle on the shores of Llyn y Fan Fach. The light was different there, he told Mam, the air thinner. Sometimes, as he sat in the shadow of those dark peaks, he fancied he heard the Fair Folk singing.

'As Ianto wandered the shores of the lake one day, he saw a sight to make him tremble. There, perched on top of the water, was a maiden—a most comely maiden, combing her long dark tresses.

'Now, Ianto might have been a dreamer, but he was no fool. Closing his eyes, he counted to ten, certain this was nothing but a trick of the light on him. Imagine his wonder and surprise, then, when he opened them again to find the maiden still present. Indeed, if he was not mistaken, she was even lovelier than he imagined.

'Ianto fumbled in his pack for the hunk of barley bread Mam had baked for him that morning. It was burned black along one edge and hardly an inducement for one so comely. But Ianto knew better than to approach the Fair Ones empty handed.

'The maiden's scarlet sandals barely rippled the water surface as she floated toward him. She stopped, wrinkling her nose at the sight of his meagre offering.'

'Oh handsome youth standing so truly,
With hard baked bread you will not persuade me.'

Bridie leaned forward, notebook and paper forgotten as Siân sang the maiden's response. Indeed, as the Welsh girl gazed upon her husband, her face alight with love and longing, it was hard not to imagine her the fairy maiden and Rhys the handsome young man who had lost his heart to her.

Glancing up, Bridie saw a gathering knot of onlookers.

'Only practising.' Rhys smiled at the group. 'I'll have my fiddle, come Friday night, and tell the whole thing properly.'

'Over supper that evening, Mam could scarcely credit Ianto's strange tale. She'd had so few dealings with the Fair Family. But seeing her handsome son in a fever of agitation, she determined to help him. Next morning, she sent him up the mountain with unbaked bread as his portion.

'All day, Ianto wandered the shores of the lake, watching the sun burn away its mists and deer drink from its waters, seeing each ripple of the wind and every tiny fish that broke its surface. Until, at last, the day's light began to fade.

'Turning to leave, Ianto took a final, parting glance across the water. There, coming toward him, was the maiden. She wore an emerald gown and the setting sun for her mantle and, as he stood on the rocky shore, Ianto thought his heart might burst with love for her. He held out the bread dough Mam had provided, but the maiden only laughed, shaking her head at him.'

'Oh handsome youth standing so truly,
With unbaked bread you will not woo me.'

'Ianto scarcely slept a wink that night. For all knew the Fair Folk only gave three chances. But Mam was undaunted. The maiden must love her handsome son. Why else would she have appeared to him? The following day, she sent Ianto up the mountain with a barley loaf baked to perfection.

'All day Ianto wandered the rocky shores of the lake, watching magpies swoop and dragonflies skim the surface of the water, hearing bird trill and the patient lowing of his cattle. Until, at last, the day's shadows lengthened into the purple of early evening.

'With a sinking heart, Ianto turned his face homeward. When he reached the first bend in the path, he heard a tinkling laughter. Unable to believe his good fortune, he sprinted back up the mountain, and held the barely loaf out to the maiden.

'"Maiden, sweet maiden, turn not your face away,
'With this perfect bread I beg you to marry me."'

'The maiden lowered her dusky lashes and accepted his offering with a slender hand.'

'*I will marry you, mortal, on one condition.*

That you make not a habit of striking me causelessly.'

'Now, being a gentle young man, Ianto could scarcely imagine crossing words with this delightful creature, let alone striking her. But before he could utter a word of protest she sank beneath the water.

'"No! Wait!" Though unable to swim, Ianto was determined to plunge in after her.

'"Halt! Do not destroy yourself," a booming voice called out to him.

'To Ianto's surprise, a hoary-headed man with a gold torque strode toward him. Floating behind him was not one, but two fairy maidens.

'"I will grant your request, mortal, on one condition. That you tell me which of these maidens you love most truly."'

Closing her eyes, Siân sang the aching chasm of Ianto's confusion—recalling the smooth curve of the maiden's breasts, the rosy depth of her blushes, the mole growing betwixt her left ear and her hairline, the way she fluttered her lashes. But though he searched the depths of his soul, calling on the timeless wisdom of the lake and mountains, Ianto could not find a distinction. The maidens were seemingly pressed from the same mould.

'But as Ianto was about to give up and throw himself into the icy depths of the lake, one of the maidens thrust her sandaled foot forward. Ianto's heart leapt, for her sandal was scarlet, whereas her sister's was only a deep maroon. He reached out, grasping the maiden's hand.

'"This—this is the maiden I love the best!"

'"You have chosen well, mortal, and I will provide a dowry. For as many head of cattle my daughter can count without drawing breath will be your portion. But hear this young man, take heed of my warning. The moment you strike a third causeless blow, she and all her dowry will return to these waters."'

'Ianto walked back down the mountain path a wealthy man. But, though he loved his fairy wife, it did not take him long to realise she was not like other women. She neither aged nor grew weary, and people from all over the district benefited from her healing remedies. She was also subject to strange, otherworldly moods. But, as the months stretched into years, and three fine sons were added to their number, Ianto grew accustomed to her difference. So accustomed, that he came to forget the strange conditions of their courtship.

'So it was, on a blustery morning, as the family rode out for church, Ianto tapped his wife on the arm with his riding crop. It was a mistake. He knew as soon as the first blow had fallen. The fairy woman turned reproachful eyes on him.'

'*Oh handsome man, take heed of my warning.*

With two more blows our marriage will be forfeit.'

'Ianto took great care over the coming months,' Rhys continued softly, 'touching his wife only in moments of great tenderness. For, despite her strangeness, he loved his fairy wife and could not bear the thought of losing her. But when she began to sob at a wedding feast, he could not contain his impatience.

'"*Hist*, wife. Why are you crying?"

'Ianto grasped his wife's shoulder, urging her not to spoil the occasion. It worked. Her sobs eased. But as the tears dried on her cheeks, Ianto realised he'd struck the second blow.'

'*Oh handsome man take heed of my warning,*

With one more blow our marriage will be forfeit.'

'The next few months were filled with days carefully trodden. Ianto took great pain never to rebuke his wife, only coaxing her gently as her moods worsened. On good days, he bought her sweets and flowers, giving her reasons to stay with him. But when she laughed wildly during a burial service, he could not contain his fury.

'"Hush, wife! Why are you laughing?"

'He reached out, grasping her roughly. As the laughter died on his wife's lips, Ianto realised he'd struck the final blow.'

'I laugh, husband, for a soul released from suffering,
As you will now mourn for a blow causelessly given.'

'All the way home, Ianto begged his wife not to leave him. White lipped, she shook her head, refusing to enter into a discussion. For no matter how deeply she loved her husband, nor how greatly she would miss her children, by the law she lived under, their marriage was now forfeit. On reaching the farm, she began to summon her dowry.'

'Come speckled cow, brindled cow,
Black cow and grey one,
Come milch cow and meat cow,
Come calf young and suckling,
Come heifer and bullock
Come oxen team ploughing,
Come beast from the field,
Come steer gently grazing,
Come wealth of Ianto,
Come turn your face homeward.'

Tears slid down Bridie's cheeks as Siân gathered the fairy woman's cattle with her song. She didn't know why. It was only a story, a fairy tale from a far off time and place. But all that love, those horrible tests, Ianto's careful restraint and, in the end, the fairy woman still left him. She heard the cattle lowing, Ianto's retching sobs as he followed them up the mountain, hooves clattering on the rocky shore line, the fairy woman's sons pleading. But nothing could persuade her. There was nothing anyone could do to change things.

'Ianto's heart was broken.' Rhys picked up the tale. 'Neither the love of his sons nor the sacraments could bring him healing. His eldest son, Rhiwallon, took his father's decline the hardest. All day long, he wandered the rocky shores of the lake in search of a solution. One evening, a year and a day from her departure, his mother appeared to him. Dropping to his knees, Rhiwallon begged her to return and save his father. But the fairy woman could not grant his request, only gift him a brown leather satchel filled with healing remedies.

'After nursing his father back to health, Rhiwallon went on to become a physician of great renown, passing his mother's remedies onto his sons, and their sons, and down through the ages. Even now, those who live in the shadow of the Black Mountains sometimes find themselves touched by the fairy woman's power.'

Bridie didn't know how long she sat there after the story finished. An age it seemed—with her chest heaving and her hanky sodden, thinking of babies called home before their time, her dad's long and bitter illness, his strange, turbulent moods, Ma's even-now bitterness. She became aware of Siân's soft humming, Rhys's dark, considered gaze, the knot of onlookers drifting away. She sniffed, dabbing at her eyes.

'Sorry. I won't cry every time.'

'No need to apologise, Bridie Stewart. There is no greater compliment to a story teller.'

'But ... Rhys? Do you think she wanted to leave?'

'I don't know, *bach*. The story doesn't tell us. Only that the maiden loved Ianto enough to thrust her sandaled foot forward and that she bore him three fine sons.'

'But, laughing at a funeral, sobbing at a wedding? She wouldn't have done those things if she'd loved him.'

'We don't know why the fairy woman laughed at the funeral, *bach*. Or indeed, why she sobbed at a wedding. Maybe she mourned for the bride, seeing problems others could not perceive. Maybe she grieved for her first life, the ones she'd left behind. But that doesn't mean she didn't love Ianto. Or that she wanted to leave him.'

'I think it does. I think she hated him.'

'Indeed, that is why you feel the story so deeply. You are not alone in that, Bridie *bach*. No doubt, Ianto asked the same questions. For they are the questions of the ages—how we tell a true story from one fashioned merely for entertainment. For in the plight of each character, we confront our heart's reasons. Do not fear those reasons, *bach*, be they ever so painful. Only promise you'll write about them in your own version of the story.'

* * *

Bridie barely touched her evening meal. Neither did she join in the after supper sing-along. When Alf suggested they start work on their voyage log, she almost snapped his head off. With an alarmed glance in Ma's direction, he turned back to his tasks. Bridie climbed into her bunk and spent a lonely evening staring at the deck boards above. She had no desire to write the fairy woman's story, or to think about it ever again. But she'd promised Rhys—and she did want to save her notebook, to learn to see with different eyes. Only, who'd have thought the process would be so painful? Or that Ianto's questions would reach down to her through the ages?

She woke the next morning in a tangle of bedclothes. Her plaits had unravelled during the night, her hair seeming to compete with the welter of thoughts in her head. It took an age to find her ribbons and to drag a comb through the mess of her curls. Added to which, her bodice seemed to have shrunk. No matter how she tugged at the laces, she couldn't seem to fasten them.

'Oh, for goodness sake.' Ma stepped onto the bench. 'Climb down and let me help you.'

'I'm not a child.'

Ma gave a knowing smile. 'Child or not, we'll need to adjust that bodice soon. You're certainly moody enough to be a young woman in the making.'

Bridie scowled, turning her back on Ma as she wrenched at the laces of her bodice. She didn't want to be a woman—made or unmade. She certainly didn't want to discuss it now, in steerage, while everyone ate breakfast. Gathering notebook, scrap paper and pencils, Bridie shoved her feet into her boots.

'Where are you going in such a hurry?'

'On deck, Ma. I'm not hungry.'

Ma's gaze flicked from the table to her notebook. 'A growing girl needs to keep her strength up.'

'I don't care. I'm not having any.'

'Suit yourself. There will be no more until dinner time.'

This wasn't true. Pam made elevenses every morning. This usually involved leftover pudding. But Bridie was in no mood to argue.

She climbed the hatchway ladder under Ma's narrowed gaze.

For once, the sky wasn't blue. It had filled with dirty lowering clouds. The wind also matched her mood. It flattened her skirts as she staggered toward the lee side of the ship. She sank down beside the cargo hatch, tucked her notebook behind her back, and balanced the wad of scrap paper on her knees. Where to begin?

This was a first draft, so she could start however she wanted. Maybe with a description, like … in the shadow of the black mountains? But, what did mountains look like? Dark, looming? She'd never seen a mountain. So what about starting with Ianto's cottage?

She gave it whitewashed walls and a flagstone floor, a small mean kitchen fire with a cauldron hanging over its coals. There were rag-rugs, made by Ianto's mam, a row of chipped yellow crockery. Mementos of his dad lined the mantelpiece.

Bridie stopped, chewing her pencil.

Mementos. What would the widow have kept? A dagger maybe? His sword belt? No. She wouldn't have wanted reminding. Besides, they were poor. She'd have sold those things. Ianto would have kept something, though—something small and secret, like a notebook.

No, that was her story. What about a brass button? Or a buckle?

She pictured their cattle, black like the Welsh drovers brought into Smithfield Market. Imagined moss and spring flowers growing along the shores of the lake. Ianto's smile when he heard the Fair Folk singing. The catch of his breath when he first saw the maiden.

The maiden. What would she look like? Indeed, how to describe

Ianto? Would he be slender and handsome, like Rhys? His wife dainty like Siân? No. She couldn't write that. Not with the story ending so badly.

She gave the fairy woman straight russet hair and clear blue eyes, like her dad's; Ianto soft brown curls and a wide, playful smile. They were happy, so happy walking down the mountain together that first evening, full of love and plans for the future as they exchanged first kisses in the moonlight.

Writing the next part was more difficult. Strange otherworldly moods? What did they look like? The fairy woman never got sick. So there was no fever or winter cough. But had she lain with her face to the wall, or wept without reason? Stayed out until late at night, perhaps started drinking? She'd loved Ianto at the beginning—Rhys had been most particular on that score—borne him three fine sons. So, what had changed things?

Did her healing powers start to wane over the years? Did she begin to feel less like a fairy and more like a human? Realise, one day, she would lose everything, even her ability to slip beneath the waters? Did she fear being left alone in the world of men and begin to plan her escape? Perhaps slipping a message into her brown leather satchel, knowing one day, in the not too distant future, she would leave them ... forever.

Bridie stopped, her fingers curling around her pencil. So much pain, so many unanswered questions. Placing her scrap paper on the deck, she slid her notebook out from behind her back. The leather felt warm and firm. She opened the cover.

When the night is dark and the wind blows hard and shadows overwhelm you—there are always stories. Write them down and think of me and how I have ever loved you.

Why? Why was she doing this? She'd read her dad's message a thousand times. Nothing had changed. The words didn't prove a thing, not goodbye, or I want to die. They were nothing, without Ma's accusations. Nothing, unless, she took her dad's behaviour into account.

Behaviour, strange otherworldly moods? Could she call them that? Though her dad was neither woman nor fairy. Is that what Rhys had meant by seeing with different eyes? If so, she didn't much like the experience. For if she took her dad's behaviour into account, his hacking won't-go-away cough, the times he'd wept without reason, the days he'd lain with his face to the wall, the nights he'd gone out drinking. Then maybe Ma was right. She would never believe he'd meant to kill himself that icy December night. But maybe, just maybe, he had given up on life.

CHAPTER 10

*N*ext afternoon wasn't so difficult. Once Rhys and Siân had practised the fairy woman's story, they told the tale of a changeling boy and how, by brewing beer in an egg cup and finding a hen without a single white tail feather, his mother managed to win him back from the fairies. The next day, they told a silly story about a man called Cadwaladr and his goat. Except, they didn't simply tell the story. They acted it out, with laughter and bleating voices, trading memories of their childhood back on the mountains.

It was the same the next afternoon, and the ones following— as if the stories worked a kind of magic. For no matter how distant Rhys was of a morning, nor how tight and white his face at the beginning of a story, once he entered the realm of the make believe, the real, storytelling Rhys returned.

Bridie had no more time for loneliness, no further need to sit with Annie and the single girls. She spent her mornings drafting and redrafting. Her afternoons participating a mystery. 'A long and noble tradition,' as Rhys explained it, 'a bardic stream dating back to antiquity.' She could never quite capture the essence. No matter how often she redrafted. But as she wrote, she fancied herself part of a chain, without beginning or end, linked only by the silver-strong words of its tellers.

It wasn't all stories and make believe. They had left the Canary Isles far behind, and brisk, northeast trade winds were pushing them down toward the equator. Bridie spent miserable steerage-bound afternoons with fat drops of rain spattering the deck.

Restless, sweat-drenched nights with heat prickling her every crevice. Stomach churning mornings like this one, when she huddled beneath the bulwarks, the wind snatching at her paper and the sea's swell threatening to bring back the nightmare of seasickness.

She also had to keep an eye out for Ma.

Bridie had made no secret of her afternoons with the Bevans. By shoving scraps of paper across the supper table, she'd managed to convince Alf they were working on her voyage log. So far he'd been too busy and preoccupied to protest. Ma wasn't nearly so stupid. She didn't often venture onto the main deck, preferring the closeness of steerage. But lately, she'd made a habit of climbing the hatchway ladder and, once on the main deck, had developed an uncanny knack of sneaking up on Bridie unawares.

Bridie shivered, glancing back over her shoulder. She heard the familiar chime of six bells. Eleven o'clock, as if on cue, Lucy's tousled head popped out from the hatchway. Pam followed with an empty quart pot. Elevenses! How could they contemplate tea with the sea bubbling like a cauldron beneath?

Adjusting her scrap paper, Bridie weighed it down with her notebook. Last night, Rhys had told the story of another magical boy. Young Myrddin hadn't been cast upon the waters by a witch. But his birth was considered cursed, nonetheless—so cursed that when Gwrtheyrn, a real fifth century British king, needed blood to strengthen his castle foundations, Myrddin was considered a powerful otherworldly sacrifice. For hadn't he been sired by his grandfather? Or indeed the devil himself! As a curious crowd gathered to witness the sacrificial rite, Myrddin saved himself with words and magic. Only he didn't summon the wind, or unearth a cauldron filled with gold. He raised two stone coffers from the depths of a lake, and unleashed two ancient, prophetic dragons whose cries foretold of bloody battles to come.

How did the Myrddin feel, standing on the castle earthworks with those dragons screeching overhead? Had he truly been cursed at birth, as people believed? Or did he simply possess a poet's soul like Taliesin? If so, what did that soul look like? Like Rhys all lit up like a candle in the middle of a story? Her dad, in the early days, making birdsong with his flute? A mistake, Ma had called their marriage, right from the beginning. Was that akin to being cursed? Bridie remembered her parents trading laughter and stories, like Rhys and Siân did of an afternoon. So, what had changed things?

'Working on your voyage log, I see, Bridie?'

Bridie jumped at the sound of Ma's voice, dropping her pencil. She dragged the notebook over her story.

Too late. Ma had clearly been standing there for ages.

'I don't know what's got into you. I used to be able to trust you. But now every time my back is turned, I find you doing something sneaky.'

'Not sneaky. Only … my writing's private, that's all.'

'Up early, skipping breakfast, busy as a squirrel with your paper and pencils, afternoons spent working with the Bevans. Yet, when Alf asks about your voyage log, you've barely a civil word for him. Is there a reason for that, Bridie? Or am I imagining things?'

'No.'

'Would you elaborate, please? I'm having trouble following your logic.'

'I don't want to work with Alf. He's silly.'

'Silly! I've seen a fair bit of silliness coming from the base of the main mast these past afternoons and it's got nothing to do with your voyage log, young lady. No matter what fibs you might be telling.'

'Rhys and Siân are my friends, Ma. I enjoy their company.'

'And Alf is good man, trying to be a good father to you.'

'But he isn't my dad. I've told you that already.'

'Oh, for goodness sake, how many times do we have to go through this? Alf pays your bills, which is more than your precious father ever did. We'd have starved if not for Alf bringing us market greens at his own expense. You didn't know that, did you? Or perhaps you chose not to notice? Alf cares about your future, young lady. He wants to guide you in the colony. But you won't even give him a chance.'

'A chance!' Bridie scrambled to her feet. 'What about my dad? You never gave him a chance. Even dead, you can't say a single good word about him. It's all about Dear-Mr-Trying-to-be-a-good-stepfather, Alf. Well, I don't like him, Ma. I never will. No matter how often you sneak up, or try to lecture me.'

'I gave your father plenty of chances. One day you'll realise. You can love a man until your heart breaks—but sometimes it isn't enough.'

Love! Not enough! The wind snatched at Bridie's paper. She brought her foot down, trying to prevent the pages from fluttering across the deck. It didn't help. Her thoughts, like her notes, had scattered everywhere. It took an age to gather them, by which time, Ma had spun on her heel and left. Good riddance, she thought; she had her friends and her stories—strange, half-true stories of cursed boys with poets' souls, who summoned dragons and raised stone coffers. Besides, she'd never asked Alf to deliver market greens, or take an interest in her future. She certainly wasn't going to let him guide her in the colony.

Bridie swiped at her eyes with the sleeve of her shift. Tears came so easily these day. Was it because of her bodice tightening? Maybe Ma was right. Maybe she was a young woman in the making?

No. She didn't want to think about that either.

She swivelled round, saw Pam still waiting at the galley. Goodness, the water must be taking an age to boil. Though it was hardly surprising in today's heavy swell. Sometimes they doused the galley fires completely. They were alight now, however. Smoke belched from the narrow chimney. Bridie watched cook hand a steaming quart pot to Pam. She grasped its handle and turned her face toward the hatchway. Bridie held her breath. It was hard enough fetching water on a calm day, let alone in today's blustery conditions. It didn't help that two-year-old Lucy tugged at Pam's skirts.

Today wasn't a day for letting little girls help with boiling water. Pam was firm on that score. Halfway along the deck, she squatted down and pointed up at the sails. Thumb in her mouth, Lucy shook her head. Pam grasped the little girl's shoulders and faced her into the buffeting wind. Lucy didn't care for that logic either. At the hatchway, Pam propped the steaming quart pot against the awning post and stepped backwards onto the ladder. Lucy jerked free and made a grab for the pot. Pam's eye caught the movement. Her hand shot out, missed. Lucy sprawled onto the deck. The pot slid sideways, slammed against the combings and overturned, spilling its scalding contents onto Lucy's hand.

Bridie heard a wail, Pam's shriek. From amid a group of married men, Tom leapt to his feet. Pam clambered out from beneath the hatch cover and grabbed Lucy. The little girl howled, writhing in her arms.

'Tom! Get Doctor Roberts, quick.'

Tom didn't hesitate. He surged across the deck, scattering books, blankets and sewing projects in his wake. He pounded on the saloon doors. They inched open. The steward peered out. Bridie saw his mouth move. Tom's red face pushed up close. The steward stepped back, slamming the door. Tom hollered, pummelled with his fists. After what seemed like an age, Doctor Roberts emerged, scowling from the saloon.

The crowd parted, as if he were Moses. Tom grabbed his elbow and steered him toward the dispensary. Bridie gathered her notebook and pencils and shoved her way to the front of the crowd. Doctor Roberts looked rather unsteady on his feet. Bridie doubted this had anything to do with the sea's bilious roll. She knew the signs.

Pam grabbed Lucy's flailing hand and flipped it over for him to see. Lucy shrieked, drumming her feet. Doctor Roberts peered down his nose as if she were a nasty insect.

'A burn. Hmm … A bad one. Keep that wretched child still.' He swung round, searching the crowd. 'Miss Bowles? Where are you?'

'Here.' Annie stepped out from amid a group of single girls. 'I'll need a dish of mutton fat. Ask the cook to oblige, please?' The sea of faces parted. A minute later, Annie reappeared with a chipped enamel basin. Lucy's wails had faded. Silent sobs wracked her little body. Even so, it took all Tom's red-faced efforts to hold her while Doctor Roberts smeared the burn with mutton fat and wrapped her hand in a thick white bandage.

'Keep her warm and quiet. We don't want her going into shock.'

'What about her thumb? She likes to suck that thumb.'

Dr Roberts' lips curled, his smile putting Bridie in mind of a weasel or a ferret. 'Well, Mrs Griggs, this should cure her of that nasty little habit.'

* * *

The Bevans didn't join them for dinner. This wasn't unusual. Siân often took Rhys's plate onto the main deck. Today, with Lucy's howls piercing the long dark tunnel of steerage, Bridie didn't blame her.

Even the wind promised better company.

They ate a tense, mournful dinner with Lucy's arch-backed form being passed back and forth between Pam and Annie. Each time, Lucy raised her thumb to her mouth and gagged on the bandage; each time brought a crashing wave of rediscovery.

Bridie ploughed through her salt-beef like a team of oxen. In between swallows, she forced down mouthfuls of chaff-dry ship's biscuit. Once she'd finished eating, she jumped up to help Annie clear the table.

'Leave it, Bridie. I'm on mess duties.'

'It's all right. You're helping Pam.'

Annie shook her head. 'It's good to keep busy. Once I've cleared these plates, we'll make a nice pot of tea.'

Tea! How could they drink tea with Lucy howling like a banshee?

Bridie watched Annie scrape and stack the plates. Tom fetched water from the galley. Pam scooped leaves into the teapot and set them aside to steep. Once she'd finished her mess duties, Annie took a turn with Lucy. But nothing could ease the little girl's fury. Bridie gulped down her tea, never mind the scald in her throat, and shoved her empty mug to the centre of the table. She rose, gathered her writing materials.

'Excuse me, miss. Where do you think you're going?'

'On deck, Ma. With Rhys and Siân.'

'We've talked about this, Bridie. You know my views.'

'But … they'll be waiting.'

'That's all very well. But Pam needs help this afternoon. You can spend time with your family.'

'Lucy's not family.'

'I won't argue, Bridie. You're staying. It'll be good practice for when the baby comes.'

Bridie stomped back to her seat. She didn't want to practise for the baby. Especially not for a big, round, pudding-faced baby that looked like Alf. Besides, Ma didn't care about the baby. She only wanted to stop Bridie working on her stories.

Bridie propped her elbows on the table and jammed her fingers in her ears. It didn't help. Lucy's howls cut through her skin and bone like a knife. Once or twice, she almost fell asleep, her cries dropping to a low grizzling drone. Then deep subterranean sobs jerked her awake and the wails started over.

'This can't go on forever,' Pam said, adjusting her skewed cap.

'No,' Annie agreed. 'She has to tire eventually.'

Bridie didn't believe them. Lucy's cries were growing shriller and more insistent by the minute. She'd bitten her lip at some point during the afternoon. A combination of blood and drool smeared her cheeks. She looked like a changeling—a grotesque other-worldly child from one of Rhys's stories. They'd have to brew beer in an egg cup or, failing that, find a hen without a single white tail feather. Otherwise, her crying would go on all night.

* * *

The Bevans came down the ladder as the ship's bells chimed the dinner hour. Arms wide, Rhys steadied Siân as they staggered along the deck. He winked at Bridie, tossing his cap onto the bed. Siân's eyes danced as Rhys undid the ribbons of her bonnet and, like a life-sized dolly-bobbin, unwound the scarf from about her neck. She clapped, stepped forward, and held her arms out to Lucy.

'Come by here, Lucy *bach*. Give your mam a rest.'

Lucy writhed and kicked, a gnome in her distress. But, eventually, they managed to make the transfer. Pam sank onto the bench with a sigh.

'It's her thumb, see. She can't suck it with all them bandages.'

'We don't even know the burn's on 'er thumb.' Tom broke his gloomy silence.

'Course it is. Doctor Roberts wouldn't have bound it otherwise.'

'It wouldn't hurt to look.'

Siân glanced from Tom to Pam. 'I can check, if you like. My aunt was a healer. She often treated burns.'

'There you are, Pam. *She* knows all about burns.'

'Not me, Tom. My aunt.'

'She'd untie the bandage though, wouldn't she? This old aunt of yours?'

'More than untie it. My aunt was a charmer. She would draw the heat from Lucy's skin with her touch.'

'Blimey! A witch.'

'Tom!'

'Don't look at me like that, Pam. We live in the age of steam, not the bleedin' dark ages.'

Siân shifted her attention back to Lucy. Snot nosed, her eyes were puffy red slits. Siân caught her flailing wrist. Rocking and soothing, she unwound the bandage, letting it fall in loose coils on the table. Opaque and jelly like, the blisters extended across the back of Lucy's hand. Silence. Her thumb found her mouth. Annie sighed, her face softening. A smile parted Pam's lips. Even Alf looked up from his plodding round of the deck. The only one seemingly unaffected by the sudden, blissful silence was Tom Griggs. He leaned forward, prodding at the blisters.

'We'll have to burst these.'

Lucy's bottom lip trembled. Tom smiled, opening up his arms. 'Come here, Lucy. Give your old dad a look.'

Lucy wasn't stupid. She wrapped her legs around Siân and tightened the one-armed grip on her neck.

Siân hummed, rocking Lucy. 'Hot is it, *bach*?'

Lucy nodded, grizzling. Siân pulled back her sleeve. 'Ask the heat to come out then, shall we?'

Tom shifted, uneasily. 'Bit daft to raise her expectations. She'll be fine now she's got her thumb.'

Siân began to circle the burn with her forefinger. 'I've not done it before, mind. Let's see if I can remember the charm. *Daeth tair angel fach o'r gorllewin.*'

Bridie glanced sideways at Rhys. He'd turned stone-still during this conversation, his eyes a coal dark gleam. It brought to mind their conversation on the main deck. When Bridie asked about the Lady of the Lake, he'd put her at ease by speaking of Rhonwen. But later, when she'd asked whether Siân knew things, he'd shut down. She saw the same flicker of alarm in his eyes now. Somehow, she didn't think a burn charm fell into the same category as healing with plants.

'Leave it be, now, *cariad*. She's got her thumb.'

Siân didn't seem to hear. Eyes closed, focused inwards, she continued chanting. '*Pob un ohonyn nhw yn profi'r tân—*'

'No!' Rhys grabbed her wrist.

Siân blinked, eyes wide open, as if seeing him for the first time. 'But … no harm surely, if I try?'

'Leave it, now, Siân.'

They sat, locked in the silent battle of each other's gaze. Eventually, Siân lowered her eyes. Rhys released his grip on her wrist. Tom held out his arms to Lucy. She hadn't forgotten about the bursting. She burrowed down into Siân's lap.

'*Hist, cariad, Tadda* won't hurt you.'

'Course I won't bleedin' hurt her. Come here, Lucy.'

Lucy held tight, her fingers digging into the soft skin of Siân's neck. Bridie wouldn't have thought she had the energy. But, as Tom tugged and Siân coaxed, the bubble popped and Lucy resumed her high-pitched wail.

It was a like nightmare, a bizarre reoccurring dream. Bridie moaned, clapping her hands to her ears. Rhys jumped up, grabbed his fiddle and raised it to his chin.

'This one's called "Counting the Goats", he called across the deck.

Tom frowned at the interruption, but gave up trying to coax Lucy into his arms. The little girl snuggled close to Siân. Rhys began to sing.

'*Oes gafr eto?*

Oes heb ei godro?

Ar y creigiau geirwon,

Mae'r hen afr yn crwydro.'

The Welsh words were impossible, but they all sang in English as Rhys drew music from the strings with his bow. Eventually, even Tom Griggs joined in. His deep voice reluctant at first, but becoming wholehearted as he sang the counterpoint to Rhys.

'*Is there another goat?*

That's not been milked?

On the craggy rocks

The old goat is wandering.'

The song was a repetition rhyme, the chorus increasing speed with every round.

'*Goat white, white, white,*

With her lip white, lip white, lip white …'

Bridie laughed and sang as the goats changed colour and the tension of the afternoon seeped out of her. Siân didn't join in the singing. Head bowed, she rocked Lucy in silence. By the second verse, the little girl's eyelids drooped. As the blue goat became a red goat, her head lolled. Her arms hung heavy at her sides. Siân rose, tiptoed to Lucy's bunk and tucked her beneath the covers.

As the song finished, Rhys launched into another, his gaze seeking Siân's. She didn't return his gaze, only slipped back up the ladder onto the main deck. Rhys drank his tea in silence. After helping with the dishes, he spent the remainder of the evening hunched at the table. He didn't lift his head, even when Siân returned, eyes red, and crawled into their bed. He sat still, silent, as if made of granite. Not joining Siân until the carpenter turned down the lamps.

In her bunk beside Annie, Bridie huddled beneath the bedclothes, trying to make sense of their strange afternoon. Had Siân been serious about the charm? Or was it simply a game made up for Lucy's benefit? No, Rhys's alarm had been real, real enough to make his troubles return. But why? What was the harm? The charm couldn't be dangerous. Not if Rhonwen had used it. But maybe it was like knowing things; something that was all right for the wise woman but not for Siân.

As the deck fell silent, Bridie heard a hissing in the bed beside Alf and Ma's. The Bevans spoke in Welsh. But she had no need of a translation. She heard fear in Rhys's voice, Siân's tear-choked replies, and knew they were arguing about the charm. For some reason the knowledge brought an ache to her throat. Hugging her notebook to her chest, she wept for the message on its flyleaf, the fairy woman's tragic tale, and the strange, bitter end to her parent's marriage—and for their love that wasn't enough.

CHAPTER 11

*L*ucy's accident was only the beginning. The following day, Thaddy, one of the little Irish boys, fell and split his lip. A week later, one of the single girls sprained her ankle. They had an outbreak of lice in steerage. No matter how often Alf swept, he couldn't rid the deck of the pests. He spent his days explaining the benefits of a washing in a basin beneath the pump, the need to air bedding, to change linen regularly; his evenings listening to the restless timbre of people's voices. For as the temperature rose, so did people's tempers. They had raised fists among the single men, complaints about hygiene from the after part of the deck while mothers bewailed compulsory salt-water baths, laundry soap that didn't lather, and the paucity of their water rations. Alf didn't dare take such petty concerns to Doctor Roberts. But, eventually, the squabbling reached his ears.

'People are bored, Bustle. They need a diversion. Fortunately, I've anticipated the situation. We have a clergyman on board, as you know. Reverend Cummings has agreed to act as schoolmaster. He can't perform the task alone. He'll need monitors. What about it, Bustle? Can you organise something?'

Alf shuffled, not meeting Doctor Roberts' gaze. He could scarcely manage his current tasks, let alone run a school for Doctor Roberts.

'I'm not asking you to be a monitor, Bustle. You're far too indispensable as cleaning constable. Just sound people out, give me a list of names. Reverend Cummings can take it from there.'

'Oh, yes, of course.'

Doctor Roberts clapped him on the back. 'Good man. I knew I could rely on you.'

Alf swelled with pride. He'd been working hard, trying to anticipate Doctor Roberts' every need. Once or twice, he'd dared to hope the surgeon was coming to rely on him. But, *Good man! Indispensable!* Those were words generally reserved for successful men. As if he didn't have the energy to organise monitors now. He'd have run the whole school if Doctor Roberts asked him, and scrubbed out the privy buckets single-handed.

'I've got important news,' he announced at supper that evening.

'Don't tell me.' Tom spat onto the deck. 'As well as having to change our linen we've got to bathe again in the morning.'

'You can scoff, Tom. But hygiene keeps disease at bay. Doctor Roberts told me.'

'Well bully for him. So, what's the news? Are we getting our wine rations?'

'No. We're not getting our wine rations.' Alf strove to keep the irritation from his voice. 'We're being offered a chance to improve ourselves.'

'I can't think of anything more improving than a mug o' wine, Alf. I'll bet your fancy Mr-Top-Hat-and-Tails surgeon would agree with me. Besides, we've been at sea more than twenty days. We're entitled to regular wine rations.'

Alf decided to ignore that comment. Wine rations were a courtesy, not a right, and conditional on good behaviour. But with all this bickering, was it any wonder they were being withheld? 'What about learning to read and write, Tom? Would that interest you?'

'No thanks. I'm doing fine already.'

'Yes, of course, you are. We all are, but ... Doctor Roberts is organising a school, here on the ship. With Reverend Cummings as schoolmaster. What about it, Tom? Will you take part?'

'I ain't a child.'

'Not an infant school. One for adults. Like a Methodist Sunday school. But you could teach Billy and Lucy afterwards.' He swiv-elled round. 'What about Pam? Are you interested?'

'Pam ain't got time. She's minding the kids.'

Alf shifted, mopping his brow. This wasn't going as he'd imag-ined. Tom ought to be jumping at the chance of an education. How did he think Alf achieved his current position? By sitting around scoffing? No, he'd worked hard, taught himself to read and write by candlelight, written an excellent application and, now look, Doc-tor Roberts had come to rely on him. He turned to Mary. 'What about you, love?'

'I can read and write already.'

This was true. But it wasn't the answer Alf was looking for. Mary had grown so pale and thin since the seasickness. Now, in this heat, she seemed to be losing interest in everything.

'You needn't be a student, love. Doctor Roberts is looking for monitors. You'd be good at that. And it would give you something to do each day. Perk you up a bit.'

'No.' Mary didn't want perking up.

Fortunately, others were less resistant. Young Annie was keen, despite her duties at the dispensary. So were Rhys and Siân. This meant Bridie also wanted to take part. The latter didn't please Alf. She was spending too much time with the Bevans already. But he couldn't forbid her attendance. Not without setting a bad example. He put her name on the monitors list.

* * *

Two days later the school was established. Alf was too busy to attend. But he insisted the other cleaners take part, happily shouldering the extra responsibilities. Alf surveyed the dimly lit deck. Mr Rolf had emptied the privy buckets. The single girls had taken their mattresses onto the main deck for airing. In their absence, Alf would disinfect the baseboards of their bunks. Steerage still smelled damp and unsavoury. He'd have to light the aromatic stoves. He'd noticed a build-up of grime at the single men's end of the table. But first, he must check on the school. Bridie had spent more time chatting to the Bevans yesterday than helping the other students. He bent and touched a hand to Mary's shoulder.

'That's it, love. I'm going to see how Bridie's getting along.'

Mary smiled, raising a hand to his cheek. 'You're a good man, Alf Bustle. One day she'll thank you for taking an interest.'

Thank him? So far she'd done nothing but evade him. 'Why don't you come with me, love? The weather's glorious.'

'I'd like to, Alf. But my ankles are that swollen. I'd better rest them.'

Lugging a bucket of water up the ladder was no easy task. Neither was carrying it across the tilting main deck. Alf tipped the miry water into the sea and threaded his way back toward the galley. He'd need fresh water for scrubbing the tables. But no point sloshing it over the students. Propping the hawse bucket against the water butt, he heard the cook singing in the galley.

'*Time for us to leave cold weather,*

Time for us to go—oh—oh …'

It was a pumping song, one of Bridie's favourites. The sailors sang it every evening as they pumped bilge from the hold. Alf remembered the night Bridie had first shown him the lyrics. He'd been so tired that night (wasn't he always tired?). She'd insisted on making a second draft and, somehow, the moment had passed. Like every other moment, now she had the Bevans for company.

Alf's worried eyes sought Reverend Cummings. The plump clergyman wore his clerical collar with pride, but Alf suspected the schoolmaster's cap didn't fit so easily. His round face looked rosy as a plum in the bright morning sun and, despite the regularity of the ship's bells, he kept his fob watch handy. His gaze kept straying toward the comfort of the saloon.

'A school in the sun,' Alf said, stepping alongside. 'Are your scholars progressing?'

'A pleasant morning with pleasing progress.' Reverend Cummings gave a beatific smile.

'And my stepdaughter, Bridie? She's working hard, I hope?'

'She is an asset to the class.'

Reverend Cummings had egg on his waistcoat. The man ate more than was good for him. But it seemed a harmless vice. Apart from that, he was an intelligent man and not unsympathetic to people's trials.

'She's a bright child, but rather lonely. Her father passed away in difficult circumstances. I've tried to make it up to her. But … her head's so full of whimsy.'

'You're right to be concerned. A young girl needs a father's guidance.'

'She'll be sixteen in the new year … and with things as they are in the colony … I can't help worrying.'

'She's a fanciful girl, Mr Bustle, but far from foolish. She'll turn to you when she needs you. Meanwhile, she's not without friendships. The young Welsh couple seem to have taken her under their wing. Let that be a comfort.'

A comfort! It was hardly a comfort. The Bevans were part of the problem as far as Alf was concerned. He'd seen them laughing and play-acting of an afternoon, caught the gist of their conversations. Knew Rhys was filling Bridie's head with nonsense. But he could hardly say that to Reverend Cummings. Not without sounding ungrateful.

'Yes, of course, a great comfort. I've come to see how they're getting along.'

As Reverend Cummings turned back to his class, Alf sidled over to where Bridie sat with her friends. They were reading from a religious tract, one of the many brought on board by a tall, thin man with a benevolent smile. Today's text was from the Psalms.

'*They that go down to the sea in ships, that do business in great waters; these see the works of the Lord, and his wonders in the deep.*'

Annie was stuck on the word *business*. Bridie struggled to explain.

'B-u-s-i-n-e-s-s. Can you see the whole word, Annie? All those letters say *business*.'

Annie grimaced. 'I know the word busy.'

'Yes, except *business* is different to *busyness*. You put an *i* instead of a *y* and it changes the meaning.'

Alf smiled. He'd taken no part in Bridie's formal education. But he'd seen the tattered book of fairy tales from which she had learned her letters, had watched her rise to the top the charity school on Hart Street. Reading, writing or adding up long lists of figures, Bridie was in her element. She'd never have stumbled over her words as Annie was doing now. Yet she was making a great deal of effort with the older girl. This was something Alf could take comfort in.

'With some words you have to sound them out, Annie, then memorise them. Have a go at reading the whole sentence. I'll see if anyone else needs help.'

Annie read slowly, her finger moving from word to word across the page. Bridie grabbed her wad of scrap paper and slithered across the deck toward Rhys and Siân. They were reading from the same text.

'The letters 's' and 'h' make a 'sh' sound in English.' Rhys explained. 'Like in the words ship or shop.'

'They that go down to the sea in *ships*.' Siân emphasised the sound as if etching it into her mind. Bridie leaned forward, pointing at the text.

'Don't you have a 'sh' sound in Welsh, then?'

'We have the sound, yes, but we don't make it the way you do.'

'Truly? How do you make it, then?'

Rhys pulled out a pencil stub and wrote the word *Siân* with a few deft strokes. He passed the slip of paper over to Bridie. She smoothed it out, running her finger over the words, as if they were a message from the queen, not a hastily scrawled note. She looked up at him, eyes ashine.

'So, the 's' and the 'i' make a 'sh' sound?'

Alf saw the light in Bridie's eyes, the animation of her face, the interest she took in Rhys's explanations, and felt a jealous bile rise in his throat. He'd tried so hard to engage her interest—talked about the weather, pointed out the wondrous birdlife they encountered on a daily basis, corrected her notes and observations. In the beginning, he'd had a chance of succeeding. Now, this soft-voiced storyteller was going to ruin everything.

Alf closed his eyes, ignoring the scald in his throat, and tried to focus on Reverend Cummings' voice.

'*For he commandeth and raiseth the stormy wind, which lifteth up the waves thereof. They mount up to the heaven, they go down to the depths: their soul is melted because of trouble.*'

The word storm had taken on new meaning since setting sail. Alf could almost hear the wind and the waves as Reverend Cummings evoked them with his voice. He breathed deep, letting the salt spray fall on his upturned cheeks and waited. He wasn't sure what for—a sign, perhaps, a shaft of inspiration, some quiet affirmation that Reverend Cummings had spoken the truth. That Bridie would turn to him, before it was too late.

Nothing came. Alf opened his eyes.

From her wide-eyed absorption, Alf guessed Bridie and Rhys were no longer studying the text.

'Siân is like the Irish, Siobhán. See how they both have an 'si' at the beginning. They're not spelled the same and they have different accents over the 'a' but, in truth, they're one and the same name— both mean God's gracious gift.'

'Oh, do Welsh names all have meanings, then?'

'Indeed. Not only Welsh ones. Your name means strong or exalted one, does it not?'

'My dad chose it. But … how did you know?'

'Well now, Bridie Stewart, before Wales had an English church, or even a Roman church, we had our own church. Bride was one of our saints too. She sailed from Ireland, the poets tell us, with only a piece of turf for her *cwch*. Once on our shores, she changed stones into honey to feed the poor, and made small boneless fish from rushes. But before Bride was ever a saint, she was one of the old ones—a goddess.'

'Yes. In Scotland too!'

'Well now, that's the beauty of a myth. It knows no bounds.'

'In Scotland, Bride was captured by the Winter Queen, who was a witch, like the green woman in 'Sili go Dwt'. To keep her youth, the witch bathed in a magic well high up in the mountains. Bride had to learn her secrets of the well in order to escape. When she did, she inherited the Winter Queen's wisdom and power.'

'Indeed, your dad named you well, naming you for Bride. She was the goddess of fire and healing and poetry. Only, in Wales, we don't write her name as you do. We write it like this: *Ffraid*.'

What a load of rubbish. Alf began to see why Bridie enjoyed Rhys's company so much. But it wasn't helpful, or even appropriate. She'd be far better employed helping the other students. He coughed, clearing his throat. Rhys glanced up smiling from their task.

'Morning, Mr Bustle. Enjoying the sun, are you?'

'Only for a brief spell.' Alf crouched down, forced a smile. 'Are we making any headway?'

'English is nothing like Welsh.' Siân pulled a wry face.

'Yes. I couldn't help overhearing. It must be quite a trial.' He turned to Bridie. 'What about you, lass? I heard you helping Annie earlier. You were doing a good job. Then you seemed to become a little ... distracted?'

'No.' Her chin rose. 'I've been learning things.'

'And ... what can you tell me?'

'Well, for a start, the letters of our alphabet make different sounds in Welsh.'

'I gathered that, Bridie.'

'No, you don't understand. Even my name is spelled differently. Look, it starts with an 'Ff'. And Rhys has been talking about its meaning and, well ... we might have talked about some other things too.'

'What kind of things?'

'Err ... nothing. It doesn't matter.'

'I think it does. Especially here, in the school. You are supposed to be helping Reverend Cummings. Not wasting your time on the Welsh alphabet.'

'I'm allowed to talk to my friends.'

'Indeed, you've been doing a lot of that lately, the afternoons in particular. You seem to be having a grand old time. Loads of drafting and redrafting in the mornings, too, and all for your voyage log, I believe?'

Bridie flushed, glancing sideways at Rhys. 'Yes, well, we talk about lots of things.'

'Really! What kind of things?'

Bridie shifted, dropping her gaze. 'Well … we don't work on the voyage log, all the time. In fact, not much at all, and sometimes, umm … well, quite often, Rhys tells …'

'Stories?'

'Yes.' She swallowed, looking up at him.

'No need to pretend, Bridie. I'd guessed as much, seeing as I'm neither blind, deaf or stupid. Though, I must say I find it disappointing, in the circumstances.'

'No, Alf. You don't understand. It's improving, even though it's fairy tales.'

'I don't see how it can be.'

'I'm working on my spelling, that's how, and my punctuation, putting all those dots in the right places. I'll be an asset to a man with a business. You've said it yourself. And Rhys is helping me.'

'It's true, Mr Bustle. She'll not put a word in that notebook until it's perfect.'

'That's all very well but—' Alf froze. He glanced from Bridie, to Rhys, then back again. 'Words? In her notebook?'

'Yes. Only once the story's perfect, mind.'

Stories! In her notebook! Alf swung round. 'Is this true, Bridie?'

No answer.

Alf sucked in breath. After all this time, all his patience, the days he'd berated himself for his busyness, letting her make second drafts, third, praising her commitment, and all the while she had been stringing him along like a fish. 'Were you going to tell me, Bridie? Or keep on lying?'

Still no answer. Bridie's face flushed pink.

'Stupid old Alf, is that what you thought? Slip him an observation, now and then. Jot down a chant. He'll never work it out. We made an agreement, Bridie. Back in Deptford. To work on a voyage log.'

'You wouldn't understand. You never do. Why should I bother explaining?'

'I understand lies, Bridie.'

'If I'd told you the truth, you'd only have tried to stop me.'

This was true. Alf paused, conscious of a sudden watchful silence. All around him, young men jabbed their friends in the ribs, single girls whispered behind raised hands, their tracts fluttering forgotten in the breeze. Talk about wasting time; he'd drawn the whole school into their argument.

'You never know. I might have surprised you.'

'You? Surprise me! I doubt it. You and Ma have been in cahoots from the beginning. That's what all this is about, isn't it? Trying to make me forget my dad—and his stories.'

'It's about helping you grow up, to see the world as it is for a change. Not as some extended fairy tale.'

'I don't want to grow up. Or see the world the way you do. It's boring.'

Alf stepped back, seeing her hate-slitted eyes, the way her body shook with fury. Dear God, how had it come to this? He'd only meant to challenge her. Not back her into a corner.

'If you've got time for fairy tales, I expect you'll have time for some sensible, nautical observations as well.'

'I won't. I'm too busy.'

'Then I'm asking you to make time, Bridie.'

'No! It's stupid.' She jumped to her feet. 'You can go on about your voyage log, you can talk about the wind and the sails and all the other foolish topics that interest you. But you can't stop me writing stories, or talking to my friends. You're not my dad, Alf. You can't make me do anything.'

She bunched her skirts, and dashed across the deck. Arms heavy at his sides, Alf watched her flight, aware of Rhys's face mute with apology, the averted gazes of Annie and Siân. He felt Reverend Cummings lay a plump hand on his shoulder. Alf's vision blurred. Bridie didn't want his guidance, or his friendship. She'd never intended sharing her notebook. Why hadn't he seen this? Why was he always so blind?

Chapter 12

*I*n horror, Rhys watched Alf stumble across the deck, his movements slow and stiff as an old dog whose master had unexpectedly turned on him. Rhys had known Bridie was supposed to be working on a voyage log, but not that she'd promised to share her notebook with Alf. How could he have known? No one had told him, least of all Bridie.

'Right.' Reverend Cummings cleared his throat. 'Where were we?'

Good question, Welsh names? The text? Rhys had no recollection. Beside him, Annie kept her gaze fixed on the deck. Siân's eyes swam with sympathy.

'Now young man, you mustn't blame yourself.' Reverend Cummings' eyes winked kindly. 'The problem started long before your friendship.'

This may have been true, but Rhys didn't find his words reassuring.

'The Lord works in mysterious ways,' Reverend Cummings added. 'We must leave the situation in his hands. But I will remember the girl and her father in my intercessions.'

God works in mysterious ways,
His wonders to perform;
He plants his foot steps in the sea,
And rides upon the storm.

Having been raised Chapel, Rhys was familiar with the words to Cowper's famous hymn. They filled his head like a refrain as he struggled through the remainder of the lesson, the lyrics melding with the sombre words of the text.

They mount up to heaven, they go down again to the depths: their soul is melted because of trouble.

For some reason, Rhys felt his father's dark-suited presence. Saw his calloused hands raised, ready to start conducting the chapel choir. Every word of the anthem directed at him, the coward, who'd run away. *Iesu, what was he supposed to do now?* Confront Bridie, demand an explanation? Apologise to Alf Bustle?

Judge not the Lord by feeble sense,
But trust him for his grace,
Behind a frowning providence,
He hides a smiling face.

No disrespect to Reverend Cummings, but he found the Almighty's ways too mysterious to fathom. As for a smiling face ... night after night, as Rhys paced the moonlit deck, he saw nothing but Tad's sneering countenance.

'*Bydd popeth yn iawn,*' Siân whispered. Everything will be fine.

'*Na fydd.*' Throat tight, Rhys shook his head.

'*Nid ti sydd ar fai.*'

Not to blame! Why was everyone saying that? He'd been so caught up in his troubles, he'd failed to notice what was happening. How could that not be his fault? His fear, the journey he'd insisted they make, the baby growing to fullness inside Siân. They were all his fault. And now, this terrible argument.

At last, the lesson finished. Rhys forced himself down the ladder into steerage. Alf wouldn't look at him during dinnertime. Bridie also seemed to be avoiding his gaze. Rhys trudged back up the ladder. What now? Slip behind the horsebox?

'No.' Siân caught at his arm. 'We should wait for her, Rhys.'

Rhys swallowed, looking down into her upturned face. She didn't care, that was the problem—about Alf or Bridie. No, that wasn't fair. Siân cared. But not enough to risk his sanity. He needed their story sessions, and Siân knew. She wasn't going to let him slip away without a fight. God knows they'd had enough of those since boarding this ship.

'It wouldn't be right to continue, Siân. Why can't you see that? Why must you always doubt me?'

'Not doubting, *cariad*. Only trying to help.'

'Help! Is that what you call it? Interfering in another man's family?'

'A crime, is it, now? To tell a story?'

'Not a crime. But still driving a wedge. *Iesu!* Think of the meddling I've endured over the years. All those friends of my father urging me not to shame him, thinking they knew best, that their words would somehow cure me. None of it helped, Siân. Only added to the burden. Now, I'm guilty of the same interference.'

'You didn't mean to interfere, Rhys. Surely that alters things.'

'Not to Alf Bustle it doesn't.'

'The rift was there, long before your friendship. Only stories can bring their healing now—for you and for Bridie.'

Rhys shivered, aware of her scent, the warmth of their fingers entwining. Dear God, all he'd wanted was a future, a place to raise their children without fear and prejudice. Yet here they were, like a skein of wool unravelling.

'He's a good man, Siân. I'll not undermine him.'

'Then you must tell Bridie yourself. She deserves that courtesy.'

Siân took her place at the base of the main mast. Rhys couldn't settle. He strode back and forth, trying not to imagine the long afternoons without stories, every bell-toll a reminder of the coming night in steerage. He rarely made it through an entire night, spent most his pre-dawn hours pacing main deck. The sailors didn't question his presence, they seemed to understand his need for space and privacy. Only when Doctor Roberts scratched on Mrs Scarcebrook's door in the early hours of the morning did he feel a need to duck behind the horsebox.

At last, here was Bridie. Stepping over the rotten wood of the combings, she adjusted her writing materials and marched toward them.

'Bridie, I had no idea about the voyage log.'

'No. I didn't want you to know. It's stupid. Alf's stupid.'

'But, can you not see? This puts me in a terrible position.'

'It's my notebook.'

'I'm an adult, Bridie. Expecting my first child. I'd not take kindly to another man interfering in my family.'

'I never asked to be part of Alf's family, or to share my notebook. Besides, I'm an adult too, a young woman in the making, so Ma keeps telling me.'

'Adults keep their word, Bridie.'

'And you promised stories.'

'Under false pretences. Without your stepfather's permission.'

'I don't need Alf's permission. I've told you already. But I do need your stories. Don't you see? They're helping. I thought they were helping you too, that we were friends. Maybe I was wrong?'

Nefi, what to do? She looked so small and lost with her eyes brimming. Not nearly the adult she claimed to be. He reached out, brushing a tear from her cheek.

'No, *bach*. You're not mistaken. I need the stories too. And your friendship. But adulthood brings responsibility. Can you not see? It wouldn't be right for me to continue. No matter how I wish it otherwise. Not without your stepfather's permission.'

'Then ask him, please, Rhys. For the sake of our friendship.'

* * *

It wasn't easy catching Alf alone. When Rhys waited at the entrance to the back hatch, Alf used the front hatch. If they were rostered on mess duties together, Alf altered the schedule. Even when Rhys squeezed onto the bench beside him at dinnertime, Alf angled his shoulder in the opposite direction. In the end, Rhys had no choice but to shove trembling hands in his pockets and confront him during cleaning.

'Watch out,' Harvey Rolf snapped as Rhys dodged a pile of sweepings. 'We've a job to do here.'

'Indeed, an important one. It's Mr Bustle I'm after.'

'He's busy.' Mr Rolf jerked his chin in Alf's direction.

'I'll wait, then. If you don't mind. I'd like to speak with him alone.'

Alf took an age to finish the cleaning. It seemed to Rhys he gave the task far more attention than necessary. But even Alf couldn't scrub forever. As Mr Rolf and the other steerage cleaners filed up the ladder for their lesson, Rhys found the older man alone.

'Mr Bustle, I owe you an apology.'

'No, you don't. Leave matters alone.' Alf hefted the hawse bucket and turned toward the hatchway.

'Please. Wait.' Rhys grabbed his arm. 'I appreciate your anger, Mr Bustle. Truly. But I ask you to hear me out. I had no idea Bridie had agreed to share her notebook. I hope you believe me.'

'I know my stepdaughter, young man. Better than you realise.'

'I don't doubt it, Mr Bustle, and I've no desire to interfere in your family. I'll be telling stories Friday nights, as people have come to expect it. But I'll not work with Bridie again without your permission. I've told her as much.'

Alf lowered the bucket, his blue eyes clouded. With what? Doubt? Confusion? Rhys couldn't tell. Only that the shadows spoke of a long and difficult journey.

'Do you know what it's like to compete with a ghost, young man, to never be funny enough, or clever enough, or even fanciful enough? To butt your head against an enormous rock of affection?'

'My father isn't dead, Mr Bustle. But I know how it feels not to measure up. Even here, on this ship, his presence haunts me.'

'I thought, once we left Covent Garden with its taverns and theatres, the cellar where her father practised, I'd stand a chance. That with time and distance, his presence would fade. But, still, she has her notebook and you are resurrecting him daily.'

'I'm sorry. I had no idea.'

'No, young man. You don't have any idea.'

'I'm an adult, Mr Bustle. I still find comfort in stories. They are like parables; the kind you might find in scripture. From an earlier time, perhaps, and somewhat more fanciful. Yet still they hold lessons. Maybe the lesson Bridie needs. She weeps, sometimes. Did you know that? And, though it may feel like you are butting your head against a great rock, I see disappointment walking hand-in-hand with that enormous affection.'

Alf shook his head. 'He didn't die well. He was a drunk and a dreamer. In the end—'

'No, please.' Rhys held up a hand. 'Let's not break her confidence. I don't expect you to understand my request, Mr Bustle. Or to give me your blessing. Only a chance, that's all I'm asking, to let the stories work their magic.'

'I'm a plain man, Rhys. I don't believe in magic. But I know when I'm not wanted. If you can fill that notebook by the end of the voyage, so that Bridie arrives in Port Phillip with a sense that her childhood, like its pages, are well and truly finished, then you'll not only have my permission, son, you will also have my blessing.'

CHAPTER 13

*O*lf and Bridie weren't the only ones arguing. By midweek, the wind had dropped and *Lady Sophia* reeled to the bark of her ship's officers. No matter how many times they dropped the speed log over the side, or how often the sailors set and reset the sails, it made no difference. They weren't going anywhere.

All day, Rhys sat on the windless main deck, his skin blistering. At night, when the sun dipped its fiery orb into the sea, he found sleep impossible. Even with windsocks set up over the hatchways, they couldn't keep the air circulating. He heard moans as he padded through steerage in the early hours of the morning, children whimpering. As one windless day gave way to another, the bickering became hostility.

Patrick O'Malley, one of the Irish lads, punched his brother on the nose for shirking mess duties. Shrill female voices accused each other of pilfering. Millie Burns, one of the younger married women, declared she no longer wanted to sleep with her husband. Alarmed, a red-faced Frank Burns took his problem to Doctor Roberts.

'If the married men could take their bedding on deck while the wind is absent, it would cool our wives' tempers.'

'Certainly not, Mr Burns. I keep a disciplined ship.'

'But my Millie's that savage with the heat. She's not slept a wink with all my tossing and turning.'

'No doubt, your wife is savage. But I'm afraid she must find another way to cool her temper.'

'Cool! As if anyone could keep cool in this heat.'

Rhys heard the snarl of discontent as he climbed down the ladder into streerage that evening. There were no maps or letter books laid out on the table, precious few sewing projects. Women leaned forward, gossiping behind raised hands. Men slapped cards down, their talk a growl of anger and frustration.

'Who does he think he is? If my wife don't get some sleep she'll murder the kids.'

'It's all right for him. He's got portholes in his cabin. A steward to bring him drinks.'

'His cabin! As if he's sleeping in his cabin!' Frank Burns slammed his cards down on the table. 'More likely visiting that matron of his.'

Rhys flipped open his violin case. They had practised 'The Fairy Ointment' for tonight—the story of an old midwife who'd rubbed an eye with ointment and realised the woman she was tending had been captured by the fairies. A traditional tale, though not exclusive to Wales. Bridie had been enchanted by the notion of seeing through different eyes. But tonight, with this mood, would it hold their audience? He glanced sideways. Could Siân feel it too? The violence pulsing beneath the surface?

She frowned, shook her head. *Please, Rhys, stick with the plan.*

Iesu, why must she always doubt him? They had other tales—tragedies to set men weeping, rousing political tales to nurse their fury. Though he doubted they would accord with Doctor Roberts' idea of a 'disciplined ship'. Maybe that was Siân's concern. Maybe she was right.

Rhys breathed deep, loosed his kerchief, and sank onto the bench. Beside him, Pam tutted as she examined a hole in Billy's stocking. Mary sat, fan in hand, listening to her prattle. Tom and Alf were squabbling, as usual, the tension between them rising. But though sweat rimmed Tom's armpits, they weren't bewailing the heat, or Doctor Roberts' refusal to let the married men sleep on deck. They were arguing the terms of Annie's employment.

'Mrs Scarcebrook ain't doing her job,' Tom jabbed the table with a stubby forefinger, 'and our Annie ought get paid for helping.'

'Doctor Roberts is a professional man, Tom, and a busy one. It's probably slipped his mind. Besides, it's not as clear-cut as you think. Mrs Scarcebrook's still doing his paperwork.'

'And Annie's working at the dispensary.'

'Annie likes helping. She told me.'

'That's not the point, Alf.'

'No? What is the point?

'Annie needs a piece of paper outlining her gratuity.'

Tom was right. They'd left seasickness behind along with the coasts of England and France, yet Annie still bathed heads and checked sores while Mrs Scarcebrook spent her afternoons promenading the quarter deck with Doctor Roberts. Frank Burns wasn't the only one complaining. Rhys had seen raised eyebrows among the families amidships, heard more than one snide comment about Doctor Roberts and his 'paramour'.

Alf wouldn't hear a word against the surgeon. Rhys couldn't help admiring the older man's loyalty. Though he doubted Doctor Roberts deserved it. He still couldn't place the thin, humourless face. But he'd seen the wad of credit notes alongside that criss-cross of calculations, felt a sharp wave of revulsion and, quite apart from Mrs Scarcebrook, he sensed Doctor Roberts couldn't be trusted.

Alf shifted, mopping his brow. 'Doctor Roberts hasn't offered to pay Annie.'

'Well, of course not. You've got to ask him.'

'Me!'

'You're her guardian.'

'I'll raise the matter, Tom. Though it's none of your business, I agree Annie deserves a small gratuity.'

'Not small, Alf. Fair. Tell him you want it in writing.'

Rhys thought Alf might burst. His mild blue eyes looked almost wild. His pulse throbbed above the open neck of his shirt.

'Oh, and another thing, Alf. About our wine rations.'

'Rations are at the surgeon's discretion. I've told you that already.'

'It wouldn't hurt to remind him. In case he's forgotten.'

Alf dropped his head in his hands, his calloused fingers threading his thinning blond hair. He'd aged these past weeks, his argument with Bridie bowing his shoulders and deepening the worry lines on his face and, although Rhys had apologised for his part in their quarrel, he couldn't resist trying to make amends.

'Is it the steerage union you're forming now, Tom? Next, you'll be drawing up a charter and asking us to pay our dues.'

'Not a bad idea, Welshman. Sure your name ain't Rebecca?'

'No dressing up for me. I've told you already.'

'That's right, your tad was a great one for politics.'

'Indeed, you are greatly like him. Though, Tad mixed politics with religion. I doubt anyone could say that of you, Tom?'

'Is that why you're running, Welshman?'

Iesu! Where had that come from? And how to answer? Tom hadn't goaded him about Tad since the night of the Taliesin story. 'Welsh politics for you, is it, Tom?'

'All politics, son. I've told you a number of times. But I'd rather you stuck to the topic.'

'The Rebecca Riots, I thought we were discussing.'

'Your tad, if I remember correctly.'

'Tom the radical.' Rhys kept his voice deliberately light. The trick was to answer questions with more questions, he'd learned over the years; steer the conversation away from his past. 'If you've an interest in Welsh politics, you'll know the name Dic Penderyn. From Aberafan, he was originally. Close to my home village.'

'I know who Penderyn was. I signed the petition for his release. For all the good it did him.'

'His cousin was luckier, though, Tom. Sentence commuted to transportation.'

'I bet that pleased your Bible-thumping tad?'

'Tad was a hard man to please.'

'Come on, Welshman, what's the story? Religion? Or something else?'

'My name's Rhys, Tom. And who says I have a story to tell?'

'No one, Rhys. It's written all over you—you and the pretty girl.'

Rhys shivered, aware of Siân's stillness on the bench beside him, the way the deck around him had fallen silent.

'We've heard all about her aunt. No mention of parents. Funny what goes on in those valleys. Better than one of your stories, I'm guessing.'

No. It wasn't funny, none of it was funny, and damned if he'd let Tom Griggs dictate the evening's entertainment. Rhys rose, grabbed his violin and called out across the deck.

'Tonight, ladies and gentlemen, we will have a story for our good friend, Mr Griggs, a unionist and political agitator who is travelling to New South Wales as a free settler. Not, as you would imagine, a prisoner of Her Majesty.'

Rhys heard the ripple of amusement as people scrambled into place. He reached down, unsmiling, and helped Siân onto the bench.

Her eyes were like black ink, underlining her disquiet.

Yes, he was angry. Yes, he was overreacting. And, yes, he would pay for this in the morning. But he didn't care. Tom wanted a tale from the Valleys; he'd give him one. Never mind 'The Fairy Ointment'. He'd give them the story of Dic Penderyn, the man hung for his involvement in the Merthyr Riots.

Eyes closed, Rhys raised an arm as anticipation ran like a fuse along the deck. He heard a scuffle of feet, creaking timbers. When all was quiet, he began to speak.

'Tonight I must tell you a tale of great sorrow.'

Rhys scanned the deck, daring his fellows to enter into the tale.

'Of tinder and sparks and embers that glow.

Think hardship and hunger,

Think profit and loss,

A rising of men, revenge, a life lost.

Sad tale whispered in valleys, softly blown on the wind,

Spoken with awe and with pride and fear tinged.

Missed son of a mother, beloved of a wife,

A miner, a unionist,
Man for a fight!'

Rhys felt the response. It was palpable. No one in steerage was a stranger to hardship. All were acquainted with loss. Hot, sweaty, and berthed like beasts in an airless compartment, Doctor Roberts' high-handed refusal to let them sleep on deck had set a match to their fury. Pacing back and forth on the bench, Rhys used short, sharp, staccato violin strokes to fan that fury into a blaze.

'Merthyr—dirt-mean and poor at the century's turn,
Barely eight thousand souls still a rural concern.
Scratch the surface, find iron ore, limestone and coal,
Add water, add timber—industrial gold!
Come Crawshay investor, stir the pot, give us cawl,
In pit, foundry, quarry employment for all.'

A roar greeted the word employment. Rhys stepped back as if from the blast of a furnace. *Give us this day our daily bread*, the most basic of human needs. *A fair day's work for a fair day's pay*, their reason for being on this ship. As Rhys's eyes raked the crowd, he saw that struggle in every face: anger, disappointment, uncertainty—they were all there. He turned to Siân, wanting her mood to match his own. To know that in this, he wasn't alone.

No. Brow creased, she shook her head.

Rhys shrugged, returning her frown. Why? What was the harm? They could control a crowd. He held out a hand. She stepped back, jerking her head toward the hatchway. Rhys followed her gaze, saw the alarmed face of a ship's officer. Siân's eyes flicked from the back hatch to the front hatch. She raised a fist, slamming it into her palm. Then he knew. *Iesu Grist*, he knew.

If things got rowdy, they would batten down.

Rhys swayed, his knees threatening to buckle. He imagined the sky all purple with dusk, a tight-lipped Doctor Roberts pacing the deck, Captain Thompson's curt, no-nonsense orders, the hatch planks slamming into place. Hard, wooden, like the inside of a cupboard. His chest growing tight, the air rationed.

He turned back to Siân. Her eyes held a question. What? What did she want him to do? Pull back, wind things down? No, he might be a coward, but he'd never pulled out of a telling. Besides, things had gone too far. People were on their feet, stamping, shouting, pressing up against him, eyes hard as bullets. He'd have to take this story to the end, no matter what it cost him.

'Population explosion, there's work for the poor,
They come in their thousand and thousands and more.
Blistering Merthyr, vision of hell,
Foundries and furnaces, smoke and foul smell.
Cheap housing, flimsy, sanitation poor,
Cholera come quickly, don't knock at the door,
Feel it to see it, don't turn a blind eye.
Filth, rancid squalor, misery, vice.'

Rhys's gaze found the back hatch. Open, thank God. The hatchways were still open. It was only a matter of time. Children bawled, forgotten in their bunks. Women stamped their feet. After Rhys spoke each line, he paused, raising his bow, letting them beat out its rhythm on the deck boards, benches and tables, their voices rising in an ocean of deep-throated guttural sound. Dear God, what must it sound like from above? As if he were starting a riot.

No one in steerage had known Dic. But all knew his story. For hadn't it been on every tongue those short weeks in 1831, spoken in pits, foundries, and quarries the length and breadth of the land? All knew a group of miners had met on Twyn-y-Waun common to discuss parliamentary reform. With the iron industry in the grip of a recession, was it any wonder those talks had grown restive? Or that workers had poured in from nearby towns of Dowlais, Aberdare and Penderyn? For hadn't a red flag been raised over Merthyr that early week in June and hadn't a troop of Highlanders been called in to quell the swirling mass of protest?

'By Castle Inn gathered in grey light of dawn,
Mob seething and restless, festering sore,
Come violence and murder, terrible strife,

Sixteen men killed, soldier stabbed with a knife,
"Black" the man's name was,
Though, no one quite saw it,
Lewis Lewis was arrested and Dic from Penderyn.'

Rhys had been too young to understand the court cases that followed. But all knew those eighty trained soldiers had fired on the unarmed crowd. He remembered the pall of horror spreading from valley to valley, Tad's fist pounding the table top.

'One soldier! Only one soldier stabbed, him not even dead! Whereas sixteen Welshmen—sixteen innocent Welshmen are, even now, being laid to rest!'

Petitions had been circulated. Men of reason and power protested Dic's arrest. But in London, Lord Melbourne was adamant. 'A unionist! And a Welshman! By God, I'll make him pay for this!'

'They killed Dic Penderyn to set out an example,
Though guilt never touched him, they forced him to wear it.
One last cry of injustice, one last dying breath,
Brought home, Aberafan, laid there to rest.
But his cry it still echoes in valley and town,
Still we do whisper it bitter and proud,
It's the cry of the poor, it's the cry of the weak,
It's the cry of our people, it's our turn to speak.'

A drub of anger, hands and feet, echoing Tad's fists. Rhys felt a jolt, an all round shudder of timbers as the first hatch plank was rammed into place. He raised his fist, letting Dic's final cry ring out over the deck.

'*O Arglwydd, dyma gamwedd! Lord here is injustice!*'

'Lord here is injustice!' the crowd roared back at him.

Another jolt, the lanterns flickered. Rhys's gaze flew to the nearby scuttle. Open. Thank God. The scuttles were still open. He bunched his fist, felt a sob rise in his chest.

'*One step.*' Tad's hectoring voice. '*Then another. That's it, son. Control your breath.*'

Rhys moaned, swaying. No airless cupboard, no Tad standing

over him, belt in hand. Only the hatch covers. The flimsy rotten hatch covers—yet still his chest heaved like the flanks of a pit pony.

'What's he done? Taken fright? Christ, see his legs tremble.'

'Nah! It's all part of the act. Wait, you'll see.'

Legs? An act? Were they talking about him? Speak, Rhys, speak. Raise the violin. Do something. Anything. Before they guess.

No. He couldn't move. His arms had frozen—and his lips. His legs, on the other hand, seemed to be turning to slush. Dear God, he was going to fall. Now. In front of them all. He staggered, reached out, pleading to Siân. She grasped his hand. In that moment, she gathered him like a hen does its chicks. Her song, not of anger, or injustice, but of grief and a terrible yearning.

'*A dream has ended,*
The fire has burned,
A young wife lonely,
A child must mourn.'

As Siân stood, her dark curls tumbling down her back, it wasn't hard to imagine Dic's young wife, pregnant and alone. Nor to experience a deep, welling sorrow as her husband's lifeless body was dragged from the gallows. Rhys found himself part of the funeral procession that walked him home to Aberafan; saw the silent avenue of faces that lined the way for his passing.

'*Come lift your voices,*
Sing deep regret,
A star has fallen,
The sun has set.'

Rhys still couldn't utter a sound, let alone raise his fiddle. Fixing his gaze on the nearby scuttle, he let Siân's words fill the icy void within. Not with courage, for he was surely craven. But with a borrowed strength, the kind that only Siân could give. Like Moses holding his staff aloft in the wilderness, or the severed head of Bran the Blessed, she kept him from foundering and, as long as she stood beside him, he could face anything—this journey, the aftermath of tonight's story. The terror that, even now, stole the breath from him.

As he stood, gathering strength, he watched her song work its wonder. Saw women turn and embrace men, reaching out to grasp work-roughened hands, handkerchiefs; many of them with red-rimmed eyes and tremulous smiles. As his face thawed and his legs began to strengthen, he at last found himself able to function.

He acknowledged Tom's nod of approval, watched Pam reach up to settle the children, saw Mary sink on to the bench, Alf stooping to pick up a battered quart pot. Glancing upwards, he saw Bridie crying alone in her bunk.

Bechod! Such sorrow, cutting her like a scythe.

For whom did young Bridie weep tonight? Not Dic Penderyn, or his young wife's plight—something older and deeper, to do with her father. A man of music and stories, who'd drunk too much in his sorrow. A man Bridie had loved deeply yet, strangely, also feared had wanted to leave her. He'd not died well, according to Alf Bustle. Perhaps he should have heard the older man's side of the story. No. Bridie must find the courage to trust him. *Iesu mawr,* who was he to speak of courage, or trust? He, who stood with knees weak and his chest wheezing like a set of bellows.

Crist, he needed Siân.

He dug his fingers into the soft skin of her palm. She didn't wince or turn away. Only held his gaze. Rhys's pulse thrummed. He closed his eyes, raised the violin, and let it speak his longing—for her lips, her touch, the warm yeasty scent of her hidden places. The need to rise above her and to feel like a man. To come home shuddering in the fortress of her arms.

* * *

Rhys couldn't sleep after their coupling, though Siân gathered and rocked him like a toddling child. If only he could stay in her arms forever with his breath slow and his *pidyn* softening, enjoying the rise and fall of her breasts and the dead sleeping weight of her in his arms.

He breathed deep, forcing air down into his lungs. Fixed his gaze on the nearby scuttle. Heard the sea's lap, a rat scuttling, muffled footsteps from the deck boards overhead.

A single bell marked the change of watch. He heard movement around the back hatch, a curse, someone fumbling with the ropes. A plank lifted, then another. Moonlight slivered in.

Open. Thank God, the hatchways were open.

Rhys drew his arm from beneath Siân. Hair mussy with sleep, she pressed herself against him.

'The baby, Rhys, can you feel it moving?'

Yes. He could feel it, her belly undulating beneath his palm. Was it an arm or leg, perfect and finely formed? He'd be a father soon, an adult calming a child's fears.

'You'll be fine,' Siân answered his thoughts. 'Grand stories you'll tell our *babanod*.'

'Not stories they'll be needing.'

'What then? A firm hand, no nonsense. Locked in a cupboard until they behave.'

'Not that either.'

'Well then … stories and songs, is it? A *cwtch* by the fire. Strong arms, clear mind, gentle faith … you'll be fine, Rhys. Brave.'

'No, Siân. I'm a coward. Jumping at ghosts, reacting to the slightest sound. That wasn't brave, what I did tonight, or clever. It was foolish.'

'Yes. It was.' Her words stung.

'Only wanting to keep you safe. You and our *babanod*.'

'What good does it do me, with us arguing, you not sleeping, and me unable to try a simple charm?'

'It's never simple, Siân. You know that. People will talk, ask questions. Our children unable to hold their heads up.'

'Is it for our children you fear, or yourself?'

'You should know. You're the one they turned on.'

'And it's you who are turning on me now.'

Rhys jerked upright, groped for his trousers and shoved his feet into his boots. He dragged a blanket from the bed and fumbled his way along the deck, keeping his movements slow, deliberately even, though none were awake to see him. On the main deck he bent double, sucking clean, fresh air into his lungs. The watch officer nodded at him from quarterdeck. A sailor winked his complicity.

Rhys swivelled away, shoving his hands in his pockets. He picked his way toward the deckhouse, slipped past Mrs Scarcebrook's cabin, and squeezed in between the boats. Settling back against the horsebox, the cold wet nose of a puppy made him startle.

What are you afraid of? Rhys laughed mirthlessly in the dark.

When they were children, boys from the village had thrown stones at Siân, calling her the devil's child. As her friend, he'd taken his share of stoning over the years. His father had beaten him for spending his days on the mountain. Yet he'd never stopped running back to Siân. Even in London, never mind the pretty girls in chapel, their fathers wanting a son-in-law to carry on the business, he'd been bound by a simple childhood promise and the sanctuary he had found in Siân.

He'd sensed her danger long before the news of Rhonwen's death ever reached him. Racing back to Cwmafan, he'd found a party of youths had burned her whitewashed cottage to the ground. It was all right for the old woman to live among them, they said, but not the devil's child. Never mind that Siân had nowhere to go. Or that she'd fled, fearing for her life. When Rhys found her hiding out in the woods, he'd had to gentle her like a foal. So, why wasn't she afraid now? Because he was. Afraid people would glimpse his cowardice. Imagining, even here, on this ship, someone would link Siân's magic with her birth.

Rhys shivered, pulling the blanket about his shoulders. They'd come so far. They need only hold on for a few months and they'd reach the foreign shore. He'd be released from his torment. They could start life anew. Why couldn't Siân see this? Why must she put the whole plan in jeopardy?

* * *

Blood. Rhys dreamed of blood—warm, thick, pulsing. He lurched toward a hawse bucket. It disappeared. Blood spilled onto the deck. He heard a moan, spun round. The blood was Siân's. He grasped her hand. So cold, her body dissolving. *Siân! Dear God, no!*

A bell tolled.

He gasped, jerked upright. Smelled salt. Felt a warmth pressed up against him. The puppy! A dream, only a dream. He shook his head, scrubbed his face. Another bell. Two. What time was that? Five o'clock in the morning. Not too late to slip back into steerage. No, he'd put that off a while longer. He balled the blanket, shoved it behind the hencoop, heard an indignant cluck, feathers ruffling. Too early for the hens, but not for the cook. Pots clattered in the galley kitchen. Tobacco smoke wafted on the breeze. With any luck, the cook might be willing to slip him an early morning cup of tea.

As he popped his head out from between the boats, Mrs Scarcebrook's cabin door creaked open. He froze. Waited. Saw Doctor Roberts step into the pre-dawn light, leather bag in hand, a silk hat perched atop his head.

Rhys shrank back into the shadows. He'd rather not face Doctor Roberts at this hour of the morning, let alone with the man in such a compromising position.

'Here, Franklin, let me tie your cravat.' Mrs Scarcebrook leaned up, brushing a kiss to Doctor Roberts' lips.

'Is that all?' His hand cupped her breast.

'For now. Look, the sky is lightening.'

'What about later, sweetheart?'

'Tonight. Certainly. I'll leave the door unlocked.'

'And in Port Phillip?'

'Well, my husband may not like the situation. But, seriously, Franklin. What about your wife and family?'

'Let's just say I've burned my bridges there, love.'

'And your practice, where was it again? Somewhere in the north of London?'

Wife? Franklin? Somewhere north of London. The words shifted like a kaleidoscope in Rhys's head. He saw Doctor Roberts' thin-lipped profile. The way he shrugged, pulling his collar up, and the pieces fell into place. Barnet, of course. Huge sums of money changed hands in Chipping Barnet. Cattle were fattened for the city markets. Welsh drovers sent letters and parcels on to their families in London. One year, Dai Phillips had brought his sister Ceinwen along—a pert, green-eyed girl, eager to work in her uncle's Marylebone dairy. She'd managed the journey well enough. Though by Barnet she'd developed an abscess. They'd tried resting her, using the local apothecary's powders. In the end, a surgeon had to be consulted—a sleek, well-dressed man with a practice on Barnet High Street.

'He's a competent surgeon,' the apothecary's wife explained, 'and not afraid to use his scalpel. But don't you go leaving that girl alone with him. He's a gambler, they tell me, and a womaniser. I'd not be trusting him with my sister's virtue.'

CHAPTER 14

*A*lf spent the morning waiting for a summons. It would come. Nothing was more certain. He would lose his position as chief cleaning constable. And why not? Doctor Roberts had tried to warn him. 'Strange and haughty,' he'd said, followed by, 'you'd do well to keep an eye on him.' Had he done so? No, he'd been too busy wallowing in self-pity. Now look! They'd almost had a riot in steerage.

Alf moaned, sprinkling the bed boards with chloride of lime and passed the hawse bucket back to Harvey Rolf. If only he hadn't argued with Bridie, or let his nagging sense of failure distract him. If only he'd looked up from his busyness, now and then, he might have noticed trouble brewing.

Good man! Indispensable! The words mocked him now. Then again, hadn't it always been the case, at the market shop, and with Bridie? He could bend and scrape, all right, bag up a delivery, but life's subtleties always eluded him. And now this riot, just when he'd promised to sort out Annie's pay.

'I'll come with you, if you like?'

Alf glanced up, forcing a smile. 'No, Harvey. You mustn't miss your lesson.'

'He'd be mad to dismiss you. And Tom's right, the lass deserves her gratuity. I've a good mind to tell him so myself.'

Alf grunted, pressing his brush into a lice-infested crevice. Mr Rolf worked with the tireless energy of a steam engine and Alf had come to rely on him greatly over the weeks at sea. But he doubted Doctor Roberts would be impressed by the young man's blunt well-meant advice. Besides, Annie was his responsibility. He should have spoken up long before this.

'Right, then.' Mr Rolf straightened up, lifting the hawse bucket. 'I'll tip this water out, shall I?'

Alf nodded but didn't look up. His head throbbed and his palms felt slick. Dear God, what a fool, to get so worked up. The whole thing was probably a misunderstanding. Doctor Roberts probably intended to pay Annie, and had simply forgotten. It was like that with the professional classes. They had no idea how much a penny meant to the workingman.

Lord, listen to that! He was starting to sound like Tom Griggs.

He would simply point out how hard Annie was working at the dispensary and ask that she be given a small gratuity. There was nothing difficult about that, nothing to get worked up about. Until now, when he was about to be dismissed.

* * *

'Mr Bustle, Doctor Roberts wants a word with you.' The ship's boy stooped, catching his breath. 'He says it's important, sir. You're to come immediately!'

So, this was it. A noose tightened about Alf's neck. He straightened up, pressing his hands into his lower back and forced a smile.

'Settle down, son. That's it. You're doing a good job. But, first, tell me … what else did Doctor Roberts say?'

'Well, sir, he were stern. I were having a boil lanced—that's when they pop it, you know—and he were stern even though it hurt.' Puffing out his cheeks, the errand boy altered his tone to imitate Doctor Roberts. '"Now, boy," he says. "Tell Mr Bustle the captain wants to see him. And tell Mr Bevan,"—that's the Welshman, you know, that tells them stories—"Tell Mr Bevan the captain wants to see him, too. And boy," he says. "I want to see them, immediately!"'

The captain! Dear God, even worse than he imagined.

Alf looked down at the murky water in his bucket. He'd never been inside the captain's cabin, let alone received a summons, and he could think of only one explanation. Doctor Roberts intended to make a formal report.

Alf surveyed the deck. The floors were scraped and the privy buckets emptied. The last of the bunk boards had been scoured clean. Steerage still reeked of bilge. He ought to have fumigated. But that wasn't his problem. At least, it wouldn't be after this morning's meeting.

He trudged up the ladder, splashed his hands and face in the water butt, and worked his way along the crowded deck. An unsmiling steward ushered him into the saloon and left him standing, cap in hand, outside the great cabin door. He knocked. The door flew open. Doctor Roberts balanced on his toes, like a pistol ready primed.

'Alone! Where's the troublemaker?'

Alf blinked in the flooding light of the stern cabin windows. 'I don't know, sir. I came straight from steerage.'

Alf glanced about the cabin. It was large and elegant with polished oak panels and gimballed candlesticks for light. A bed, an oval table and a mahogany bookcase were the only items of furniture in the room, apart from the captain's ornately carved, high-backed chair. Captain Thompson inclined his head, but didn't rise. Doctor Roberts filled the remainder of the space with his pacing.

'How big is this vessel, Bustle?'

'Perhaps the messenger couldn't find him, sir.'

Doctor Roberts flicked open his pocket watch. 'Ten minutes to walk the length of this ship.'

'The deck's crowded. And I didn't see him at breakfast time.'

'I'm not surprised. The scoundrel's probably hiding. But the cabin boy knows where to find him. I've seen to that. We'll soon know who's boss around here.'

Alf glanced sideways. Captain Thompson didn't seem alarmed by Doctor Roberts' strange behaviour. If anything, he seemed slightly amused. Maybe things weren't as bad as he thought. A dismissal, perhaps? Without the formal report? In which case, he should ask about Annie's pay now, while he still had the opportunity.

'Young Annie's doing well at the dispensary, sir.'

Doctor Roberts grunted but didn't reply.

'We'd never have managed without her, not with Mrs Scarcebrook being so delicate. She's a good girl, too, Doctor Roberts, and all alone. She'll have her work cut out for her in the colony.'

'She's competent, Bustle, though rather ghastly to look at. No doubt someone will take pity.'

'Yes, of course, and in the meantime my wife and I will do our best. She won't starve, not if we have anything to do with it. But, well, if you'll forgive me for mentioning it, Doctor Roberts, with the girl being so competent, and you having come to rely on her so greatly, I wondered, whether, well, perhaps you'd consider … offering her a small gratuity?'

'A gratuity!' Doctor Roberts' eyes bulged. 'The morning after a riot and you come asking for a gratuity.'

'I know it's not the best time, sir. But I mightn't get another chance.'

'Good God, man. Whatever are you blathering about?'

'I don't blame you, sir. Honestly. You tried to warn me. "Haughty", you said, and "you'd do well to keep an eye on him". But I've been that busy with the cleaning and my stepdaughter—'

'Enough! This is absurd.' Captain Thompson slapped the arms of his high-backed chair.

'No, not absurd.' Alf swung round to face him. 'I'm not good at explaining things. But I ask you to hear me out. I deserve what's coming. But young Annie's a different matter. I'd not see her miss out on my account.'

Captain Thompson blinked, shook his head. 'Are you quite well, Mr Bustle?'

'Yes, sir. Only I'm a little nervous. It's just … with things as they are this morning and with Annie being under my care, I wanted to speak now, before … well, before I lose my position.'

Captain Thompson leaned forward, eyes narrowed. 'Surely you were not the instigator of this riot?'

'Certainly not.'

'Right, now we have established that important detail, let me ask you a simple question. Are you able to see into the minds and hearts of your fellow travellers? Or somehow direct their consciences?'

'No, sir.'

'Then, I think that absolves you of all responsibility.'

Consciences? Absolution? Alf had never imagined Captain Thompson a religious man.

'We're dealing with a dangerous rebel.' Doctor Roberts leapt back into the conversation. 'One who is no doubt fleeing a legal entanglement. Personally, I'd like to throw the nuisance overboard. But Captain Thompson tells me this is not an option.'

'Sorry, sir. I'm still not following.'

'Dear God, Bustle, have you not been listening to a word we've been saying? The young man is a unionist and, no doubt, a criminal, and as we can't get rid of him, we must somehow manage the situation.'

'We? Manage! You mean … I'm not being dismissed?'

'No, Bustle, you are not being dismissed.'

Not dismissed, or reported. Warmth stole over Alf, as if he stood with his back to a blaze. He had no idea why he had been summoned. But Doctor Roberts had used the words 'we' and 'manage' in the same sentence. As if they were colleagues. Alf held the idea gently, as if it were warm and freshly laid. He'd heard of such things happening in the colonies, places where workingmen were able to rise above their humble beginnings. So, why not here, on this ship, where he was Doctor Roberts' *eyes and ears in steerage*?

* * *

A rap on the door interrupted Alf's reverie. As if on a pin, Doctor Roberts' head swung round. He crossed the cabin in two strides and flung the door wide.

'Mr Bevan. How good of you to come.'

Rhys's eyes were darkly shadowed, his boyish face guarded. To Alf's surprise, he ignored Doctor Roberts, addressing the captain. 'You asked to see me, sir?'

Captain Thompson inclined his head, but let Doctor Roberts reply. 'Quite a performance you gave us last night, Mr Bevan.'

Rhys bowed. 'Glad, I am, you enjoyed it, Doctor Roberts. You and Mrs Scarcebrook, was it?'

'Mrs Scarcebrook has no interest in the doggerel you produce.'

'Indeed, not with her being so delicate and needing extra care of a night time. Mind, you've quite a reputation with the young ladies, I believe?'

'We are not discussing my affairs, Mr Bevan.'

The surgeon spoke firmly without lowering his gaze, but his face flushed puce above his cream silk cravat. Alf couldn't help noticing his hands were also balled into fists.

'Doctor Roberts is right,' Captain Thompson interrupted from his high-backed chair, 'as interesting as his proclivities may be. We are concerned about your political persuasions, young man. Rebellion is a dangerous force on board a ship.'

Rhys's expression lost some of its intensity. 'A storyteller, I am, Captain Thompson. Not an agitator.'

'And last night's story?'

'About a man called Richard Lewis.'

'Otherwise known as Dic Penderyn,' Doctor Roberts all but pounced. 'The scoundrel hung for stabbing a soldier during the Merthyr Riots.'

'Penderyn was innocent,' Rhys said, still addressing the captain.

'You question Britain's judicial system, Mr Bevan?'

'I don't need to, sir. The story speaks for itself.'

'And not about any political aspirations you may hold?'

'He died when I was seven.'

'You aren't seven now, Mr Bevan.'

'Nor am I politically motivated.' Rhys passed a hand across his face. 'I'm a teller of tales, sir. Truly. I'd not intended to tell that story last night, or, indeed, to cause a commotion. But … things got out of hand.'

Captain Thompson turned his shrewd gaze on Alf. 'What do you make of the situation, Mr Bustle? Doctor Roberts tells me you're a solid sort of fellow. Not prone to hasty judgments. Perhaps you can shed some light on the matter?'

Solid! Not prone to hasty judgments!

This was it, a chance to prove himself to the captain, and justify the surgeon's faith in him. But … how? He searched the men's faces. What exactly was expected? He saw the flare of Doctor Roberts' nostrils, Captain Thompson's narrowed gaze, Rhys standing like a poker before him, and he had no idea what was happening.

'I'm not a clever man, Captain Thompson.'

'We're not asking for cleverness, Mr Bustle. Only the truth of the situation.'

The truth. Ah. Alf could manage that. 'Well, to be honest, sir, he generally tells stories about the past, legends and fairy tales. Quite ridiculous, in my opinion. But others enjoy them.'

'Yet, last night was different?'

'Yes, completely.'

'Can you tell me how, Mr Bustle?'

Alf closed his eyes, casting his mind back to the previous evening. He'd been sitting in steerage—hot, disgruntled and tired, as always, with Tom Griggs pestering. At his wits end, if he were honest, until Rhys stepped in …

Wait! Stepped in? Was that the truth of the situation? He opened his eyes. Yes, possibly. Then what? Alf pursed his lips, recalling the banter, the sly malice in Tom Griggs' questions, Rhys's attempts to evade them.

'We've a man in our mess who's quite annoying.' He glanced at Rhys. 'He asked some pointed questions, about your wife. That's right, isn't it, lad?'

'Yes. Sorry, Mr Bustle. I never meant to cause trouble.'

'It's all right, son. I believe you.'

And he did. For some inexplicable reason, Alf believed him, about the riot and the stories—even his friendship with Bridie.

'Good God! This isn't a Drury Lane.' Doctor Roberts pointed a gloved finger at Rhys. 'Look at him, pale, contrite, quite the performer. But he's running, I'm guessing, and a seasoned agitator. The question is what to do until we can hand him over to the authorities.'

'Not so hasty.' The captain rose, pushing back his chair. 'I think you're forgetting who is master on this ship.'

'With all due respect, sir. I must answer to the immigration agent at the end of the voyage.'

'Anyone can make a mistake, Doctor Roberts. And, if I remember correctly, this young man brought the incident to a close without intervention.'

'It's hardly a mistake to cause a riot.'

'We all have secrets, Doctor Roberts. And he who protesteth the loudest is often the guiltiest.'

Hands behind his back, Captain Thompson walked the short, tense line of men, past Rhys with his pale face and wary shoulders, and Doctor Roberts with his gilt buttons and fiery accusations. Alf had the uncomfortable notion that the captain read his mind as he stood, cap in hand, submitting to his scrutiny. He came to a halt in front of Rhys.

'The question is: will it happen again?'

Rhys didn't answer. Only held his gaze.

'Very well. We will leave it there for the time being. But I suggest you stick to legends in future, Mr Bevan, regardless of your messmates' awkward questions. I will not take kindly to a repeat of last night's performance.'

* * *

Back in steerage, Alf had no desire to talk about the interview—especially not with Rhys seated at the table opposite. But Tom

Griggs had no such reservations. Pushing his empty dinner plate aside, he bared his yellow teeth.

'Come on, Alf. Spill the beans.'

'There's nothing to spill.'

'Go on! After last night, there must have been hell to pay.'

Alf didn't answer. Shovelling salt-pork into his mouth, he glanced sideway at Rhys. The Welsh lad sat in his usual white-faced silence, barely touching the food on his plate. Was he a criminal, as Doctor Roberts suggested, fleeing some terrible past misdemeanour? Alf could scarcely credit the notion. Nor could he imagine the Welsh lad causing any more trouble. Indeed, if the smudges beneath his eyes were any indication, Rhys wasn't so much a troublemaker as the one troubled.

Still, who was he to question Doctor Roberts' judgment? He'd been warned once and had failed to heed that warning. He wasn't about to make the same mistake twice. Whether Rhys was a troublemaker, or troubled, Alf intended to keep an eye on him.

'Did you ask about Annie's pay?' Tom broke into his thoughts.

'Yes. I did, in fact.'

'And ... what did he say?'

'Nothing specific. We have an understanding.'

Alf smiled as he said the words, though they weren't strictly true. Doctor Roberts hadn't promised anything. But who needed promises? Doctor Roberts had called him *solid, not prone to hasty judgments.* As a colleague, Alf could raise the matter anytime and be certain of a fair hearing.

'An understanding? What's the good of that?'

'Doctor Roberts had more pressing things on his mind. There wasn't time for lengthy discussion.'

'Meanwhile, Annie works for nothing.'

'Doctor Roberts is a reasonable man. I think we can assume her pay will be backdated.'

Tom appeared somewhat mollified by this statement even as Alf's own quiet confidence surprised him. He felt puffed up, important, as if someone had worked a bellows in him.

'What about our wine rations?'

'I didn't ask about the wine.'

'We can't let him keep it.'

'I'm not suggesting we let Doctor Roberts keep our wine rations. But the morning after a riot was hardly the time to raise the matter.'

'When is a good time?'

'I don't know. Doctor Roberts is a busy man. I'll have to work out the best way to approach him.'

'What about a letter? We could all sign it?'

Alf reached for his mug and took a swig of tea. Despite his new-found calm, a knob of salt-pork had lodged in his throat. 'I doubt he'd take kindly to that strategy.'

'Then we'll go to Captain Thompson.'

'He won't interfere. Rations are the surgeon's responsibility.'

'He will, if I tell him Doctor Roberts is stealing our wine rations.'

'Don't be ridiculous. What would Doctor Roberts want with our wine?'

'Well, he might be gargling with them, Alf, or washing his socks in them. But my guess is he's drinking them.'

'That's absurd. You've got no proof.'

'No proof!'

'None.' Alf glared back at him. Why did Tom look so smug? And why was Rhys smiling? He took another swig of tea, glanced from Rhys to Tom and back again. 'Well, you haven't, have you?'

'Come off it, Alf! You could light a lantern with his breath.'

Alf coughed, spluttered, the tea gurgling in his throat. For some reason, it wouldn't go down. His throat was like a drain clogged up with salt-pork. Rhys thumped his back. It didn't help. Alf's eyes streamed. Tom was right, damn it; Doctor Roberts' breath stank. Why hadn't he realised? Why did others always have to point these things out to him?

Tom grinned, rubbing a hand over his stubbly chin. 'So, who's going to write the letter then?'

Alf's stomach churned. He stared down at the gristly pork on his plate. So what if Doctor Roberts' breath stank? It didn't prove a thing—apart from Tom Griggs' meddling, suspicious mind. Besides, he was surgeon superintendent. He could pilfer the entire wine ration if he wanted. Alf wasn't about to question him.

'Count me out. I want nothing to do with it.'

Tom fixed his yellowing smile on Rhys. 'What about you, Welshman? Is your pen as silvery as your tongue?'

'No! Please Tom. I promised to keep an eye on things.'

'Well, bully for you.'

'Why not write it yourself?' It was unkind. Alf knew the question was unkind. But he was sick of being pushed around by Tom Griggs.

'I don't have a good hand.'

'Practise makes perfect, Tom. Or have you tried already? Found you couldn't get on with it? Is that why you didn't attend Reverend Cummings' school? Because you're too proud to admit your weakness?'

'At least I don't bow and scrape like other people on this ship.'

'I've got priorities and I'm working toward them. If that means bowing and scraping, I'll do it. Damned if I'll let you, or anyone else, spoil my chances.'

'Hah! By the time you've worked up the guts to ask Doctor Roberts, I'll have a hundred signatures.'

'You'll have the signatures. But no letter.'

'No, that's where you're wrong. Young silver tongue here's going to write it for me.'

Alf shook his head. 'I stood up for him this morning. He owes me a favour.'

'I owe you an apology,' Rhys's soft voice interrupted. 'Honesty and fairness must bring their own rewards.'

'See, Alf! He's not as lily-livered as you think.'

Alf swivelled round. 'No, please, son, don't do this. I'll have to go to Doctor Roberts, don't you see? He'll make trouble. You know that, don't you? You've had dealings with him in the past.'

'Yes, Mr Bustle. I've had dealings. Which is why I don't trust him. But I'll not see you shamed, or jeopardise your position. I'll write Tom's letter on one condition—that he hand it over to you once he's collected the signatures. That way, you can decide whether to approach Doctor Roberts, or take the matter straight to the captain.'

CHAPTER 15

*B*ridie didn't wait for Rhys and Alf to finish their dinner. She barely made it through her pudding. So much trouble, confusion, the still-now sorrow of last night's story. She shoved her bowl to the centre of the table and made a dash for the hatchway ladder.

Siân sat in her usual place at the base of the main mast, her eyes darkly shadowed. But she held her back straight, as if determined to face the afternoon squarely. Bridie felt no such compulsion. She had no desire to talk to Rhys, or work on her stories. She certainly didn't want to see with different eyes. Her own were quite enough. Her vision suddenly altered.

She sank down beside the quarterdeck stairs, her mind a roil of memory and emotion. Was it shock? Or disappointment? She had to admit last night's story frightened her. One minute, Rhys had been talking to Tom Griggs; next, he'd been stoking the fire of people's fury. He'd regretted his actions almost at once. She'd seen that, and it was hardly surprising. There had been no magic in last night's story, or life lessons, only a terrible dredging up of memory, along with the cloying heat of steerage. Rhys had been affected too. She'd seen the tremor of his limbs, Siân's hand snaking out to save him and, now, this terrible tension, much worse than after Lucy's accident.

'*A dream has ended,*
The fire has burned,
A young wife lonely,
A child must mourn.'

Even now, Siân's words brought a wedge of sorrow to Bridie's throat. They might have been her own words, written to her own life's melody, a song for her even-now stubborn ache of grief. Although, her dad had been no martyr. Only a handful of theatre friends had turned out for his passing. Yet today, for some reason, she saw it all clearly, as if through the window of a peep box—the song, the sorrow, last night's story, bringing each tiny image into focus. She remembered anger and raised voices, the long fear-filled night of waiting, Alf organising a party to search the Boxing Day streets. He'd run ahead, when the men had found her dad, and helped with the medical expenses. But, by then it was too late. Ma's face was a plaster cast of fury.

Bridie had done her best—raising his head, spooning broth into his mouth, heating bricks and laying them at his feet. But Ma wanted nothing to do with him. She remembered Alf laying a hand on Ma's shoulder, the grateful quiver of her lips, Ma's fingers curling around his. Bridie moaned, pressing her hands to her face. Had she known? Or had she only just realised? For this changed everything. Mr trying-so-hard Alf didn't look so good now, or his boxes of market greens. As for Ma—it was worse, so much worse, than she'd imagined. For not only had Bridie's dad given up on life, but Ma had given up on him. And, if that wasn't bad enough, she'd also loved another man in place of him.

* * *

At supper time, Thaddy, one of the little Irish boys, wouldn't stop crying. His high thin wails threaded a needle up Bridie's spine. Slumped at the table, she jammed her fingers in her ears, her own misery enough without Thaddy's competing woes.

'Oh, for goodness sake,' Ma snapped. 'Have some pity. The poor little mite is probably sickening.'

Pity! Since when had Ma shown pity? Not Christmas night when Bridie's dad given her the notebook, or later on when he lay dying. But as she glanced along the deck, the angry words died on Bridie's lips. Hunched over Thaddy, his ma's anguished face was a pitiful sight.

By lights out, Thaddy's sister Maeve had started to whimper, along with the rabbit-toothed Hilary, whose head was pounding.

'Dim the lamps,' Hilary moaned, clutching her temples. 'Sweet Jesus. It's like someone's put a nail in me head.'

Dimming lights didn't help. Hilary moaned, Maeve and Thaddy wailed. In the fierce, unforgiving heat of the tropics, the blackened deck sounded like a scene from hell. Bridie woke the following morning to a smell of fresh, ripe vomit and the news that five others had joined the list of sufferers.

'It's like the smallpox,' Annie whispered, white-faced, as they set the table.

Bridie shivered, peering along the deck. 'Why? Has someone got spots?'

'No, but this is how it started, with one person, then another. Until everyone in our lodging house was sick. Then people started dying.'

At breakfast, no one spoke, or ate. Bridie's hands shook as she scraped bowls of cold grey porridge into the waiting slop-bins. She didn't grab her notebook once mess duties were finished, or head for her spot on the main deck. She sat as if chained to the bench. When the bells rang for surgery, she trooped up the ladder and joined the whispering knot gathered at the dispensary.

'Good God. This is not a circus.' Doctor Roberts gave an impatient flick of his hand. 'Be off, all of you. Go about your business.'

No one moved, apart from Thaddy's ma. She knelt, laying Thaddy on the deck. He whimpered, unable to raise his head. His calico shirt plastered to his ribs, his tiny body bathed in a feverish sweat. How old was he? Three? Four? About Billy's age. He still had the little-boy roundness to his cheeks.

Doctor Roberts raised a white lace handkerchief to his nose. His gaze darted over the heads of the crowd.

'Miss Bowles, where are you? Ah, there you are. Unbutton his shirt, please.'

'No. Wait!' Bridie grabbed Annie's arm. 'You might get sick.'

Silence. Doctor Roberts' flinty eyes. He lowered his hanky. Bridie wished a star trap would open up and let her plunge from his sight. But, no, if this was a serious illness, like the smallpox, then Annie could indeed sicken.

'She's right.' Bridie heard Alf's stiff apologetic tones from behind. 'Annie mustn't touch him.'

'Don't be ridiculous. The girl's my assistant.'

'Yes, I know that, sir. And I'd not like to spoil her chances. Especially now you're organising a gratuity.'

'Gratuity!' Doctor Roberts blinked. Clearly this was news to him, though Alf was too agitated to notice.

'Annie's in my care, sir. I promised her aunt I'd see her safe. And there was no great risk, lancing boils and checking heads for lice but, if this is an epidemic—'

'Epidemic! Who says this is an epidemic?'

'No one, sir. I just thought—'

'The last thing we need is panic.' Doctor Roberts turned, forcing a smile, and addressed the crowd. 'You must rest. Do you hear me? Eat well, attend your lessons, sing hymns of an evening. Nothing undermines the health so much as fretting.'

'It's all right for him,' someone muttered. 'He's nowt to lose but his gratuity.'

'He could sicken. Look how he holds the cloth to his nose.'

'Him! Not likely! He ain't cooped up like a beast in steerage.'

All around Bridie, people murmured their agreement. Doctor Roberts' face flushed scarlet. Was he hot, in his fancy frock coat? Or shamed by the lies he'd just told? For this could well be an epidemic. It was spreading so fast. That's how epidemics started, Annie said; first in one family, then in another. Until people started dying.

'I suggest you leave the thinking to me in future, Bustle. You are quite out of your depth on medical matters. Meanwhile, where's that girl? Miss Bowles! Unbutton his shirt please.'

Annie stepped forward, her eyes soft with concern. Alf stepped forward, grasping her shoulder.

'No. She mustn't get involved.'

'Good God, Bustle. Are you determined to thwart me?'

'Please,' Thaddy's mum interrupted. 'Can someone help my boy?'

'I intend to, madam, once this nuisance stops interfering.'

'No,' Alf stammered, 'not interfering. I respect your position, Doctor Roberts, and your knowledge. But I'm Annie's guardian. I'd never forgive myself if she got sick. I'll take her place at the dispensary.'

'What about the cleaning? That's how these things start, you know, with poor hygiene. It's possible you've overlooked something.'

Alf drew himself up to full height.

'If I have, I'm not aware of it. But if you'd like to carry out an inspection, Doctor Roberts, I'm happy to take your advice.'

'Oh, very well. If you must play the martyr, take the girl's place. But don't blame me if you succumb to this illness.'

Alf? Sick! No, Bridie gasped at the notion; he was solid as a brick. He hadn't coughed during the long winter months while he was stealing Ma's affection. Or vomited like everyone else at the beginning of their journey. But if this was an epidemic, like the smallpox, and it was serious enough for Doctor Roberts to lie about the situation, then even Alf was at risk.

* * *

Three days later, Thaddy started to tremble. When Alf pulled his shirt up during surgery there was a deep purple rash leaching beneath his skin. The word *typhus* was spoken in hushed tones. Thaddy's body barely made a splash when it hit the water, only flashed white in the morning light before being swallowed up by the sea. Within hours, his sister Maeve joined him in a watery grave.

Steerage filled with a high, keening wail.

'Dear God, what's to become of us?' Ma's hands curled shell-like around her belly.

'If only we knew what caused it.' Alf shook his head. 'If only we knew what we were fighting against. I'll never forgive myself if something happens to you or Bridie.'

Hilary, who'd fancied Mr Rolf, died later that evening. Next morning Eunice, who'd dreamed of marrying a squatter, joined her in the deep. Terror tightened like a nutcracker around Bridie's breastbone—the same hard, pinching terror she'd felt that long, fear-filled night in December. What if Alf did get sick? Then Ma might catch it, or Rhys and Siân, or even Annie. What if his ship became their coffin? There would be no new baby then. No new life. She would never get to grow up, or choose a husband. Let alone make the most of her opportunities in the colony.

Thaddy's ma sickened next, followed by three Scottish brothers who were berthed at the single men's end of the deck. An eerie silence followed this fresh outbreak of illness. No one complained about airing their bedding now, or sweeping the baseboards of their bunks. Bridie scoured their plates after each meal and helped Alf scrub their narrow section of the long table. In between, she lathered her hands and face in the basin on the deck. Though no one knew if these measures were helping. Or who would sicken next. It was like a man with a scythe walked the deck, cutting down his victims at random.

Doctor Roberts suspended the deck school. Cabin passengers were ordered to stay in the saloon. Reverend Cummings read burial services from the safety of the quarter deck. But in steerage there was no escape.

No way to separate the well from the sick.

As they neared the equator, strange fish took flight. Shimmering phosphorescent seas conjured up images of Neptune's kingdom beneath the waves. But Bridie didn't saunter in the night air marvelling at these wonders, or even try to work on her stories. Maps, voyage logs and recent arguments were forgotten. When Alf sank onto the bench of an evening, Tom Griggs didn't even try to badger him. Only the sailors seemed unaffected by the illness. As *Lady Sophia* inched her way toward the equator, they began to prepare for their traditional Crossing the Line ceremony.

'It's not right,' people muttered. 'People are dying.'

Mr Burns and a group of married men approached Doctor Roberts. 'It's not respectful, sir, to go ahead with this mummery.'

'Ordinarily, I would agree with you, Mr Burns.'

'Then why not put a stop to it?'

'The sailors set a great store by these heathenish practices. It's a rite, to them, a form of initiation. If we do not seek Neptune's permission to cross the equator, they fear it will bring bad luck down upon the ship.'

It didn't seem possible for their luck to worsen. But no one was willing to take the risk. At noon the following day, they all trooped onto the main deck. Bridie found a place at the base of the quarterdeck stairs. Annie stood alongside with Lucy balanced on her hip. Billy huddled in a heap at their feet. All around them, the sea lay utterly still, a mirror to the piercing skies. Taking a deep breath, Bridie blew air up onto her cheeks.

'It's hot, luck or not. I wished they'd hurry up.'

'They shouldn't be long,' Annie said, pulling Lucy's bonnet down over her face.

Bridie stood on tiptoes and peered over the heads of the crowd. Captain Thomson stood amidships, his coat freshly brushed, his stance determined. Beside him, Doctor Roberts smiled widely, like an actor in a pantomime.

'My head hurts,' Billy whined.

Bridie shot Annie a worried glance and squatted down beside him. 'Neptune'll be here soon.'

'Don't care. My legs are tired.'

Bridie wriggled her bottom onto the step and pulled Billy onto her lap. He felt strangely puppy soft and compliant.

'Is he all right?' Annie asked.

'No. He's burning up.'

Above her, the crowd shifted and stirred. Pam? Where was she? Bridie dragged Billy to his feet. So many faces, so many bonnets and cloth caps. Even if she could find Pam, it would be impossible to worm their way across the deck.

'Look, Billy. Here's Neptune. Please, Billy? Stand up!'

A wigged figure with a blackened face and flowing green robes strode along the deck. It was old Joe, the bosun's mate. Bridie must have seen the wizened sailor a thousand times. But with Billy's hot little body slumped at her side, his grim visage ran a finger up her spine.

'Silence!' Neptune rapped his trident on the deck.

The sailors raised a ragged cheer as Captain Thompson clicked his heels together. 'Hail, Neptune, King of the Sea.'

'Who dares enter my dominions?'

'The good ship, *Lady Sophia*. We seek permission to cross the line.'

Neptune inclined his head, casting an eye over the assembled crew. 'First, I must claim my children.'

It was a signal. Paul, the new ship's boy, dashed along the deck. The crowd roared as Neptune's retainers sprinted after him.

'Run,' Bridie yelled. 'Run!' Though all she wanted was to get the whole thing over with. Another part of her wanted Paul to escape, to run forever free, because she was frightened and Billy felt leaden at her side and, as long as Paul remained unfettered, she wouldn't have to look down at his flushed little face, or think about the possibility of him dying.

Up the shrouds Paul scrambled, along the yard arm and down again, his shrieks eerie, as he wove in and out of the closely packed bodies.

At the base of the main mast, Neptune's retainers brought him down.

'Billy.' Bridie shook his dead weight. 'Look, Paul's been caught. They're going to shave him now, and dip him in the sea, then our luck will turn.' Except she didn't believe that anymore, for herself or Billy.

* * *

Within days, Billy developed a rash. Pam wept as she carried him up the ladder to the dispensary. She wasn't the only one crying. Five new patients lay on the main deck, their families a hover of grey weary faces. Alf moved among them, offering words of comfort. But today, Bridie couldn't help noticing, even his movements held a slur of fatigue.

Please God, don't let him die! The thought broke from her throat with a gasp. Her shock, not so much that she'd had the thought, but how deeply she'd meant the words. Meant them? Surely not! She didn't want Alf in her life. They'd managed fine before he came along. No, this wasn't about the past, it was about the future, and, no matter how she resented Alf's presence, or how slyly he'd gone about stealing Ma's affection, she didn't want him to die at the height of a typhus epidemic.

Doctor Roberts looked weary too, though not from overwork. He'd probably stayed up all night, recalculating his gratuity. His face glistened with sweat. The sharp downward pull of his mouth suggested the dispensary was the last place he wanted to be. He turned his hard smile on the Griggs family.

'On the deck with him, please. That's right, unbutton his shirt.'

Doctor Roberts squatted down, holding a hanky to his nose. 'Typhus,' he said, running a gloved finger over the mottled skin on the Billy's chest. 'The rash confirms it.'

This wasn't news to anyone. By now the symptoms were so familiar, Bridie could have made the diagnosis herself. Seven emigrants had left them already—seven in less than a fortnight. Now, they had five more with headaches and fever chills, along with three single men who'd taken leave of their wits.

'I ain't daft. I don't need a fancy, Mr-Top-Hat-and-Tails surgeon to tell me what's wrong. The question is, what are you gonna do about it?'

'There's not much we can do, I'm afraid. You've seen the others and, as you have correctly pointed out, you are familiar with the course of the illness. But ... in this case, although it may look hopeless, your son does have youth on his side.'

'Youth! Is that it? Ain't there a pill or a powder you can give him?'

'A powder—of course, Dover's Powder. I have it in my supplies.'

'Dover's Powder!' Tom's red-rimmed eyes bulged. 'Call yerself a bleedin' surgeon. You gave us that last night.'

Doctor Roberts' lips thinned. He raised the hanky and squatted down, pushing a hank of hair back from Billy's forehead.

'He's hot. And his colour's high. But he's not showing signs of delirium. That's a good sign.'

'Oh, good. Let's all dance and clap our hands.'

'Look here. Blaming me isn't going to help, Mr Griggs. What you need is to get your boy out of the sun. It'll be cooler between decks.'

'It's like a bleedin' inferno down there, Doctor Roberts. Not that you'd know what it's like.'

The surgeon's nostrils pinched. A clenched fist suggested what he might like to do with Tom's face. 'I understand you're upset, Mr Griggs, but I really must advise—'

'Advise! What! What do you advise? That I give him a dose of powder and everything will magically be all right?'

'No, not at all. I can't guarantee any such thing. But we mustn't let emotion cloud our judgment. In many cases, as long as there are no complications, the fever will run its course. Meanwhile, you must—'

'Make him want to get better,' Pam interrupted. 'Make him want to stay alive.'

'Precisely.' Doctor Roberts nodded. 'Keep him warm and comfortable. Let him know you're there.'

'Well, that's marvellous. They promise us medical attention and all we get is a feller in a frock telling us to keep the boy alive.'

'I know it sounds like nonsense, Mr Griggs. But it's true, nonetheless. One of the first things typhus does is break down the will to survive. If you can get your lad past that, give him a something to hang onto, he may yet recover.'

Doctor Roberts measured out a dose of powder and handed it to Pam.

She looked worn out, her face soot-grey with fatigue, as if any minute she might join Thaddy's ma at the bottom of the sea. Looking down the long, thin line of his nose, Doctor Roberts seemed to reach the same conclusion.

'Mrs Griggs, I know it's hard. But do get some rest. There's no point running yourself into the ground.'

'It's all right for some,' Tom muttered, scowling. 'If you'd wanted us to rest, you'd have set up a proper hospital and looked after us yerself.'

* * *

The afternoon was a ball of string unravelling slowly; steerage, a dustbin rotting and souring in the heat. The smell clung to Bridie, swirling in her nostrils and making her stomach heave. Slumped at the table, she found herself straining for the sound of the ship's half-hourly bells, their doleful chimes marking every half hour of continuing life.

Annie washed Lucy's face and settled her down for an afternoon nap. Alf kept steerage clean and quiet. Even Rhys and Siân stayed between decks. Though there was nothing anyone could do. It was simply a matter of being there, sharing their concern, as all along the deck, groups cared for the afflicted, or lived through the horror of watching someone die.

'Here, Pam,' Alf coaxed. 'Plum duff, left over from dinner. Have some, for my sake.'

Pam shook her head, unwilling to break her tuneless song. Tom simply couldn't keep still. He cursed and paced, his red-rimmed eyes putting Bridie in mind of a creature from the underworld.

'Here, Tom, have some tea.'

Tom paused, seeming to consider Alf's offer, then resumed his restless tread.

Alf stepped in front, blocking his path. 'Drink it standing, if you must. But have something, before you collapse.'

Tom came to a reluctant halt. Sagging onto the bench, he ran a hand through his grizzled hair. He looked a fright. The internal horror, the possibility of Billy dying was etched into the lines of his face. He couldn't eat. He wouldn't rest, and all the while Billy lay in a stupefied sweat while Pam sang to him endlessly, tunelessly.

'Give the poor little bugger a rest,' Tom called out from the bench. 'I'm all right.'

'Stop your singing, then, Pam. It's giving 'im a fright.'

'It's you that's taken fright, with all your cursing and pacing. I've been nursing him day and night.'

'Give it a break then, old girl. He ain't going anywhere.'

This wasn't true. Billy might go to a place forever beyond their reach. Pam knew this, even if Tom wouldn't admit to the possibility. She was hanging onto him with all her might—by her voice, her touch, her presence, engaging in a desperate tug-of-war with God.

Bridie knew what that was like. She'd waged her own tug-of-war with God—chafing her dad's hands, stroking his stubbled cheek, whispering stories, songs and rhymes, anything to bring a flicker of life back into his face. Would it have helped if Ma had spoken softly? Told him she loved him? Or did her dad already know Alf had stolen her affection? What came first: the sadness, or the betrayal? Did it even matter? Her dad died, though she'd begged him to stay alive. So maybe Ma was right, maybe he didn't love them enough to stay alive, and, if he didn't love them, then maybe he had meant to die that icy December night.

Bridie shivered, hugging her notebook to her chest. Billy wasn't sad. He was sick, like Hilary and Eunice and all the others who had died. He hadn't given up on life. Despite what Doctor Roberts said, it took more than love to keep a person with typhus alive. Bridie didn't know what—some strange, misty element that allowed one person to slip away and gave another the will to survive. Her dad never found it. But she hoped Billy would, before it was too late. Lest she see Ma's bitterness mirrored in Pam's plain, honest face.

Siân rose and pushed her mug to the centre of the table. 'Give you a rest, shall I, Pam?'

Pam's song halted. She peered out from the shelter of Billy's bunk. 'I can't ask that of you, Siân.'

'Only a short while, not wearing myself out.'

Pam glanced at Rhys. He shrugged, not meeting her gaze. It didn't take much imagination to guess his thoughts. If Siân caught typhus it would kill her and the child.

'Sing to him, shall I?'

'Well … if you don't mind. I am a bit tired.'

Siân clambered into the bunk and drew Billy on to her lap. Pam sank onto the bench, wiping her nose with the back of her hand.

'I wouldn't mind so much if we were on land. If he were to die, he'd have a grave and … I could visit him.'

'Gawd! Do we have to talk about this?'

Pam sniffed, ignoring Tom's interruption. 'Only here, they run a needle through their nose, you know … to make sure they're dead, and you've seen how they weigh them down with lead—'

'Enough!' Tom roared. 'Our Billy ain't going to die.'

'A fat lot of help you've been, if he does.'

'What good does your singing do, woman? Apart from driving me mad.'

'Doctor Roberts said it, Tom. We have to make him want to stay alive.'

'It's miserable. All the boy needs is peace and quiet.'

'No, he doesn't. Death is quiet.'

Tom looked set to explode. Bridie didn't blame him. She didn't want to think of Billy's body growing stiff and cold, his freckled face setting into a bland last smile.

'I'm not saying he will die. But if he was to, you know ... slip over the side, well, at least he'd know I was with him, right to the end.'

'Look at him, Pam. He don't know what the bloody hell's going on.'

'That's not true,' Rhys interrupted softly. 'Siân's great aunt, Rhonwen, said nothing's a waste while a body's alive.'

Tom's lips curled. 'Ah, that's right, the witch.'

'Not a witch, a healer. She knew things.'

Tom froze. 'Say that again, lad?'

'She knew things.'

'No, before that.'

Rhys paused, perhaps sensing a shift in the other man's mood. It wasn't surprising. From where she sat, Bridie fancied she saw the cogs turning in Tom's head.

'Not a witch, a healer.'

'She'd have known all about typhus, I'm guessing?'

Rhys shrugged, his face a wary blank. 'I don't know. You'll have to ask Siân.'

'I will.' Tom shot Pam a withering glance. 'Ain't no one going to blame me if Billy dies.'

Tom leaned toward the bunk. Bridie saw him swallow, once, twice, uncertain in the face of Billy's dwindling life.

'So, what did your old aunt know about typhus, then, Siân?'

Siân stopped mid-song. 'No typhus up on the mountains, no filth or overcrowding, not where I lived. Only in the bigger towns like Merthyr and Penderyn.'

'She must have heard of it, though?'

'I don't know, Tom. It's unknown to me, see.'

'Well, that's bleedin' marvellous.' Tom's anger beat the air like a stick.

'Fair play,' Rhys snapped back. 'Siân's not the wise woman, only her aunt.'

'Besides,' Pam added, her lips a bitter twist, 'you said we lived in the age of steam. "Not the bleedin' dark ages."'

Tom swallowed, his lined face, haggard. 'Well, of course we do. It's just ... well, I'm a bit desperate now, aren't I?'

'We all are.' Rhys placed a hand on his forearm. 'But there's nothing we can do. Only watch and wait, as Pam said. Let him know we're here.'

'There's one thing.' Siân peered out from the bunk. 'One small thing I could try.'

'Blimey! Why didn't you say so before?' Tom's face took on signs of life.

'I've not done it before, mind.'

'Don't matter. At least we've got something to try.'

There was a surge of action, a wave of relief. Pam climbed back into Billy's bunk. Siân rummaged in her bag and produced a small wooden box. She prised open the lid and pulled out a red velvet pouch. Loosing the drawstring, she drew out a smooth rounded stone and held it up for their inspection.

'*Ble gest ti hi!*'

Rhys gave a startled cry. Bridie swung round, saw the flail of his hands, his too-wide eyes.

'It was Rhonwen's. I found it after she died.'

'She didn't give it to you?'

'No.'

Rhys lunged, grabbing for the stone. 'It won't work then, Siân. Not if she didn't give it to you. It's not yours by right.'

'We'll let the stone decide.'

It took forever—a contest of dark eyes, granite faces, and absent smiles. In the end, Rhys shoulders slumped. His hands fell slack at his sides.

Siân turned to Bridie. 'I'll need a pan of water, *bach*, and a small cup for pouring.'

Bridie's heart divided, like oil and water inside. Rhys was her friend and he was frightened. She saw it in the hard knob of his throat. The way his hands clenched white at his sides. But ... Billy was dying and Siân might be able to help him. With an apologetic glance in Rhys's direction, Bridie scurried along the deck and returned in no time with a pan of water as directed.

Siân set the pan upon the table and placed the shiny, egg-shaped stone in its centre. It didn't roll. It was mounted on a tiny silver pedestal. But it seemed to glow, if that were possible, in the murky light of the lamp and, although only small, in its presence they fell silent.

'It's crystal,' Siân said. 'Been in my mam's family for generations.' She smiled round at them. 'Its use is rare, mind. Only the gifted can invoke its powers.'

'It's beautiful,' Pam whispered.

It was. Antiquated and elegant, it sat in the centre of the pan, and not one of them could take their eyes from it. As they gathered in the warm, hushed half-light, Siân began to chant.

'*O garreg braint a chadarn*
  Oh thou stone of might and right
Gad i fi dy drochi di mewn dŵr
  Let me dip thee in water
Yn nŵr ffynnon pur neu don
  In the water of pure spring or wave.'

Siân held the stone aloft like Reverend Cummings held the host, except she was a woman and her chin didn't wobble, and what she did seemed right somehow, her movements so fluid and graceful.

'*Yn enw Dewi Sant*
  In the name of Saint David
Yn enw'r Apostolion
  In the name of the twelve Apostles.'

Siân placed the stone back in the middle of the dish and, in the flickering light of the lamp, she looked like a goddess from another time and another place—a solitary taper kindling a blaze.

'*Yn enw'r Drindod Sanctaidd*
   In the name of the Holy Trinity
A Mihangel a'r angylion
   Of Michael and all the angels
Yn yr enw Crist a Mair ei fam!
   In the name of Christ and Mary his mother!'

No one moved as Siân reached for the water and began to pour in a thin clear stream above the stone.

'*Bendith ar y garreg glir disglair!*
   Blessings on the clear shinning stone!
Bendith ar y dŵr clir a phur!
   Blessings on the clear pure water!
Iechyd i bob salwch corff
   A healing of all bodily ills
Dyn ac anifail!
   On man and beast alike!'

Bridie didn't need Siân's translation. The sound was enough. Sweet and pure, her words were like incense pervading the deck. Once poured, she transferred the water to a cup and passed it to Pam. Billy gagged, his tongue thick and heavily coated. But Pam wouldn't let him spill it, not a drop.

'Here, Billy boy, it's a special drink. Siân made it with her magic stone. Like the charm she wanted to do for Lucy's burn. She didn't finish that time, remember? Rhys made her stop. But it was magic all the same.' Pam paused, her eyes willing Billy to show signs of life. 'This water's magic too. It's going to help you fight the fever and make the headache go away.'

Once Pam had finished, Siân refilled the cup and walked along the deck, offering it to others. It was a simple gesture, a sacrament of sorts, as one by one frightened relatives foisted water on those they loved.

They stood round Billy, waiting for something to happen—a

lightening of his symptoms, relief in the lines of his face. Nothing came. As Billy lay in a stupor of sweat, their hopes began to fade. Only it was worse now, much worse. They had exhausted all their options. There was nothing anyone could do but wait through the remainder of the day and, if they were lucky, into the long, dark hours of the night, with only the bells for solace.

CHAPTER 16

*B*illy's recovery wasn't rapid. For days, he lay on his own personal equator, drifting neither to the north or the south. But he didn't get hiccups like the ones who'd died. And he continued to pass fluids. These were good signs, Doctor Roberts told Alf. They proved he was destined for life.

Alf knew Billy's healing wasn't magic. Yet the crystal water marked a turning point in the epidemic. As they headed toward the milder Cape climate, the sea rolled and swelled like a proud man's chest. The wind bore them valiantly across the waves. With strong south-easterlies and no fresh outbreaks of typhus, Doctor Roberts was confident they'd left death behind. Though he wasn't taking any chances. They would sail into Table Bay under a yellow quarantine flag.

The mood in steerage remained low. People sang hymns of an evening. In the morning, they trooped up the ladder to hear prayers read out from the quarterdeck. No need for a flag to remind them; they were living like cattle in a shed. Each sneeze brought a flare of white to people's eyes, the mere hint of fever a sickening dread.

The only one unaffected by the sombre mood was Tom Griggs. As Billy recovered, he bounced back like a hideous piece of Indian rubber. Never mind people's fear or the fug of sorrow hanging over steerage. He turned his thoughts to their missing wine rations and started badgering people for signatures.

'It's callous, Tom. Can't you see people are grieving?'

'We've faced death and won, Alf. We oughta be celebrating.'

'Not everyone has cause to celebrate.'

'I know that. Gawd, why do you think I'm persisting? If I'd lost me wife and child, I wouldn't wanna be sober of an evening.'

Rhys took his time writing the letter, for which Alf was grateful. But once the ink had dried, Tom laid the petition before him.

'There it is, Alf, with fair warning. If you don't raise the matter with Doctor Roberts, I'll take this letter straight to the captain.'

* * *

Next morning, Alf stood in the dispensary queue with his mouth dry and his palms sweating. Lord, why was he getting so worked up? Because he'd known about the letter for ages, and should have raised the matter long before this. No matter how he justified his inaction, Doctor Roberts was going to be furious.

Alf wiped his sweaty palms on his trousers as Pam Griggs stepped up to the dispensary.

'Good morning, Mrs Griggs. How's your lad coming along?'

Pam nudged Billy forward. The little boy wasn't a pretty sight. A mask of skin and bone had replaced his baby face. But his skin was warm, thank God, his bones coming back to life.

'I'm nursing him like you said, Doctor Roberts, giving him plenty of reasons to live.'

'Well done. I'm sure it's making a difference.'

'That and the crystal water.'

'Yes, well, as I've explained, Mrs Griggs, typhus isn't always a death sentence. Sometimes it's simply a matter of letting the illness run its course.'

'I'm sure you meant well, and we don't hold it against you, Doctor Roberts. But our Billy would have died if not for Siân's magic stone.'

Doctor Roberts' lips thinned. For a moment, Alf thought he might argue the point. But he turned round with a twitch of his shoulders, and started to stopper the jars in his cupboard. As Pam slipped away, Alf stepped forward.

'Ah, Bustle. How are things below?'

Alf swallowed, licking his lips. 'Well, to be honest, sir, I'm a tad concerned.'

'I'm not surprised, with all the mumbo jumbo flying about. Honestly, I'm going to throttle the next person who mentions magic stones during surgery.'

Alf didn't know what to say. He agreed with Doctor Roberts, of course. Siân's stone wasn't magic, only a foolish ritual. Yet, for all its foolishness it had brought hope—a hope that for all his lecturing Doctor Roberts had failed to provide.

'We need a diversion, Bustle. Something to take people's minds off death for a while.'

'I quite agree.'

'I'm glad, sir, because—'

'People are weak and feeble minded. Yes, but we must make allowances. Working people need levity to ease their drudgery. That's why I have a concert in mind.'

A concert! Did the man have any idea? Of their grief, the daily hardship of life between decks? Alf shifted, dropping his gaze. 'You may be right about the concert, sir. I'm not saying it isn't a good idea. But, if you'll pardon me for speaking freely, people might not be ready and, well … it is rather … cramped between decks.'

'I'm not suggesting a three-ringed extravaganza, Bustle.'

'No, sir, I understand, but—'

'There are no *buts* about it. I've heard you all singing of an evening.'

'Hymns, sir, for comfort.'

'Then why not carols? We'll make it a Christmas concert.'

'Yes, carols are a good idea, though it may feel a little strange with the sun shining overhead. However, before that, in prepara-tion, perhaps we might start with something a little less drastic … you know, to raise people's spirits?'

'Less drastic?' Doctor Roberts peered down the long thin line of his nose.

'Yes. Like issuing our wine rations.'

'Rations! I'm proposing a concert to raise people's spirits and you are quibbling about wine rations.'

'It may seem unimportant to you, sir, but—'

'Enough!' Doctor Roberts raised a gloved hand. 'I'll not hear another word on the subject.'

Alf sighed, bracing himself for the onslaught. 'I'm sorry, Doctor Roberts, I'm loath to persist but, well, it's only … there's a letter.'

'A letter?'

'Yes … everyone's signed it.'

'A letter! With signatures! Dear God, why didn't you say so earlier?'

'I've been trying, Doctor Roberts.'

'A petition.' The surgeon's eyes narrowed. 'So much for sadness and grieving. Whose idea was it? I want names, Bustle. The ring leaders.'

'I'd rather not say.'

'Oh, you'd rather not say. That's very noble of you. Is it the Welsh lad? Our regular troublemaker? He's rather good friends with your daughter, I've noticed.'

'He's not the instigator.'

'I'd never have picked you for a rebel, Bustle, or a turncoat. But this sheds a different light on the matter.'

'I'm not involved, Doctor Roberts. You have my word on that score. I may have acted too slowly, in hopes that things would blow over. But I've come to you now and given you fair warning. If you don't issue our wine rations, the letter will go straight to Captain Thompson.'

* * *

That night, steerage received its first ration of wine. From Tom Griggs' crow of triumph, anyone would think he was solely responsible. Not Rhys, who'd written the letter. Or Alf who had faced Doctor Roberts' ire. In the end, he'd volunteered to organise the Christmas concert in order to placate him. Dear God, what a muggins, doing other people's dirty work. Then again, what was organising a small concert, against Doctor Roberts' backing in the colony?

Alf wasn't a man for grand announcements, despite Doctor Roberts' expectations. He had no intention of shouting the news across the deck, not with Tom Griggs in such fine fettle. He only had to mention the concert and, like a foghorn, Tom would blare the news into the night.

'Your singing sounded good this evening, Tom.'

'Thanks, Alf. I rather like the sound of me own voice.'

That was an understatement. Across the table, Rhys gave the ghost of a smile. It was a rare sight. The crystal water may have brought healing to some. But it hadn't helped Rhys. He sat beside Siân in his usual white-faced silence, but things weren't right between the Welsh couple—they were cautious as a set of scales.

'Did you sing hymns in London, Tom?'

'Gawd, no! I ain't been near a church since me great aunt Mabel died.'

'You never sang in a public?'

'Never, unless you count me union hymn.' Tom tilted his head back and sang out loud:

'*God is our guide! From field from wave,*
From plough, from anvil, and from loom.'

A stirring sound, it echoed the length and breadth of steerage as others linked arms and joined him.

'*We come our country's rights to save,*
And speak a tyrant faction's doom.
We raise the watchword liberty,
We will, we will, we will, be free!'

It wasn't what Alf had in mind but it confirmed his strategy. 'Never mind, you'll have your chance at the Christmas concert.'

Tom's silence was a direct contrast to the defiant mood his song had provoked. 'All right, you've got me attention, Alf. What's this about a concert?'

Tom wasn't the only one interested. Like Chinese whispers, the idea began to work its way along the deck.

'It's Doctor Roberts' idea. He thought it might lift our spirits. He understands some of us might not be ready.' Alf nodded to one or two whose children had died. 'But for the rest of us, it may prove a distraction.' He swivelled back round. 'What about you, Tom? Will you be giving us an item?'

'Not on your life. I'd be dead shy.'

Shy! Alf couldn't believe his ears. It was unthinkable to put the words shy and Tom Griggs in the same sentence. 'Go on. It's like your union song.'

'No, it ain't.'

'People hear your voice.'

'Yes. But it's not a performance. We're supporting the cause.'

Alf shook his head. Tom was right; of course, people marched and sang to protest against their working conditions, not to draw attention to themselves. 'But ... you like singing?'

'Not on me own. But ... I've always wanted to sing in a choir.'

'A choir? You'd need a conductor to start a choir.'

'Well, I know that, Alf.'

'We haven't got one, unless ... Reverend Cummings.' Alf paused, aware of the trap he was falling into. 'Reverend Cummings might be able to help out. Why don't *you* ask him, Tom?'

'That's not a bad idea.' Tom's smile widened. 'But I won't be asking Reverend Cummings anything.'

'Well, I'm not asking.'

'You don't have to, Alf. Not this time.'

Alf eyed him warily. A trick. It must be a trick. He sat waiting for a rabbit to pop out of Tom's battered cloth cap. To his surprise, the other man turned his yellowing smile on Rhys.

'Perhaps you'd like to help out, son?'

Rhys's smile flickered. 'Why don't you ask him yourself, Tom?'

'Not ask, son, conduct.'

Rhys blanched, shaking his head, as if the question pained him. 'My … my father conducted a choir.'

'There you are. You'll do him proud.'

Rhys didn't look heartened by this comment. He looked rather like he was going to throw up. Alf wasn't surprised. It was hard enough standing up to Tom Griggs at the best of times. Let alone when, by his own admission, he'd always wanted to sing in a choir.

'Perhaps Rhys needs time to think.'

'Go on. What's there to think about?'

Tom Griggs had the sensitivity of a sledgehammer. Alf knew what it was like to fall under his blows and, something told him, there was more to Rhys's caution than met the eye. What had he said about his father that day in steerage? *I know what it's like not to measure up.*

The deck fell silent. Everyone waited. Not only their mess. Others had gathered in small murmuring knots. Rhys glanced sideways, his eyes seeking Siân's. She grasped his hand, waited.

After what seemed like an age, Rhys nodded. 'All right, I'll give it a try.'

Shouts followed Rhys's announcement, back slaps all round. Alf stood, waiting for the excitement to die down. He'd carried out Doctor Roberts' instructions, let Tom Griggs announce the concert, and avoided organising the choir. This was indeed a night for celebration.

'A toast!' he said, raising his cup. 'To the steerage choir.'

CHAPTER 17

*A*s days lengthened into weeks, with no fresh outbreaks of typhus, the ship seemed to heave a great sigh. Diaries, letter books, and sewing projects were pulled out. People fell back into the steady rhythm of bells, deck lessons, and mess duties. Steerage buzzed with plans and preparations for the concert.

The choir would take part of course. Rhys was working on a version of the fairy woman's tale set to the haunting strains of 'Ar Hyd y Nos'. Some of the single girls were planning to recite verse, while groups of single men had decided to try their hand at playwriting. Time would tell whether they had any talent in this department. But hoots of laughter from the forward part of the deck told Bridie they considered themselves great wits. Only the families who'd lost loved ones kept themselves apart. As *Lady Sophia* approached Table Bay, Bridie fancied she heard their grief echoed in the mournful cry of the Cape Pigeons.

Rhys and Siân were slow to restart their story sessions. The typhus seemed to have worsened the tension between them. Bridie heard hissing after lights out, Siân's soft weeping. She knew without being told they argued about Billy's healing. But why? The stone had helped, hadn't it? Brought an end to the epidemic? Yet, she heard pressed steel in Rhys's night time voice. The word *sori* being demanded. From Siân's emphatic *nage,* she gathered the Welsh girl felt no need to apologise.

Bridie wasn't worried by the delay. The typhus had set her own thoughts churning. Over and over, she found herself reliving that final Christmas night, seeing the strange mix of anger and hurt in her dad's eyes, a wind stirring the ash in the fireplace, hearing the stab of Ma's final words:

Don't come back. We're better off without you.

Had he thought of her, when he staggered through the streets that night? Or had Ma's treachery already drowned out love's voice? Did he fall? Or simply lay down in the snow? And how was that different from actually killing himself? What about later on, when Bridie chaffed and spooned and begged him to stay alive? Did he hear her voice? Or even try to get well? Or was it too late, by then, matter how hard he tried? Was he simply too sick to fight?

She couldn't answer these questions. Neither could she ignore them. They hissed and coiled like a snake in her head. But the typhus had given her a chance to school her face. By the time Siân once again beckoned from the base of the main mast, she had her mask firmly in place.

Rhys looked pale and drawn, Bridie noticed, even worse than before the typhus, his hands a knot of anguish. But he managed a wan smile as she sank down beside him.

'Siân says we owe you an apology, Bridie Stewart.'

Her? An apology! 'It's fine. You've had things to discuss. I understand.'

Rhys's brows rose. 'Discuss! Is that what you'd call it? No doubt we've kept you awake with our squabbling.'

'Not much,' Bridie lied. 'We've all been upset since the typhus.'

Rhys smiled. 'You're a good friend, Bridie Stewart, and sorry I am to have ignored you for so long. What do you say? Shall we resume our story sessions?'

Bridie shrugged, not quite meeting his gaze. 'I'd like that. But only if you're ready.'

Rhys swallowed, glancing sideways at Siân. 'Will we ever be ready? I'm not sure anymore, about anything. But I suspect Siân is right. There is nothing to be gained from arguing.'

Once their stories resumed, Bridie's days once again throbbed with purpose. She settled back into a pattern of hearing, drafting and redrafting. To her relief, she found Rhys's stories less intense than before the epidemic, as if he'd sensed a shift in her emotions. Though, more than once, she glanced up to find his dark gaze fixed on her, as if trying to gauge the weight of her burdens.

* * *

One morning, about three weeks after crossing the equator, Bridie woke to an ache in her tummy and a strange absence of sound. She winced, rolling over, no flap of canvas, no lines clanking against the mast. The deck seemed flatter somehow, not tilted, and there were voices, from beyond, not overhead. She heard a lapping against the sides of their vessel; a rhythmic splash that could have been anything; high, shrill laughter that made her think of a market ... or a town.

A town! She jerked up, cracking her head on the overhead beam.

'Yes, exciting, isn't it?' Annie smiled in the bed beside her. 'We're in Cape Town. We arrived about an hour ago. I heard them run out the anchor chains. But you were sleeping like a babe.'

'It doesn't smell any better.' Bridie wrinkled her nose at the stale, overnight odour of bad breath and ripening privies.

'Not down here. I expect it will on deck.'

As if on signal, Bridie heard the clang of six bells. They were louder without the trinity of wind, waves, and canvas. Their measured chime shattered the stillness of early morning. She heard groans from the bunks around her, a breaking of wind, saw capped heads pop up over the surrounding partitions.

'In port!' Someone gave a crow of delight.

'Either that, or we're back in the doldrums.'

'Nah, don't be daft. There's singing. Listen!'

Bridie raised her head, trying to catch the snatch of song drifting in through the scuttles. It was in a different language, the sound altogether foreign. It brought to mind the clatter of the Sunday

School collection box, stories of brown-skinned girls who lived in mud huts and balanced earthenware pots on their heads.

Bridie moaned, biting down on her lip as she drew back the covers. The pain in her tummy was worse this morning, jagged, as if someone had snipped at her insides with pinking irons. She hadn't mentioned the pain to Ma, fearing the Spanish inquisition. But she'd noticed things were slippery last night when she'd gone to the privy.

She sat up, shrugged out of her nightgown and clasped a blanket to her chest. Her skirts, bodice and petticoats had slipped from their pegs. She crawled to the bed end, rummaged amid the tangle of blankets and turned her bodice the right way out. She slipped into it, tugging at the laces, reached for her petticoats. A gasp, she saw Annie's hand fly to her mouth.

'What's wrong? Did you bang your head, Annie?'

'No. It's just … well, you've got a stain on your shift.'

'A stain?' Bridie twisted, craning her neck. 'What sort of stain?'

'Turn round. Let me have a look.'

Bridie did as requested. Peering back over her shoulder, she saw Annie bite down on her lip.

'What's wrong? Tell me?'

'Well, it's not bad. At least, it's nothing serious.' Annie leaned forward, lowering her voice. 'I think you might have started your monthlies.'

Monthlies!

No. It wasn't possible, not here, on board ship. Bridie reached round, her fingers finding a wet patch on her shift. She clawed at the fabric, dragged it into view. Sure enough, there was a stain, about the size of a soupspoon. It looked an awful lot like blood. No, it was blood. She smelled the coppery tang on her fingers.

'Please, don't tell anyone.'

'Don't be silly. Your ma will guess.'

Bridie flopped onto the bed and dragged the covers up to her chin. 'I'll pretend I'm sick.'

'She won't believe you. Besides, you're on mess duties.'

'Please, Annie, cover for me?'

Annie shook her head. 'It's not a disaster. No doubt your ma's expecting it. Your bodice is getting that tight. Surely you've noticed?'

Bridie whimpered, pulling the blankets over her head. Balling her shift, she tried to staunch the bleeding between her legs. Why? Why was this happening? She didn't want to get her monthlies, or to be a woman. She certainly wasn't ready for rags and pins. At least not here, in steerage, with hundreds of eager ears listening in.

* * *

Bridie focused her racing thoughts on the familiar sounds of morning—a rattle of plates, the clank of spoons being laid out along the table, thuds as people jumped down from their bunks.

'Morning, Tom. How are you?'

'Fine, thanks. Slept like a top.'

It sounded so normal, so business as usual. At least the morning had remembered its script. She heard a distant cry of 'hot water!', followed by Ma's sharp, no-nonsense tones.

'Bridie! Get up, please. You're on mess duties.'

'It's all right, Mrs Bustle. I'll do Bridie's chores this morning.'

'She's not a baby, Annie. She needs to take responsibility. Come on, Bridie.' Ma grasped her ankle. 'I'll not have a lazybones in the family.'

'No, please, Mrs Bustle. She's poorly.'

'Poorly!' Ma's voice took on a note of alarm. 'What do you mean?'

'Nothing serious. Truly.'

'No headache? What about a rash? Maybe Alf should climb up and check?'

'No!' Bridie jerked up, cracking her head for the second time that morning. She winced, rubbing at the sore spot with the heel of her hand. 'Please, Ma. I'm fine.'

'Then I suggest you get up, young lady.'

'No. I can't.'

'Why ever not?'

Silence. Bridie glanced sideways, saw heads cocked, spoons raised, hundreds of big pink ears flapping. Tears welled. 'I've got a ... tummy ache.'

'A tummy ache.' Ma's eyes narrowed. 'What kind of tummy ache?'

Bridie shrugged, heat creeping her cheeks. 'You know, the usual sort that girls get. Annie says you're expecting it.'

'Ah.' Ma gave a quick sideways glance. 'You'd better rest then, love.'

Bridie heard Ma's feet shuffling on the bench, a murmur as she hissed the words 'tummy ache' to their mess, imagined nudges and knowing winks as the news worked its way along the deck.

'Fresh bread!' She heard a whoop. 'Lord, can you smell it! And butter while we're in port.'

Bridie's stomach rumbled at the warm yeasty scent.

In the horror of the morning's discovery, she'd forgotten the promise of such luxuries. They'd have fresh meat delivered to the ship for dinner, and potatoes. Meanwhile, she'd be sitting on the bench, with a marquee of rags and pins beneath her skirts, try-ing not to meet an eye or act differently, while everyone on board knew she was a woman now, at fifteen-going-on-sixteen years of age, ready to marry and have babies.

* * *

'Right, madam. Let's have a look at you.'

Ma stepped onto the bench.

Raising her head, Bridie eased back the covers and peered along the deck. Only Alf and a handful of cleaners remained in steerage, all with their eyes trained on the forward part of the ship.

'I can't get down. I've got a stain on my shift.'

'No one's looking. Alf's explained the need for privacy.'

Bridie's cheeks flamed at the thought of Alf's stuttering,

red-faced explanations. But there was no help for it. She couldn't stay in bed forever. She shoved her feet into her boots, wrapped a blanket round her waist, grabbed a clean shift, and shuffled along the deck. Ma followed, carrying a lumpy drawstring bag and a ball of twill tape.

Bridie held her breath as she squeezed into the privy cubicle and slammed down the lid. She stepped toward Ma, letting the blanket fall to the ground. Ma nodded, tutting at the stain on her shift.

'That'll be a job to scrub out. But there's no help for it, what's done is done.'

Ma opened her arms, ran the tape around Bridie's waist, and cut it to length. She tied a knot, pulled it tight with her teeth and drew a long, thick wad of fabric from the bag on her wrist.

Bridie's mouth fell open. She knew what it was. She'd seen monthly pads often enough. But this one seemed to have grown like a turnip over the months at sea. 'I can't wear that, Ma. It's like a baby's clout.'

'Never mind the size, Bridie. It'll save your shifts. We'll need extra pads, now you've started your monthlies. Nothing permanent, seeing as we have to toss them overboard. Once we're in Port Phillip you can make yourself a regular set.'

Bridie shuddered, her mind filling with a gloomy image of herself stitching monthly pads in the glow of a rush light while, outside, a line of big dull men stood waiting to claim her hand in marriage.

'You needn't look so long-faced. Even the queen gets her monthlies.'

The queen!

What did the queen have to do with it? She hadn't started her monthlies in the steerage deck of an emigrant vessel. Or had to sit beside her mother making regular sets. Bridie blinked, pressing her lips together, determined not to weep. The tight, no-nonsense set of Ma's mouth told her there would be precious little sympathy.

Ma showed her how to pin the pad to one end of the tape, twist it round to the back, and draw it up between her legs. Slipping out of her shift, Bridie folded it around the tell-tale stain and shrugged into a clean one. It felt stiff and scratchy from its salt-water washing. Bridie held the soiled shift out to Ma.

'You're a woman now. You can start by washing your own linen.'

Bridie nodded, eyes on the deck. This sounded ominous, like the beginning of a lecture.

'You'll need to be careful from now on. Having your monthlies means you can fall pregnant. You know about that, I presume?'

'Yes, Ma. You've told me already.'

'Good, bear it in mind. One day, you'll meet a handsome young man and, although you probably can't imagine it this morning, it will be difficult to resist his advances.'

'Yes, Ma. Can I go now, please?'

'No, Bridie. This is important. You're lucky to have a mother to tell you these things. My own ma died before I got my monthlies. I had no one to stop me making foolish choices. I want better for you.'

'Yes, I know. But can we talk about this another time?'

'There's no time like the present, especially with the deck half empty. You'll begin to feel desire, Bridie, long before you marry.'

'Please, Ma. I don't want to talk about this. It's embarrassing.'

'Nothing to be ashamed of, it's all part of the process. Once you find the right man, someone strong and reliable, you'll no doubt find it quite pleasant to lie beneath the blankets and … let him touch you privately.'

Urgh! Bridie couldn't think of anything worse than a big dull man fiddling with her private parts. 'I'm only fifteen. Alf says there's no hurry.'

Ma's brows arched. 'Alf! That's the first time you've heeded his good advice.'

'Well, it's true, isn't it? I don't need to talk about these things. I'm not ready. So, there's no danger.'

'No danger? Really! You could have fooled me.'

'What's that supposed to mean?'

'Well, it's not seemly is it? Spending so much time with a married man, and all under the pretext of those ridiculous stories. It'll have to stop now you've got your monthlies. Don't you see? Siân won't want another woman making eyes at her husband.'

Rhys! Did she mean Rhys? What did this have to do with him? 'Rhys is my friend. Siân knows that. I've never made eyes at him.'

'Really? That's not what I see.'

'Well, you'd know, I suppose.'

'Me! I have no idea what you're talking about.'

'You do!' Anger surged. 'You know exactly what I mean. You and Alf were making eyes at each other long before my dad died.'

'Don't be ridiculous.' Ma's face paled.

'That's why he gave up, isn't it? Maybe even killed himself. Because you stopped loving him.'

'Your dad gave up because he was weak and fanciful, like your friend Rhys.'

'No!' Bridie backed away. 'You can say what you like, Ma. But I loved my dad, right to the end, even if he didn't love me. But you wouldn't understand that, would you? Because you hated him. Well, not everyone is like you. Some people keep faith with the ones they love. Rhys and Siân love each other like that. And I'm not going to let you spoil our friendship.'

* * *

The deck school had already started by the time Bridie clambered out from beneath the canvas awning. Bridie saw Rhys and Siân amid the group of students, but she had no intention of joining them. Not with her eyes puffy and her cheeks still slick. Annie would only squeeze her hand and ask about her tummy ache. Rhys and Siân's eyes would soften with sympathy while, all around her, people would nudge each other whispering: *monthlies, monthlies, monthlies …*

Bridie fumbled for a hanky and blew her nose. She picked her way through the groups of women and toddling children seated amid ships, trying not to waddle around the great wad of cloth pinned between her legs. It must be possible to walk normally. All over Covent Garden, women had managed their monthlies. Now it was her turn to learn. She turned toward the shore.

Lady Sophia had anchored apart from the other ships. Yet all around her, at a safe distance, the harbour teemed with life. Small boats plied their wares alongside other, non-quarantine ships. Sailors loaded vessels. Men black as soot rowed smartly dressed ship's officers toward a huddle of official buildings.

She'd seen black men before. Only here, there were so many of them, with wide-white smiles and brightly coloured bandanas. The air seemed to thrum with the sound of their stop-me-start language.

Bridie wrinkled her nose. Annie was right. It did smell different—all fruit and earth and flowers, like Covent Garden on market morning. Except this place was nothing like home. Stone buildings lined the shore, one of them a fort. Though its shape was foreign, unlike anything she had ever seen before. The whole town seemed to be held in the grip of the surrounding mountains.

Mountains? So, that's what they looked like—tall and brooding and magnificent, even the one with the sliced-off top made the town buildings look like dollhouses.

'Beautiful, isn't it, Bridie Stewart? As if the land itself held stories?'

Bridie startled, dropping her hanky. She'd been so absorbed in the sights, she'd missed Rhys coming alongside. She took a deep breath and glanced sideways. Was Ma right? Had she been guilty of making eyes at him? No, she hadn't, and she wouldn't let Ma spoil things. Besides, even if she had been guilty, Rhys appeared not to have noticed. He stooped to pick up the hanky and handed it back to her, the gesture easy and brotherly like it had always been— toward her and Annie and all the other single girls in steerage.

He nodded to indicate a mountain on the right side of the harbour. 'That one's called Lion's Head. Can you guess why?'

'No.' She sniffed, pocketing her hanky.

'See its nose and eyes, like a lion's head? Table Mountain, the flat one's called. The clouds lay over it like a tablecloth. On the left you have Devil's Mountain. The sailors tell me a pirate, called Van Hunks, met the devil there for a smoking contest. Whenever a wind blows from the southeast, the cloud hovers and people say, "Van Hunks and the devil are smoking again." What do you think, Bridie Stewart? Does it look like smoke to you?'

Bridie shrugged, not ready to trust her voice.

He chuckled. 'I'd not normally be letting you off so easily but … you've had a difficult morning, I'm guessing.'

Bridie flushed at the veiled reference to her monthlies.

'I'll not press you, *bach*. But I'm here, and Siân, if you need to talk.'

Bridie nodded, a sob swelling in her chest. There was so much to say—a great aching need that cleaved her breast like an axe. But where to begin? It was all so mixed up and sordid, especially with Ma's most recent accusation. Even if she left that out, told Rhys only about Alf and Ma and her dad, there was nothing he could do, nothing he could say to change things.

'My dad told me a story once, an African story he'd heard it at the theatre. You know, from one of the sailors.'

'Not about Van Hunks, the pirate, I gather?'

'No.' She shook her head. 'A different story. About a crocodile. I didn't write it down. I don't know why. Perhaps, I didn't like it, even then.'

'But you do now?

'No. But I can see it differently.'

She looked up, noting his silence, the shadows beneath his eyes, the way he watched her, even now, with a trying-to-understand smile.

'It was a long time ago, you know, when the animals could still talk. Though it couldn't have been that long ago because the Dutch people already lived at The Cape. Anyway, that's beside the point.' She gave a shaky laugh. 'No need to worry about where the story starts or where the history ends.'

'Indeed. You are learning, Bridie Stewart.'

'In that day, not so long ago, when the Dutch were still new in the land, a crocodile grew weary of the other animals coming to drink from his section of the river. He hated the smell of their droppings and the way they muddied the banks with their hooves. Being a fiendish creature, he came up with a plan to rid himself of the other beasts.

'He called a meeting and persuaded them that the river was drying up. He said they must make a trek across the plains to a better water source. The animals were alarmed, for none could live without water. Only the wily jackal sensed deceit in the crocodile's plan.

'No one heeded the jackal's protests. The crocodile was so convincing. He'd arranged everything for their safety, he assured them with great earnest tears that made it impossible to doubt him. In the end, all apart from the jackal voted in favour of making the trek.

'It was a long journey and hazardous. But the animals set out bravely. They walked for many days and nights, with the elephants carrying the slender meerkats and the lions keeping pace with the tortoises. At last the new river came into sight.

'It was so big and beautiful, that river. It took their breath away. Yet, as soon as they entered the water, the first shots rang out. For the jackal was right. It had been a trick all along—a great big ugly trick, like my dad and his stories, like Alf and Ma. Like everything.' She waved her hand over the strange rocky vastness of their surroundings. 'For the crocodile had been in cahoots with the farmers all along.'

Rhys didn't reply. He stayed silent for so long, Bridie feared he wasn't going to answer. Hands tight on the rail, he stood gazing out over the glittering bay. When he did finally speak, his words were laced with sorrow.

'Growing up is never easy, *bach*. I'll not lie to you. Or, indeed, seeing with different eyes. Sometimes, I think the process will never end. But I do know one thing and, trust me, this is a lesson sorely learned. Whether it be a person, a situation, or a truth you are running from—even a truth that sends you half round the world, the fear is often worse than the reality. It may not feel like it at the time, Bridie *bach*. But, if you face that fear—I mean truly face it, then I think over time the hurting will ease. At least, I hope so, for you, and for me.'

CHAPTER 18

They didn't stay long at The Cape. Once they had taken on food, water and livestock, *Lady Sophia* once again put out to sea. The open waters were a shock after the stillness of Table Bay. As the Atlantic Ocean met the Indian Ocean, seasickness once again drove Bridie into her bunk. Huddled beneath the blankets, she heard shouts, drubbing feet, and snapping canvas as the sailors battled against competing seas.

After rounding the Cape of Good Hope, the wind settled on a strong, westerly direction. Her sickness eased as *Lady Sophia* picked up her skirts and fairly danced across the waves. They wouldn't see any more land until they reached the far off coast of Australia, precious little shipping. They now faced the longest, uninterrupted sea stretch of their voyage. It was a halfway point, of sorts. Time to pull chests from the hold, retrieve musty clothing and stow dirty items for the remainder of the journey.

Bridie was shocked upon opening their battered wooden chest to find her clothes looking older and shabbier than remembered. Annie was right—her bodices were getting tight. Even with the new set of stays Ma produced, she couldn't seem to fasten them. Ma and Siân faced a similar problem. Their bellies had swollen like melons over the months at sea. Shaking of heads and exclamations told Bridie their mess weren't the only ones affected.

'There's no help for it,' a plump matron declared. 'We need privacy for fitting and fixing, without the men gawking at us.'

A meeting was held, a decision made, action taken. Men were

banished from steerage between four and eight bells on the afternoon watch, children thrust into the arms of reluctant fathers, and a hive of activity commenced in which gossip seemed to be the primary ingredient.

Bridie had no desire to be part of a sewing circle. But there was no point trying to wriggle out of the situation. She was a woman now. She belonged with the women. She stripped down to her stays and petticoats, trying not to think about the small breasts budding beneath her shift. Once her measurements were taken, Ma thrust a bundle of rags into her hand.

'Here. Stitch some monthly pads. We'll need extra now you've started.'

'Hush. Keep your voice down.' Bridie glanced sideways, heat flushing her cheeks.

'Don't be ridiculous, Bridie. We're all in the same situation here.'

Ma had a point. Bridie wasn't the only one stripped down to her small clothes. She saw rolls of dimpled flesh, hairy armpits, and nipples of all shapes and sizes poking through sheer white shifts. She didn't know where to look, or how not to listen as, all around her, women discussed the intimate details of their bodies.

Mrs Reid had piles (Bridie didn't need to know that), and going to the privy was like passing canon balls. Mrs Burns had terrible pain with her monthlies, like her insides were coming apart at the seams.

Bridie knew what was like. Her own innards had scarcely recovered from the experience. But she saw no reason to talk about it. Though Mrs Scott certainly warmed to the topic. Telling anyone who cared that she hadn't bled for three years.

'Only twenty-seven,' she added with a sigh, 'and already going through the change.'

Well, lucky Mrs Scott. If only Bridie's body had been so obliging, she wouldn't be sitting in steerage making monthly pads among a gaggle of half-naked women. The Griggs family were expecting another baby. Pam thought it might have been conceived during the typhus epidemic.

'Honestly,' she gave a low chuckle, 'I don't know how Tom managed in all that heat. But once Billy started to recover, well, you know how it is, girls. He wouldn't take no for an answer.'

Gasps of amazement greeted this happy news. Though Bridie wasn't surprised. She'd heard the Griggs' grunts and moans after lights out and, although she'd scrunched her eyes tight and pressed her hands to her ears, she'd gathered they were pleasuring each other beneath the blankets.

She lost focus momentarily, jabbing herself with the needle, at the memory of their quivering bunk. She glanced up, sucking her thumb, as Ma took a deep, tell-all breath. With a horrified shudder, Bridie feared she was about to hear about Alf and Ma's under-blanket activities.

'I knew a Welsh woman back in England, Siân. Blodwen, her name was. She lived down by Lambeth. Had a stall at Taffy's Fair.'

Siân nodded. Clothed only in her chemise and petticoats, she was unpicking the seams of her skirts.

'You didn't know her then, this Blodwen?'

'No, sorry. You liked her, Mrs Bustle?'

'Not so much the woman, her craft. She was a healer like your aunt.' Ma's brows rose as if to indicate the delicate nature of Blodwen's remedies. 'I visited her a number of times, and always to great effect.'

Bridie wriggled forward on the bench. Now, this was interesting, and so far no mention of baby making.

'You'd not have needed her yourself, Siân. Knowing the methods, as you do.'

'Methods?'

Ma leaned forward, voice low. 'You know ... tricks to make yourself conceive.'

'But ... surely, there's only one way to conceive.'

Warmth, like a flame, ran up and scorched Bridie's cheeks. Her mind filled with a sudden sharp image of Rhys—his slender hand tracing Siân's face in the dark, her mouth finding his, their bodies moving together, skin on skin. For some reason, her abdomen turned liquid at the thought.

She jerked a pin from her half-finished pad and stabbed it into her pincushion. How had the conversation taken this uncomfortable turn? She preferred the intimate details of Mrs Reid's piles. Or the animal antics of Tom Griggs. Anything was better than ... well, better than thinking about Rhys ... and Siân.

But there was no help for it. Ma was talking again—more loudly now, it seemed. Bridie could do nothing but listen, with a strange heavy drawing in her belly and blood thrumming in her ears.

'It was Blodwen who helped me conceive.'

Bridie peeped up from beneath her cap, saw Ma pat her bulging waistline. Her mouth fell open. She snapped it shut. How did someone have help making a baby? Still, it made sense. Alf was pretty hopeless. But, no. She didn't want to think about that either—not Alf and Ma.

'Bridie too. I've always had trouble.'

Her dad too!

Bridie startled in her seat. She knew how women fell pregnant; of course, she did. Though she'd never expected it to be such a noisy, grunting activity. Her knowledge didn't include Welsh women ... or charms. She paused, mid-stitch, waited. Siân glanced sideways, her lips a knowing twitch.

'What herb was it, Mrs Bustle? Do you remember?'

'Mandrake, I think she called it.'

'I know the herb.' Siân nodded. 'Gathered at the full moon, picked with the left hand, never cut, mind, and drawn under a clean white cloth. *Planhigyn yn peri cyfog*, we call it. A powerful herb.'

'The same! You'd know how to use it then?'

'I might, if we could find it in the colony.'

Ma leaned close, lowering her voice. 'I've got the seeds. Only, I wouldn't know the words of the charm.'

'You're wanting another child, Mrs Bustle?'

Ma sighed, her voice heavy with sorrow. 'Not so much another child, Siân. A healthy one. I love Alf, you understand. He's a good man. And I'd like to give him a son. But I've had that much trouble in the past. Even if I do carry this baby to full term, I might lose it at birth. If that were to happen, I'd like to try again, for Alf's sake.'

* * *

Fortunately, the conversation soon took a different turn. Bridie was left alone with her body's strange reactions. As the afternoon drew to a close, gossip gave way to a determined silence as, all along the deck, women stitched against the hourglass. Bridie finished her fifth monthly pad and started on a sixth. Siân stitched her skirts waists back together and started lengthening the drawstrings. Annie stood, arms outstretched while Ma refitted her new gown.

The garment, a simple cotton mantua, had been a second-hand gift from Annie's aunt. She'd unpicked it and with Ma's help tacked it back together. Now was time for final adjustments before finishing off the seams. Pincushion in hand and a measure tape around her neck, Ma was in her element, her mind mercifully focused on nothing more intimate than Annie's lack of sewing experience.

'Surely this isn't the first time you've remade a gown, Annie?'

'It is, Mrs Bustle. I've stitched my own pinafores and caps. But never remade a complete gown. My mum died when I was young, remember? My dad could barely thread a needle.'

'Couldn't your aunt have helped?'

'Perhaps. But she wasn't interested. She was too busy organising my emigration.'

Bridie eyed the soft green dress tacked close to Annie's form. Its tight waist hugged Annie's slim figure, its well-placed darts moulding around the modest swell of her breast. The fabric was good quality, her aunt clearly wealthy. Flushed and excited as she was now, Annie looked, well … almost pretty.

Pam was clearly of the same mind. 'You look a treat, Annie. That gown sets your figure off to perfection. You'll be swamped with marriage proposals in Port Phillip. You mark my words.'

'Thanks, Mrs Griggs. But I doubt even Mrs Bustle's dressmaking will help my prospects.'

'Men want more than a pretty face, Annie.'

'I've got scars all over me.'

Pam chuckled. 'Trust me, a man with his trousers down won't even notice. Look at me, pregnant on an emigrant vessel, and I'm no oil painting. Tom's not much of a romantic either. Though, he is rather keen on the under-blanket activities.'

'How did you meet him, Mrs Griggs? If you don't mind me asking?'

Bridie smiled at how neatly Annie steered the conversation away from herself. Pam didn't seem to notice. She dimpled, enjoying the limelight.

'He was a customer,' she wagged a finger, 'and no, girls, not that kind of customer. I worked in a cook shop, back then. Tom started walking me home of an evening. Lord, the man could talk! But I liked that about him. One day, right out of the blue he said: "Pam, I've had enough of waiting for the situation to improve. There's opportunities opening up in a place called Port Phillip. It'll take time, and there's no guarantee of success. But ... what do you say, old girl? Would you like to apply with me?"

'Well, you could have knocked me down with a feather, Annie, right there in High Street. But I thought, Pam, here's a man with an eye for the future. So I agreed, right then and there, to marry him.'

Ma sniffed, tweaking at an organ pleat in the waist of Annie's gown. 'Pam's right. Looks aren't everything. You want a good, sensible man who will provide for you.'

Annie nodded, as if taking the advice to heart, though doubt still puckered her brow. She clearly didn't think she'd have much choice. Or maybe she didn't fancy marrying an ageing, yellow-toothed builder who mistook emigration plans for a marriage proposal.

'What about you, Mrs Bustle?' Siân interrupted with a smile. 'Had you known Mr Bustle long before you married him?'

Now it was Ma's turn to blush. So she should, turning to Alf while her husband was still alive.

'An awfully long time, in fact, Siân. He lodged in the same house as my first husband, Archie, and me. I knew him to be a kind, sensible man and I couldn't help admiring him. Though,' she fixed Bridie with a withering glare, 'there was nothing improper in our friendship.'

'Oh, no. A good, honest man, is Mr Bustle. Not one for anything improper. Bridie knows that surely?'

Bridie didn't look up, though the question was directed at her. She wouldn't give Ma the satisfaction of answering. Siân was right, of course. Alf didn't have the nouse to plan anything improper, let alone carry it out. But it had happened, whether he'd meant it to or not, and she wasn't about to let Ma off the hook.

'Well, Bridie, what do you say? Siân has asked you a question.'

'I suppose not.'

'Alf was a good friend to your father. I can't count the times he helped him up the stairs, or listened to his maudlin ramblings. But you don't remember that, do you? Perhaps I should have told you more at the time.'

Alf? A friend to her father! Head down, Bridie didn't respond.

Ma shrugged, turning back to Siân. 'My first husband was a musician and a dreamer, gentle, softly spoken, poetic, not unlike your husband. Not that I wish to insult you, Siân. I hope you'll not take it unkindly. But I hope, for your sake, that Rhys has more spine than Archie did.'

'I know my husband's weaknesses, Mrs Bustle, and lack of spine has never been one of them. Rhys would do anything to keep me from harm—anything, though it be at great cost to himself.'

Ma sniffed, clearly unconvinced. 'I hope you're right. These handsome dreamers are so appealing. My father warned me not to marry Archie. I didn't pay him any heed. Though, looking back, it was a fool's choice from the beginning.'

'No!' Bridie jerked up, slapping her half-made monthly pad

down on the bench. 'You loved him once. I know you did.'

'I thought I loved your father, Bridie, I truly did. He was a handsome man … so handsome, and a fine musician in the early days. His stories and ballads fair turned my head at the age of seventeen. But those things didn't last. Once his cough started and he couldn't play his blessed instrument, the real Archie Stewart emerged. He wasn't so fine then, was he? Or romantic? His foolish dreams didn't help much at all.'

'They might have … if you'd believed in him.'

'Ah, no, girlie. Love isn't a fairy tale. I think even Siân would agree with me. It's about getting up each day, though your heart is breaking, taking a job, any job, if only to see your wife and daughter fed. I'm not saying Rhys would do the same to you, Siân. I'd not wish that on anyone. But Annie should think twice before marrying and, when she does, choose carefully.'

Annie blanched at being dragged back into the conversation. 'It's all right, Mrs Bustle. Lovely as this dress is, it won't be working any miracles. I mean, my own aunt didn't want me … because I'm ugly. Even for a man with his trousers down, that's a pretty hard thing to overlook.'

There wasn't much to say after that. Their afternoon had soured. Ma snipped at her thread with her teeth. Siân flipped her skirts right-way-out and struggled back into them. Annie slipped out of the half-made mantua and shrugged into her old gown. Bridie rose and started laying mugs out along the table. As the men came tramping down the ladder, Siân slid onto the bench beside Annie. She leaned close, pitching her voice low. But Bridie couldn't help overhearing.

'Cursed, I was, in my village, Annie *bach*. Never mind a bit of scarring. They called me the devil's child. I'd be an old maid still, if not for Rhys. He might be handsome, as Mrs Bustle said, and a dreamer. But he saw beyond my ugliness. Someone will do the same for you, one day, Annie *bach*. Wait now and see.'

CHAPTER 19

othing more was said of Siân's confession, or Ma's bitter advice. But Bridie wasn't able to forget their conversation. How could a girl be born cursed? Especially one as lovely as Siân. Was this the shadow hanging over Rhys? And what about her dad? She remembered hunger, of course, their coats hanging in the pawnshop window, Ma stitching until her fingers bled. But her dad had been sick. They'd had no choice. Or so Bridie thought. Now, she wasn't sure.

Maybe he could he have tried harder? Done something, anything, to keep them warm and fed. He hadn't. He'd turned his face to the wall and let them suffer. Why? Because he was a dreamer who didn't love them? Were all dreamers weak? All big, dull men reliable? Siân didn't think so. She'd called herself fortunate. Yet, anyone could see she was worried about Rhys. The hiss had gone from the Bevans' late night arguments. But by day, tension still hung like a cat's cradle between them. Bridie saw it in the twist of Siân's hands, their too-careful conversations, the way Rhys's face seemed to be growing thinner and paler by the minute.

One afternoon, as they sat in the shadow of the main mast, Siân seemed to reach a decision. Squaring her shoulders, she placed a hand on Rhys's knee.

'I'd like to tell today's story, *cariad.*'

Rhys glanced up, his eyes dark, wary. 'The one about Macsen Wledig? As we promised Bridie?'

'No. That is not the story for today.'

Bridie straightened up, glancing from Siân to Rhys and back again. This was odd. Siân never told stories. She always performed the songs and dialogue, leaving the narration to Rhys. She wasn't the only one surprised by the sudden change of plan.

'What story did you have in mind then, Siân?'

'I'd like to tell the story of March ap Meirchion's ears.'

Rhys winced as if the idea pained him. 'No. Please, Siân. Not that one.'

'We can't go on like this, Rhys.'

'And you think this will help? After all these miles, these terrible months at sea, to throw away the chance of a fresh start?'

'I can't see the future anymore, Rhys. I don't know how this voyage will end. Only that we must make our peace now … before it's too late.'

She turned to Bridie. 'You'll not mind, I hope, *bach*? I'll not tell the story as well as Rhys. But you are part of his journey now and,' she smiled, tilting her head, 'I've a sense you too need to hear March ap Meirchion's story.'

Her, part of Rhys's journey? Something in Siân's voice brought a spidery dread to Bridie's spine. Yet the Welsh girl's smile was compelling. She found herself nodding in agreement.

'March ap Meirchion was a good king, Bridie *bach*, always gentle and kind. But, alas, he'd been born with a set of horse's ears on his head. Over the years, King March took great pains to hide his deformity—wearing a parade of fancy bonnets and hats. For, if the ears were discovered, he feared he would lose the respect of his subjects. Indeed, no one but his barber knew of the curse, and that poor man was sworn to secrecy.'

Secrets! Bridie searched Siân's face. From Rhys's earlier response, she'd imagined the story was about the curse. Now she wasn't so sure. Maybe it was also directed at her?

'You needn't fret,' Rhys answered her thoughts. 'You'll soon realise I'm both the king and the barber in this story.'

'The barber was a simple, honest man,' Siân continued, 'and, by-and-by, the weight of his knowledge caused him to sicken. What if he let the truth slip out? Would the king accuse him of treason? Eventually, he broke down under the strain. King March called for a physician. After careful examination, he made his diagnosis:

"'You, my dear man, are labouring under the weight of a terrible secret.'"

'This was no surprise to the barber. But fearing for his life, he dared not breathe a word of the curse. Fortunately, the physician was wise as well as learned.

"'I can see you are sworn to secrecy. Here, then, is my advice. If you daren't tell a living soul, why not whisper your burden to the earth?"

'The earth? Of course! The barber almost skipped for joy. On leaving the castle, he squatted beside a clump of reeds and whispered King March's secret to the ground.

'Not many moons afterwards, King March planned a feast. He summoned bards, tumblers and musicians for his guests' entertainment. One of them, a piper, couldn't help noticing his instrument was getting past its prime. On seeing a fine clump of reeds growing outside the walls of the *Castellmarch*, he decided to fashion a new pipe for the occasion.

'The feast went well, for King March was both wealthy and wise. As knife went into meat and drink into horn, the hall filled with wonder and stories. At last, as the evening drew to a close, the piper stepped forward. Bowing to the king and honoured guests, he raised his pipe to his lips. But, oh, the horror! His new pipe was bewitched. No matter how he pressed his lips to the reed, nor how artfully he arranged his fingers, the pipe spoke with its own accord.

"'Horses ears for March ap Meirchion," it shrilled, over and over. "Horses ears for March ap Meirchion."'

Head in his hands, Rhys gave a low moan.

Siân nudged him, her smile gentle. '*Hist, cariad,* it's not such a bad ending.'

Rhys didn't look up, only shook his head.

'King March rose, furious,' Siân continued softly. 'He drew his sword, determined to slay the piper.

'"No! Please, sire? Have mercy. My pipe is bewitched."

'King March halted, lowering his sword. He had no desire to slay the innocent. Besides, only a fool would resist the promptings of such a powerful enchantment. King March raised his hat and exposed his hairy ears to his guests.'

Siân reached out, lacing Rhys's trembling fingers with her own.

'And it didn't matter, did it, *cariad*? After all his fear and shame, March didn't lose the respect of his subjects.'

'I don't know, Siân. Like you, I can no longer see our journey's end.'

'Then you must choose, Rhys. Tell the story as you want it to finish.'

Rhys raised his head, his eyes meeting Siân's. As if they were alone, in private, the air between them static.

'Some mocked the king, Siân. People can be cruel like that. But those who mattered stood beside him, seeing beyond the curse and the cruelty. For he was a good man, March ap Meirchion, though proud and foolish. He'd only been trying to do his best. In the end, those qualities mattered more than his deformity.'

'You're not the only one at fault, Rhys. I hid the stone, remember.'

Rhys shook his head. 'I knew, Siân. It seems to me I've always known. Right from the beginning. Yet I fought against the knowledge, thinking I could outrun a curse, forcing you to emigrate against your wishes, refusing to acknowledge the truth, even when it brought healing to others.'

'And I knew you would take me away, Rhys, before you ever came back to Cwmafan. I looked into Rhonwen's stone and foresaw a great journey. I'll not live in fear, Rhys. Or deny my heritage. But,' she reached out, cupping his face in her hands, 'I'd rather be here with you, than anywhere else on the earth.'

* * *

They had forgotten her presence. Eyes soft, foreheads touching, sunlight burnished their slender faces. Their hearts had gone to a land far away. Bridie hugged her knees, gazing up beyond the ratlines. She watched a white-winged albatross soar in the sky overhead, heard waves thud against the prow of their vessel, men whistling on the yard arms, the exultant cry of a cabin passenger wheeling in fish.

Eventually, Siân yawned and stretched, wriggling her toes. 'Move Rhys, this deck is hard.'

'Rest for you now, is it, *cariad*?'

Siân rose, touching a finger to his lips. She was close to her time and, though her ankles weren't puffy like Ma's, she often took to her bunk of an afternoon, leaving Rhys and Bridie alone with their stories.

'There's more to this tale, Rhys. You may tell it with my blessing. Bridie is woman enough to hear your confession. Perhaps, make one of her own? Like a pair of miserable old packhorses, you are, each carrying your own secret burdens.'

Rhys tensed, holding his breath, as Siân stepped backwards onto the ladder. Bridie imagined him counting as her swollen belly negotiated each slippery rung. *Four, five, six*, there, she was down. He leaned back against the main mast and closed his eyes.

'Right then, Bridie Stewart. Let's have it.'

'Have what?'

'I don't know what you made of all that, *bach*. But I'm sure you have questions.'

Bridie didn't know what to say. Of course she had questions—about the curse and how it was related to Siân. Why Rhys had been so set against Billy's healing? But he looked so peaceful, shoulders soft, eyes closed, a half smile curving his mouth. She had no desire to bring the tension back to his face.

'It's all right. Tell me another day.'

'It won't be easy, *bach*. I'll not lie to you. I'll take no pleasure in the telling. But Siân's right. It's time I whispered my secrets to the ground.'

'Well, she didn't come out of a lake. I know that much. But she knows things, like Rhonwen. Things that have nothing to do with plants.'

'Clever girl. What else can you tell me?'

'You didn't want Siân to know things, or to be magical, because you feared it was linked to a curse—a curse she somehow inherited at birth. But she is magical. No one can deny it, after what she did to Billy.'

'You are right. No one can deny it.'

Bridie shifted, studying his face. Why wouldn't he look at her? He wasn't normally so evasive. It must be a terrible secret. Yet it had brought healing. 'Please, Rhys, I don't understand.'

'Remember, I told you. Rhonwen was the seventh child of a seventh child.'

'But ... Siân was her mother's first child. You told me.'

'She was, indeed. I can't fault your memory. With us, there are other ways for a child to inherit unnatural abilities.'

'Through their father?'

He nodded, opening his eyes. 'Siân's mam was young, Bridie *bach*, so very young. Shameful, it was, to conceive out of wedlock. Yet no one stepped forward to claim the child. Siân's mam left the village, alone, and without a word. There was a reason, they said ... a terrible reason for her silence ... and her flight. Why else would a mother leave her child?' He stopped, swallowed, sweat beading his forehead. 'You'll know the situation, perhaps? From the dragon story?'

'Dragons!' Bridie blinked.

Rhys leaned forward, eyes intent. 'Remember the boy considered a powerful, otherworldly sacrifice?'

Myrddin? The boy with a poet's soul like Taliesin? Who'd saved himself with words and magic? How did that relate to Siân? Taliesin had been conceived of a witch's vengeance. That's why he'd been thrown into sea. But who was Myrddin's father? What had she written in her notebook?

'"For hadn't he been sired by his grandfather," Rhys provided the answer, 'or indeed the devil himself?'"

The devil! She stared open-mouthed at him. No, that wasn't possible. But a grandfather? How could a grandfather also be his sire? They were two separate people. Unless ... oh, the meaning hitting her with a thunk. A father forcing his daughter! Bile rose in her throat. She'd heard whispers of such things, children born horribly malformed. But Siân was beautiful. Perfect. How could she spring from such a union?

'And you believe this?' Her voice shook.

'You heard the story, *bach*. I've run myself half round the world in denial of the possibility. But, now Billy is healing. Yes, now, I have to believe.'

'And it changes things, is that what you're saying? It shames you?'

Rhys shook his head. 'I knew Siân before the words had meaning. So, in one sense, no, it doesn't change a thing. But in another, it does, because she's my wife and will bear my child. I don't want them suffering. I thought if we stayed away from the Valleys, no one would know. But even in London the Welsh community is small. There were whispers. So, I thought, if we emigrated ... sailed far across the sea, the whispers would cease. But fool me, even here I can't escape. For the whispers are within me.'

Whispers!

Bridie knew all about whispers. Some days she didn't know where to turn for the hissing questions in her head. She knew about fearing the truth, too, and being afraid to ask, forever weighing up words like given up, goodbye, and wanted to die. But a father forcing his daughter—that was horrible, too horrible to contemplate.

'It's a shameful secret, Rhys. Thank you for telling me.'

'The shame isn't Siân's. I was a fool to try to make her live a lie.' He raised his cap, his dark curls ruffling in the breeze. 'What do you think, Bridie Stewart? Are my horses ears ridiculous?'

She smiled, trying to match his mood. 'Hmm ... let me think, am I the reed? Or one of your subjects?'

'You are the friend that matters, Bridie *bach*. Helping me see beyond the curse and the cruelty.'

Bridie nodded, throat tight. 'Then I think we can safely say your ears are perfect.'

* * *

For a while, neither of them spoke. It was indeed a shameful secret, even if the shame wasn't Siân's. Many would despise her for the knowledge. Though it only made the Welsh couple more wonderful as far as Bridie was concerned. Rhys loved Siân so much he'd tried to rescue her from a curse—that was beautiful, so beautiful it made her throat ache and, although Rhys had dragged her half round the world, Siân hadn't turned against him. If only Ma could have loved like that.

'May I ask a question of you now, Bridie Stewart?'

'Me?' She gulped, looking up at him. Had he read her mind?

'You needn't look so concerned. I'm only wanting your help with the Christmas concert.' He picked up her notebook, turning it over in his hands. 'Siân may be confined, as you know. Our baby is due around Christmas time.'

'And you want me to take her place?'

'Why not? We could practise in the afternoons. While she is resting.'

'But … what would we do? One of your stories?'

'No. I wouldn't recommend it. People might compare.'

Yes, of course, that would be dreadful, everyone whispering and pointing. There's Bridie Stewart, with her bodice let out round the chest. Who does she think she is? A woman, now, with her monthlies. She ought to know better than to spend so much time with another woman's husband.

'I expect Siân will be fine.'

'We could prepare an item anyway. Write a ballad, perhaps? Or a poem?'

'A poem! What sort of poem?'

Rhys shrugged, settling back against the main mast, and fixed his gaze on the pile of canvas at their feet.

'Anything. A topic of your choosing. Though ... I had the sails in mind.'

She didn't know anything about sails. Alf had wanted her to learn the names, write them in her notebook. But she wasn't interested. Hang on a second? Alf? The sails! Her mind did a hop and a step. She jumped. 'You don't care about the sails!'

'Your stepfather is a good man, Bridie.'

Bridie looked from his not-quite-there eyes to his hands clutching her notebook, and saw him flush.

'He's annoying and interfering and always makes me do stupid things. I thought you understood.'

'I do, but—'

'You think it'll be clever, me writing a poem about sails?' She snatched her notebook back. 'You think people will listen and enjoy it?'

'Please, Bridie, you and me, together. It'll be fun.'

Why? Why was he even suggesting this? And why was the sun so hot? And why did her stomach swim? And what about Alf? Yes, Alf—this was all his fault in the first place. Everything was his fault—*everything*. It all came back to Mr-trying-to-be-a-good-stepfather, Alf.

'Sometimes, when a thing means a lot to another person, it can be worth doing, *bach,* even when you don't feel like it, and I'd be there to help you.'

'He doesn't care. You know that, don't you? He and Ma can't say a single good thing about my dad. They want me to hate him. As Ma already does.'

'So you, in turn, must hate Alf.'

'No!'

'Though he was a good friend to your father.'

'So Ma says. That doesn't mean I have to like him. Or let him guide me in the colony.'

'Alf's not a monster, Bridie *bach*. He knows how much you loved your dad and, although it may feel like he's forcing a friendship, in his own way, he only wants to help. Only he doesn't know how to go about it. So, I know this may sound difficult. But I think you may have to show him.'

'Why?' She turned furious eyes on him. 'Why are you making me do this?'

'Not making, asking. It would put my mind at rest.'

'I don't know what you mean.'

'I think you do.'

'What do you care, anyway? About Alf and me?'

Rhys sighed deeply, rubbing a hand across his face. 'It's for him and for you and, perhaps, also for me. I miss my own tad, see; I would do it for him.'

'Why, did he make you do silly things?'

'Tad was never silly.'

'He wasn't your *step*father either, was he, Rhys?'

'Tad was strict man,' Rhys continued, as if she hadn't spoken. 'Fair in many ways, but strict with it. Only one thing he asked of me, one thing I wouldn't, well … I couldn't do.' He stopped, hugging his arms to his chest. 'I've fear of enclosed spaces, surely, you've guessed.'

She hadn't. But it made sense. The hours he spent behind the horsebox, his nightly absence from steerage, his cheeks leaching of colour between decks. So much hurt this afternoon, so many secrets. But, no, she wouldn't give in.

'What's it got to do with me, Rhys?'

'It's a bit of a liability, don't you think? I'm a miner's son.'

'So?'

'I couldn't work underground.'

'Why didn't you work somewhere else?' It didn't make sense. The fear did, but not Tad's insistence, or the husky shame in Rhys's voice.

'Twelve, I was, Bridie. Tad wouldn't allow it.'

'That's stupid.'

'Not to Tad.' Rhys's anger rose to meet hers. 'He was a miner and his father a miner before him. They worked the old Waunlas level, scraping a living from the valley before its wealth was uncovered. When the investors came, he saw it as a reward for his years of hard work. I was to work beside him, as my brothers did, as they are … even now.'

'But … surely he wouldn't make you? Not if you were frightened?'

'You think not! He beat me, Bridie, locked me in the cupboard, took me down the pit regularly. Said it was a cowardice, something I must overcome.'

'What did you do?'

'I left, without a goodbye.'

'Oh.'

'And I miss him, see, every day.'

'How can you miss him? He sounds like a brute, worse than Gwyddno Longshanks.'

Rhys shook his head. 'Tad wasn't a bad man. Only he cared what others might think more than he cared about the fear in me. In the end, he managed it the only way he knew—with prayer, his belt leather, and with an iron will. But if that makes him like Gwyddno, then, I too am guilty. For I did the same to Siân, forcing her to emigrate against her wishes.'

Bridie didn't answer. Rhys had good reasons for making Siân emigrate, even if she hadn't welcomed them. They were nothing like locking a child in a cupboard, or forcing him to work underground.

'People are not wholly good or bad, Bridie, like eggs and apples. Despite what your Ma says, they are more complex—like me and Tad, like Alf and your ma. Perhaps … even a little like your dad.'

Still, Bridie didn't say anything. Blood hammered in her ears.

'I know you'd rather not talk about him, *bach*. I'll not press you against your wishes. But Siân's right. Some burdens are too heavy to carry alone.'

This was it, a chance to whisper her secret to the ground. Rhys would understand, even if he couldn't help her, and it would stop the churn of questions. But where to begin? With her dad giving up? Or Ma giving up on him? The reasons she'd given him to stay alive? The knowledge they weren't enough—that she wasn't enough. Or simply with the final, terrible words: *my dad killed himself.*

No. She couldn't say it—no matter how deep Rhys's concern or how soft the sympathy in his kind dark eyes. For once those words had been spoken there was no turning away from them. They would be in the world, like a curse, or the thin reedy voice of a pipe, and, like Rhys, she would do anything, even run to the ends of the earth, rather than face that truth.

'Did you see him, when you went back for Siân?'

Rhys shook his head. 'I am dead to him, Mam said. As if he'd never had a third son.'

'I'm sorry, Rhys.'

'And me, for interfering.'

'It's all right. You were only trying to help.'

He gave a wistful, half smile. 'You'll likely think me foolish. But every morning, I think today he will relent. Today a letter will come. Even here on this ship. And I tell you Bridie, if that letter did come, I'd build me a coracle and sail home on the ninth wave, if only to put things right with him.'

Bridie heard the ache in his voice, saw the desperate working of his throat, and her heart twisted. He'd trusted her with his secrets, called her the friend that mattered, for surely this too was a curse—this fear and estrangement, and there was one small way she could help him. 'All right! I'll play your silly game.'

'Game!'

'Yes, you know, the one in which we prepare an item for the Christmas concert, in order to please Alf, without me having to apologise. It's a clever ploy, Rhys, and I thank you for the opportunity. I'm sure Alf will grin like an ape when he hears of it, not to mention Ma's gloating. It will be dreadful, truly dreadful. I will therefore do it one condition—that I do it for you and Siân. Oh, I know,' she held up a silencing hand, 'you don't want my thanks. But those are my terms.'

Rhys grinned. 'It seems you have me backed into a corner, Bridie Stewart. Though, I think, you'll have to explain the rules. For I must confess, I'd not thought of it in terms of a game before.'

'Oh, that's easy. Fancy you not working it out. We're going to send a message to your dad. Not via the postal service. It's too unreliable. Besides, he wouldn't read a letter from you. Therefore, we'll send your message via a friend. For as you help this friend with her stepfather, it will work a kind of magic, and, one day, because of it, someone will do the same for you and your dad.'

'Clever girl. Though, I must say, it's a strange kind of magic. Do you think it'll help?'

Bridie laughed. It wasn't real magic, not like Siân's, and she had no idea whether it would work. But she was willing to try, for Rhys's sake. Indeed, if he'd asked her then to spill her secrets, she might have found the courage to utter them. For she would do anything, she realised—*anything*, for this gentle young man at her side.

* * *

Okay, so maybe not *anything*. At least, not during supper that evening. When Alf plonked down onto the bench, Bridie's mind spun a web of excuses. She flushed, seeing Rhys's brows rise. She shrugged, mouthing the word *tomorrow* across the table.

She woke the next morning with a flood of recollection. Peeling back the bedcovers, she jerked her bodice and petticoats from their overhead pegs. This was going to be dreadful, truly dreadful. For a moment, as she sat shivering in her nightdress, she wished she hadn't agreed to the scheme.

By the time she'd dressed and clambered down from her bunk, breakfast had already started. To her surprise, Rhys was seated at the table. How odd. He never came down for breakfast and, by the tight, whiteness of his face, he wasn't enjoying the experience. She sighed, slipping onto the bench beside him.

'What are you doing? Checking up on me?'

'Good morning to you, too, Bridie Stewart.'

She saw his fingers clench around the raised table edge, the uneaten ship's biscuit on his plate. 'It's all right. You don't have to be here.'

'I'll admit. I'm hoping not to have to join you a second time.'

'Then, why? Don't you trust me?'

'I told you, some burdens are too heavy to carry alone.'

Right. Bridie took a deep breath and blew out through her puffed cheeks. She was going to have to ask, now, over breakfast, with everyone else listening. She eyed her stepfather. He looked bleary-eyed and placid. But what if he ignored her?

She glanced sideways at Rhys. He raised an eyebrow, a smile playing about his mouth. Oh, yes, it was all very amusing. But the pallor of his face was truly alarming. Who'd have imagined steerage could have such an effect on someone?

She swivelled round. 'Er ... Alf?'

Nothing. She raised her voice. 'Excuse me ... Alf?'

Still no answer. She glanced at Rhys. He jerked his chin upwards. She waited for a lull in the conversation, cupped her hands around her mouth.

'Alf!'

Their mess fell silent, all eyes on Bridie. She ducked her head, heard Ma's hiss of indrawn breath, felt the quiver of Rhys's laughter. Alf turned, fixing his miserable old-dog eyes on her.

'Yes, lass?'

'Sorry. I didn't mean to shout.'

'Not this time,' Ma muttered.

Bridie flushed, ignoring Ma's comment. 'I was ... well, I mean ... Rhys and I were wondering whether we might ask a favour of you?'

'A favour? The nerve of it!' Ma bristled in Alf's defence.

'Now, Mary.' Alf laid a hand on her arm. 'Let's not be hasty. What did you have in mind, Bridie love?'

Bridie! Love!

Was he being kind? Or just plain stupid? She looked up into his round, earnest face. She thought, perhaps, kind. Which only made the whole thing more awkward.

'Actually, we've been thinking about the Christmas concert. Well, actually, Rhys has. He's convinced me to take part.'

'Excellent. Very educational. Is it a story you've been working on?'

'No, actually, we've decided to write a poem.'

'A poem?' Alf's gaze flicked from her, to Rhys, and back again.

'Yes. We thought you might help.'

Alf shook his head. 'It's a kind offer, lass, but I might have to let you down. I've no great talent for verse.'

'Oh, it's okay. I know you can't write verse. Or imagine things. But, we thought, well … we might do a poem with a nautical theme and you could help … you know, with the names of sails and things.'

'The sails?' Alf's creased blue gaze found Rhys.

He nodded. 'I've very little nautical knowledge, Mr Bustle. But with your help, we could make it a team effort.'

Alf shook his head. 'Nice try, son, and I appreciate the gesture. But I think we both know my expertise is lifted straight from the pages of a penny magazine.'

'It's more than I have, Mr Bustle.'

'Then you'd best ask the sailors. They'll fill your page in a minute.'

'Looking forward to it, Bridie was. And, as you said, educational, to try her hand at some composition.'

Alf rose, pushing his plate to the centre of the table. 'I told you to leave matters alone, son. Why are you doing this?'

'Perhaps you should ask Bridie that question.'

Bridie gulped. Things weren't going as expected. Alf was

supposed to be thrilled, Ma triumphant, herself squirming with virtuous embarrassment. Instead, she saw pain in Alf's eyes, defeat in the sagging line of his shoulders. Her heart plummeted.

'I won't lie to you, Alf. At first, I wasn't keen. I'm still not that interested in ships, if I'm honest. But I do want your help.' She shrugged, glancing sideways at Rhys. 'I can't explain my reasons. You'd likely think them fanciful. But, sometimes, a thing is worth doing, if it means a lot to another person.'

* * *

Bridie would need charts, she told Rhys, before she could start working with Alf, one for each sail, with a name box for each relevant part. For some reason, she couldn't get started. She chewed her pencil, gazing up at the shrouds. How had it come to this? Alf wasn't her dad. She'd never asked him to take an interest. Yet maybe he did care about her future, like Rhys said. Was offering her a friendship, like the one he'd given her dad?

These questions didn't help her motivation. Only made her feel small and shabby. But there were only so many times she could sit with her brow creased in concentration, or scrub at diagrams with an eraser. Eventually the charts were finished. She laid them before Rhys at the end of their story session.

'There you are, all done. Alf had better be impressed.'

'He'll see the care in these drawings. Mark my words. We'll see magic this evening.'

'No, Rhys. I will see magic.'

'Miss Determined, now, is it?'

'I'm not joking. If you even set foot in steerage after supper, I won't bother asking.'

'Rest assured then, Bridie *bach*, I'll not hinder you with my presence.'

He didn't. But when Bridie shoved her diagrams across the table that evening, Alf sighed deeply.

'You meant it then, lass?'

'Yes.'

'And I can see you've gone to a great deal of effort ...'

... for Rhys. The words hung unspoken between them. Bridie squirmed, looking down at the charts. 'I'm sorry, Alf.'

'For what?'

She shrugged. 'Everything.'

'You can't pretend an interest, lass. I was a fool to try to force a friendship. But perhaps we can start again ... with something you're interested in?'

She had no desire to start again, only get the charts filled out and start writing her poem with Rhys. But as much as she resented Alf's presence in her life, she wasn't going to lie to him again. 'I'm not sure. Let's see how this goes, shall we?'

Alf flinched, as if taking a blow. His big blunt fingers curled. He'd understood, the words spoken and unspoken—and it hurt. For some reason, Bridie was shocked to find the knowledge pained her too.

CHAPTER 20

*R*hys smiled to see Bridie and Alf standing on the main deck together the following morning. Alf's face glowed with pleasure as he pointed out the various squares of canvas. Rhys couldn't say the same for Bridie. Her scowl could have manured a garden. But over the following days, as she listened and scribbled down terms, resentment gave way to a determined jut of her chin.

It wasn't the answer. Bridie still harboured secrets, secrets with which for all Rhys's effort, she'd chosen not to confide in him. But in the absence of her confidence, this shared project with Alf was the best he could offer. And although Bridie sometimes pouted, dismissing Alf with a hard shrug of her shoulder, at other times, they worked together long and hard and, true to her word, she never asked Rhys to join them.

It was a kindness, in truth. He had no desire to spend extra time in steerage. He'd made his peace with Siân. They were ready to face the challenges of a new land. But his fear of enclosed spaces was worsening. He spent most of his waking hours on the main deck now, having given up all pretence of sleeping in steerage. Yet even curled up behind the horsebox, he'd begun to have dreams—vivid, blood-filled dreams, involving Siân and Doctor Roberts' scalpel. As *Lady Sophia* made her snail-like progress toward the western coast of Australia, he'd begun to dread the prospect of her giving birth, on board ship, with Doctor Roberts in attendance.

His fears weren't logical. Doctor Roberts was a cold, selfish man who preyed on young women. But he was a qualified surgeon who needed his gratuity and that required live bodies at the end of the voyage. Then why the nightmares? Were they a premonition, like he'd had in London? Sensing Siân was in trouble before the news of Rhonwen's death ever reached him? Or were they the haunt of her simple admission?

I don't know how this journey will end.

He couldn't see the future either. Only a dark empty space where determination once lived. Perhaps he was finally losing his wits. The nightly drub of his boots suggested the latter—that he would arrive in Port Phillip a gibbering idiot, unable to care for his wife and child. Rhys shivered, despite the warmth of the December night, and pulled the blanket tight about his shoulders.

What if it wasn't madness? He'd made an enemy of Doctor Roberts from the outset. *Crist!* What a fool—and a coward. If he hadn't been so pathetic, he'd not have missed the cleaners' meeting or been forced to beg for second chances. If he hadn't been so defensive, he'd not have overreacted, by telling Dic Penderyn's story in steerage. If he hadn't been quivering like a blancmange the following morning, he'd not have taunted Doctor Roberts with the knowledge of his past. But he had done all those things. Now Siân might pay for the looseness of his tongue.

Rhys closed his eyes and took a long steadying breath. Land smelled close. A strange, mingled scent of earth and foliage hovering above the sea's briny offering told him victory was at hand. If he could only get Siân through the travail of childbirth, they might yet build a future in the new land. But how to keep her safe from Doctor Roberts' scalpel? Ask to be present at the birth? No, Doctor Roberts hated him, as did Mary Bustle. Pam was too sick with her own pregnancy. Which left only one other option: Annie Bowles.

* * *

It wasn't hard catching Annie alone. Over the past weeks, as Siân's balance had grown precarious, Annie had taken on extra mess duties to compensate. Rhys often found himself working alongside the shy, damaged girl. This morning was no exception. They stood, side by side on the leeward half of the deck, awaiting their allocated meat ration. Everyone else—those not rostered on mess duties—crowded the bulwarks awaiting a first glimpse of the foreign shore.

The western coast of Australia was visible from the crow's nest. This was causing a frenzy of excitement below. People stood on tiptoes, craning their necks as each windward tack brought them closer to the shore. Cape Leeuwin was the name being bandied about, the point at which the Indian Ocean met the Southern Ocean. Awesome and mysterious, the words were like a doxology to Rhys.

He could scarcely keep from dropping to his knees.

It was too early for celebration, however. They still had to sail from Cape Leeuwin to Port Phillip, a considerable distance, even as the crow flew. But within weeks, he'd be spewed from the belly of this great fish and crawl shivering onto the shore. He'd been a fool from the outset, thinking he could outrun a curse, let alone manage the closeness of steerage. But if they arrived safe, none of it would matter—the arguments, the pacing, the overreacting.

They could start life afresh in a new land.

Rhys leaned back, his shoulder against the deckhouse, and smiled at the antics of the steward. The man's movements were slow, exaggerated, as if he too were infected by the festive atmosphere. He jabbed his long-handled fork into the harness cask, speared a lump of salt-beef, held it aloft, and read from a metal disc attached to the joint.

'Six pounds, six ounces.' The steward's sandy whiskers opened to reveal a row of untidy teeth.

Doctor Roberts ran a bored finger down the list, searching for a group whose allowance matched the weight on the disc.

'Mess seven!'

A representative from mess seven, a group of Scotsmen who often traded their rice and pease for oats, jostled forward.

'Ah, it's the Oat Eaters.' The steward's eyes gleamed over the flourish of his beard.

'Haggis, too, when it's on offer,' a member of mess seven hollered. 'You don't know what you're missing, Cat's Whiskers.'

A trill of laughter ran through the crowd. The steward liked to poke fun, enjoying the return of banter. Though no one had called him Cat's Whiskers to his face before.

Rhys glanced sideways. Annie was a calm, sensible companion, not prone to idle chatter. But she seemed subdued this morning, neither smiling at the antics of the steward, nor glancing shoreward. Her hands gripped the metal rim of the meat pan as if she found the prospect of land unsettling.

'Not looking forward to it, Annie?'

'No. What about you?'

'Me? I can't wait to get off this ship.'

Annie's eyes searched his face. 'What about Siân? You'll want her giving birth before we arrive, with Doctor Roberts in attendance?'

It was the last thing Rhys wanted—a man who seduced young women, who'd registered as surgeon superintendent on an emigrant vessel to escape a host of creditors, who was most likely travelling under an assumed name. Wilson, Rhys thought the surgeon's name was: Doctor Franklin Robert Wilson. At least, that's what he recalled of the fancy brass nameplate on Barnett High Street.

'I've a favour to ask of you, Annie.'

She smiled, her grey eyes softening. 'Of course, you only have to ask.'

'I want you to look after Siân … during her confinement.'

'But,' Annie flushed, dropping her gaze, 'I don't know anything about babies … or birthing. Only what I've heard in passing.'

'Doctor Roberts relies on you greatly.'

'For lice and boils, yes, but … hardly for a birth. He'll want Mrs Scarcebrook in attendance.'

'I'd like you there too, Annie.'

'Goodness. Whatever for?'

Rhys shifted, face in the shadows. How to explain his fear to this sensible, hardworking girl? The terror jerking him awake at night? Say, *Doctor Roberts hates me because I know things. I fear he will take revenge on my wife and child*? 'Say you want to learn about birthing, perhaps.'

'Well, it would be handy but ... why, Rhys?' It was a good question. She deserved an answer.

He turned slowly to face her. 'I'm frightened, Annie.'

'Well, of course you're frightened. But Doctor Roberts is a good surgeon. Not a kind man, I grant you. But experienced. Siân couldn't be in better—'

'Land! There it is. I can see it!'

Annie's words were interrupted by hoots of triumph. Men thumped each other's shoulders, women planted kisses on their mess mates' cheeks. Others jumped up and down, waving scarves and handkerchiefs, as if someone on the shore might see. Beside him, Annie's eyes were a wash of tears.

'Are you all right, Annie?'

'Yes, I'm fine.'

'Are you sure? I didn't mean to upset you. Here, give me the meat pan.'

'No!' She jerked it from his grasp.

Rhys stepped back, palms raised. 'Whoa, steady *bach*.'

Annie flushed, biting down on her lip. 'Sorry, I didn't mean to snap. Only ... I've been so happy on board ship.'

'And now it's all coming to an end?'

'Yes.'

'It's all right. I understand.' Rhys gave her arm a gentle squeeze. 'Fear takes us all differently. Go, join your friends.' He pointed to a group of single girls staring wide-eyed at the shore. 'No, doubt some will share your misgivings.'

Annie took two steps toward the group, halted. Swung back round. 'What about Siân?'

'I'm a fool, Annie, letting my fears run away with me. Take no notice. Go now, have fun. Look at the land. We'll talk about the birth another time.'

Annie smiled, shaking her head. 'You're not a fool, Rhys. Only a first-time father. I doubt I'll be of much use to Siân. But I'll ask Doctor Roberts, if it'll ease your mind, and do what I can for her when the time comes.'

CHAPTER 21

To Bridie's surprise, Alf knew a great deal about *Lady Sophia*'s rigging. Anything he didn't know, he asked old Joe the bosun's mate. Between them, they managed to name every yard, sheet, and sail. It was a mammoth task, and not the least bit interesting. But working with Alf wasn't as miserable as Bridie had imagined. As they grappled with the workings of the ship and sought to understand the sailors' feverish activity on the yards, she found it easier to speak to him without snarling.

As Christmas approached, the excitement in steerage mounted. It felt odd with the day's heat smarting their noses, but the deck rang with carols of an evening. The single men threw themselves into auditions and rehearsals. The choir took every opportunity to practise Rhys's version of '*Ar Hyd y Nos*'. Clusters of single girls stood on the after part of the deck reciting stanzas of verse. Bridie and Rhys started work on their item.

Bridie had collected so many nautical terms she doubted they'd be able to fit them into a poem (at least, not one worth listening to). Rhys assured her it would be fine. They would pick and choose, using the odder terms to add an element of surprise.

Once the poem was written, they set about turning it into a performance. Rhys sought permission to use the captain's speaking trumpet. Into this, Bridie would call commands like: *Trim the sails!* Or: *Square the yards!* For every command, Rhys came up with a response, mostly in the form of sea shanties, which he would play on his fiddle while Bridie urged the audience to sing along.

Ya-ho-hup-la haul there ha-ho-now-ho-hup-yaho-hoy-ya was her favourite. Rhys liked the pumping song: *Haul the bowline, Kitty, you're my darling, Haul the bowline, the bowline, haul.*

When Rhys practised these songs, Bridie shut her eyes and tried to capture the rise and fall of his melodic voice. At other times, she focused on his slender face, memorising its shape, the tilt of his head, the smile that sometimes lit his eyes. She had begun to treasure their moments together, like bright beads, slipping through her fingers and puddling at the bottom of her memory's purse. For it was vast land, this Great Southern Land. As they tacked between open sea and distant shore, Bridie had begun to suspect a person might disappear forever into its greyish, green unknown. And she realised, once they reached Port Phillip, she might never see Rhys or Siân again.

Despite the flutter of preparation, Bridie's stomach clenched like a fist at the thought of standing up in front of an audience. Not a small fist either—a great, meaty dockworkers fist that tightened its fingers around the dwindling days of Advent. By Christmas Eve, she could barely eat for its size, let alone sleep.

'*Course, topsail, main-gallant, royal,*
Sails on each mast: mizzen, main and fore.'

Curled in her bunk, Bridie's head pounded with remembered lines. She heard two bells. Five o' clock on the morning watch. She'd been awake half the night and, now, on top of it all, she was going to vomit. She moaned, her cheeks watering. The dockworker's fist expanded. She jolted upright, grabbed her shawl, lurched from her bunk. She made a dash for the hatchway. Scrambling out from beneath the canvas awning, she saw the startled face of a sailor, felt a thump as she hit the side of the ship and leaned out over the bulwarks, hurling the contents of her stomach into the sea. Again she heaved, and again, her innards emptying like a wine skin. She pressed her forehead against the cool dark wood, their carefully constructed lines coiling in and out of her mind.

'*Fiddle-block, snatch block, deadeye, sheave,*
Lanyard and halyard: vang, ratline and sheet.'

She straightened up as the wave of nausea passed and scanned the horizon. It was early—far too early to see clearly. A faint rosy tinge whispered the promise of early morning. Bridie shuffled across the deck, scooped a pannikin of water from the water butt, and drank deeply. Wiping her mouth with the back of her hand, she surveyed the empty deck. A scuffle came from beyond the horsebox. She peered into the semi-dark, trying to make out a form. Was it the horse? Or Rhys? She strained her eyes, hoping to see movement in dawn's waking hour.

Nothing. Perhaps she'd imagined it? Bridie blew warmth into her numb fingers and turned back toward the lightening sea. No. There it was again. More scuffles, a cough. She spun back round. Heard footsteps, definitely footsteps. Tiptoeing across the deck, she peered around the boat end.

'Rhys!'

'Bridie!' Wrapped in an old grey blanket, Rhys crawled out from behind the horsebox. 'You might have told me you were going to rise for *plygain*.'

'*Plygain*?'

'An early morning watch to celebrate the birth of the Christ.'

'That's not why I'm here—and you know it!'

Rhys laughed, chafing his hands. 'Nerves, is it?'

'Don't laugh. I haven't forgotten whose idea this was in the first place.'

'Your stepfather's, I believe.'

Bridie grinned, stamping her feet. It was cold on the main deck—not the sleety cold of an English Christmas morning, a clear, missing-the-sun kind of chill, peculiar to these southern climes.

'Aren't you nervous?'

'About today? No.' He shook his head. '*Nefi!* There's frozen, you look, Bridie. Here, take my blanket.'

'I feel awful, Rhys. My stomach's a bucket of earthworms.'

He chuckled, draping the blanket about her shoulders. 'It's always like that the first time.'

'First. And last. I'm never doing this again.'

'I'll ask you afterwards. You might change your mind.'

Bridie doubted that very much. She'd enjoyed writing the verse, bringing together different combinations of word and sound. Watching Rhys turn their poem into a performance had also been magical. But she wasn't enjoying herself now.

'I must have been to the privy at least a thousand times.'

'*Duw!* That'll keep the cleaners busy. *Nadolig Llawen*, by the way, Bridie *bach*. I'll help you greet the dawn.'

'Oh, yes. Happy Christmas to you too.'

Three deep chimes interrupted their season's greetings. The ship stretched and yawned. Dawn filled with waking sounds. Bridie could now make out a dark line of coast. Was it Cape Otway? One of the points they must pass between to enter the treacherous waters of Bass Strait? Alf had described the narrow entrance during supper last night. As they stood in the stiff early morning breeze, Bridie watched the red-tinged clouds lighten to a dusky mauve.

She turned to Rhys. 'What story will you tell today?'

'Today? Can you not guess?'

'Hmm ...' Bridie pursed her lips. Rhys had been reticent to choose a story for the Christmas concert, as if by uttering the name he might bring on Siân's labour pains. But he'd told the story of Pwyll and Rhiannon the previous Friday and, although Bridie had already heard the tale, she'd thrilled, along with everyone else to hear of Pwyll chasing a stag and encountering Arawn, King of the Underworld; blushed at the idea of Pwyll sharing a chaste bed with Arawn's wife; and cheered loudly at the cunning defeat of Hafgan, his foe. The remainder, the story of Pryderi's birth, the giant claw that ripped him away from his mother, and brave Teyrnon who'd waited up all night to rescue him, would make a fitting finale for their Christmas concert.

'Will you tell Pryderi's story, perhaps?'

'In Wales, we have a custom called *Y Fari Lwyd*.' Rhys stood, legs apart, braced against the sea's rising swell. 'Between Christmas and New Year, groups of mummers go from house to house with a beribboned horse skull, singing riddles and verse. On outlying farms, a procession bearing cakes and ale makes its way to the stable of the finest ox. I suspect these customs are related to the story of Pryderi, wrapped in swaddling clothes, and found in Teyrnon's stable.'

'But Pryderi wasn't found at Christmas.'

'No, indeed. It was May Eve, another night when the door to the otherworld swings open.'

Bridie's stomach swilled. Not just nerves—a rolling sensation. She clutched at the bulwarks. Rhys's blanket slithered about her feet. Bending to pick it up, she bumped against the side of the ship. The sea's mood was changing. No longer gentle, it slapped against the sides of the ship. She tilted her head back, letting the wind buffet her cheeks—thinking of May Eve, cursed births, stolen children, and of course, behind it all, the shadowy figure of her dad.

She would never know how he had fallen. But she suspected he had gone out courting death that final Christmas night. Was it Ma's fault? She had no way of knowing. But, she thought, perhaps Ma had spoken the truth that sewing afternoon. If he'd loved them, he would have tried harder. He hadn't, not nearly hard enough. She would live forever with the weight of that betrayal. But she wasn't alone. She thought, perhaps, it was like that for everyone— for Rhys, with his fear of enclosed spaces; Siân with her shameful heritage; Annie's scarring; Ma's even-now bitterness; Alf, who tried so hard. What had Rhys said on the main deck that day? *People are not eggs and apples. They are more complex.* Maybe he was right. Maybe that was part of seeing differently—knowing they were each walking around with a set of horse's ears on their heads. She reached out, laying her hand on top of Rhys's.

'Thank you.'

He smiled, squeezing her fingers. 'Remember, I told you the ancient Britons associated time and place with the activities of the otherworld? In the valley where I come from people still believe that between eleven o'clock on Christmas Eve and one o'clock Christmas morning, the cattle bow in reverence to Christ.'

'Truly? Has anyone ever seen it?'

'No,' Rhys raised his voice to compete with the rising wind, 'for the person who sees it will surely die. But imagine if they had, Bridie *bach*. If only one of us had the courage of Teyrnon. Had been willing to wait up all night in the stable. Imagine what wonders we might have seen.'

Bridie swallowed, a lump like candle-wax forming in her throat. She gazed out over the rapidly changing sea. How did Rhys do this? How did he make his words pierce so precisely? She felt the weight in her chest shifting, a strange levering sense that it wouldn't take much to lift it, that even if there was nothing Rhys could do to change things, this was the real magic, this friendship and, no matter how painful her secrets, she must find the courage to trust him.

'I haven't been honest with you Rhys.'

'Yes, *bach*. I know.'

She shook her head, tears pressing. 'Not only about my notebook. About everything—Ma and my dad, his accident, all of it. Right from the beginning.'

'Then we are two of a kind, Bridie Stewart.'

She nodded, felt the tell-tale quiver of her lips. No, she mustn't cry. Not this time. 'I've wanted to speak, Rhys, for ever so long. Only, it hurt so much …'

'And you were frightened.'

'Yes.'

Rhys smiled, stepping back, and placed his hands on her shoulders. 'You've made a start now, Bridie *bach*, and, rest assured, I'll not let you wriggle out of the telling. But no matter how greatly I value the gift of your confidence, I'm afraid you'll not get a chance to offer it this morning. Look!' He pointed to the sky behind her. 'Storm clouds coming from the west.'

Bridie followed the direction of his pointing finger. The sky had indeed blackened, its rosy tinge mired up by a dark bank of approaching cloud. She heard a peel of thunder, felt the deck heave beneath her feet. A storm? They would have to batten down the hatches, postpone the Christmas concert, spend the day holed up in steerage.

The weather was changing, even as these thoughts skimmed through her mind. An icy wave broke over the bows of the ship. She heard the yards creak, sails straining against their sheets, the rallying cry of: 'All hands on deck!'

Sailors poured from the fo'c's'le and swarmed up into the rigging to set small rugged sails against a gale. Clutching Rhys's arm, Bridie staggered across the deck. She saw his face leach of colour as he stepped backwards onto the ladder, heard the overhead snap of canvas. As she plunged back down the ladder into steerage, the morning seemed to reel and shudder, as if a giant claw had ripped away its promise. Despite Rhys's assurances, Bridie sensed she'd need the courage of Teyrnon to find it again.

* * *

Ma's waters broke with the storm, at five bells on the morning watch, as seawater came gushing down through the hatchways, and Bridie didn't have time to worry about courage, claws, or confessions. The floors were awash. People pushed and shoved, anxious to secure their belongings. Ma stood, mid-aisle, her skirts dripping.

'Lord, Alf. The baby's coming.'

'Christ!' Alf stopped mid-flight.

It was a shock. Alf never blasphemed. His round face glowed red as a chemist's lamp.

'Sorry, love. You gave me a fright.'

'There's worse to come. I'd not be worried about a bit of cursing.' Ma shook her skirts, her trickling fluids joining the swirl of seawater underfoot.

'I'd best get Doctor Roberts then, love.'

'No rush. The baby won't be born for hours.'

'They'll batten down the hatches.'

As if on cue, the carpenter slithered down through the hatch and started to worm his way through the wigwag of legs and arms. He unlocked the lamps and began to snuff them out, one by one. Alf adjusted his grip on the bedpost. His gaze flicked from Ma's sodden skirts to the hatchway.

Ma seemed to guess his thoughts. 'I was in labour two days with Bridie.'

'Lord, Mary. We might be stuck here for two days.'

Ma's smile faltered. Her face blanched white in the half-light. Wrapping her notebook in her petticoat, Bridie shoved it to the bottom of her bag and slithered down from her bunk. Alf swivelled round, grabbed his jacket, and wrapped a scarf around his neck. Ma's voice rose, panicked.

'Be reasonable. He won't come out in a storm.'

'He will for me. I'm his chief cleaning constable.'

It was ridiculous, as if he were discussing a stroll across an open deck. It would be a torrent out there, waves at sucking all in their path.

Alf scanned the deck. 'Annie? Where's Annie?'

'Here, Mr Bustle.'

'Ah, there you are. Good girl. I want you to take Mrs Bustle to the hospital. Yes, that's right, grab her shawl. Tell the carpenter we'll need a lamp, do you hear me? Don't let him snuff it out. I'll be back soon with Doctor Roberts.'

Annie nodded, taking Ma's arm. Bridie stepped alongside and grasped Ma's other hand as Alf began to force his way through the press of people.

Ma's voice rose, shrill. 'He won't come. Please, Alf. It's too dangerous.'

Alf wasn't listening. For once, his solid good sense appeared to have left him. He reached the hatchway as the last plank was rammed into place. Stormwater oozed through the cracks, plastering his hair. He yelled, thumped with a fist. A plank lifted, then another. Alf bellowed through cupped hands. The bosun's mate shook his head, his weathered face incredulous at whatever was being suggested. Alf gave a shove. The mate raised a fist.

Ma's voice rose to a shriek. 'He's going to drown. Drown! And we'll be alone again.'

CHAPTER 22

*A*lf crouched in the surge of wind and waves flooding the deck. The bosun's mate fastened a line to the hatch post and leaned into the bullying wind. Head down, Alf followed him, bracing, knees bent as a towering wave broke over the ship. He scrabbled for a foothold. As the wash subsided, he made a dash for the saloon doors. Shaking water from his eyes, he stumbled dripping into the saloon. He reached for the oak table. Edged crab-like around the perimeter. Stopped halfway, fumbled for the doorframe. Found a latch, raised his fist, hammered.

No response. He waited, nursed his knuckles. Thumped again. Still nothing. Why wasn't it opening?

Wait. What was that? Alf's eye caught a movement. The latch? Or the wind? Alf felt a jarring thud. Seawater swirled around his ankles. He hammered again, louder. The door snicked open. Doctor Roberts peered out through the gap.

'Bustle?'

'My wife!' Alf yelled.

'Sorry?' Doctor Roberts raised a cupped hand to his ear. 'Can't hear you.'

Alf leaned closer. 'The baby's coming.'

'Baby! Are you mad?'

Alf staggered against the swell. Smelled sherry on Doctor Roberts' breath. Saw him step back as if to swing the cabin door closed. Alf sprang forward, wedged his foot in the gap. 'It's your duty!'

'Duty! To get myself killed! For one panicky woman.'

Doctor Roberts planted a hand on Alf's chest. He stood firm. 'I'm your chief cleaning constable.'

'Yes. Worth every penny. But I can't help you!'

He gave a shove. Alf stumbled backwards, grabbed for the table. Missed. On hands and knees, he beat the door with balled fists. *Dear God, what now?*

'Doctor Roberts!' He pounded again. Why wasn't the door opening? He wrenched at the latch. It wouldn't lift. Why not? Was the man holding it? He hammered. 'Please, sir. I beg you!'

It was no use. Even as he hammered, Alf knew the door wouldn't open.

He shivered, icy seawater swirling about his knees, aware of his clinging shirt and bruised fists. He dragged himself to his feet. What now? Go back? Apologise to Mary? *Sorry love, it seems, the surgeon can't make it after all.* Dear God, what a fool. Mary had tried to warn him. But no, he'd fancied himself the surgeon's favourite.

Sou'wester streaming, the bosun's mate waited for him at the base of the quarterdeck stairs. Alf dragged himself back across the deck, the waves tugging at him with icy, persistent fingers. The mate lifted the swollen hatch planks. Alf stepped onto the ladder. The mate grasped his shoulder, held up a knife, made a sawing motion, nodded at the ropes and canvas. He swung round, pointed to a line he'd strung across the deck. It was a kindly gesture, though a waste of time. If Doctor Roberts wouldn't come out now, he wasn't going to come out later as the storm worsened. Alf took the knife anyway, nodded his thanks, and plunged back down into the welcome dark of steerage.

* * *

Alf peered into the gloom. Had Annie and Mary made it to the hospital? He saw a faint, rectangular seam of light at the far end of the single girls' quarters. Yes, well done. She'd kept the lamp burning too. Alf fumbled his way aft, and heard Mary's curses through the thin planks of the hospital door.

'Bloody man! Look after you, he says. Then dashes out in a storm.'

'Here, Mrs Bustle. The lower bed's made up.'

'Kill him. I'll kill him. If he doesn't drown.'

Alf winced, bunched his fingers and knocked. The door creaked opened. Annie's white face peered out.

'Mr Bustle …? Where's Doctor Roberts?'

The ship lurched. Alf clutched at the doorjamb with swollen fingers and saw two sets of bunks, a stool, and Bridie bent double, puking into a hawse bucket. Bridie! What was she doing here?

'Mr Bustle?' Annie's eyes flicked to the knife in his hand.

Alf swallowed, moving his lips. No sound came out. He heard a moan, pushed past Annie, and sank down on his knees beside Mary.

'You've come back then, Alf?'

'Yes.'

'And, what can you tell me?'

'He … he wouldn't come love.'

'Of course he wouldn't come. Only you were fool enough to think otherwise.'

Alf slumped, as if a puppeteer had loosed his strings. Yes, he was a fool, a cringing ineffective fool, who couldn't even fetch a surgeon when his wife needed one. 'The bosun's mate gave me a knife, Mary.'

'What for, Alf? To cut the cord?'

'Mrs Bustle,' Annie pleaded. 'This isn't helping.'

'Neither will the knife, Annie.'

'You'll be ages. You said so yourself and, if there's an emergency, we can still fetch Doctor Roberts.' Annie's anxious eyes sought Alf's. 'That's right, isn't it, Mr Bustle?'

'No, she's right. It was a fool's errand.'

Confusion knotted Annie's brow. Mary's mouth hung down at

the edges. Long fingers of lamplight stroked the oozing walls of the cabin. Alf swallowed, licking his lips. 'Doctor Roberts is a difficult man, Mary.'

'And you shouldn't have left me.'

'No, enough!' Bridie thumped the hawse bucket down on the deck. 'You can say what you like about my dad, Ma. He, well ... maybe he deserved it. But Alf's come back safely, as you wanted. That's all that matters.'

'You've picked a fine time to realise who your father is.'

'Alf's not my dad. I've told you already. But your nastiness scares me.'

'Your ma's scared too, lass. Fear sharpens her tongue. You've realised that, surely?'

She hadn't. Realisation flooded her face. The ship pitched. Bridie moaned, clutching the bedpost. Alf grabbed the hawse bucket and shoved it under her nose. Eyes closed, she nodded her thanks. 'You'd best be getting back to your bunk, lass.'

'No. I'm staying.'

She looked so young, defiant, chin jutting, eyes brimming. He'd spent the entire voyage urging Bridie to grow up. But now, as he looked down into her upturned face, he found himself wanting to preserve her innocence.

'You're not ready for this, lass.'

'I'm a woman now. So Ma keeps telling me.'

'A young woman, yes, and I'm proud of the steps you've taken. But childbirth is violent, Bridie, gruelling.'

'What about Annie? She's staying.'

'Ideally, neither of you would be here. But Annie's had preparation. She's been working with Doctor Roberts. Besides, it's not her ma who's birthing.'

'Please, Alf. I can't lie in my bunk not knowing.'

CHAPTER 23

*T*hunder, all around, no light, no air, the ship jarring, shuddering, crashing. Rhys gripped the end board of the bunk, his other arm wrapped around Siân. *It'll pass*, he told himself, over and over, jaw clenched, teeth chattering. *It's a squall. Nothing more.* No worse than the last. Or the one before. At least he had Siân. He told himself that too. Not like Alf Bustle, whose wife laboured behind closed doors.

Rhys hadn't heard the older man return to his bunk. But he must be down there somewhere. Either that, or he'd stayed crouched outside the hospital door. That's what Rhys would do if they took Siân away. Never mind that people glimpsed his fear. He was nothing without Siân. Nothing. Rhys's arm tightened about her. She cupped his face in her hands.

'*Heddwch!* Rhys.'

Peace? His chest was heaving like an old man with black lung. Any day, their time would come. Siân would face the violence of birth. Please God, they'd be on dry land. He'd be able to pace like a man while his child was being born.

'Need to go to the privy,' Siân yelled in his ear.

'Too dangerous, *cariad*. You'll have to hold.'

Siân moaned, drawing her legs up. Rhys pressed his hand to the hard ball of her belly. *Duw!* It was tight. How long had they been lying there? Hours. With the babe pressing down on her bladder. She was normally up to the privy three times a night.

'Giving me pain, it is.'

'Only worse, you'll get, moving about.'

'I can't hold!' She wriggled free, crawled to the bed end.

'Siân, wait!' Rhys followed, yelling from behind as she slid from their bunk. She staggered, front heavy, against the sea's heavy swell. Rhys stepped close, shielding her from the cups, beakers and quart pots beating a tattoo along the deck. 'Never mind the walk, Siân, *twti* down here.'

'I'm not a beast.'

'Please. It's dangerous.'

The privy buckets were still standing, thanks to the last minute efforts of the steerage cleaners, who'd lashed them in place with stout ropes. But in the pounding seas, nothing could contain their contents. It oozed sticky about their feet.

'Careful!' Rhys bellowed. 'Please, Siân, don't slip.'

No answer. The deck pitched. Air jammed in Rhys's throat. He spun round, arms flailing. Felt wood, hard, unyielding. A crash, like the sound of a cupboard door slamming.

'Help! Please, Siân! Don't leave me.'

'*Heddwch!*' Like an answering spirit she came alongside.

Rhys clung to her, sobbing in the dark. Without the urgency, she seemed to have weakened. More than once Rhys had to stop her from falling. Arm about her waist, he groped from bed to bed. Almost there. *Crist*, what was wrong? She felt floppy as a cloth doll.

'I'm fine,' Siân answered his thoughts.

The ship reeled and Rhys stumbled, scrabbled for a handhold. Managed to regain his balance. Palms sweaty, he grabbed the bedpost. Ducked. A pot struck his back. He took a firm hold of Siân.

'Ready? I'll hoist you onto the bench.' He grasped her about the waist. 'Almost there. Can you step up, do you think?'

She nodded and braced.

'Right, on the count of three. *Un, dau*—'

A lurch. Rhys's hands slipped. He clutched at her bodice, felt it rip. The ship tipped. *Iesu*, it was dark. Down on one knee, Rhys groped for the bench. Missed.

'Siân! Where are you?'

No answer. Rhys lunged, arms wild, groping. He found her rammed up against the table. Breath ragged, soaked. He pulled her close, hands desperate about her arms, her belly, her face. She whimpered, bent double. Terror squeezed his chest.

'Siân? Are you hurt? Please, Siân, speak to me!'

No words. Only groans.

'Up now, *cariad.* Let's get you onto the bed.'

Rhys fumbled for the bench, hooked her under her armpits, and dragged her across the narrow companion way. Siân cried out, hands clutching her belly.

'*Crist!* What's happening? Tell me.'

'Nothing. I'm fine.'

Rhys rocked and soothed, willing her to be unhurt. He smelled dirt, and fear, felt a warm moisture oozing through her skirts. 'Take you to Doctor Roberts, shall I? Have him check? Close by, he is, Siân. In the hospital.'

'No,' she panted. 'I'll not be leaving you at the height of a storm.'

'It doesn't matter. Nothing matters, if you're hurt.'

'*Heddwch!* Rhys. We'll have hours before this baby is born.'

CHAPTER 24

*A*lf clung to the end board of the top bunk. He no longer heard the ship's bells above the hammer of the sea. The growl of his stomach told him they had gone long past dinner hour. In the bunk opposite, Annie lay pressed against Mary. Had she slept? How could she, with Mary writhing like an eel on the bed beside her? Maybe he should fetch one of the other women. No, it'd be hours before anyone was well enough to stir. Look how sick Bridie was. She'd scarcely moved since crawling into the bunk beneath. Though every so often a sob told him her rest wasn't easy.

Alf saw Mary's jerk of pain, her fingernails biting into Annie's arm. After what seemed like an age, she relaxed, panting.

One, two, three … Alf resumed his steady count.

He couldn't give an exact number, but the pains seemed to be coming before he reached four hundred, each time. Was that close? He had no way of knowing. Please God, it meant they had a few more hours. At least until the storm eased.

How long had Annie been lying in Mary's bunk? She must be worn out. Meanwhile, he was doing nothing. Alf grasped the bed end and swung down onto the deck. His breath caught. Icy seawater seeped through his boots.

'How are you, Mary? All right?'

'No, your baby's tearing me apart.'

'Sorry, love.'

'It's a bit late for sorry,' Mary bawled back at him. 'You should have thought about that nine months ago. But I'll tell you one thing, Alf Bustle. You can keep your trousers on in future, do you hear me?'

Alf stiffened, heat flushing his cheeks. 'Hush, Mary. The girls are listening.'

'They can listen all they like. If you so much as come near me in the future, I'll cut your bits off!'

Alf grimaced, turning to Annie. 'Sorry, lass. You shouldn't have to hear this.'

Mary gave a low moan. Annie massaged her arching back. As Mary flopped panting onto the bed, Alf mouthed the words 'how long?' over the top of her head.

Annie shrugged, mouthed 'don't know' back at him.

'No, need to whisper, you two. I can see your lips moving. You'll not miss it, Alf. I can assure you. That's when I'll really be cursing.'

CHAPTER 25

*R*hys woke with a start. Dark, so dark, a weight pressing down on him. He heard a sob. His own? He fumbled beneath the bed covers. Siân? Still there! Thank God, she was still with him. Come morning they'd take her away. Her pains were coming hard and fast. The mattress beneath them was now sodden. The warm metallic scent oddly familiar. She tensed, hands scrabbling among the blankets. Gasped, panted, fell back onto the mattress.

Rhys moved in close. 'How is it with you, *cariad*?'

'Fine. Still plenty of time.'

Fine. She was fine. Rhys let his breath go with a sigh. She knew, of course. She'd seen birthing often enough, with Rhonwen.

Coward! A mocking voice in his head. *Only you, she's thinking of!*

Rhys rocked her gently. 'Sorry, I didn't mean to fall asleep. Help, you're needing, is it?'

'Hold me,' she whispered. 'Only hold me, Rhys.'

He wriggled close, gathering her spoon fashion. 'Not long now, you'll be Mam. I'll be Tad.'

Dear God, where had the years gone? Only yesterday they were children—dancing in hay meadows, tickling trout in sunlit pools, running home with them slippery and fresh for Rhonwen to cook. Now, that same laughing girl would bear his child.

'I've a fear on me, Rhys.'

He was not surprised, with the pains coming often.

'Time for the hospital, is it?'

'Not the pains I'm worried about.'

'What then, *cariad*?'

'I can see things in the dark.'

'Things? What kind of things?'

'*Cannwyll gorff*, Rhys. Coming for me.'

'No!' The hairs on the back of his neck rose. 'No corpse candles at sea, Siân.'

'I can see them, Rhys. Blue for me. Yellow for a child.'

He grabbed her arms, shook her hard. 'I can't see them, Siân. Not real, are they, if I can't see them? Only phantoms?'

Iesu, who was he to speak of phantoms? He who'd clung to her, sobbing in the dark.

'A sign, it is, Rhys. You have to believe to see a sign.'

'Then don't! Not for a minute!'

He dragged her upright. Her head lolled. *Crist*, when had she grown so weak? He pushed the hair back from her face. Leaned his forehead against hers.

'Listen, *cariad*, we're going to be brave now. Strong. No more arguments, do you hear me? No more pandering to my stupid fears. We're going to climb from this bunk, walk along the deck, and leave you in the hospital. You'll be safe there, with Annie and Mary. Nothing to harm you.'

CHAPTER 26

*B*lood. Bridie dreamed of blood, rising, oozing, pulsing. She reached out, tried to cup it in her hands. No, she couldn't move. A giant claw held her, dashing, crashing, smashing her against the face of the deep. She heard a wail, Ma calling down curses. Fear! All fear. Why hadn't she realised? Like a whetstone to Ma's tongue. Fear for Bridie's future, fear for Alf, fear for this baby crushed in the grip of a storm.

No! She lurched upright. They couldn't lose another baby.

Her head swirled. She moaned, sank back down onto the bed. What time was it? How many hours had she been huddled in this bunk? She stretched her cramped legs, tried again to raise her head. The room swam. She blinked, tried to bring the cabin into focus. Saw Ma's head rise in the bunk opposite.

'Am I alive, Alf? Or dead?'

'You're alive, Mary love, and I'm still here.'

Bridie heard words, not clear, but definitely words. Her ears pricked to a subtle change in sounds. The storm still raged. It wasn't over by a long shot. But the wind had dropped to a child's keening wail. Bridie raised herself on one elbow and listened for signs of life beyond the hospital door. Nothing. No scuffle of feet, or cries of alarm, everyone still tethered to their bunks.

She watched Alf clamber from Ma's bed. Heard the slosh of his feet, a sigh, his warm yellow stream hitting the pot. He stooped, replacing the lid, and buttoned his trousers. Annie's tousled head popped up in the top bunk opposite.

'Sorry, lass. I didn't mean to wake you.'

Annie blinked, her bleary-eyes flitting from Alf to the flooded the cabin. She jerked upright.

'Mrs Bustle? How is she?'

'Not good, lass. The pains are coming two hundred and fifty beats apart. But the storm's easing.'

Annie yawned and pushed back the covers. She wound her hair into a loose coil, fastened her cap, and climbed down from the bunk.

'Enough, do you think?'

'Not yet. But soon, perhaps—'

Alf staggered, grabbing the bed end as a gust of wind buffeted the ship. Bridie heard a harsh, tearing sound, followed by an almighty thump. Annie reeled, staggering at the impact.

'Goodness! What was that?'

Alf grimaced, shaking his head. 'Sounds like a mast, or one of the yards coming down. The deck will be a mess of cables.'

Annie stepped forward, touched a finger to his arm. 'We'll manage, Mr Bustle. It's not her first time.'

Alf shook his head. 'I'd rather it wasn't her last either, Annie.'

As if on cue, Ma began to moan through clenched teeth. 'I'm going to die. I'm bloody well going to die before this baby is born.'

Annie squatted down, grasping her hand.

'You won't die, Mrs Bustle. I promise.'

Ma moaned, tension roping her throat. Alf clenched his fists. Bridie swung her feet out onto the watery deck. Alf stooped, wiping the sweat from Ma's brow.

'Not long now, love.'

Ma glared back at him, her eyes slits. 'You're not the surgeon, Alf. Or a midwife. So, I don't suppose you've got any idea.'

Alf swallowed, licking his lips. 'Isn't it normally like this then, love?'

'No.' A tear slid down Ma's cheek. 'It's worse, much worse.'

Bridie swayed, gripping the bunk. What if Ma was right? They had a bucket and towels, the mate's knife. But neither Alf nor Annie knew anything about birthing.

As if reading her thoughts, Alf's gaze found the mate's knife lying on the floor. Bridie stooped, grabbed the knife, and lurched toward him. 'Alf, you have to go, now. She might be dying.'

A rap on the hospital door. Annie jumped, her hand striking the lamp. Ma gave a sob. The room spun. Bridie lunged for the door. She heard raised voices, an urgent pebble of a fist. Dragging the door across the water-logged deck, she halted, mid-step, arrested by the tableau confronting her.

'What? What is it?' Ma broke the silence.

Rhys stood in the doorway, supporting Siân's sagging form. The Welsh girl's skirts were sodden. Blood-red rivulets trickled over her bare feet, the water around them a ruddy swirl. Rhys's gaze darted about the cabin.

'Siân's had a fall. Where's Doctor Roberts?'

'He wouldn't come, lad. Sorry.'

'Wouldn't come!' Rhys turned disbelieving eyes on Alf. 'What do you mean, he wouldn't come?'

'Said it was too great a risk.'

'*Iesu*, Mr Bustle. You should have made him come.'

Annie smoothed the sheets of the lower bunk and held back its covers. 'Here, Siân. Come lie down, quick.'

Siân trembled as Annie peeled away her sticky outer garments, revealing a heavily stained chemise. It seemed to Bridie that she used the last of her flickering strength to crawl into the bed. Ma wailed as another contraction took hold of her. Rhys pressed bloody fingers to his face.

'Dear God, I'll have to fetch him.'

Annie tucked the blankets around Siân. She pulled a towel from the cupboard, moistened it with water from the harness cask and dribbled it onto Siân's lips. 'She's thirsty. You did right to bring her.'

'I have to get help, Annie. I've waited too long already.'

'I'll go.' Alf squared his shoulders. 'It's my fault. I should have been strong hours ago.'

'Sorry, Mr Bustle. I can't take the risk.'

Alf flushed, his face turning pink. 'You think you're clever, don't you?' He laughed, jabbing a blunt finger at Rhys. 'Go on then, story boy—succeed where I failed.'

'He's cruel, Mr Bustle. Selfish. He'll not come without persuasion.'

'Forget it, son. I don't want your pity.'

'It's not pity. Only, I know things … about Doctor Roberts.'

'Hah! Know things, do you? Well, I know things too. There's a line strung from the back hatch to the saloon doors. You didn't know that, did you? And I've got this,' Alf raised the mate's knife, 'and I'm not afraid to use it.'

'Stop!' Bridie thrust herself between them. 'This isn't helping.'

She saw the determined gleam in Alf's eyes, the pale tension of Rhys's face. Realisation flooded. They were scared. Both of them. Fearing they'd brought their wives to sea to die, knowing the guilt would be on their heads. Two men, one a dreamer, the other solid and reliable, both terrified. But who should fetch Doctor Roberts?

'This thing you know, Rhys, will it bring him … definitely?'

'Without bloodshed?'

'Yes.'

'Then I think you'd better go.' She prised the knife from Alf's fingers. 'It's not going to help Ma, or Siân, if Alf attacks Doctor Roberts.'

CHAPTER 27

*R*hys stood, hands splayed, back pressed to the thin wood of the hospital door. He swayed, giddy. His knees trembled. A cold like black vice squeezed his chest. Dark, so dark, like the inside of a cupboard.

No! This had nothing to do with Tad. He was a man, not a child. No bolt held him captive. No one stood over him, belt in hand. There was only Siân, whose blood stained his fingers. Who'd always believed in him. Who even now might be dying because of him.

He groped for the bench; its cheap, splintery wood felt solid beneath his fingers. He found a bed post, took a halting step— followed by another. Past the single girl's bunks, the long narrow table. He stopped, bent double, gasped for breath. Took two more steps. Had he reached the ladder? He swung round, arms outstretched, a desperate game of blind man's bluff.

Warmer, you're getting warmer. He heard Siân's laughing voice in his head.

His arms quivered as he hoisted himself onto the ladder. For a moment, he feared he'd not have the strength. He closed his eyes, sucked air into his lungs. Found the rung. Was this courage? Not a courage Tad would recognise. But it would serve. And maybe that's all that mattered? Maybe that's all courage was anyway—terror honed to a point.

He fumbled for the mate's knife, forced it up between the hatch planks. The canvas ripped. He hacked at the ropes. One severed, another, a board lifted. He heaved the remaining planks upwards.

A plume of salt water broke over him. Head back, arms flung wide, Rhys let the rain pelt his cheeks.

'Get down! It's not safe.' He heard a bellow.

Not safe! Here? The open deck was a haven to Rhys. But Alf was right. One of the yards had come down; the main deck, a trapeze of splintered wood and cables. Rhys grabbed the line and dragged himself hand over fist through the wreckage. At the saloon doors, a gnarled hand jerked him backwards.

'What're you doing, you mad Welsh bastard?'

'My wife,' Rhys yelled. 'She's bleeding.'

The bosun's mate shook his head. 'You're wasting your time. He'll not come out in this.'

Rhys jerked free and pushed through the saloon doors. He paused, letting the familiar wave of nausea pass, grasped the table and worked his way around, stopping in front of Doctor Roberts' door. He knocked once. Didn't bother waiting for a reply. He lifted the latch, stepped into Doctor Roberts' cabin. Smelled sherry, and the musky scent of Mrs Scarcebrook's perfume.

'Who's that?'

'Me, Rhys Bevan. Light a candle, Doctor Roberts.'

'I can't come out. It's madness. I've told Bustle already.'

'He's not asking. I am.'

'My answer's the same.'

'You don't remember me, do you, Doctor Roberts? Or the pretty young Welsh girl whose abscess you drained. We were warned, you see, by the apothecary's wife. The surgeon wasn't to be trusted. He's a womaniser, she told us, and a gambler.'

'Another of your stories, is it, Welshman?'

'Does your wife know you're here, Doctor Roberts?'

'My wife!' A bark of laughter. 'You'll have to do better than that. She asked me to leave.'

'Light the candle, or I'll be asking the captain to join us.'

'He won't care. The whole ship's falling apart.'

'You had a little girl, if I remember correctly. A babe in your wife's arms. They'd be anxious for news, I'm guessing.'

'You're Welsh, son, from a mining village. Yet for some reason, you don't like steerage. A bit odd, don't you think? Hiding behind the horsebox all day? Sleeping out at night? Then again, maybe it isn't. Some men are cowards.'

So he knew. What did it matter? What did anything matter compared to the enormity of losing Siân?

'I know my weakness, Doctor Roberts. As I know about the credit notes in your strong box. Made out to a Doctor Franklin R Wilson, I believe. The captain may be interested in that small detail, maybe even the immigration agent. A crime, it is, to falsify documents. And to flee creditors. Maybe enough to put you in prison.'

Rhys heard the flint strike. He blinked in the sudden flare of light, saw Doctor Roberts' scowl, Mrs Scarcebrook's deer-wide eyes.

'What do you want from me?'

'I gave you a penny, remember, at the beginning of the voyage? Lest my wife require your services. She's labouring now, Doctor Roberts. She and Mary Bustle need your assistance. Bring Mrs Scarcebrook, seeing as she's in there.'

Rhys watched unsmiling as Doctor Roberts pulled on his coat. Was it wise to include the matron? She looked so ill. Perhaps he should leave her behind. But no, the burden of two birthing women was too great for Annie's shoulders.

Doctor Roberts fastened Mrs Scarcebrook's bonnet, his hands fumbling with the ribbons.

'This isn't Easter. No need to fuss over her bonnet strings.'

Doctor Roberts spun round, his eyes a blaze of hatred. 'You think you're clever, don't you? Blackmailing a ship's surgeon? You'll get away with it now. But not in the long term. So watch your back, miner's brat. I'll make you pay for this, eventually.'

* * *

The first thing Rhys noticed on re-entering the hospital was the fresh ripe smell of vomit, with Mary Bustle up on all fours and heaving her guts onto the floor. Alf squatted alongside, stroking her face with a calloused hand.

'You're doing fine, love. Fine. Look, Doctor Roberts is here now.'

Mary wailed, rocking back and forth. 'It's coming. I tell you the baby's coming. Never mind the bloody surgeon.'

'Now then, Mrs Bustle. I expect a better welcome than that.'

Mrs Scarcebrook sank down onto the stool. Rhys shoved past her and dropped to his knees beside Siân. *Iesu*, she was pale, her face a white mask of pain. And the blood ... Dear God! It was dripping onto the floor.

'Siân? It's me, *cariad*. Can you hear me?'

Siân's head turned at the sound of his voice, her lips moving, soundless.

'Here.' Annie thrust a bucket and sponge into his hand.

Rhys moistened the sponge, lifted Siân's head, drizzled water into the corner of her mouth. Her lips moved again. He leaned close. 'I'm here. Please, *cariad*, speak to me.'

Still no sound.

Over the roar in his head, Rhys heard Mary's wails, Doctor Roberts' snapped queries. Annie's calm, matter of fact replies.

'I've been counting, like you told me. Mrs Bustle's pains aren't far apart. She's been pushing for a while but can't seem to get the baby out. And Siân, well, she's had a fall. As you can see, she's bleeding.'

'Right.' Doctor Roberts clapped his hands. 'Out. Everybody. Out. No, Bustle, I won't have arguments. Your stepdaughter as well. This isn't a family picnic.'

Alf bent, pressing his forehead to Mary's.

'Be strong, love ... trust the surgeon. It's almost over, I promise.'

'Oh, for God's sake, Bustle, leave me to my business.'

Alf rose, his face wooden. For a moment, Rhys thought he would reply. But he only nodded, lips pressed thin, and left the hospital with jerky steps.

'And you, Welshman. Leave the poor girl alone, for Christ's sake. She's enough on her plate without your craven need for comfort. Annie, you too.' He swung round. 'This is no place for a young girl.'

In the doorway, Rhys froze, fingers tight on the latch. This was it, the moment he'd feared—and with Doctor Roberts' recent threats still ringing in his ears.

'Please, Doctor Roberts. You promised.'

'This isn't a schoolroom, Miss Bowles, despite your macabre desire to be present. I might have to intervene. Use a scalpel and forceps.'

'I'm not afraid of blood.'

Doctor Roberts' mouth turned down at the edges. 'Dear God, you ill-favoured girls are all the same. Desperate to hold other women's babies. It won't be pretty, girl, I tell you. No matter what you've heard to the contrary.'

From the corner of his eye, Rhys saw the Annie's chin lift.

'Lancing a boil wasn't pretty, or checking heads for lice. Besides, I might be ill-favoured but you'll need my help with two babies coming.'

CHAPTER 28

$\mathcal{B}$ridie had never seen so much blood, on the bench, the floor, in the deep red soak of Siân's mattress. Away from the hospital, Rhys sat, shoulders hunched, his back to their sodden bunk. Alf slouched on the bench beside him as, all around, steerage took on signs of life.

The carpenter dragged himself away from the splintered yard to relight the lamps. Tom fetched boiling water from the galley. Pam scooped leaves into the teapot and jammed on the lid as if determination alone could improve the situation. Once the tea had steeped, she slid a steaming mug across the table.

'Here, Alf. No. Don't shake your head. I was in labour two days with Lucy and, as you can see, we're both fine.'

She passed a second cup to Rhys. 'You too, love. No point getting upset over a drop of blood.'

Rhys didn't answer. He had his gaze fixed on the hospital door.

'I knew a woman once. She had a fall. Lord, you'd have thought she'd been bled dry. But it wasn't all blood. Only her waters.'

Still, Rhys didn't say anything, though Bridie couldn't help noticing his skin quivered at the mention of blood. That was a good sign, surely? Meant he was listening. She didn't know why that was so important. Only that he looked scooped out, hollow, his back a curl of anguish. She had seen her dad in that posture too many times.

'Here.' Pam pushed the mug right under his nose. 'Keep your strength up.'

Tom took the cup from Pam's hand. 'Give over, love. Can't you see he wants to be left alone?'

'It's not good for anyone to be alone.'

'Well, he ain't alone, technically. He just don't want to be bothered, that's all.'

Pam nodded, blinking back tears, and squeezed Rhys's hand.

At the far end of the deck, Bridie caught a stirring. She swivelled round and saw the hospital door flung wide, Annie in the doorway. By the clasp of her hands, Bridie guessed she was pleading. Though it didn't work. The door slammed in her face. Rhys lurched to his feet and shoved his way along the deck. Bridie watched him beat an urgent tattoo on the hospital door. It didn't open, no matter how hard he pounded. With a final despairing thump, he sank to his knees. Beside her, Bridie heard Annie trying to explain.

'She's fine, Mr Bustle. They got the baby out.'

'And ... is it alive?'

Annie's chin quivered. 'There's something wrong. Doctor Roberts covered the back of its head ... as if there was something dreadful he didn't want me to see. And, well ... there was no crying.'

'Mary? What about Mary?' The question rasped from Alf's throat.

'She'll be all right, I think.'

Got it out? What did Annie mean? Had they lost another baby? Bridie turned to Alf. His face held the worst possible answer. She sat down with a bump. Ma was all right. At least, Annie thought she was all right. But the baby hadn't cried. Which meant it must have died ... before it was born. Another stillborn child.

Bridie's vision blurred. Through a wash of tears, she watched Rhys rise and give a final despairing thump on the hospital door. He stumbled back toward them, then stopped alongside Annie and rested a hand on her shoulder.

'You did your best, Annie *bach*. I couldn't have asked for more.'

Tears slid down Annie's cheeks. Once the mugs had been cleared, she made the weary transition to her bunk. Mr Rolf and the steerage cleaners set to work on the wreck of their quarters. Alf didn't join them. He sat, head in his hands, staring at the table.

Annie woke at six bells and began to sob silently in her bunk. Bridie had never seen anyone so upset. She didn't know why. Anyone could see she wasn't to blame. Pam was clearly of the same mind.

'Come on down, Annie love. I've kept some tea.'

'I t-t-tried to stay.' Annie wrapped her hands around the steaming mug.

'Well, of course you did.'

'B-b-but something was wrong with ... with the baby's head.'

'You're tired,' Pam pulled a grubby hanky from her pocket, 'imagining the worst. But Doctor Roberts is with them now. He's not a good man, Annie. Or a kind one. But he's a qualified surgeon. We can trust him, I think.'

* * *

It was hours. At least it seemed like hours before Doctor Roberts finally emerged. To Bridie's surprise, Ma was bundled up, leaning on his arm. Behind him, Mrs Scarcebrook nursed a swaddled form.

'Mary!' Alf sprang to his feet.

'Mrs Bustle needs rest,' Doctor Roberts interrupted Alf's clumsy joy. 'I'm moving her down to the men's hospital. She's not to be disturbed, on any account. The other girl will stay where she is.'

'She's all right?' Pam's homely brow creased.

Doctor Roberts paused, mouth tight. 'She'll need care.'

That was good news—better than expected. Siân was alive and she was going to need care. Bridie looked round to see how Rhys had taken the news. But he was gone—sprinting along the deck.

'The child?'

'The child is dead.'

Ma's face crumpled at his words. She clutched Doctor Roberts' arm as if her knees would give way. The bundle in Mrs Scarecbrook's arms squirmed; a tiny fist escaped the swaddling. A seal dark head.

Alive! Their baby was alive, moving. Its head perfect. What was Annie thinking?

'And Siân?' Alf asked quietly.

'Will need nursing.'

'She'll be all right though?' Bridie blurted the question. 'She'll get well?'

'I doubt that,' Doctor Roberts said, after a long pause. 'I doubt that very much.'

Annie wasn't the only one sobbing now. Bridie heard a wail, realised it was her own, the sound echoing as the news began to work its way along the deck. Siân dying. Rhys's lovely, gentle fairy wife leaving him. She'd never wanted to die, or given up on life. Yet, here she was dying; amid blood and chaos, on the far side of the world.

CHAPTER 29

*R*hys paused at the hospital door. Eyes closed, hand claw-like on the latch, he tried to gauge the horror within. There were no clues. The cabin lay silent, voiceless. He pushed open the door.

Iesu! He recoiled. Sweet Jesus, she was lifeless as a corpse. 'Siân,' he croaked. 'How is it with you, *cariad*?'

She didn't answer, though for a moment, Rhys fancied he saw her eyelids flicker. He crossed the room. Her fingers cold, so cold—icy as a new fallen snow. He rubbed them, trying to summon their warmth.

'*Sut wyt ti cariad?* Please, Siân, speak to me.'

Nefi, how slender she looked beneath the covers, hardly a bump to the sheets. Slender! Dear God, the baby. Where had it gone? Rhys spun round. Saw the hawse bucket filled with blood. Siân's blood, dripping out of her, slow, measured, like a heart beat. He scanned the tiny cabin, found their baby tucked on the other side of the bed. Still. Cold. Rhys leaned over and lifted the lifeless form. A waxy face stared back at him—perfect the nose, the mouth, the cheeks. But dead. Tears welled as he laid the baby on the bed and began to unwind the sheet.

'Stop!' He heard Doctor Roberts' clipped tones. 'Sometimes we want to know things. But afterwards, we realise it would have been better not to know.'

Rhys paused, but only for moment.

Doctor Roberts sighed, stepping into the cabin. 'If you persist, I must tell you, before you ask, the child didn't suffer—'

'*Arglwydd mawr!*'

Rhys bent, retching onto the deck. A girl, the child was a girl, perfect, apart from the back of her head, which was open at the back—a ruddy gore of tissue bulging out.

The room whirled. Rhys retched again.

A curse? From Siân's birth. Why else would his child be so horribly malformed? No! This was his fault, all of it. He'd kept Siân away from the hospital, allowed her to fall, and now ... He'd killed their tiny, perfect baby daughter.

Doctor Roberts coughed, his manicured hands reaching down for the baby.

'No! Leave her. She's mine.'

'Come now. You can see for yourself the child is dead.'

'I said leave her! I'll wrap her myself.'

Rhys stooped, picked up the baby and kissed her forehead, her eyelids, the tip of her nose. He spread the sheet out on the bed. Placed his daughter at the centre, rewound the swaddling and placed her alongside Siân.

'Right. I will step outside while you say goodbye to your wife. Call me once you're finished. I'll take over from there.'

'I'd not leave a dog in your care, Doctor Wilson.'

'I'd watch my step if I were you, Welshman.'

'No need. You've taken all that I value.'

'I didn't kill her, if that's what you're implying. The girl started to bleed long before you brought her to my attention. A fall, the Bowles girl tells me, though for some reason you didn't seek medical assistance. No prizes for guessing why, are there, Welshman?'

* * *

Rhys didn't know how long he sat there, listening to Siân's slow rattling breath. The bells resumed their half-hourly toll, but he didn't keep track. Once, twice he heard laughter, plates clanking on the table. Mostly he sat numb, silent, with nothing but the slow spat of Siân's blood to mark time's passing. He heard the latch lift, Alf's hesitant tread behind him.

'Rhys, lad. Do you want someone to sit with you?'

Rhys shook his head, tears blurring his vision.

'I'll be outside if you need me.'

Some time later, Pam popped her head around the door. She had Siân's stone in her hand.

'I thought this might help. Tom didn't want me to bother you, but I couldn't sit there doing nothing. Here.' She thrust the stone at him. 'It'll give her strength.'

Rhys nodded as Pam backed out of the cabin. He weighed the stone in his palm, considered dashing it against the cabin wall. No, that would only bring people running. He'd send it to the bottom of the sea later. But not with Siân. She would not be meeting her maker with the evidence of a curse in her hand.

Crist! He'd have to watch her sink to the bottom of the sea, the ship moving, ever moving, even as her body hit the waves. She'd lie alone, unmarked, fish would nibble her face.

'Siân, can you hear me? I should have stood up to Tad. Not made you emigrate. *Duw*, the cost. I'd no idea of the cost. Can you hear me?' He choked on a sob. 'We'll go back home, Siân. I'll find a way to make it happen. Save every penny.' He grasped her hands, rubbed, chafed. 'Please, my lovely girl. Stay with me.'

Rhys heard the ship's bells chime; another round of mess duties. How could that be? How could the commonplace still be happening? Here, now, when his lovely Siân was leaving him? Never again to press her cheek to his, or whisper love words in his ear. No more songs, or laughter. Her silvery voice gone. Forever. Silent.

He kissed her lips, her face, the soft pale place where her hair met the nape of her neck. Her eyelids fluttered. He waited, hardly daring to breathe. Then, like a butterfly's wings, they opened. She was there in the room with him.

'Rhys.'

'I'm here, *cariad*. Don't try to speak. I know you're hurting, all that time in the storm and me too selfish to realise. But I'm here now, holding your hand. Can you feel it, Siân? I'm holding you tight.'

He heard the sloughing of her breath. Saw tight lines of pain about her mouth. Felt a shudder work its way through her body. Her breath caught. Held. Her eyes widened, fixed on something beyond him. Then she was gone—her warmth, her love, her laughter, all gone from him.

Rhys laid his head on her chest and wept.

CHAPTER 30

'*I*'ll not have her buried in English!'

Alf pushed open the hospital door, saw Rhys's swaying body blocking Doctor Roberts' path.

'You don't have a choice. Reverend Cummings doesn't speak your tongue.'

'I'll bury her then, read the service myself.'

'That is clearly ridiculous.'

Rhys trembled, though with fatigue or fury, Alf couldn't tell. There was a fragility about him that was new and alarming.

'I have said it once and I will say it again. We must commit your wife and child to the deep.'

'I am not disputing the need for a committal, Doctor Roberts. Only its manner and timing.'

'It doesn't matter, man. None of it. Your wife is dead.'

Alf winced at the malice in Doctor Roberts' voice. There was an undercurrent to this conversation he didn't understand—something dark and savage. What had Rhys said? *I know things about Doctor Roberts.* Alf had no idea what those things were. He had no desire to find out. But even a fool could see Doctor Roberts resented the knowledge.

Alf glanced from Doctor Roberts' hate chiselled face to Rhys's wild, darting eyes. The Welsh lad looked dangerously close to coming unhinged. And who could blame him? He'd lost his wife and child within days of reaching their destination. Alf couldn't begin to imagine the despair he was facing.

'Tell him, Bustle. Tell him his wife and child must be buried.'

'Rhys, son, we have to go through with this.'

'Not now, Mr Bustle. And not in English. The last sound she hears must be Welsh.'

'But … can you not see? Reverence Cummings doesn't speak your tongue.'

Rhys shivered, pressing a hand to his face. 'I've done so much harm, Mr Bustle. So much harm … and this is the last thing I can do for her. These burial customs are important to me.'

'A funeral is for the living, Welshman. Not the dead.'

Rhys spun round, his eyes a blaze of hate. 'I am the living, Doctor Roberts. My wife and child are dead.'

That was the crux of the matter. Rhys had lost everything, his wife, his child, his very reason for emigrating, and the manner of their committal was significant to him. So significant, if Rhys's pale face, crazed eyes, and twitching limbs were any indication, the Welsh lad stood in danger of losing his wits.

Alf glanced at Doctor Roberts, surprised at how loathsome he now appeared. To think he'd spent the entire voyage trying to impress this man, only to find it wasn't worth the effort. It never had been. For some reason, the knowledge steeled him.

'I know it's a strange request. But I think, perhaps, we should let him read the burial service.'

'Bustle! Have you taken leave of your senses? He can't bury his own wife and child.'

'Not on his own. In cooperation with Reverend Cummings.'

'It's ridiculous. I won't allow it.'

Alf shuffled, looking down at his feet. 'I think … if you don't mind me saying so, Doctor Roberts. This is a matter of respect.'

'Respect? To override the responsibilities of an ordained man?'

'Not for Reverend Cummings.' Alf spoke slowly as if to a dim-witted child. 'Respect for Rhys and his dead.'

'Good God,' Doctor Roberts spluttered. 'Have you forgotten yourself? All you stand to gain in the colony? It won't look good to have sided with a troublemaker, Bustle.'

'I'm sorry to hear that, sir.'

'Sorry! Is that all you have to say? After all I've done for you?'

'You left my wife without assistance.'

'Ah, so that's what all this is about. Spite. Because I failed to single you out. Poor old Bustle, thought he was the surgeon's favourite. No one will attend. You know that, don't you? Not to some burial service in a God forsaken language.'

'I disagree.'

'Oh, disagree, do you? Since when did you learn to think? Not under my tutelage. I hired a cleaner, not an esteemed adviser. Someone who would pay me respect and carry out my wishes. I thought you were the man, seriously, Bustle. Considered backing you in the colony.'

'I've supported you, sir, to the best of my abilities, and carried out your wishes.'

'But you don't respect me, is that what you're saying?'

'Respect must be earned, Doctor Roberts.'

'And if Reverend Cummings doesn't agree? Have you *thought* about that, Bustle?'

'Reverend Cummings is a kindly man. He knows Rhys and Siân from the deck school. He saw them helping my daughter, advised me to take comfort in the friendship. I didn't. I regret that now.'

'Oh, please! Spare me the confessions.'

'Reverend Cummings may still be feeling bilious,' Alf pressed on, undaunted. 'Which means we don't have to act immediately. But once his stomach settles, perhaps we could ask him to join us?' He turned to Rhys. 'Reverend Cummings may not like it, son. But I think he'll give you a fair hearing. Then, we'll help you send Siân off properly. You have my word on that score.'

CHAPTER 31

*B*ridie had no idea what was happening in the hospital. Only that Siân was gone. Dead. Through a judder of sobs, she heard raised voices from within the hospital. Saw the door fly open, a tight-lipped Doctor Roberts stalk along the deck. He didn't return. Hours later, Reverend Cummings appeared. There was no shouting after he entered the hospital. Only a murmur of voices to interrupt their hushed supper preparations, the occasional rasp of Rhys's anguish.

After supper, the carpenter climbed down the ladder with the burial board. He didn't turn down the lamps as he had every other evening. He helped lift Siân and the baby's bodies onto the board. They were sewn into a white shroud. The bier was lifted shoulder high. Rhys and a group of men began to walk the bodies along the deck, their pace solemn, measured, as all steerage rose for their passing.

Bridie hadn't seen Rhys since Siân's death. The first word that sprang to mind was haunted, followed by smudge-eyed and hollow-cheeked. He was determined not to let Siân down, Bridie saw that too—in the rigid set of his jaw, the taut, upright lines of his body, step after determined step as he walked her along the deck. All through the night, he walked in that strange, silent procession. Up one side of the deck, down the other, neither resting by turns, nor taking a break, as the other men did. His rhythmic tread was punctuated only by the high, keening wails of the Scots and the Irish.

* * *

Morning dawned grey and bleak, the very elements suffused with grief. Breakfast was served at the usual time but Bridie couldn't eat. She sat in bleary-eyed silence, her throat raw from a night of endless sobbing. Siân, gone. Even now she couldn't believe it. Her melodic voice forever silent. Never again to touch a hand to Bridie's cheek. Or call out from the base of the main mast, eyes ashine. Yet it must be true. For there was Rhys, walking her body along the deck.

'It's to keep her company,' Alf broke the gloomy silence, 'and to chase away evil. That's why the men walk. Women don't usually attend burials in Wales. Rhys is making an exception on this occasion.'

'As if we'd let her go without a farewell.' Pam gave an indignant toss of her head.

'You'd have had to, Pam, if he'd forbidden it.'

'No, Tom, I wouldn't.'

Bridie agreed with Pam. It would have been impossible to stay away from the burial service. Only a thin layer of wood separated steerage from the main deck. No doubt, Rhys had reached the same conclusion. Though, this morning, with his gaunt face and haunted eyes, he didn't look capable of reason.

At eight bells, Reverend Cummings climbed down the ladder. After a short prayer, he managed to prise Rhys's hands from the bier. Alf stood at the back hatch with a dish of salt to ward against further evil. After taking a pinch, Rhys and Reverend Cummings climbed the ladder. One by one, the line of mourners followed them, jostling into a horseshoe formation on the main deck.

Siân's bier passed up through the hatchway.

Rhys stepped forward, his slender body swaying in the buffeting wind. With trembling hands, he took the prayer book from Reverend Cummings. He opened it to the marked page and nodded. A hush fell on the assembled crowd.

'*Dysg i ni felly gyfrif ein dyddiau fel y dygom ein calon i ddoethineb.*'

'So teach us to number our days that we may apply our hearts unto wisdom,' Reverend Cummings translated.

'*Dychwelyd, Arglwydd, pa hŷd? ac edifarhâ o ran dy weision. Diwalla ni yn fore â'th drugaredd; fel y gorfoleddom ac y llaweny- chom dros ein holl ddyddiau.*'

'Turn thee again, O Lord, at the last and be gracious unto thy servant. O satisfy us early with thy mercy. So shall we rejoice and be glad all the days of our days.'

Rhys stood rigid in his determination. Though anyone could see he faced a mountain of grief and, after a long night between decks, the effort of reading the burial service was costing him.

Not long now. Bridie closed her eyes, lending him strength. Once they'd said the words of the committal, Rhys's torture would end. It would be dreadful, of course, and final. She'd seen it often enough during the typhus epidemic to know how final. It would also bring release.

'*Gan hynny yr ŷm ni rhoddi ei chorff hi i'r dyfnder, i'w droi i lygredigaeth,*' Rhys continued. '*Gan ddisgwyl am atgyfodiad y corff, pan roddai'r môr ei feirw i fynu.*'

'We therefore commit this body to the deep, to be turned into corruption. Looking for the resurrection of the body, when the sea shall give up its dead.'

Hang on. Something was wrong. Those were the words of the committal, but the bier wasn't lifting. Rhys fumbled, passing the prayer book back to Reverend Cummings. The clergyman placed a hand on his arm. Rhys shook it off. Oh, God, no. A murmur rip- pled through the crowd.

Rhys was going to sing.

He closed his eyes, gathering strength, as Bridie had seen him do so many times. Jaw clenched, his throat corded with emotion. But as he raised his arms, an energy seemed to pulse through him.

'*Unwaith carais i forwyn lledrith,*'

Once I loved a fairy maiden,
Ar hyd y nos,
All through the night,
Gwallt hir tywyll, sgidiau flamgoch,
Long dark tresses, sandals scarlet,
Ar hyd y nos.
All through the night.'

The fairy woman's story, set to the haunting strains of '*Ar Hyd y Nos*'. Siân's favourite. A natural choice. Though not easy words to sing. Bridie didn't understand the Welsh but her mind produced the English lyrics Rhys had taught the choir.

'*Ger y llyn ei cherais hi,*
On the lake shore I did woo her,
A'i charu hi yn wir addawais,
Promised e'r to love her truly,
Yn ofalus o'r telerau tad,
Mindful of her father's promise,
Ar hyd y nos.
All through the night.'

It was a lovely gesture, bold and extravagant, so typical of Rhys. It was also a punishment. As if he somehow blamed himself for Siân's death. Maybe he did. Maybe that was why he'd chosen the fairy woman's song.

The wind gusted, bringing a fresh spray of rain. The deck heaved beneath Bridie's feet. On and on, Rhys sang, through the excruciating lines of the next verse. Men wept openly now. Women clung to each other, sobbing. The Irish women had resumed their high-pitched, keening wail.

'*Trwy'r blynyddoedd fi'n esgeulus,*
O'er the years did I grow careless,
Ar hyd y nos,
All through the night,
Tan cyrhaeddon mawr ergydion,
'Til the blows had reached their zenith,

Ar hyd y nos,
　All through the night.'
It was a torment—nothing like Rhys's lovely tenor voice. His white lips forced the words out with the concentration of a habitual stutterer. His voice began to falter. Bridie saw Alf's wince of pity, Reverend Cummings' eyes soft with sympathy. Heard Annie's long, thin wail of grief. Bridie clung to the older girl, her chest heaving.
　'*Ohonof aeth ei hud bŵerau,*
　　Gone from me her fairy powers,
　Plymiodd hi o ddan y dyfroedd,
　　Plunging down beneath the waters,
　Nawr rwyn crwydro'r bryniau unig,
　　Now, I roam these lonely mountains,
　Ar hyd y nos.
　　All through the night.'
At the end of the second verse, the men began to lift the bier. Reverend Cummings edged close, a hand beneath Rhys's elbow, girdering. It didn't help. Tears coursed Rhys's cheeks. He'd come so far, but he wasn't going any further. The will, the courage, the strength, were all leaving him. The men tipping the bier halted, faces uncertain. Tom Griggs stepped forward. His work-roughened hand grasped Rhys's shoulder.
　'Enough, Welshman. I'll take it from here.'
Eyes closed, Rhys shook his head. Bridie feared he might try to continue. But as Tom's deep, bass voice rang out, Rhys's shoulders slumped. He pressed trembling hands to his face.
　'*One day soon she'll come to find me,*
　All through the night.
　Offering her healing powers,
　All through the night.
　Bound in leather, filled with longing,
　Then will I find peace and courage,
　'Til at length I forfeit sorrow,
　All through the night.'

CHAPTER 32

ridie couldn't find Rhys after the funeral. He'd probably ducked behind the horse box. If so, he wouldn't want to be disturbed. The bleak windy conditions drove everyone else between decks. As they sat in gloomy silence waiting for the dinner bell to ring, Ma emerged from the hospital.

'Ma! What are you doing up? Doctor Roberts said you were to rest.'

'I won't stay long. I only came out to pay my respects.'

'Rhys isn't here.' Bridie patted the bench. 'Sit down. You shouldn't be on your feet.'

'My feet are fine. But your concern is appreciated. You'll be wanting to see your brother, I expect?'

The baby? Did she want to see the baby? How could she possibly with Siân so recently dead? How could she ever take pleasure in anything ever again?

Ma held out the tiny swaddled form. 'Careful, now. Mind you support his head.'

Pam patted the bench, sliding a mug across as Ma handed the baby to Bridie. Arms wooden, her back mast-straight, Bridie nudged the shawl from the baby's face. A pair of dark, barely focused eyes stared back at her. A face so tiny and perfect, from its porcelain fine skin, to its delicately sculptured nose and pursed pink lips.

'He's handsome.' Pam looked on admiringly.

Pam was itching to have a hold. Strangely, Bridie had no desire to hand the baby over. She hugged him close, marvelling at his sweet, warm, newborn baby scent.

'Does he look like Bridie?' Pam asked.

Ma jerked, as if caught off-guard, her tea sloshing onto the table. 'Well, yes, of course. In the … well, the shape of his forehead.'

Interesting. Bridie eased the shawl back further, touching a finger to the baby's forehead. He arched his back, a tiny wishbone-thin arm escaping. His shock of downy black hair brought a smile to Bridie's lips.

'He's lovely, Ma. Like a little pixie. Did I have this much hair when I was born?'

'No. Yours was thinner.'

'And curly?'

'Course it was curly.' Ma's brow knit with annoyance. 'It's curly now, isn't it?'

'I might have changed.'

'Oh, for goodness sake. You've seen babies before. Use your common sense.'

Fortunately, at that moment, Pam intervened. 'Leave it now, Bridie. Your ma's tired.' She whipped the baby from Bridie's arms and thrust him at Alf. 'Here, proud father. Have a hold.'

Alf's hands closed around the baby, his face pinking with pleasure as a miniature finger curled around his thumb. He'd worked so hard to make the funeral a success, his joy at being a father overshadowed by a genuine concern for Rhys. He deserved a chance to revel in the baby's possessive gesture.

Pam leaned forward, clucking like a mother hen. 'You must be proud. Have you thought of a name yet?'

'Alfred or John,' Ma answered on Alf's behalf.

'Alfred's nice. Who is John for then?'

'Oh, John was my father. But Alf isn't keen. He wants to give the baby a foreign name.'

Well, whoever would have imagined? Bridie stared openmouthed at Alf. He looked the same—big blunt hands, round earnest face but … a foreign name? Where would he have got such a novel idea?

She wasn't the only one surprised. Head to one side, Pam's nose wrinkled.

'Would a foreign name go with Bustle, do you think?'

At this point, Alf took a strong interest in the baby. Head lowered, he stroked the tiny curled fist, the back of his neck turning a ruddy pink. Bridie wasn't the only one to notice his sudden discomfort. From across the table, Tom Griggs crowed his delight.

'Come on, spill the beans. Is it Pierre? Jose? Or Alfonso?'

'Nothing that foolish.'

'A Welsh name,' Ma blurted out. 'He wants to give the baby a Welsh name. Have you ever heard of anything so ridiculous?'

For a big man, Alf looked suddenly very small. Head bowed, shoulders hunched, shame burned the space between his hairline and kerchief.

Tom recovered first. He nodded, approving. 'Not bad, Alf. Quite considerate really.'

'Yes, well, it's only an idea, and, as Mary said, probably ridiculous.'

'No!' A curious warmth flooded Bridie's chest. Alf was a good man, big, dull, boring and definitely annoying, but kind, and always good. Rhys had tried to tell her that day on the main deck. She'd refused to listen. But now, for the first time, she saw it clearly. 'We don't have to give the baby a Welsh proper name, though do we?'

'See!' Ma turned to Alf, triumphant. 'Even Bridie agrees with me.'

'No, Ma. I don't agree. It's a kindness and, I think, Rhys will appreciate the gesture.' She stopped, heat flushing her cheeks. 'But ... I think, perhaps, we should call the baby Alfred, officially, you know ... because of who his father is. But he could have a Welsh pet name—that would honour Siân's memory.'

Alf coughed, clearing his throat. 'That's kind of you, lass. Is there a name you had in mind?'

Bridie paused, chewing her lip. 'We don't have to decide straight away. But Dylan is a name from a legend. It means Son of the Sea.'

'Dylan ain't bad.' Tom chuckled. 'And it's darn easier to say than Llewelyn or Gruffydd.'

'Alfred John Dylan.' Ma swallowed, blinking back tears. 'It's been awful, Alf. Truly. I'd hoped, in time, to forget.'

'I don't think we can, love. But I hope, one day, to remember with less pain than this.'

* * *

'More tea?' Pam's sensible voice broke the silence.

'No, thanks. I'd best be getting back to the hospital. This young man will need a feed soon.'

Alf rose. 'I'll come with you, love.'

'Tom. Pam.' Ma nodded to each one in turn. 'Give my regards to Rhys. Tell him I'm sorry for … well, sorry about everything.'

'Where is Rhys, anyway?' Tom rose, scanning the deck.

Alf pointed. 'Last I saw, he was down with the single men. But look, here's Harvey Rolf. Why don't you ask him?'

'Morning all.' Mr Rolf gave a broad, good-natured smile. 'So this is the latest addition.' He leaned over, peering. 'Lord, he's puny, isn't he?'

'No.' Ma bristled. 'He's a good size.'

'Well, of course, he is. No offence, Mrs Bustle. Only, it's funny to think of starting out so small.' He paused, as if searching for words. 'Not him, I mean, me.'

Bridie eyed Mr Rolf's solid, tree trunk form. It was hard to imagine him as anything other than substantial, let alone swathed in lacy shawls.

He beamed round at them, his face radiating good intent. 'What is it you're wanting to ask me, Alf?'

'Only wondering where Rhys might be.'

'Down our end.' Mr Rolf jerked his head. 'Funny you should ask. I've come to get his things.'

'His things.' Alf blinked. 'Whatever do you mean?'

'He's being moved, isn't he? Down with the single men.'

'But ... we're almost in Port Phillip!'

Mr Rolf shook his head. 'Odd, I know. It's Doctor Roberts' orders. As you know, Alf, he's a hard man to cross and, just between you and me, he doesn't seem to like Rhys.'

'Even so, he must have given you a reason.'

'Well now, let me think. "Damn Welshman ... sneaking about the ship ... can't have him near Miss Bowles." I think that pretty much sums it up.'

'Annie?' Alf's brows rose. 'What's she got to do with this?'

Mr Rolf shrugged. 'He's not married anymore, is he?'

Alf shook his head. Bridie wasn't surprised. How could anyone be so dense? To move someone's belongings without asking their permission! Maybe Mr Rolf did indeed have nothing but sawdust between his ears. Though Alf had grasped the awfulness of the situation.

'I suggest you go back and speak to him then, Harvey. Tell him if he wants to move berths, he can collect his own belongings.'

'Well, now.' Mr Rolf ducked his head. 'I won't argue with you, on principle, Alf. It's Rhys's business to organise his luggage but—'

'But what?'

'Well ... he can't, can he?'

Alf's eyes narrowed. 'Why ever not?'

Mr Rolf shrugged. 'I'd hoped not to mention it with the ladies present. But, well, seeing as you're insistent. I don't mind admitting, he's ... legless.'

'Legless?'

'Blind. Drunk. Snookered. Whatever you want to call it.'

'Rhys? Drunk! I don't believe it.'

'I'm not joking, Alf. Some of the single men pooled their wine rations, you know, thinking he might want to drown his sorrows. Seems they were right.' Mr Rolf gestured along the deck. 'He can't even stand at the moment.'

Bridie rose, her heart punching like a fist. Steerage was gloomy, as always. Packed with bodies. All along the table, steaming mugs and teapots fogged up the moist, dank atmosphere. Beyond them, she could just make out Rhys's limp form. Suddenly, she wanted to run, to scream, to lash out and hit. To do anything other than watch Rhys being heaved bodily onto the bed.

'But ... Rhys hasn't shown any tendency for drunkenness.'

'These handsome dreamers are all the same.' Ma's voice clotted with spite. 'Too weak and fanciful for their own good.'

'Come now. He's lost a wife and child. Don't be too hard on him.'

Too hard!

Memories clutched at Bridie's throat. She remembered her dad's stumbling gait on the stairs, the whisky on his breath, Ma's nagging, his drunken-all-day shape on the bed. Now it was happening again, to Rhys, her friend with soft dark eyes, who'd tried to rescue a fairy. Who'd shared his secrets and taught her people were complex. Who'd understood the importance of her stories. That same, musical, magical Rhys, was now drunk, as her dad had been so many times.

CHAPTER 33

*R*hys was drowning his sorrows, only once. It wouldn't happen again, Bridie told herself as she lay awake in her bunk that night. He'd shown no tendency for drunkenness. Alf had said so and, for the second time in her life, Bridie agreed with him. She'd wake tomorrow and find everything back to normal.

Well, as normal as it could be with Siân dead.

Then why did the words *too fanciful for their own good* coil like a snake in her head?

Bridie didn't see Rhys the next morning, or during the long drizzling afternoon that followed. She presumed he was sitting behind the horse box, which was a good sign, surely? Seeking space and privacy to settle his thoughts? But when she peered along the deck later that evening and saw a row of mugs lined up in front of him, she knew he was drowning his sorrows again.

Was Ma right? Did all handsome dreamers lack spine? Were they all destined to struggle and give up on life? Siân hadn't thought so; she'd seen beyond Rhys's fear to the love and courage that had motivated him to emigrate. But what about now, when Siân was gone? Who would pull Rhys back from the brink?

When he didn't climb down the ladder for dinner the following noon, Bridie slipped a ship's biscuit into her pinafore pocket. He needed someone to look after him and feed him, as Siân would have done. Someone who knew of his guilt and fear and all he hoped to achieve from the voyage to tell him drowning his sorrows was not the solution.

At the narrow entrance between the longboats, Bridie paused, her heart banging like a drum in her chest. She heard dogs whine, their chains dragging against the kennel, the rhythmic grate of the carpenter's saw further along the deck. But no sound from Rhys.

She crawled into the narrow space.

Eyes tight, face buried in the crook of his arm, Rhys's body shuddered as if caught in the grip of an inner scream. The moment was so intense, so private, she gasped, jerking backwards. Her shoulder hit the longboat. Dogs yapped, a cacophony of clucking hens. Rhys's head rose. His eyes so dead and dull, they might have belonged to someone else.

Bridie froze, staring at him open-mouthed. A biscuit? Why on earth would he need a biscuit? How could he possibly eat when he was being torn apart from within?

'Sorry. I didn't mean to pry. I'm here, if you need to talk. I wanted you to know, in case you'd forgotten.'

Silence. His gaze blank, uncomprehending. Did he even know who she was?

'Rhys? Can you hear me?'

'Yes.' One word, dry, husky, as if dragged from his throat.

She swallowed, the biscuit crumbling in her hand. 'I'll wait, shall I? Until you're ready?'

'Yes, please. I've no desire for company.'

* * *

Huddled at the base of the main mast, Bridie trained her eyes on the longboats, lest Rhys change his mind and come looking for her. She heard the heave and chant of the sailors lifting the newly repaired yard arm into place, watched the ship's officers squinting up at the leaden sky. But no matter how they adjusted their sextant and quadrant, the noonday sun would not grace them with its presence. At night, when grey gave way to a starless black, Bridie saw another round of drinks lined up in front of Rhys.

She ached to hold baby Dylan, to feel his soft warm skin against hers, to marvel at his sweet newborn baby scent. To remind herself that one good thing had come out of the voyage. But Doctor Roberts said Ma needed rest. Only Alf was allowed to visit her in the hospital. Alf was kind. Bridie could admit that now. He brought Dylan out to her more than once. But each time Bridie took him in her arms, tears slid down her cheeks. What kind of world awaited her baby brother? A world in which dreams and wishes and fairy tales were nonsense, where only the strong had a chance of survival. What if this baby wasn't one of them? What if, one by one, all the people she loved were taken?

* * *

At twilight, four days after the funeral, *Lady Sophia* finally approached the entrance to Port Phillip Bay. It was too dark to enter at dusk. Strong tides guarded the entrance, shoals to navigate in a treacherous stretch of water called 'The Rip'. Despite this, people crowded the bulwarks, hoping for signs of life on the foreign shore. Bridie stood apart, listening to the whispers of the jostling crowd.

'Wait! What was that? Movement! Was that movement?'

Yes, there it was, she saw it too—sparks, followed by more sparks, a flame widening, lengthening, licking the dark. All around her, people gasped and pointed. Bridie stood in silence, her eyes fixed on the shore. She felt too numb for wonder, too numb for anything.

'It's a signal,' Alf said, stepping alongside. 'Showing us where to heave-to for the night.'

'How do they know we're here?'

'There's a pilot station with a lookout inside the heads. It's manned around the clock.'

Bridie nodded, fixing her eyes on the shore. She saw figures moving about on the beach—one, two, maybe three shadow puppets against a bright, backdrop of fire. Others had seen them too. They laughed, standing on tiptoes, pointing. One of the shadow men took a branch from the fire and waved it above his head.

'Ahoy!' The sound came drifting out across water.

Bridie shivered, pulling her shawl tight. Like a hearth fire banked up for the night, or a candle left on the windowsill for weary travellers, the beacon on the beach would have been perfect, if not for losing Siân. The sheer hopelessness of her friend's death washed over her anew. There was no blaze strong enough to heat the chill at her core. Her friend was gone. Dead. Taking her kindness and her magic, her fierce love for Rhys. Yet as Bridie stood beside Alf in the stiff evening breeze, she knew it wasn't Siân's absence so much as Rhys's withdrawal that was making her heart freeze.

* * *

Bridie didn't know how long she stood on the windy main deck. Only that tired and chilled others drifted below. She didn't follow, preferring the wind and waves to the close dark warmth of steerage. What was it about the sea that called to her tonight? The choppy uncertainty of Bass Strait, or the wild entrance they called The Rip? Maybe the human hand of fire reaching out to them in the dark? Whatever the reason, Alf stayed alongside, like a rock in the ocean, sharing her grief.

'It's a difficult time,' he said, breaking the silence. 'I won't pretend to know how you feel. But … he'll be all right. Rhys, I mean.'

Bridie nodded, sorrow clogging her throat. She didn't want to talk to Alf, even if he was kind. He had no way to make things better, nothing beyond the bleak lessons Siân's death had taught her.

Alf shuffled, looking down at his feet. 'I know you set a great store by Siân.'

'She was beautiful, like a fairy.'

'Yes, she was.'

And then, because she wasn't sure, not really, and she did so want to be, she turned slowly to face him. 'Do you really think so? About Rhys?'

'Yes, I do.'

'You don't think …?' She stopped, swallowed, the ache in her throat pulling her eyes tight. 'You aren't worried about, you know, about the drinking?'

'I'm surprised. I won't lie to you. But I think he'll pull clear.'

'What if it's, you know … like Ma said, because he's a dreamer?'

'The truth is, I don't know what will happen to Rhys. Neither does your ma. But he's young, healthy. He can make a fresh start.'

'I don't suppose he wants to.' The knowledge stabbed Bridie anew. 'He only emigrated because of Siân and the baby.'

'Yes. It's a crushing blow.'

'What if it's too much for him? What if he doesn't cope? He'll be alone. In a strange land. With no one to talk to. Or tell him stories. No one to even nag him like Ma did my dad.' She stopped, swiped at her eyes. Saw the awkward heft of Alf's shoulder, the nervous swallow of his throat.

Maybe it was too much for him, despite his kindness. Maybe she'd been right about Alf all along. Maybe he was stupid—and here was no one in the whole world who could answer her questions.

'Your ma loved your dad, Bridie.'

'Really! And he loved her too, I suppose?'

'Yes, I think he did.'

'He picked a funny way of showing it then, didn't he? Letting us go cold and hungry, watching Ma pawn our belongings. He might have taken a job, any job, if only to ease our suffering. But he didn't. Not once. Not even for me.'

'Things weren't always that bad, lass.'

'Yes, well, thanks to you and Ma, that's how I remember them.'

'Your dad was a handsome man. Clever too. When I first met your ma, I thought her the happiest girl in the world. She waited up for him every night. Did you know that? No matter how late he came home from the theatre, I heard her tripping down the stairs.'

'Well, it didn't end that way, did it? I was there too, remember? I heard their arguments. Saw everything *you* did for Ma. Before, and after my dad died.'

'No, lass, you've got it wrong.'

'I haven't, Alf. Admit it! You and your boxes of market greens.'

'I was there, Bridie. I'll admit that much. But … you have to understand. Your ma and Archie were beautiful. Happy. Not unlike Rhys and Siân. When things went wrong, I only wanted to help. I never courted your ma's affection. Or imagined she would see me differently. I'm too big, dull and stupid remember?'

'Well, she did see you differently, didn't she? Despite your ever-so-good intentions. That's why she gave up on him.'

'No, lass. They both gave up.'

'Ma gave up first.'

'There are no easy black and white answers, Bridie, despite your ma's claims. Or neat fairy tale endings. Life is messy and uncertain. That's why we feared for you, tried to curb your fancies. Maybe we got that wrong. But I do know one thing: your dad loved you, and your ma, and, I think, in his own strange way, he thought he was doing the best for you that Christmas night.'

'His best! To go out and kill himself!'

'He was dying, lass. You know that, don't you? He'd been coughing up blood for years. Maybe it was losing the babies early on. Or the thought of leaving you and your ma alone, without support. Maybe it was, as you say, partly my fault. The truth is, no one knows why Archie Stewart gave up on life. Only that somewhere, at some point, something inside him broke and no one, not you, not him, nor even your ma, was able to fix it.'

'But … he could have tried harder.'

'He did try, Bridie.'

'Truly? As hard as he could?' She looked up, searching his earnest face. 'You're not lying, just to make me feel better?'

'I would never lie to you, Bridie.'

She shivered, fury draining out of her like the blood from a beast. He was dying. Her dad was dying. Why hadn't she seen this before? It made him sad. So sad, he'd given up on life. But before he gave up, in the beginning, when he'd first got sick, he'd tried hard, as hard as he could, because he loved her. Even after he'd given up, even if he had laid down in the icy street, he'd still loved her. She turned, eyes blind, felt the solid wrap of Alf's arms, his big, clumsy hand patting her back.

'That's it, lass. Have a good cry.'

Which was awkward, and soppy, and made her cry even harder. For Rhys and the road before him, for Siân, who'd lived under a curse, for Ma, who'd once been happy, and for Alf—yes, even poor old Alf, who'd never meant to spoil things. But mostly she cried for her dad, whose best wasn't good enough. Knowing there were no easy answers, only love and people who were complex, while Alf held her fast above the treacherous waters of Bass Strait.

* * *

She stood for an age in Alf's arms, her tears wetting his shirt and the moon laying its silvery tracks across the water, aware of his solid warmth, the chill of the night beyond her. Eventually, she sniffed, dabbing her eyes with a hanky.

'Sorry. Your shirt's soaked.'

'Never mind, I've got a spare one between decks.'

She stepped back, eyeing him sideways, unsure how to walk in this new, uncharted territory. 'I never wanted to be friends.'

'I gathered that, Bridie.'

She shrugged. 'I'm not sure how to begin, if I'm honest.'

'The truth is a good place to start.'

'Of course, Alf-the-honest. Well, I like that about you and … let's face it,' she pulled a wry face, 'I've got no one else.'

'Rhys is still your friend, lass.'

'No. Friends talk to each other.'

'He's lost, Bridie, heart sore. Give him a chance.'

'A chance.' Head to one side, she smiled up at him. 'Funny, he said that about you, once.'

'And ... what did you do?'

'I ignored him.'

'Then don't ignore him again, lass.'

CHAPTER 34

Supper was finished by the time Bridie and Alf clambered down the ladder into steerage. All along the deck, people cleared mugs from the tables and stowed cards, maps, and letter books for the night. Bridie joined the privy queue, only tiptoeing back to her bunk as the carpenter turned down the lamps. She loosed her bodice, slipped out of her skirts, and slid into bed beside Annie.

But her thoughts wouldn't stop churning. Her crackling mattress joined the chorus of after-dark snoring. She heard the watch change on the deck above, the half-hourly bells tolling midnight. She sat up, fumbled for her notebook, and lay back down again, hugging it to her chest.

Fancy Alf understanding about her dad. He was right. She had to talk to Rhys. After all they'd been through, they couldn't part in silence. But where to begin? And without Siân's help? The Welsh girl had been their link, reaching out to her even when Rhys didn't have the strength. Now she'd have to forge her own connection and, with Rhys so sad and distant, she didn't how to approach him.

With your notebook—and stories. The answer came in Siân's tinkling fairy voice.

Stories? Of course! Bridie sat up, gathered her writing materials, and wriggled along the bed. The carpenter always left a lamp burning over the hatchway. Dimmed, so as not to disturb people's rest, but bright enough for her purposes. She tiptoed along the deck, found a hazy circle of light, and slid onto the bench.

She opened her notebook, eyes snagging on her dad's message. *When night is dark and the wind blows hard and shadows overwhelm you—there are always stories. Write them down and think of me and how I have ever loved you.*

Was it true? Had stories helped him right to the end? Or were they like love against typhus? Something that helped, sometimes, but not always, with life so big and complex that people died, no matter how much they wanted to stay alive? Bridie couldn't answer those questions. At least, not in any way she could have explained. But as she leafed the notebook's pages and saw story after carefully penned story, the words *how I have ever loved you* ran like a refrain in her head. Beneath it, ever so faintly, she fancied she heard the echo of her dad's Scottish bur again.

There were five blank pages at the end of the notebook, enough for one final story. But ... where to begin? With Rhys? Or Siân?

Rhys had come first, that evening on the Thames.

Once upon a time, she wrote, *in the gathering dusk on an emigrant vessel.*

She stopped, chewed her pencil. Once upon a time—could she write that even though this wasn't a fairy tale? Yes, why not? The evening had been magical. Her friendship with Rhys and Siân had been magical. She blinked, pressing her lips together. She mustn't cry. She had to think clearly. No time for rough copies, or second drafts. She must write freely, as the words came into her head.

She started with 'Ar Hyd y Nos'. Remembering how she'd seen a struggle in the lines of Rhys's body that went beyond the music, though she hadn't understood it at the time. Had told him about the lament for a fairy who was dying and found herself not waiting to appear foolish before him. How she needn't have worried because he'd understood—about everything. How kind Siân had been during the seasickness, how she'd longed for their friendship, longed for it so much that she'd pretended to tie her bootlaces in front of them. Not understanding their troubles, or how they might be able to help her. Until Rhys had stood up for her and told the story of Taliesin.

She'd known then that he valued her friendship. It had given her the courage to crawl behind the horsebox and find him. She wrote about the web of lies and half-truths she'd told him. How even, despite them, he seemed to be able to read her mind. The way she'd treasured their moments together. How shocked she'd been at the Dic Penderyn story. How it had altered the weave of her memories, altered them so much that she'd lost the courage to trust him. How she'd carried her burdens all through the horrors of the typhus epidemic, only to find he and Siân also harboured secrets.

She wrote about how he'd tried to help her with Alf, the magic they'd woven between them. How, even then, she couldn't find the courage to trust him. Though, she almost did, early Christmas morning, until the storm came and ripped her chance away. About how much she'd loved Siân, thought her the most beautiful girl in the world, with Rhys the handsome prince who'd tried to rescue her. How much she'd wanted him to succeed. How, even now, she wanted to help him, despite the shock of his drunkenness. How frightened she was for his future. How icy the world felt without him, until Alf had encouraged her to speak, though she couldn't think how to begin, apart from writing this story—the story of their friendship. Which she wasn't even sure he would welcome. Though she had to try because she loved him, more than anyone else in the world.

Bridie stopped, shocked. What had she written? She scanned the page. The words *love* swam before her eyes, followed *more than anyone else in the world*. Truly? Had she written that? She shivered, glancing about. Whatever did it mean?

She loved Rhys. Of course, she did. She'd loved Siân too. Though she'd never dreamed the two loves might be different. They were. She saw that now, completely different. She'd never made eyes at Rhys. Or thought about him like … well, like Hilary and Eunice and the other single girls. But from that first night in Deptford, his words, his voice, even his troubles, had drawn her like a lodestone. Was that love, like Alf's love for Ma? Something that had grown unknowing? And had Siân suspected? Is that what she'd meant by *you are part of Rhys's journey now?*

So much confusion, so many questions. Bridie pocketed her pencil and crept back along the deck. Saw dawn's palette leaching through the scuttles, heard the yards creak, the scrape of an anchor chain. Soon the carpenter would climb down the ladder and launch the day on its course. She'd have to face Alf, the friend she never wanted, who was nowhere near as stupid as she'd imagined. See questions in his big, blue eyes, the kernel of an understanding. Meanwhile, her skin would be tight and her heart pitter-pattering as she tried to make sense of these strange new realisations.

CHAPTER 35

No one commented on Bridie's tired, white face at breakfast the following morning. Or the way she sat, hugging her notebook to her chest. Once the dishes were washed and stacked, the steerage cleaners set about their duties. Everyone else swarmed up the ladder and onto the main deck to await the arrival of the pilot.

Bridie went in search of Ma and baby Dylan.

That Ma wanted to go on deck and greet the pilot was a good sign. She'd been so sad since Dylan's birth, her eyes constantly red with weeping. Bridie found this odd. When did Ma build up such an affection for Siân? She'd spent most of the voyage trying to keep Bridie away from the Welsh girl. Still, maybe giving birth next to a dying women changed things?

It had certainly altered Doctor Roberts' behaviour. Over the last few days, he'd paid Ma frequent hospital visits, and although Ma was now strong enough to venture out on occasions, he'd kept visitors to a minimum. Bridie was surprised, on reaching the hospital, to find its door ajar. She heard a raised voice within. Not Ma's or Doctor Roberts', but Annie's, and from its pitched timbre her friend was crying again.

'I thought there was something wrong, Mrs Bustle ... with the back of the baby's head.'

'Well, as you can see, the baby is fine.'

'Yes, but in the hospital. Mrs Scarcebrook's hand flew to her mouth, as if, well ... as if she'd seen something dreadful.'

Dreadful! Their baby? No, Dylan was perfect. How could Annie say such a thing? She'd so wanted to attend a birth, had apologised over and over to Rhys. Did she think she could have prevented his baby's death?

'Mrs Scarcebrook is a fool, Annie. Even without the bucket of blood, she'd have needed her smelling salts.'

'Please, Mrs Bustle. I'm only trying to help you.'

'Then go away. Do you hear me? Leave us alone! It's too late to change things.'

Bridie lifted the latch as Ma's calm started to dissolve. Before she had a chance to step through the door, fingers pincered her shoulder. Bridie stumbled backwards, dropping her notebook as Doctor Roberts strode into the cabin.

'Miss Bowles. What are you doing here?'

'Visiting.'

'And upsetting my patient.'

'Not intentionally.'

'Your intentions are immaterial. The effect is all I see. Here, Mrs Bustle, do sit down.' He patted the nearby stool. 'Yes, that's right, dry your eyes, you've nothing to fear. Young women like Miss Bowles are meddlers, desperate to hold other women's babies. Sometimes, when a young woman dies, they try to endear themselves to the bereaved by raising ... well, let's just call them false hopes. I've seen it all before, Mrs Bustle, and trust me, no one will believe this girl's stories. Indeed, if she is not careful, Miss Bowles will find herself quite unemployable.'

Annie blanched, her pockmarks livid against the sudden pallor of her cheeks. She opened her mouth as if to argue, then snapped it shut. She glanced from Ma's stony face to Doctor Roberts' scorn twisted lips. With a wail, she gathered her skirts and dashed from the cabin. Doctor Roberts turned furious eyes on Bridie.

'Out! Get out! Your mother is too frail for company.'

Bridie fled the hospital cabin, saw Annie jerk her canvas bag from the hook above their bed, grab her blankets, and lug them down to a vacant bunk at the single girls' end of the deck. Bridie watched, stunned. First Siân, then Rhys, now Annie. Their mess torn apart within hours of reaching the foreign shore.

* * *

By the time Bridie was once again permitted to visit the hospital, Ma's fragile calm had been restored. Bridie's fingers itched to pull back Dylan's shawl and search his downy head. To ask what the words *leave us alone* and *it's too late* meant. But Ma's eyes were huge, tear laden, and for some reason Bridie found herself unwilling to plumb their depths.

'Sorry, Bridie. I don't know what's come over me.'

'It's all right.' Bridie picked her notebook up from where it had fallen. 'We've both had a difficult journey.'

'Yes, we have.'

'It's going to be all right now though. Alf and I have sorted things out. He's explained about my dad. So that's one less thing for you to worry about.'

'Oh, Bridie.' Ma pressed a hand to her lips.

'No, Ma, please don't cry. Alf's waiting on deck. Truly, I'm not making it up this time. He'll worry if we don't join him. You wouldn't want that, would you? He's worked so hard for this moment.'

* * *

Lady Sophia's main deck was festive as a fair ground. Her patched, every day canvas had been replaced by clean white sails, her signal flags strung along the rigging like bunting. As they stood beside Alf, watching the sun's upward climb, the last of the morning mist evaporated.

A whaleboat rowed out through the heads.

The pilot, a young man with a thatch of mud-blond hair, climbed the ladder under the microscope of hundreds of watching eyes.

He was the first new person Bridie had seen since Cape Town, his bronzed face, dusty black trousers and checked shirt as wondrous as opening night at the theatre. After greeting Captain Thompson, he raised a blue flag to show that *Lady Sophia* was now under his command.

It was sweltering on the main deck. Sweat trickled beneath Bridie's bodice—her wool dress, stays, and petticoats quite unsuitable for the weather. Ma's forehead glistened in the blinding sun. She leaned forward, shielding Dylan's face.

'What are we waiting for, Alf love?'

'The entrance is narrow like a bottleneck. We're waiting for slack water, which occurs three hours either side of high water, in order to go through the heads.'

'How do they know it's slack?' Bridie peered at the smooth green waters beneath.

'They watch the tides, lass.'

'Oh yes, of course.' She wasn't interested in the tides. But these small courtesies were part of the new order of things. Strange to think she and Alf were now friends. Last night had a shifting, mid-summer-night quality. But no, it was real. Her notebook burned like a brand in her hand. Her anxious eyes scanned the deck for Rhys.

'Why do they call it The Rip?' Ma asked.

'Because a strong ebb tide runs across the entrance to the bay. As it meets the waters of Bass Strait, it ripples the sea. The entrance is about a mile and three quarters wide. But there are shoals on either side.'

Bridie wrenched her gaze from the crowded deck and peered at the approaching heads. A hummocky strip of land jutted out from one side of the entrance, its sandy shore covered with a straggle of distorted shrubs. On the other side was the place Alf had called Shortland's Bluff. Someone had built a red and white obelisk beside the weatherboard pilot station. It looked garish amid the strange beauty of their setting.

'There are two channels. The west one, heading over that way. But by the looks of it, we'll be taking the east channel. We'll have to hug the shore until we get in line with that hill over there. It's called Arthur's Seat.'

'Who was Arthur then, love?'

Bridie didn't hear Alf's reply. She'd just caught sight of Rhys. He stood alone, looking out over the bulwarks, as if grief was somehow catching. She wasn't sure, even now, what she would say to him. Funny, how fast a friendship could unravel. Only a week ago, Siân had been alive and there had been no awkward silence to breach, or welter of strange emotions. Now, he was like the muddy island blocking the entrance to Port Phillip Bay.

Something to be carefully navigated with care.

He pulled something from his pocket and turned it over in his hand. What must today feel like for him? He'd dressed for arrival, a good sign, and seemed steady on his feet. But he probably couldn't wait to leave the ship. There would be no groups of single men willing to pool their wine rations in order to help him drown his sorrows. Neither would there be an overhead deck. He'd be able to grieve in the open air.

But, what was he holding in his hand? Something small, heavy, by the way he weighed it, brows arrowing down to his nose. Slipping his other hand into his pocket, he pulled out something small and red. Where had she seen that slip of red velvet before? Never mind the confusion, or welter of emotions. She shoved her way toward him.

'No, Rhys, don't!'

He startled at the sound of her voice, his hands closing around the stone and pouch. He gave a wan smile. His eyes looked huge, bruised, so much darker than usual.

'Please, Rhys, don't throw the stone into the sea.'

He swung away, training his gaze on the bay. 'Beautiful, this land is, Bridie. *Prydferth!*'

It was. Bridie could only agree. The clear blue waters of the bay shimmered like a chandelier in the bright morning sun. The shores on either side were wreathed in smooth yellow sand. Beyond them, steeply wooded hills were clothed in dusky shades of green. She raised her hand, pointing.

'That hill's called Arthur's Seat. But ... I don't know why.'

'It's named for a place in Scotland. Mt Martha, the hill beyond, is named for a man's wife.'

'Oh.' Bridie didn't know what to say. Though he clearly expected an answer. Head cocked, his dark eyes studied her face. She dropped her gaze. 'I didn't think you'd like it here.'

'Lovely, the land is, and Siân dead. Two unalterable truths. I can't change them and I've no mind to try. What about you? Do you like what you see?'

'Yes. I like it fine.'

'Glad, I am, to see you happy. And your baby brother, how is he?'

'Oh, Rhys, I'm sorry ... so sorry.' Her lips quivered like flummery. She stopped, took a deep breath, determined not to cry.

'There's sorry, I am, too. To be so pathetic.'

'It's fine. I understand. You've lost everything.'

She meant it, too. At least, she thought she did. Except he didn't smile or reach out to her—no gesture, or word of comfort, nothing like her old friend Rhys. Despair washed over her. Maybe it was too late. After all her thinking and writing and realising, maybe she'd lost him already. Their stories and magic and seeing things differently, nothing but the flotsam and jetsam of a difficult voyage.

'Please Rhys. Don't throw Siân's stone into the sea.'

'It's cursed, Bridie. Like her life. I only made things worse by making her emigrate.'

'You weren't to know. No one knew. How could they?'

'Siân knew.'

'And she chose to come with you.'

'If she'd not been on this ship, she'd not have fallen, or started to bleed. I made that happen.'

'It's horrible when someone dies. You blame yourself. I did, after my dad died. I thought, if I'd tried harder he mightn't have drunk so much or felt so sad or ... given up on life.' She stopped, her heart tapping like a mallet. 'I've never told you how my dad died, have I, Rhys?'

'In an accident, like Siân's. Is that what you're trying to say, Bridie Stewart?'

'No. I lied. Ma told me the morning we left Deptford. My dad didn't die in an accident. He was a sick man. Dying. One night, after he and Ma had argued, he went out and killed himself.'

She saw his face soften, his eyes fill with understanding.

'*Sori, bach*. I should have realised.'

'Their argument was about my notebook. That's why Ma hated it. That's why I was desperate to save it. But Ma's words hurt so much. I couldn't bring myself to tell you. And now, I think, perhaps ... I wasn't meant to.'

'Yet you just have.'

'I can now because I know the whole story. Alf told me. He was there. He said my parents were happy once. That even if my dad did give up on life, he still loved me. Not the words you would have given me—magic words that would conjure a mighty wind or unlock shackles. But the words I needed in my day of trouble.'

'So, Alf was not big, dull Elffin, he was Taliesin?'

'Elffin, Gwyddno and Taliesin, that's the way it works, isn't it? Each of us in every character, the stories shifting and changing as we learn to see differently.'

'A great lesson, you've learned, Bridie *bach*. There's glad I am to hear you say it. But it's different for me.'

'Why?'

'Because Siân's life was cursed.'

'I don't think she saw her life that way. I think she liked being a fairy woman. Your fairy woman.'

'Even so.' He jerked the stone from his pocket. 'I'd rather not have this to remind me.'

'No!' Bridie caught at his arm. 'Don't you see? I almost threw my notebook into the sea, I was so desperate not to share it with Alf. If I had, I'd have lost everything, the words, the magic and the chance to see differently.'

He paused, arm aloft, his hair ruffling like feathers in the wind. '*Nefi!* Why are you doing this to me?'

'Because we're friends, Rhys, and ... because Siân would have wanted me to.'

His shoulders sagged, his arm lowered. She took the stone from his slackened fingers. It felt cool and heavy in her palm. She slipped it into her pocket.

'I'm taking this because you're grieving. But if you ever want it back, you only have to ask me.'

'Thank you.' His words little more than a whisper.

This was it. Time to read him her story—the final, most important story in her notebook. But was it the right time? Rhys looked so worn and wan, at the end of his strength. How could he possibly see in such a dark place? He'd have to wait, through the worst of his grief, and wait some more. It might be years before he was ready to hear her story, let alone see with different eyes. Meanwhile, he needed something to hang onto. Something to give him strength in the days ahead.

'I've a gift for you, Rhys. Something magic to help you remember our friendship.'

'I don't need magic to remember you, *bach.*'

'It's not real magic. I'm not a fairy woman, like Siân. But I would like to know you are all right.'

'I could write. I'm sure they have a postal service in Port Phillip.'

'No. Not penny post. This is magic we're talking about.'

'Indeed.' He found the ghost of a smile. 'I think you'd better explain yourself.'

'I don't pretend to know how you feel, Rhys. I've never lost a wife or a child. But I have known grief and I have watched someone give up on life. I know, for a while, your stories are going to be all broken up inside you. There will be no one to remind you. No magic cellar where you can sit and feel Siân's presence. So I think,' she held out her notebook, 'you'll have to use my stories for a while.'

'No.' His smile vanished. 'I'll not take your notebook.'

'I'm not giving it to you, Rhys. Only offering it on loan. I hope, one day, you'll bring it back to me. But if you don't, I'll understand. You can rely on the postal service in that instance.' She smiled, jiggling the notebook. 'Here. Won't you take it?'

'No, please, *bach*, Don't make me do this.'

'You'll not want to get out of bed, Rhys, or look after yourself. So, you see, my motives are purely selfish. I want to know you're alive somewhere in the world. You won't want to read my notebook either, not for a long time. But when you are ready, there are rules. I expect you to abide by them.'

He raised his head. Uncertainty flickering across the thin drawn contours of his face. 'May I know the rules, Bridie Stewart, before I enter into this contract?'

'You must read the stories, one at a time, in the order in which they were written. You must think of each one as a test, like in a fairy tale. You must never, ever skip ahead, or fail to heed their lessons, lest you suffer the consequences.'

Silence. Bridie heard the drumming of her pulse, the raucous cry of a seabird overhead, felt a slackening as *Lady Sophia* entered the calmer waters of the bay. The hiss of Rhys's indrawn breath.

'*Iesu*, Bridie Stewart. You're a shrewd magician.'

CHAPTER 36

There were no big, dull men waiting to claim Bridie's hand in marriage when *Lady Sophia* dropped anchor in Hobson's Bay. Not even a wharf for her absent suitors to stand on. Only a wooden jetty poking out from a squalid settlement called Williamstown. That's if you could call the stone warehouse, gaggle of wooden huts, severed trees, pigs, dogs, sheep and rough looking men a settlement. It smelled worse than Covent Garden after market day—a ripe, rotten stench of privies, animal slaughter and tanneries.

Bridie stood on the main deck that first night and watched dusk soften the outline of its buildings. A punt crossed the nearby river mouth, an offender released from the stocks with a good-natured slap. Men read notices from Williamstown's single remaining tree. She shivered. How would they live in such a strange, desolate place?

Returning to steerage, she spent a gloomy evening staring at the deck boards above. There was no light after-supper chatter to lift her mood. All talk of employment prospects seemed foolish against the bleakness of their setting; all notions of cookery, shepherding, domestic service and needlework strangely out of place.

Bridie lay awake for hours after the lamps had been dimmed. A strange absence of snoring told her she wasn't the only one affected. She heard sobs and whispered words of comfort, couples hissing their disappointment. A strange, subdued silence from Alf and Ma's bunk.

Sometime during the graveyard watch, a fight broke out on the nearby shore. She heard shouts, dogs snarling, and the crack of a rifle. She fell asleep to the haunting cry of a night fowl.

Steerage rose early the following morning. Once mattresses were rolled and the breakfast dishes stacked away, Bridie stood on the main deck to await the arrival of the immigration officers. Two men arrived at the nearby river mouth on horseback. They signalled a punt, crossed the river, and joined the harbourmaster on the pier. A pair of surly convicts rowed them out to the ship.

Bridie, Alf, and Ma took their turn before the inspectors. The harbourmaster, a scruffy old man with a bulging red nose, explained they were entitled to two free weeks of shipboard accommodation. The immigration officer asked Alf about *Lady Sophia*'s sanitary regime. Alf twisted his cap as he outlined his cleaning duties. The immigration officer asked about Doctor Roberts' role. Alf's answers were honest, critical. More critical than Bridie would have imagined.

Once steerage been given a clean bill of health, fresh meat and vegetables were delivered to the ship. One of the single men bought a newspaper called the *Port Phillip Gazette*. Its anecdotes rolled from tongue to tongue, gathering gloom with each retelling. Things weren't good in Port Phillip. Bridie's suitors were not the only ones absent. There were no jobs either. Terms like influx, foreign capital, land speculation, and depleted government revenues were bandied about. Bridie didn't know what they meant. But Tom Griggs did, and he had quite a lot to say about the situation.

'It's a cock-up! A right bleedin' cock-up! All them placards, all them bills. A colony in need of labour, they called it. Now we're here, it's all a con. A great big bleedin' con!'

He stopped, having exhausted his vocabulary of frustration, and ran a hand through his grizzled hair.

'You can always do odd jobs, Tom.'

'Odd jobs!' Tom's eyes bulged. 'I didn't come twelve thousand miles to do odd jobs, Pam.'

'Just for the start, love.'

Tom clutched his head in his hands, emitting a low growl. 'I came here to improve meself. Not to struggle.'

'And you will love, it's just … a bad beginning.'

Tom jumped up, waving his arms. 'There's no money. Or jobs. Didn't you hear what I just said?'

'Tom. You're frightening the children.'

And me, Bridie thought from the privacy of her bunk. If Tom had been given a script and told to act like a man in great distress, he couldn't have improved upon the performance. Beside him, Alf sat ashen-faced, silent. Ma nursed baby Dylan and wept. Over the next few days, as the situation failed to improve, he tried to explain the situation.

'The squatters have been buying land, lass. Lots of land, even though they don't need it, and reselling it at a higher price. They've borrowed money to set up their runs, forgetting how long a fleece takes to grow and how far they are from home. Now they've run out of funds and they can't pay the interest on their loans.'

'So … they don't need us anymore?'

'Some are still employing shepherds and hut keepers. But they want single men without dependants.'

Single men could still find work, if they were willing to travel to the remote settlements. But no one wanted a shopkeeper or an ageing builders labourer. Immigrants were starving, the *Port Philip Gazette* told them, sharing tiny wattle and daub huts with other families. There was no parish relief to fall back on. Even Ma's needlework wouldn't help them. There were more needlewomen in Port Phillip than female customers. By the end of the first week, Alf and Tom started to consider their options.

'We mustn't panic,' Alf said at teatime.

'Of course, not. We're English. Let's stay calm in the face of our ruin.'

'They are not going to let us starve. They brought us out here. They'll look after us until we get on our feet.'

'You're a fool if you believe that, Alf Bustle.'

'There are public works. One of the single men told me. Men with families are being employed to build roads and dams.'

'Like felons! Like the bleedin' convicts assigned to the water police. No wonder they stopped transportation. No need to send out convicts when daft buggers like us are willing to come of our own accord.'

'It's not like that, Tom, and you know it. The public works are only a temporary measure until things pick up. Meanwhile, we have each other—we can rent a cottage with the money I've earned from my gratuity.'

Tom deflated like a spent balloon. 'That's big of you, Alf. I've got funds set aside, too, if I'm honest.'

'Right.' Alf nodded, his eyes a steel blue gleam. 'We've got money to be going with and we'll work like felons if we have to. But no one is going to starve. Do you hear me, Mary, Pam, Bridie? We'll get through this together.'

* * *

It took days for Alf and Tom to find a cottage and, from the straight line of Alf's mouth, Bridie gathered Melbourne's streets were no more appealing than Williamstown's. Alf gave notice of their departure, by which time Rhys had also decided to leave the ship. Only Annie would remain on board. As they stood amid trunks, boxes, and bulging canvas bags, Alf fixed her with his concerned blue gaze.

'Are you sure you won't come with us, lass? I told your aunt I'd see you safe and I meant it. No matter how bad things are.'

'I'll be fine, Mr Bustle. They're setting up tents for the single girls.'

'Well, you know where to find us if you need us.'

'Yes. Thank you.'

Ma gave Annie a curt nod, passed Dylan to one of the sailors, and stepped backwards onto the rope ladder. Bridie hugged her friend tight.

'Come and see us, please.'

Annie glanced toward the ladder. 'I can't. Your Ma wouldn't like it.'

Why? What had gone wrong between them? Bridie longed to ask. But Ma's emotions were still too fragile. She nodded, throat tight, and clambered down the ladder. Rhys followed, settling himself to the rear of the longboat, his eyes trained on the shore. He'd decided to take his chances in the Portland Bay District, he'd told Alf earlier. They needed bark cutters down there, as well as shepherds and hut keepers. He hoped to pick up work at the whaling station over the winter. It sounded harsh and dangerous. What if he got injured or, worse, died? She would never see him again, or even know his fate.

The morning sun seared their skin. The convict oarsmen heaved and panted, the armpits of their faded calico work shirts drenched with sweat. They pulled onto the beach, close to the river mouth. The convicts shipped oars, jumped from the longboat, dragged her up onto the soft dark sand, and passed trunks, bundles, and bags from the boat to the shore. Tom arranged for their trunks to be ferried up the river. Alf hailed the punt. They turned to take their farewell of Rhys.

'Good luck.' Alf pumped his hand.

'Thanks. I'll need it. We sail on the evening tide.'

'Let's hope you find work down there.'

'I'll not be needing much, with only one mouth to feed.'

This was true. In a strange twist of fate Rhys had become one of the 'lucky' ones—a single man without dependants. Yet as he stood, wan and weary in his patched grey jacket, she knew neither Alf nor Tom would have traded places with him. If their families held them back, it also gave them a reason to keep going. For Rhys, and poor Annie who'd fallen out with Ma, life was empty beyond their basic needs.

'Keep in touch,' Pam said, hugging him tight.

'Yes, of course.'

'I can't think how.' Pam sniffed, dashing a tear from her cheek. 'None of us knows where we'll end up.'

Rhys turned to Ma. 'And here's baby Alfred, come to say goodbye.'

'Alfred John Dylan.' Ma nodded.

'Fine strong names to live by, and two fine parents to help him grow.'

Rhys touched a hand to Dylan's downy head. Ma shrank back, clutching his swaddled form. Alf reached out and took the baby from her arms.

'Here, Mary, love. Let Rhys have a look at him.'

Ma stepped back and released her hold. Shifting from side to side, her hands were a convulsive twitch. What did she think Rhys was going to do? Run away with him?

Fortunately, Rhys didn't seem to notice Ma's odd behaviour. He pulled back the shawl, his face softening. 'He's a handsome boy, Mrs Bustle.'

Ma nodded, snatching Dylan back, clearly not trusting herself to speak.

Tom stepped forward. 'You're off then, Welshman.'

'Yes.'

'Well, good luck.' Tom thumped his back. 'Looks like we're all going to need a bit of luck.'

'Bridie.' Rhys touched a hand to her shoulder.

She couldn't speak, only nodded, her throat tight. Tears spilled onto her cheeks. Rhys smiled, passing her his hanky. She buried her face in its folds.

'That's it,' she heard him say.

And it was. He was going to disappear forever into the immense wooded land they'd seen from their passing ship. Violin in hand, he hefted his canvas bag to his shoulder and trudged along the beach.

Bridie could have sat down to wait for the punt, like Ma, or walked to the river mouth like Pam. But for some reason her feet were rooted to the spot. The rest of her felt soft and fluid as the sea-weed she'd seen wafting in the water beneath their ship. She wasn't sure how long she stood there. Or how long it took for her mind to register the approaching punt. Only that she knew it wasn't enough. Not nearly enough.

'I'm going to say goodbye,' she called as her legs began to move of their own accord.

'Bridie!' She heard Ma's shout.

'Leave her be, Mary, love.'

'No, Alf. She's making an exhibition of herself.'

'She's fine, love, fine.'

Bridie didn't hear Ma's reply. She ran, feet pounding, arms flail-ing, dodging driftwood and sand ridges, until her lungs were lit by an inner fire. As if she had run a great distance. All the way from England to this place on a black sand beach.

'Rhys!' she called out. 'Rhys, wait for me!'

She stopped, bent double, watched him walk back toward her. His face so drawn and sad that she wanted to cup it in her hands, as she'd seen Siân do so many times. To hold him, rock him, whisper words of comfort in his ear.

He lowered his bag and fiddle. 'I'll miss you, Bridie Stewart.'

'I'll miss you too, Rhys.'

'I'll have your notebook, though, lending me strength. That means a great deal ... unless,' he stopped, head to one side, 'you're wanting it back again?'

'No. It's yours ... for as long as you have need.'

'Are you sure, now, *bach?*'

'Yes. Only promise me you'll read it, Rhys. All of it. Right to the end.'

He paused before answering, his dark eyes searching her face. She swallowed, not daring to meet his gaze. Wondering what he saw, whether he could still read her mind. Perhaps guess at the hurdy-gurdy of emotions playing inside.

'It'll take time, *bach.*'

'I don't care how long it takes. So long as you bring it back to me.'

She watched him walk away, the shells a tiny white crunch beneath his feet. Crabs scuttled along the sand. A tumble of weeds blew in the wind. Oars dipped and pulled as the longboat made its way back to the ship. He halted at the far end of the beach, hefted his bag a little higher, and raised a hand. Bridie's heart took flight, trusting she would see him again, one day, in the not too distant future, if fairies were real and magic still happened, and that by then his vision would have altered.

GLOSSARY OF WELSH WORDS

Arhoswch	Wait
Baban, babanod	Baby, babies
Bach	Little, used to convey the term 'little one'
Bechod	Shame
Ble gest ti hi?	Where did you get it?
Bydd popeth yn iawn	Everything will be fine
Cannwyll gorff	Corpse candle
Cariad	Love, sweetheart, dearest
Cawl	Broth
Crist	Christ
Cwch	Boat
Cwtch	Cuddle
Daeth tair angel fach o'r gorllewin	Three small angels came from the west
Diawl	Devil
Duw	God
Heddwch	Peace
Hist	Hush
Gelli di wneud e	You can do it
Iesu Grist	Jesus Christ
Llyn y Fan Fach	Lake of the Small Peak
Nadolig Llawen	Merry Christmas
Na fydd	No, it won't
Nage	No
Nefi	Heavens

Nid ti sydd ar fai	You are not to blame
Noswyl Mai	May Eve
O Arglwydd, dyma gamwedd	Oh Lord, here is injustice
Pidyn	Penis
Prydferth	Beautiful
Pob un ohonyn nhw yn profi'r tân	Each one tried the fire
Seisnig	English
Sut wyt ti, cariad?	How are you, sweetheart?
Tad	Dad
Twp	Daft, stupid
Twti	Squat
Y Fari Lwyd	The Grey Mary

For a recorded pronunciation guide to these words, visit
http://elizabethjanecorbett.com/novels

Historical Notes

'*Ar Hyd y Nos*' is a traditional Welsh folk song sung to a tune
that was first recorded in 1784 in Edward Jones' *Musical and
Poetical Relicks of the Welsh Bards*. However, the Welsh words now
associated with the tune were written by John Ceriog Hughes,
much later in the nineteenth century than the setting of this book.
In his useful reference book, *Caneuon Enwog Cymru/Famous
Songs of Wales*, Hywel John describes its use in *The Beggars Opera*.
I can find no evidence of its inclusion in modern versions of the
play but, as it was a ballad opera and therefore subject to change,
I have decided to trust Hywel's research. Especially as, according
to Arfon Gwilym of *Cwmni Cyhoeddu Gwynn*, it was a well known
tune in nineteenth century England and used in other operas such
as Dibdin's *Liberty Hall*.

I am indebted to Marie Trevelyan's *Folk-lore and Folk-Stories of
Wales* for Siân's folk remedies and lore. Faleiry Kockzar, my Welsh
teacher, translated her charms into Welsh for me. She also made
the fairy woman's song so much better than the original Welsh
learner's version I wrote for the choir.

Rhys's stories come from a number of sources. The most used of
which were: W Jenkyn Thomas' *Welsh Fairy Book* and the excellent
National Galleries and Museums of Wales publication, *Welsh Folk
Tales*. I read Sioned Davies' new translation of the *Mabinogion* as
well as the earlier Charlotte Guest version. I was also privileged to
attend Dr Gwilym Morus-Baird's Welsh language course on the
first four branches of the *Mabinogion* and to hear Gwyn Evans talk

about the *Tylwyth Teg*—Fair Family in Welsh. The specific links between incest and magic are the product of my own imagination. In W. Jenkyn Thomas' chaste children's version of the tale, *Why the Red Dragon is the emblem of Wales*, Myrddin (Merlin) is simply called a 'boy without a father'. However, in *Mabon and the Guardians of Celtic Britain: Hero Myths in the Mabinogion*, Caitlin Matthews says: 'The incestuous parentage of the hero is well attested in Celtic folklore. Such a union produces a special child with superhuman abilities, yet he is generally outcast by being thrown into the sea, as in the case of Mordred or Taliesin.' I therefore felt justified in making the link.

I first heard about Dic Penderyn from the local history librarian at Port Talbot Library. Alas, it was so long ago (when I imagined this was simply a practice novel) that I have lost her name, so I cannot thank her publicly. You can read about Dic Penderyn online and in a number of publications. Though, of course, Rhys wrote his own version of the story.

Lady Sophia is an imaginary emigrant vessel, although I have tried to keep the conditions between decks as close to the historical reality as I have understood them to be. For those interested in reading about nineteenth century immigration to Australia, I can recommend: *The Long Farewell* by Don Charlwood; *Life and death in the age of sail: the passage to Australia* and *Doctors at Sea: emigrant voyages to colonial Australia* by Robin Haines; as well as Keith Pescod's *Good food, bright fires and civility: British emigrant depots of the nineteenth century*. Thanks to digitalisation projects, original documents such as *Instructions for Surgeons on Emigrant Vessels* are now available online.

The Tides Between is of course a work of fiction. If I have misunderstood, misquoted, or misrepresented, it has been without intention. Any mistakes are my own.

Acknowledgments

The journey to publication has been long and arduous. There are so many people to thank. I'll attempt to do so in chronological order. With thanks to my husband, Andrew, who encouraged me from the outset. Carine who helped choose the names of my characters. My cousin Joyce who played tourist guide on my early visits to Wales. Cousin Gwyn who believed there would be another writer in the family. My Welsh class who have been such a huge part of this journey. Steve who believed in my potential before it was ever evident. Faleiry, who transformed my learners Welsh into the far lovelier versions of songs and charms you have read. The team at Say Something in Welsh, who turned me from a language learner into a Welsh speaker. The members of Balwyn Writers who put up with my truly dreadful first drafts. Salli Muirden for her early encouragement. Alison Goodman who did my first manuscript assessment. Euan Mitchell who taught me heaps about story structure. Anne Bartlett who assessed one of my later drafts. To my writing buddies, Denis, Leisl, Chris, and Laura who offered words of truth and mop-up support in equal measure. My colleagues at City of Boroondara Libraries who have supported me unfailingly. Damien who annually asked: So, Liz, how is the book going? Joe, Bea, and Ella who looked after my dog while I finished my novel in Wales. Veronica Calarco who founded Stiwdio Maelor, took me on as a coordinator, and mentored me as a creative artist. Cindy Steiler for my stunning blog header photo, Erin Curry who helped revamp my website, and all the other Stiwdio Maelor residents who walked the creative path with me during my time in Wales. Inge who proofread my initial submission. Adam and Andy for wi-fi and great coffee. Brian for letting me buy cups of tea in the Slaters Arms and never once muttering the words: stingy Aussie! My mum and brother for their unfailing love. My children, Jack, Phoebe, Seth, and Naomi Priya who let their mum spread her wings and fly in mid-life. Their partners who accepted the chaos of our household. My three overseas daughters for being part of my rocky path to publication. Michelle Lovi at Odyssey Books for believing in my manuscript. The God of grace who holds me together (not an easy task). Finally, back to my husband Andrew who has been with me almost since childhood—thank you, thank you, thank you for letting me grow up and become a writer.

ABOUT THE AUTHOR

When Elizabeth Jane Corbett isn't writing, she works as a librarian, teaches Welsh at the Melbourne Welsh Church, writes reviews and articles for the Historical Novel Society, and blogs at elizabethjanecorbett.com. In 2009, her short story, 'Beyond the Blackout Curtain', won the Bristol Short Story Prize. Another, 'Silent Night', was short listed for the Allan Marshall Short Story Award. An early draft of her debut novel, *The Tides Between*, was shortlisted for a HarperCollins Varuna manuscript development award.

Elizabeth lives with her husband, Andrew, in a renovated timber cottage in Melbourne's inner-north. She likes red shoes, dark chocolate, commuter cycling, and reading quirky, character driven novels set once upon a time in lands far, far away.